Also by Sara Cate

T0036597

Give Me More

SARA CATE

sourcebooks
casablanca

Published by Sourcebooks Casablanca, an imprint of Sourcebooks
P.O. Box 4410, Naperville, Illinois 60567–4410
(630) 961-3900
sourcebooks.com

Originally self-published in 2022 by Sara Cate.

Cataloging-in-Publication Data is on file with the Library of Congress.

Printed and bound in Canada.
MBP 10 9 8 7 6 5 4 3 2 1

For my readers who enjoy good smut without shame.

Trigger Warning

Dear Reader,

This love story deals with the journey of coming out, discovering bisexuality, and exploring polyamory. Please be aware that there are some themes of internalized homophobia, child abuse (mentioned), and child neglect. There is no on-the-page abuse or harm to minors, just the fight to overcome trauma and come out stronger and happier.

Love is love.

Prologue

"So, I HAD A FISTFUL OF HER HAIR IN MY HAND, AND WE WERE both in the moment when I looked her right in the eye and said, 'Suck my cock like a good little girl.' The next thing I knew, she reared back her fist and clocked me right in the face."

My eyes widen in shock and I nearly choke on the whiskey that just passed through my lips. To say I didn't expect those words to come out of my friend and co-worker's mouth would be an understatement.

"Damn!" I reply to Emerson, setting my glass back down on the table.

Next to me, Isabel bites her lip as she tries to stifle her own laugh. This is only the third time I've brought her to our little Thursday night "bitch-about-work" outings, and I can't quite tell how she feels about the vulgarity of my friends' conversations.

She's not even old enough to be in here, and even though we've been seeing each other for almost three years now, I don't generally invite her out with the others much. She's too…pure for this crowd.

Not including Drake, of course. He's always around us.

Except for right now, since he's currently throwing darts with a group of girls who look like they're celebrating someone's birthday.

I snake my hand under the table to take Isabel's, throwing her a tense smile as she blushes at me.

She laughs quietly at Emerson as he uses his cold glass like an ice pack against the bruise forming around his eye.

"I don't think she liked that," Maggie says. She too is watching Emerson with a playful grin on her face.

"You think?" Emerson replies with a wince. "I mean...I thought we were getting along great. She seemed kinky enough, and she definitely appeared into it, but I guess I was wrong. Not a fan of a little sexy degradation apparently."

It's never *not* surprising to me how candidly my friends talk about sex. Don't get me wrong—I'm not a prude by any means, but I was raised by a somewhat conservative father—who touted righteousness in all things convenient to him but never the things that weren't. He did a piss-poor job of keeping a roof over our heads, which meant I saw and did some pretty shady shit back in the day just to stay alive.

But now? I've got a steady paying job, two promotions in the company in the last six months, and a girlfriend I plan to marry someday as long as I can keep my shit together.

So yeah, when our Thursday happy hours get raunchy, I get a little uneasy. Isabel isn't like me and Drake. She comes from the side of town with white picket fences and purebred dogs. And I plan to keep her there. These guys getting all vulgar with their stories has me a little on edge, that's all.

When my friends aren't talking about sex, they're complaining about the entertainment company we work for. Which is fine because sure, I hate it too, but I can't lose this job. I don't want to see the company go under, no matter how inevitable we all know it is. If I want to propose to Isabel, which I do, after she turns twenty-one, then I need to have enough put away for a down payment on a house and to get her the ring she deserves.

The others might hate the company and want to leave, but they don't seem to understand just how much I'm relying on it to secure the rest of my life.

A chorus of giggles catches my attention from the other end of the bar, and I glance up to see Drake doing body shots with the birthday girl. I don't know why, but I catch myself grinding my molars. I don't know why I'm surprised. He's been like this since we were teenagers.

It makes me wonder how long I'm going to be the only permanently attached guy in the group. Emerson and Garrett take full advantage of working parties and events and get laid on a regular basis. But something's gotta give after a while, right?

I'm zoning out when Garrett's rant catches my attention. "It's bullshit that there isn't a way to match people up by the kinky shit they like to do in the bedroom."

Isabel joins in with the rest of the group as they laugh at his ridiculous ideas. I find myself squeezing her hand under the table. I want to ask her if she's comfortable or if she wants to leave, but she seems okay. Even if she is only twenty and inexperienced, Isabel has a sexy curiosity that I love. She loves sex, but I try to keep things vanilla for her since she's still so young.

"I'm fucking serious," Garrett argues. "How nice would it be if you could meet up with someone who likes the same twisted shit you do? You wouldn't have to hide it or be embarrassed by the kinks that get your panties wet."

"You're fucking crazy, Garrett," I joke, and suddenly, the grip on my hand gets tighter. I glance her way as she furrows her brow at me as if I said something wrong.

"I am not," Garrett replies, defending himself. "Who here doesn't have some freaky bedroom desires you've always wanted to do but are too afraid to ask? I mean, obviously, Emerson isn't afraid to ask."

Emerson winces again, frowning at Garrett's joke.

Garrett seems lost on a tangent, emphasizing this idea as if it could ever really work. But since Isabel frowned at me the last time I made fun of him, I keep my mouth shut.

"Out of all the shit you've done, what is the one thing you wish you could ask for?" he asks. "You know you have something. So let's hear it."

"You first," Maggie replies with a smug grin. Maggie is the only woman in our company, but she's not what you'd expect from a woman who keeps three horny men in line. She's surprisingly timid and reserved, which explains why she's pushing this question back on Garrett.

"Fine," he says.

And while Garrett unveils his, slightly unexpected, bedroom desires, my attention bounces back and forth from this conversation to Drake. He's now standing so close to the woman wearing a white sash that says *It's my birthday* and a tiara on her head that it looks like their mouths might collide at any moment. My stomach starts to sour as I watch her run her hands along the length of his chest, then up his neck. My grip on my whiskey glass tightens.

Just as their lips are about to meet, I'm pulled from the display by a soft voice announcing, "I want to be in a threesome."

"Yes!" Garrett exclaims as I gawk at my sweet, innocent girlfriend, who just told all of my friends that her kinky desire is a ménage à trois. "See!"

"Isabel!" I stammer.

"What?" she asks, giving me a shrug. "Garrett's right. It's normal to want kinky stuff. I don't feel bad about it."

"Good for you," Maggie replies.

I notice the slight blush of Isabel's freckled cheeks as she reveals a tight-lipped smile.

"I can't believe you just said that..." I gawk at her, half-amused and half-horrified.

"Wait," Garrett replies, pushing the issue. "Threesome with another girl or threesome with another guy?"

I rub my temple as I fight the urge to drag her out of here, so she can't be corrupted by my horny friends anymore. But her mouth is twisted as she considers this question.

"Um…I think either."

"Nice," he replies.

I stare at her with a look of surprise. Three years I've known this girl. Three years I've been in love with her and two since we started having sex and never have I heard about this kinky threesome desire of hers.

"All right, Hunter. Your turn," Garrett says, but I instantly shake my head.

"I don't have anything."

"Come on. I said mine," Isabel argues.

But I shrug in response. "I really don't have anything."

A look of disappointment blankets their faces before we move on. I wish I could tell them my deepest desires, but I don't ever let that thought enter my head. As I glance back over to the corner of the bar, I watch as Drake makes out with the birthday girl against the wall, and I grind my molars again.

They can joke about secret desires all they want, but none of them will ever truly know how agonizing it is to keep yours in forever because mine will never *ever* come out. I won't let it.

By the next morning, everyone else in the group gets their wish because the company has filed for bankruptcy, and we're all out of a job. The panic that ensues inside me is relentless. I'm already scouring the job sites when Emerson calls.

When he first tells me about his new business idea, developing a dating app based on kinks and sex, I figure it's crazy and will never work. I almost turn him down. The words are actually on my lips. I have too much at stake—a future with the woman I love—and I'd be better off taking a corporate job with benefits. But as I look over at her where she sleeps next to me in bed, I think about what she said last night. How cute she was declaring her desire for a threesome, and I realize that I'd rather live a wild life with this girl in an apartment than a boring one in a house. And if she can live out loud like that, then so can I.

Against my initial judgment, I agree to take on the role of finding and managing developers for the app. And I make a promise to myself to give it a shot for one year. And honestly, I don't expect it to last the year, but boy was I wrong.

Salacious Players' Club lasted far longer than a year, and it became so much more than an app.

Rule #1: When you can't be the third wheel, have a threesome instead.

Drake

I'M A FUCKING SCOUNDREL. I GUESS THAT'S AN OLD-FASHIONED term, but I don't really like the modern-day translation as much. Playboy. Man whore. Fuck boy.

I get around. I don't do relationships, and I can't stand the idea of commitment. The only people I've been with for any amount of time, I cheated on—multiple times. The first one being my high school girlfriend, whose name I can't even remember, and I didn't just cheat on her, I cheated on her with her best friend… only hours after taking her virginity.

I told you, scoundrel.

I'm not proud of it. I don't think it makes me a good guy and I'm not the kind of douchebag to flaunt it, but that's just who I am. I like to fuck, and while I respect every single person I'm with, it's not really a priority to me to learn shit about them. We can have a good time together and part ways, and no one gets hurt.

So it comes as a shock to no one that when my best friend offered me a job as head of renovations at his new sex club, I said sign me the fuck up. I paved the bricks of my own paradise. Finally in the prime of my life, I should be set to live out my days exactly like this. At Salacious, I don't have to worry about sex partners who want tomorrows and forevers. I get to fuck as much as I want. Be as kinky as I want. With whoever I want—girls or guys.

Which leads me here. With one beautiful set of lips around my cock while another petite brunette rides my face. She's howling like she's been possessed by the devil as her clit grinds against my tongue. I'm about two seconds away from yanking my cock out of her friend's mouth and shoving it down her throat just to shut her up.

I was going to let her come first, but she's getting out of hand, so I toss her off of me and pull her friend's lips off my cock to replace one mouth with the other. This isn't their first rodeo… that much is obvious.

Sometimes when it's their first threesome, you can tell by the way they stumble through the transitions, not quite knowing where to go when we change positions or where their parts belong, but these girls are seasoned. I can tell when the quiet one starts going to town on the other girl like she's in a pie-eating contest.

How exactly did I get here?

Well, technically, I got to this Phoenix rental house with Hunter and Isabel yesterday afternoon.

But more specifically, I landed here in pussy heaven after my aforementioned best friends decided to ditch me to celebrate their anniversary with a night on the town, leaving me to hunt down some mattress ornaments at the local nightclub. Obviously, it worked like a charm.

I mean…it's not like I wanted to celebrate their anniversary with them. Not even their wedding anniversary, but their ten-year *dating* anniversary. Who even celebrates those after getting married?

I don't know why I sound bitter because I'm definitely not. I mean…I'm about to shoot my load down a twenty-two-year-old's throat. Why would I complain?

Being the third wheel with those two is getting old anyway.

I've been the third wheel for the entire decade of their relationship. Fuck, I was there the day they met too. I remember the look on my best friend's lovestruck face when he locked eyes with the demure four-eyed redhead carrying her books across the street.

I was there for everything after too. Hunter cleaning up his act. Getting a job for her. Climbing his way up the corporate ladder *for her*. Making himself the owner of a club *for her*.

Maybe if I had been the kind of guy to settle down with a beautiful girl of my own, I would have flown a little farther from their nest, but since I'm not, they practically treat me like their thirty-four-year-old love child, keeping me around for their holidays and birthdays, and as you can see, vacations.

It's not like I insert myself in their lives, but they are the only family I have. They're *all* I have.

And on that thought—not exactly sure why—I come, shooting straight down the loud girl's throat, and she swallows it down like a good little girl. I'm not sure either of them has come yet, so after my dick is spent, I collapse onto the mattress and let them finish each other.

In my post-orgasm state, I'm drifting off as I hear the front door open in the distance. There's some low chatter and movement across the small house until I hear their door close down the hall.

Something heavy weighs on my chest at the thought.

"You're not done yet, are you?" the quiet girl asks.

"Give me a minute, darlin'." Heaving a sigh, I relax flat on my back as the one with the nose ring—I think her name starts with a K—starts kissing her way up my body. She's already stroking my cock, trying to bring it back to life. Kristy, Kelsey, Kyla?

Seriously, woman. It's been like five minutes. Ever heard of a refractory period?

Then, there's a high-pitched moan in the distance, and I tense up. There's only some drywall between my room and theirs, and it's abundantly clear just how thin it is when I hear Isabel cry out again.

"Here he comes," the girl says as my dick thickens under her eager tugs. The other girl is in her own post-orgasm recovery next to us.

"Sounds like a party next door," the sleepy one replies as the bed starts thumping against the wall in a slow, rough cadence.

"Maybe we should ask to join them. Make this one *big* party," the girl on my cock adds.

"You talk too much." I flip her over and grab a rubber off the nightstand. Sheathing my already hard cock, I listen to the sound of my best friends fucking as I slam into the girl on her knees in front of me. She lets out a husky cry, so I grab her by the hair, pulling her up so her ear is next to my mouth as I mutter, "Louder."

And she does, but it's not enough to drown out the sounds of the woman in the next room. The one I should not be hearing, thinking about, or getting off to.

Rule #2: A little competition never hurt anybody.

Isabel

My husband looks unhappy. Actually, I take that back. He looks happy because Hunter is good at putting on a smile and faking it for me when he needs to, but I can tell these things. I can see the subtle glances of regret and sorrow on his face.

"Are you sure you like your steak?" I ask.

"Yes, baby. I love it." He reaches across the table and takes my fingers in his hand, stroking my knuckles gently. I smile back at him.

I'm not the kind of woman to devote myself to being what society would consider *a good wife*. I don't even know what that means. In my younger days, I was so opposed to marriage. The idea of devoting my life to one relationship seemed irrational and daunting. How could I promise one person that I would love *only* them for the rest of my life? How on earth could anyone make that promise? Like we can see the future. Like any of us knows what's waiting around the corner.

But then I met Hunter Scott.

Hunter makes loving him easy. He worships me, makes me

better in every way, encourages me, inspires me, and makes me fall in love with him a little more each day.

So naturally, I want him to feel that same radiating happiness he makes me feel, but I can tell by the way he's twisting the wedding ring on his finger and chewing on his lower lip as he stares down at the red wine in his glass that something is up.

"Should we have invited him?" I ask.

His gaze dances up to mine. "No. It's our anniversary. He understands. Plus, I'm sure he's already shacking up with someone at the rental right now."

I swallow down the unsettling feeling that image brings. Drake is a grown man, single and gorgeous. He can do whatever he wants. But is he really going to screw his way through our cross-country road trip? I'm sure it doesn't help that we are touring four different sex clubs on our business trip-slash-mini-vacation. I feel like we're taking our little boy to Disneyland.

An image of Drake in a hat with black mouse ears and his name embroidered on the back makes me giggle.

"What's so funny?"

"Oh, nothing. Just wondering why we brought Drake, of all people, on this trip. There's a good chance we will lose him somewhere along the way."

"He always does this on our vacations," he replies with a laugh.

"We should know by now not to share a rental with him," I reply playfully.

"We really should." His fingers squeeze mine.

"You know…we should have brought him to dinner. Since he was there the day we met."

"Was he?" Hunter replies. "I only remember you."

I roll my eyes as I try to hide my blush. "Stop."

"No. Isabel, that was the best day of my life—the first of many. Seeing you on your way to the library, carrying that stack of books while your glasses started to slip down your nose." He's smiling, and it's infectious.

"You're mocking me," I reply.

"No, I'm not. I remember the exact thought that went through my head at that moment."

"Was it 'who still goes to the library?'"

"No. It was… 'I wish I could get a girl like that.'"

Leaning forward, I meet him halfway before our lips meet. "And somehow you got a girl like that."

When he sits back again, he's wearing another serious expression. "Because I changed."

"No," I argue. "Because I love you unconditionally."

He fidgets with the sleeves of his shirt, tugging them down as a habit to hide his tattoos. They crawl all the way up his arm from his wrist to his neckline. My husband seems to think that making certain choices from sixteen to twenty-three makes him undeserving of love. And I see the self-consciousness.

When I met him, I was a doe-eyed seventeen-year-old virgin. He was a twenty-three-year-old tattoo-covered criminal who did what he had to, to survive. We came from two different sides of town, two different worlds, two different paths. But those paths became one, and although our histories were different, our futures were the same.

Suddenly, Hunter was everywhere I turned. Afraid he would scare me, it took him months to gather up the courage to even talk to me. He figured out pretty fast that I could be found at the public library at least three days a week. And when he finally did approach me, he was so nervous, I could see him trembling. It was adorable.

But Hunter never scared me. Even with the tattoos and the reputation, there was a soft kindness in his eyes. The truth was…I saw him long before he saw me.

Ironically, I always told myself I could never get a guy like him.

"I love you," I mumble softly as I rest my elbow on the table, placing my chin in my hand like a lovestruck teenager. In some ways, I guess I still am.

He smiles, those bright-white teeth making my insides turn

all gooey and hot. Why does he have to be so handsome? So charming and fun to look at.

"I love you too, Red."

My cheeks blush, and I know my neck and chest are brighter than my hair. "Hunter…" I say in a low whisper as my foot rubs softly against his leg.

His spine straightens and his head tilts, giving me that lust-filled gaze.

"Let's go back to the rental now."

"Check, please," he calls to the waiter, and I'm smiling so hard, it hurts my cheeks.

We both hear the moaning before the front door even opens. It's just a small two-bedroom condo in downtown Phoenix, near the club we're touring tomorrow night. It was the smartest option since there are three of us. Instead of getting two hotel rooms, for the same price, we could just rent a small place.

But as I set my purse down and hear what sounds like a woman in the throes of a very intense orgasm, I'm starting to reconsider our options.

"Cancel the rest of our reservations," I joke.

"Jesus…I'm sorry."

I laugh. "Hunter…stop apologizing. You own a sex club. Do you really think this even affects me anymore?"

He corners me against the counter, placing both hands on either side of me, blocking me in. "Are you sure it doesn't affect you at all? Not even a little bit?" His lips land gently against the skin of my neck, just under my ear, and I hum in response. He knows all of my weak spots.

"Okay…maybe it does…a little."

His hands wind their way around my waist as he squeezes me closer. Pressing his mouth against my ear, he mutters darkly, "Should we give them a little *stiff* competition?"

"Oh, baby. You know I can do way better than her."

At that moment, another female voice whimpers in the next room, and Hunter pulls back as we stare at each other wide-eyed.

"Them," I correct myself.

With that, Hunter hoists me over his shoulder and carries me squealing into our bedroom. As he slams the door closed behind us, the moaning and groaning in the next room is suddenly louder. I guess we share a wall…wonderful.

Quick to distract me, Hunter drops me onto the bed and yanks me to the edge. My legs quickly wrap around his waist as he pulls his jacket off and then starts unbuttoning his shirt while I watch.

Licking my lips, I feast on the sight of my husband slipping the white cotton from his shoulders, revealing black, white, and red ink covering his skin like a second suit. Then, with a rough jerk, he yanks my dress up to my waist and tears down my panties.

Growling, he drops to his knees and nibbles his way up the insides of my thighs. I'm squirming with anticipation by the time he reaches my center, lapping and licking in fierce strokes as I moan loudly.

"Come on, Red. You can do better than that."

On that note, he plunges two fingers inside me, and my back arches with a guttural cry. His mouth is rough, and his fingers brutal as he sucks and nibbles at my clit.

The blankets are clenched tightly in my fists, and my heels fall with a clunk against the tile floor while my husband wears my thighs like earmuffs, not even coming up for air until I'm screaming.

My orgasm is fast and fierce, but before I've even recovered, he's flipping me onto my knees and crawling onto the bed behind me.

Grabbing onto the headboard, I brace myself for the impact as he slams home.

Hunter is rough in bed. It's probably my second favorite thing about him—just after that kind heart of his. And it's probably the dichotomy of his personality that makes the sex so delectable. He is warm and kind and quiet in person, but in the bedroom, he lets loose. He's wild and rough and almost primal. He growls and commands and dominates in a way that lets me know he wants me and only me. That he *needs* me.

"Louder," he grunts.

I cry out again, our bed smacking against the wall, and I swear I hear the cries on the other side get louder. Then, for some reason, I imagine what he's doing to them in that room. I picture Drake pounding into that girl the way Hunter is me. I picture sweat dripping across his bare pecs and over the ridges of his abs. I picture his dirty blond hair barely touching his shoulders. I picture his face and wonder what it looks like when he comes.

My body is flooded with heat and pleasure as I come again, my fingers straining in their tight grip around the headboard as I scream.

Behind me, Hunter pounds into me two more times before he groans through his own orgasm. And when I open my eyes again, I breathe through a wave of shame with the image of Drake still frozen in the forefront of my mind. And feeling for one second like the hands currently gripping my hips are his.

Quickly, I reach back and latch onto Hunter's hand. Turning toward him, I shake myself out of my imagination and feel relief when I lock eyes with my husband. The *only* man I should be thinking about when I climax.

So…what the hell was that?

Rule #3: Midnight kitchen meetings can be very enlightening.

Hunter

TEN YEARS. *TEN YEARS.*

Still feels like yesterday. I still feel like that drug dealer in the driver's seat of my dad's beat-up SUV. Twenty-three years old and just scrambling to get by.

Ten years in fancy suits and nice cars and a beautiful house I bought and paid for, for my beautiful wife.

I'm not going to spout some bullshit like how I don't deserve this, because I know I fucking do. I worked my ass off to trade a life of selling MDMA for one selling BDSM. I haven't lost touch. Somewhere inside, I'm still that stupid kid who's lucky he never ended up behind bars. But I don't feel bad about that. I did what jail would have done. I rehabilitated myself, and this woman next to me was my sentence.

Isabel is breathing softly, her messy mop of amber hair half covering her face. Reaching down, I pull back the strands and kiss her forehead as she sleeps. Then, I carefully roll out of bed without waking her.

The red light of the old alarm clock on the nightstand shows

3:22. Life at the club has turned me into a night owl, wide-awake all night and falling asleep at dawn. And when I hear a cabinet close in the kitchen, I know I'm not the only one.

"You really keep bad hours for a construction worker." My voice carries across the dark space, and the glass rattles on the counter when Drake hears me.

"Jesus Christ, brother. You scared the shit out of me."

I can't hold in my gravelly chuckle as I reach for a glass just behind him, his bare shoulder brushing mine. "Sorry."

"Couldn't sleep?" he asks.

"You know me," I reply in a lazy mumble. Filling the glass with water, I look over at my best friend bathed only in the light from the tiny bulb above the stovetop. As I set the drink down against the counter, I smile. "I thought for sure you'd be out cold. Sounded like a real workout in there."

He grins wide, leaning back against the marble, his broad hands bracing the surface as he hoists himself on top of it. In nothing but a pair of jeans, his bare feet hanging out of the bottom, he looks almost proud of himself for all the noise he was making tonight.

Technically, it was the girls making all the noise, I guess.

"Oh, you heard that?" he replies with a mischievous smile.

"Come on, Drake. Emerson and Maggie probably heard that back at the club. It's a small miracle the neighbors didn't call the cops. It sounded like you were drowning feral cats in there."

He's chuckling now, his chest rising and falling quickly with each breath. It must be nice to have a manual labor job like construction. Even at thirty-four, he's remained in perfect shape, without having to work out every day. Meanwhile, I had to install a full gym in our basement and live down there, part-time, to keep my physique.

His work on job sites is his weight training and sex is his cardio.

"These Arizona girls are crazy." He laughs. "I was only at the club for an hour before they had me sandwiched in an Uber. Can we stay?" he jokes with a toothy smile like a child.

"*You* can stay. Iz and I have three other clubs in three different states to see between now and next week. A few of them I know for a fact you don't want to miss out on."

"Yeah, that sounds more fun. Besides, the sounds coming from your room weren't much tamer than mine." He raises an eyebrow in my direction.

"Were you listening to my wife's sex sounds?" I reply with a glare in his direction.

"Oh, like it was the first time. Remember when the only place you two had to do it was in the back of the SUV and I had to wait outside? Or when we had that apartment in the city and I worked nights, trying to sleep through your morning sexcapades."

I'm chuckling into my water glass when I hear soft footsteps coming from the bedroom. "What are you boys still doing up?"

Isabel emerges from the hallway in her pajamas, a revealing pair of shorts and a skimpy tank top that shows off her perky nipples through the fabric. By this point, I've gotten over any jealousy where Drake is involved. He's seen Isabel in underwear before. It was a little hard to avoid when we lived together for those few short years before he started construction on our new house.

But when she leans over the counter smiling at us, and her tits are pressed together and practically hanging out of her top, I tense up.

"So you had a fun evening, didn't you?" she teases him. "Was that *two* girls I heard?"

"You heard correctly," he replies with pride in his tone. He's smiling at her, his eyes firmly set on her face. I can only imagine the feat of strength it's taking him not to even glance down at her cleavage.

"And they didn't wear you out?" she asks.

"Isabel…you don't think I can handle a couple twenty-three-year-olds?"

"You're getting up there in age. Can't keep hanging with those sorority girls," she replies with a sarcastic smile.

"Oh, I could handle the *whole* sorority."

She laughs. "I'm sure you could, Drake."

Meanwhile, I'm leaning against the fridge, watching them go back and forth, a subtle smirk tugging at my lips. I could watch these two go on like this forever. Isabel and I can make jokes and laugh together, but we'll never have the playful relationship she has with Drake.

And I'm not jealous of that. Because I know that's all it is. They joke like brother and sister…or at least like best friends.

Which makes sense. The moment she became my girl, he took her on as his friend too. Always looking out for her, treating her like I would, and bringing her right into the fold. As if she always belonged.

But it won't always be like this. That's my pessimistic, grim brain talking, but I know deep down that the clock is ticking on our youth. At some point, Isabel will want kids or Drake will settle down. And this family that I have now will change.

And as much as I do want to start a family with Isabel—and for Drake to settle down—I hate change. If things could just stay the way they are between us right now, I'd be happy.

They are still going at it, both laughing and jabbing at each other with sarcastic insults, and through it all, his eyes have stayed on her face, never raking over her body or lingering too long on the parts of her I see other men gawk at. I mean…she's a yoga instructor. She lives in Lycra. And she's a fucking masterpiece. Who wouldn't want to look?

But Drake never does.

It's *her* expressions I'm not quite sure I can read. My wife is more discreet than Drake…or men in general. So when she lets her eyes drift to his pecs or bites her lip as she smiles at him, I start to wonder what is going on in that mind of hers. I'd pay anything to know. Even if it meant she was checking him out.

Again…I'm not sure I could blame her. Drake is as easy on the eyes as Isabel. His chiseled abs, golden sun-bronzed skin, dirty blond chin-length hair, and bright as lightning smile…make it fucking hard not to stare.

And I'm straight.

Isabel yawns as she straightens up and reaches for my hand. "Let's go back to bed. We have a busy day tomorrow."

Technically, today. We're meeting with the owners of a sex club here in the city, and it's the first of four clubs that we'll tour on this trip to collaborate, share ideas, and discuss brand affiliation. I'm not just here to scout for Salacious, but this is really about the opportunity for expansion. Emerson is considering a second location, and buying out a preexisting club would be easier.

"Come on, Red," I whisper, placing Isabel under my arm and kissing the side of her neck. We wave good night to Drake, and just before I disappear down the hallway, I take one last glance backward at him, and I'm surprised to see his smile is gone, and he's watching us leave with an expression of longing on his face.

As Izzy and I crawl back into bed, I ask her, "Does he seem okay to you?"

She laughs. "Is that a serious question?"

"Yeah. I just noticed him looking almost sad."

"I'm sure he's just tired. He looked fine while I was talking to him," she replies, cuddling up on my chest.

"Yeah, that's because he's always smiling with you."

She lifts her head. "What's that supposed to mean?"

"Nothing," I reply. "Just that you two always seem to make each other laugh. But when no one was looking, he seemed a little down."

"So why don't you talk to him tomorrow?" she asks.

"Okay." With that, I plant a kiss on her mouth and squeeze her tighter against my body. With her heart beating softly against my chest, I start to drift off. Her soft hair brushes against my arm and her delicate breath kisses my skin.

Looking down at her, I smile, then kiss her again on the top of the head. How the fuck did I get so lucky? Ten years and I still can't believe it.

I just wish Drake could find someone like Isabel. I know I wasn't imagining that sad look on his face, and it's not the first time I've seen it. He pretends sleeping with random people every night is a dream, but if he could have what I have, I know he'd be happier.

Rule #4: Keep your friends close and your husband's best friend even closer.

Isabel

I MIGHT BE A LITTLE BIASED, BUT I THINK SALACIOUS PLAYERS' Club has to be the best sex club in the world. Okay…I don't have much to compare it to. Or *anything* to compare it to. Truth be told, I've never stepped foot in another sex club.

Tonight will be my first.

Hence why I might be a tad bit nervous. It's one thing to walk into the sex club your husband owns and his best friend built, but it's very different walking into a strange club, where you don't know a soul.

At least I'm walking in with two hot-as-hell men at my side. I shouldn't be so anxious.

But suddenly I'm reminded of the first time Hunter brought up the idea of opening a sex club with his business partners and the fact that I thought it was a crazy idea. A nightclub is one thing. Hell, even a strip club would be a stretch, but a full-on sex club? I guess I never really saw myself as a sex club owner's wife, but I knew the moment I fell in love with Hunter that I was in for a wild ride.

A quiet, yoga-loving book nerd with accountants for parents

is suddenly in marital possession of the freakiest establishment in Briar Point. I was never cut out for straitlaced anyway.

"You're shaking," Hunter whispers in my ear as we pass through the front doors of Fire Palace, the seven-year-old kink club in downtown Phoenix. It's more discreet than Salacious, almost like a speakeasy with a downstairs entrance, under a seemingly normal bar. It was so quiet on the street outside that I thought we were in the wrong place, but once we pass through the door, I see why.

Fire Palace isn't a loud dance club and I can't hear sex anywhere. Even at our club, if you listen hard enough, you can hear the soft hum of sex in the background. I mean…it's happening in almost every room of the building. Drake could only make the rooms so soundproof. Not to mention…some of them *aren't* soundproof on purpose.

As we stride up to the hostess stand, a beautiful blond man with hair longer than Drake's and blue eyes focused directly on him, greets us. I smile and try to hide behind the two men.

"Hunter Scott. I'm here to see Mirabel Santos."

"Oh, yes, Mr. Scott. She told me you were coming." The man reaches under the counter and pulls out a key. It's not a key card like we have. This is a real key and it's hanging on a black key chain that reminds me of the kind old hotels used.

"Fire Palace is organized by rooms to ensure maximum privacy and safety. She's informed me to give you a key to a VIP suite where she will meet with you in promptly one hour. You are welcome to use the suite"—his eyes dance between the three of our faces, and my eyes widen when I realize what he's implying—"however you'd like until she can meet with you."

Drake stifles a laugh. "Isn't there a bar I could wait at?"

"We don't serve alcohol, I'm afraid, but there is a lounge upstairs that might quench your thirst."

Wow, do we sound this uptight at our club?

"Are we not able to look around? Isn't there a place where people…mingle?" Hunter asks.

"Mingle? We have group activities on Thursday and Saturday nights from—"

"Never mind," Hunter interjects, grabbing the key from the man. "You have water or something in the rooms for my wife, right?"

He seems tense, so I gently squeeze his arm against my body to try and calm him. It's too early for him to lose his temper and Hunter has a bit of a short fuse.

"Yes, sir."

"And please tell Ms. Santos that we do not need an hour. We're here to see the Shibari demonstration at ten, so I'd appreciate it if she wouldn't keep us waiting in our…room."

The man behind the counter looks uncomfortable. "Yes, sir."

"Let's go," he grumbles, pulling me to the door.

"I guess I'll be upstairs at the lounge," Drake says, moving toward the stairs that lead to the street, and I feel a twinge of disappointment at seeing him leave, alone.

"Come on, Drake. You don't want to miss the demonstration."

"Come with you…into your sex room?"

"We're not—Will you just come on?" Hunter barks. With a laugh, Drake follows us through the doors into the club. So much for being quiet. The moment we enter the long dark hallway, the sounds of sex behind each door mingle with the loud thumping bass of the music. I'm actually quite impressed that we couldn't hear any of this in the lobby.

The vibe of this club is nothing like Salacious. Instead of entering one large room, we're left to meander through a labyrinth of hallways with doors on each side, numbered in gold letters. It takes us a few moments to find ours: room thirty-three.

Holding Hunter's hand, I stand by, letting him unlock the door, and glance back at Drake when I hear a thunderous roar coming from the room across the hall. Drake and I lock eyes and both resist the urge to laugh before rushing into our room.

The moment the door closes behind us, it's a little more quiet.

A little. The music is still loud in here and I can't tell if the pounding sound is the bass or the headboards.

"This place is weird," Drake mutters as he looks around our room.

Hunter is still clenching his jaw, which I know means he's annoyed. He clearly doesn't like that they ushered us into a room like prisoners, but I know it was just a business tactic. We're technically their competition. They *will* show us respect, just after they humble us.

"I don't like it," Hunter mutters.

"Oh, it's not so bad…" I say. The room is nice. It's a good size, and it smells clean, like jasmine and cotton. There's a giant bed on the right and a couch along the wall with a minibar and a cabinet against the opposite wall. It's dark in here, giving the room a sexy vibe. Which I guess makes up for the fact that the room itself is a little…boring.

Walking over to the cabinet, I open doors to find exactly what I expected to: ropes, cuffs, tiny bottles of lube like hotel shampoos, and a bowl of condoms. In the drawers are sealed and unopened sex toys—butt plugs, dildos, anal beads. It makes me laugh that this stuff really doesn't faze me anymore.

"This is bullshit," Hunter mutters as he paces the room.

"Baby, relax," I reply, approaching him and running my hands over his chest. Drake drops onto the sofa behind us. "We have an hour," I joke, trying to lighten the mood for my husband. "Just because Drake is in here doesn't mean we can't still use the room."

"Be my guest," Drake says with a laugh.

My husband just rolls his eyes, but his shoulders do relax a little as his hands slide down my back. "This lady better hurry. I'm not sitting here cooped up for an hour."

It doesn't end up being an hour before there's a knock at the door. In a rush, Hunter walks over and opens it. A beautiful woman with large green eyes and sleek black hair smiles politely at us.

"I'm Mirabel," she says with a small bow. "I hope you enjoyed your room."

"We didn't request a room," Hunter replies through clenched teeth.

As she peeks in, she notices the large man on the sofa, and her eyebrows rise in surprise. "Pity. I was unaware you were bringing a third. I would have been happy to accommodate him in the singles' lounge."

"There's a singles' lounge?" Drake whines from the couch.

"I'll have a talk with my front desk host. My apologies," Mirabel says with a sweet smile. She doesn't strike me as a sex club owner at first glance. She looks so nice and normal.

"Thank you," Hunter replies, and I notice the way he relaxes a little into my arms.

"In your email, you mentioned the Shibari demonstration. Are you still interested in that?"

"Yes, please."

"Absolutely. You three can follow me."

I glance back at Drake again, and we share an expression of surprise as we step in line behind Hunter and Mirabel.

"Our members appreciate discretion," she says, glancing back at us. "That's why we keep it very private with the keys and doors. There are social events and spaces in our club for members to mingle, but they like that they can come here, for whatever reason, and not risk seeing anyone they would know outside the club."

"At Salacious, we promote an open and nonjudgmental approach. They have nothing to hide in seeking their pleasure at our club."

"How liberated you are to feel that way," she replies with a coy smile, and Hunter's brow furrows. Then Mirabel glances back at me. "Have you asked your wife or any woman, for that matter, how comfortable *they feel* being seen in a sex club? The societal expectations are quite different."

I avert my eyes when I notice Hunter glance my way.

"We're working to dismantle those expectations, Ms. Santos. Not cater to them."

"I admire you for that," she replies, and I feel Drake's gaze on me this time. Glancing his way, our eyes widen as we fight back our smiles again. I guess we *both* find this incredibly uncomfortable, but I'm glad he's here to share the humor in it with me.

When we reach the end of the hall, Mirabel pulls out a key from her wristlet and unlocks the door. It opens to a large area that reminds me of a small concert hall. The room is wide and narrow with a stage at the other end. There are people mingling in small groups as they watch the performance. There are pillars in the way, so I can't quite see what's going on yet, but as we make our way into the room, I let out a gasp when I see a young man suspended in the air. He's hanging upside down, bound in tight black rope. There is an older man behind him, slowly spinning the rope, so the suspended man twirls. When he returns to facing the older man, he pulls him close to show that his mouth is perfectly aligned with the other man's groin.

I'm sure he did that on purpose.

"This is Maxwell," Mirabel says with a smile. "He's an excellent Shibari instructor. Be sure to stick around for his workshop. He'll pull someone from the audience to demonstrate."

I step a little closer to Hunter.

"We'll stick around then," he replies.

When I glance back at Drake to see his reaction to the idea of being pulled onstage to demonstrate, he's too busy eyeing a woman giving him a flirtatious stare. I have to bite back my envy at seeing his attention on someone else. I want to be bitter about it, but I guess I can't expect him to stay by my side all night.

He just took two girls home last night...does he really need to find someone else so soon? Doesn't he ever tire of it all?

Who am I kidding? Of course he doesn't. He's young and gorgeous and women are obsessed with him. If he can have a different one every night, why would he stop?

We watch the demonstration in silence as Maxwell slowly unravels the man suspended in the air, pulling the ropes in a way that allows him to slowly descend to the floor safely, without falling on his head.

Before he's done, I hear Mirabel speaking to Hunter, her voice just barely carrying over the music.

"Your guests are welcome to stay and watch the next demonstration if you'd like to come to the office with me, so we can talk business."

Hunter glances sideways at me. "Is that okay?"

"Of course," I reply with a smile. Glancing toward Drake, he nods, and in return, Drake steps a little closer to me, as if he instantly understood his best friend's silent request to protect me. Suddenly, his interest in the other woman is gone. It's not the first time Drake has had to *watch* me in a club. Hunter doesn't like me walking around alone, even in Salacious. Even if it's perfectly safe with cameras and bouncers at every turn.

So if he needs to step away, he hands me over to his best friend, like I'm a child who needs a babysitter. It grates on my nerves, but I don't argue. He just wants to protect me, and I know that's just how Hunter shows his love.

Hunter presses his lips to my cheek, squeezing me close to his body. "Be good," he growls in my ear, and chills run down my spine at the dark rasp of his words, which sound more like a sexy promise than a serious warning.

"Or what?" I reply, glancing back at him through my lashes.

He smacks my ass and kisses me on the lips, pressing his tongue between them and owning my body until I'm breathless in his arms. Then he tears himself away, leaving me disoriented and staring up at the stage.

The suspended man is no longer suspended. He's now standing front and center, completely naked, showing off the intricate rope marks all over his body. The crowd *ooh*s and *ahh*s at the performers like they are an artistic masterpiece.

"Looks like it hurts," Drake mutters next to me.

"What's wrong, Drake? Afraid of a little pain?" I tease, glancing up at him. He's standing closer than before, almost stationed behind me like some sort of bodyguard.

He leans down, until his mouth is closer to my ear, and replies, "Not at all. Are you?"

"Nope," I reply with my chin held high.

"You're telling me you wouldn't mind being strung up there like a piñata?"

I bite my lip as I stifle a laugh. "It doesn't look that much different than the aerial yoga we do in my studio."

His deep chuckle vibrates against my back. "I guarantee this is much different."

The man with rope stamps all over his body is gone now, and it's only Maxwell, the demonstrator, left onstage, and I look up just in time to see him staring at me. I'm struck silent as I wait for him to speak. I feel like I've been caught by the teacher talking in class.

"You two," he calls to me and Drake.

"Us?" I ask, pointing to my own chest.

"Yes. You two would be perfect for my next demonstration. Would you like to come up here and try this next one together?"

"I'm not—" Drake starts, but the man cuts him off.

"I won't touch her. Only you."

Drake stiffens behind me.

I'm speechless as I stare at the black ropes hanging from the ceiling. On the one hand, this could be an excellent training opportunity to learn what we need to know for Salacious, and I'd love to see how we could get our members involved in these demos. I've also always wanted to try Shibari. It's harmless. I mean…we are here to learn.

On the other hand, if Hunter sees me onstage, he might not react well.

But I'll be with Drake.

"Okay," I call as I take a step toward the stage.

"Really?" Drake replies quietly.

Turning around, I reach a hand toward him. "It's just a demonstration. We should learn this stuff. Come on."

He hesitates as he takes my hand but still lets me pull him up the three steps to the top of the black stage, where we meet Maxwell under the bright pink can light shining from the rafters.

"Beautiful couple," Maxwell greets us as we meet him in the middle of the stage.

Drake's hand is still in mine, so I give it a quick squeeze as I glance up at him with a tight-lipped smile. He only shakes his head in return. This is making him uncomfortable already, I can tell.

"Thank you," I reply to Maxwell.

"I'd love to show you how to tie the pentagram harness on this beautiful woman. Would you like to learn?" he asks.

Drake clears his throat. "Sure."

"Excellent. This dress is lovely, but the harness would fit better without it. Would you mind removing it? You can say no."

My mouth goes dry. Remove my dress? Onstage?

I scan the gathering crowd for any sign of Hunter or Mirabel, but I don't see them. I'm in a bra, and this is a sex club. I mean…it's hardly inappropriate here to be half-naked. And I am with Drake.

It's just a demonstration.

"Yeah," I answer quickly. Pulling the straps off of my shoulders, I let my dress fall down to my ankles. When I pick it up and turn to drape it over the chair to the left, I catch Drake's expression, and he looks downright livid. His cheeks are red, and no, that's not just the bright pink light shining on us. His eyes are wide and his jaw is set. He takes a step closer to me, keeping his eyes laser-focused on my face and not my nearly see-through bra.

"Beautiful," Maxwell says. Then he steals Drake's attention as he hands him one of the black ropes. "Now stand behind her," he tells him, and Drake obeys. He's so close behind me, I feel the warmth from his body against my skin.

"With the rope doubled, run the length between her breasts and around to the back."

I'm relaxed and standing there proudly, staring at the audience as Drake reaches around me and sets the rope against my skin. Even when he lays it between my breasts, I'm fine. But as the demonstration proceeds, each step adding another layer of rope around me, between my breasts, cinching them tighter until they begin to protrude through the layers of rope, my body begins to react in nervous arousal.

I can't quite sense how Drake is feeling, but every time his fingers swipe over my bare skin, goose bumps erupt, and I swear I almost imagine his touch lingering every time we connect. Even through the bumping music, I hear his breath in my ear as he works to bind me.

It's only a harness over my top half, wound around my breasts and torso. I look down to see a star pattern at the top of my chest.

"Please turn to show the audience the knot at the back," Maxwell tells him, and I flinch a little when I'm spun around. In nothing but a thong and this harness, my backside is on display for the audience and the cool confidence I felt a moment ago is gone.

As Maxwell demonstrates to Drake how to finish the knot at my back, I focus only on Drake's touch and his calming presence, weaving the rope in and out of itself until it's finished.

"Perfect," Maxwell announces when it's done. I glance up at Drake and we share a long moment of eye contact that's not like anything we've ever shared. It's not our usual inside jokes or laughing at awkward moments. It's intense and intimate.

"Please rotate for the audience," Maxwell says, and I do, spinning slowly to show off the harness. I might be wearing a bra, but I might as well be naked with the way this harness exposes my breasts.

The crowd applauds, and I think it's over, a feeling of relief washing over me.

But Maxwell doesn't show us how to take it off—not yet.

"This harness is great for different positions of domination. Simple and effective." Then, he looks at Drake as he says, "Take her by the front of the harness and pull her toward you."

My wide eyes meet Drake's before I discreetly nod. Then with an intensity shining in those blue eyes he has trained on my face, he grabs the harness directly between my breasts and jerks me toward him.

The air in my lungs is practically punched out of me as I collide against his hard body. Heat pummels my insides, lighting a fire in my lower belly.

The crowd reacts in a way I don't expect. There's no applause, but someone reacts loudly with something that sounds like a moan, and I start to feel dizzy with this strange new arousal I wasn't expecting.

"This is a great harness for lifts as well. Care to try it?" he asks, looking at Drake.

"Like this?" he asks, and he's no longer angry looking. He's not hesitating or holding back either. There's something in Drake's expression that shows just how much he's enjoying this now. Something about this really has him turned on—maybe rope bondage is one of his kinks.

Drake then reaches behind me, holding the tight knot on my back as the other hand reaches down to take my thigh as he lifts me easily, and my legs instinctually go around him.

The moment I have my thighs wrapped around Drake, something happens to me.

His waist is broader than Hunter's. The feeling of another man between my legs is foreign, but it is just Drake. He's my friend… my *best* friend. He's like family to me, and there is nothing sexual between us, but right now…the feeling of being weightless in his arms is intoxicating.

"Are you okay?" he whispers as he holds me effortlessly, our faces only inches apart.

Without a word, I nod. Because I am okay, and I'm not quite

sure if that is wrong or right. It doesn't feel wrong, but I'm a little worried by how good it feels. Even if we're not really crossing a line, I definitely should not feel this aroused in my husband's best friend's arms.

"You can set her down now," Maxwell says, and I tear my eyes away from Drake as he lowers me to the ground. "Turn her around, please."

Drake spins me so my back is to him, and once again, I think we've reached the end of the demonstration, and I'm only moments away from taking this rope off and being able to put my dress back on.

Wrong again.

"One last position," he says, and I glance up at Maxwell as he tells Drake, "bend her over."

My mouth goes dry. Because somewhere in the room, I feel Hunter's eyes watching us. I scan the room again, but I don't see him. I *feel* him, though. He's out there. He can see me exposed and tied up with his best friend, and my heart pounds wildly in my chest at the thought.

With a hold on the knot between my shoulder blades, Drake nudges me forward until I'm hinging at my hips. Then I glance up again, and this time, I do find those dark eyes in the crowd. He's standing at the edge of the room, next to Mirabel, staring at me and Drake. Where there should be rage and jealousy is an expression of awe and intrigue. Why isn't he stopping this?

"With the harness, control and thrusts are much more powerful. Care to demonstrate."

Drake and I tense at the same time. But the eyes of the crowd are on us and the energy in the room won't allow us to back out now. We've gotten this far and we're almost done, but even with my husband watching from across the room, I *feel* Drake behind me. I feel the sexy energy of his body holding mine. Overpowering and dominating and controlling me in a way that has my panties wet and my body on fire.

After clearing his throat, Drake jerks me backward but doesn't quite make contact with my backside the way I expected him to. I probably shouldn't be as disappointed as I am.

"Oh, I think you can do better than that. Really show her," Maxwell says, and there's a whoop from the crowd, urging Drake on. I hear him growl behind me as he tightens his grasp on my harness.

Then, I'm being violently jerked backward until I feel him slam into my backside, and I let out a howling yelp at the sudden impact. Boiling hot arousal swims through my bloodstream at the unmistakable sensation of his rock-hard length wedged roughly between my cheeks.

The crowd reacts again, this time clapping and hollering at our display.

As quickly as Drake slammed against me, he is gone. I suddenly miss the weight of his cock against my ass, and I can't seem to stop thinking about it. Even as I glance back up at Hunter across the room, watching with more of a blank expression on his face now.

Then Maxwell is walking Drake through removing my harness, and I can't think through a solid thought. My mind is swimming. I keep feeling him hard against me and the undeniable power of the thrust.

There's more applause as we rush off stage, and when we meet Hunter by the door, I glance up to see Drake shifting uncomfortably.

"That was impressive," Hunter says as his arms go around my waist, now safely covered by my dress. Although the rope still burns like an echo of our time onstage. I keep glancing at Hunter's face, looking for anger, but there is none. He seems calm, and I wonder if he's just storing up his anger for when we're in private or if seeing his best friend dry hump his wife onstage wasn't as upsetting as it probably should be.

"I need a drink," Drake mutters.

"Me too," I reply.

"Then let's go," Hunter adds, and with that, the three of us quickly move toward the door.

Rule #5: Why be jealous when you can be turned on?

Hunter

THE CAR RIDE TO THE RENTAL FROM THE CLUB IS QUIET. ISABEL IS next to me in the passenger seat with her hands folded in her lap, and her eyes are glued to the passing city through the window. Behind us, Drake is brooding. Every time I glance in the rearview mirror, I catch his eye contact for only a second before he looks away in a rush.

I find their strange sense of shame amusing. They look as if they've both been caught with their hands in the cookie jar, and maybe if I were an insecure man or thought for one moment that these two would ever even think about betraying me, I would be more worried. But I'm not.

What happened onstage was just a demonstration, and the presenter, Maxwell, clearly misjudged them as a couple. The little show they put on was entertaining, more so to me than anyone else, since I was the only one in the audience who knew just how uncomfortable that was for them.

Seeing them up there, my half-naked wife in the hands of my best friend…didn't quite have the effect on me I expected.

When I walked back into the main showroom, I paused at the door when I recognized the two people under the pink light. And while my mind echoed a cadence of *what the fuck*, my body didn't react the same way.

Maybe I should have wanted to charge the stage and tear my woman out of Drake's arms. I probably should have been boiling with anger at the sight of his fingers running the length of her spine, brushing over her barely covered breasts, and tickling the underside of her rib cage. But I didn't hate it.

I didn't hate it at all.

Isabel looked so small next to Drake's six-three frame. Her warm copper hair shone even brighter under the rose-colored lights. And I couldn't help but wonder what was going through his head during their little rope-tying exploration. I didn't have to wonder long because the moment Isabel moved to the side, everyone in the room, including me, got a view of his impressive reaction.

He was hard. Very hard, if I was judging correctly from my vantage point.

My best friend was visibly aroused while touching my rope-bound and scantily clad wife.

I should be fucking furious…but I'm not.

"What did you and Mirabel talk about?" Isabel asks in a meek voice as we pull up to the rental.

"Cross-promotion. She told me a little about how they handle their contracts and freelancers."

"Oh. Good," she replies, and then goes quiet again. She's acting strange.

"Did you like that demonstrator? We can talk to him about coming to Salacious."

"He was too formal and stuffy," Drake grumbles from the back seat.

"Never mind then," I joke.

"I don't know…I sort of liked him," Isabel adds with a sweet smile. My wife likes everybody, making her judgment a little hard to trust sometimes. But it makes me love her that much more. She doesn't have a vicious or cruel bone in her body. Reaching across the console, I squeeze her hand.

Once we get back to the rental, it's after midnight, and we should probably be exhausted, but the three of us have spent the last year adjusting our schedules to accommodate the late hours of the club. Isabel even hired staff to open her studio and switched to teaching the sunset classes instead of the sunrise ones.

So when we enter the small living space, none of us move toward the bedrooms. Instead, Drake pulls out the bottle of tequila he bought at a local shop today and pops it open with a determined look on his face.

"I'm going to get in my pajamas. Maybe take a bubble bath," Isabel says, eyeing Drake's sour mood at the kitchen counter.

"Sounds good, babe," I say, kissing the back of her hand before she disappears into the bedroom.

Returning to the living room, I watch Drake skeptically as he pours himself a glass.

"Better make that two," I say, and he does so without a response.

After handing me the glass, he throws back his shot, then lets out a weighted exhale and slams his empty glass on the counter. "Can we talk, please?"

"You okay?" I ask, swirling the golden liquid in the glass.

"No, I'm not okay. I tied up my best friend's wife in her underwear, and I feel like an asshole for it."

For the first time tonight, he finally looks me in the eye, and his expression is shrouded in remorse.

"Drake, it's fine. Relax. It was just a demonstration."

His brow furrows as he glares at me. "Stop it," he mutters.

A chuckle erupts out of my chest. "Stop what?"

"Being too fucking nice to me. Treating me like a fucking kid. You should want to wring my neck right now. You want to punch me? Fine. Just do it."

I'm laughing even harder now. "You're being fucking stupid. I'm not being too nice to you because I'm not fucking mad at you. What? Do you think I'm really worried you tried to grope my wife onstage with me in the room? Jesus, Drake. I've known you my whole goddamn life. If I thought for one second you were ever out to take Isabel from me, do you think I would have kept you around as long as I have?"

"If that were my woman up there, being touched by another man...gawked at by a whole room full of people...I'd lose my shit," he mutters over another glass of tequila. "I never should have let her get up there like that."

"You're beating yourself up over nothing."

His eyes find mine over the rim of the glass and he watches me for a long time before he slips the drink into his mouth. When he speaks again, he does it a little more quietly. "Everything okay with you guys?"

I flinch before glaring back at him. "Of course. Why would you say that?"

"Because you're strangely calm about all of this."

"Because it wasn't a big deal!" I argue. When he doesn't relax or say anything for a minute, I grab the bottle from his hand and set it on the counter. "Listen, I'm as surprised as you are, but seeing you with Isabel didn't make me mad. Maybe it's because the three of us practically grew up together, so I've seen you with her so long that it doesn't have any kind of effect on me. You can't get all worked up over one little mix-up and an accidental brush of a tit. It's not like you fucked her."

"Hunter!" he bellows, his head snapping up to stare at me in horror. "I would never. You know that."

"I do know that. Hence why I'm not even a little worried. Now will you just chill the fuck out?"

"Fine," he mutters. "It was just weird. That's all."

"Couldn't have been that weird. I mean...everyone saw how much you were enjoying it," I reply with a slight chuckle.

"Jesus Christ!" Drake snaps, pulling away from the counter like I punched him. "You saw that?"

Maybe the tequila's starting to set in because I probably shouldn't have admitted that to him since he looks slightly mortified.

"She's hot," I reply. "You think I'm going to fault your dick for noticing?"

"You're so fucking sick," he replies, this time actually cracking a smile.

And I'm relieved by that. I hate to see my best friend so upset, which might explain why I'm not as upset as I should be.

"I'm going to go check on her," I say, leaving Drake in the kitchen. He starts browsing through his phone, and I can tell by the softness of his expression and the slight loss of focus in his eyes that the tequila has set in. Which tells me he's not going to be upset about it anymore.

"Yeah, okay," he mumbles as I leave the room.

When I enter our bedroom with an attached en suite bathroom, I instantly pick up the smell of lavender, a scent that immediately has my cock stirring because it means she's near. These lavender baths are almost a daily ritual for her. Each night she escapes into her warm bubble bath, soaking in the calming scent, which she then brings to bed with her so our sex and my dreams are laced with the familiar smell. It's calmly infiltrated itself into my life, and I'm so not complaining.

"Hello, beautiful," I whisper, peeking my head into the foggy bathroom to find her with a book in her hands and bubbles up to her chin.

"Hey," she says sweetly, drunk on the heat of the water.

With a laugh, I sit on the side of her tub and brush a hand over her head. "Red, it's like a hundred degrees outside. How can you take a hot bath right now?"

"You know I love my nightly soaks. Besides, I wanted to give you a few minutes to talk to him. Is he okay?"

"He's fine. Why are you two making a big deal out of this?" I ask.

She sits up a little taller. "You're not mad?"

I shake my head. "Not at all. If anything…" I say, letting my hand skate over her cheek and down the moist skin of her neck. She hums in response. "That whole thing got me a little turned on."

"Seeing me being touched by your best friend turned you on?" she asks in a teasing tone.

And I know she's joking because that is ridiculous. I wouldn't be in my right mind if that turned me on, but she voices the exact thought in my head, except in my head…I'm not kidding.

Seeing Drake with my wife *did* turn me on. The sight of his hands on her body had my blood racing more than I'd like to admit. It's not exactly something I want to unpack right now. Or ever.

Because, deep down, the arousal that swept over me at that moment makes me feel like less of a man. Like Drake said, I should have been raging. I should have claimed her, punched him, and turned into a feral, territorial caveman. But I didn't. Instead, I watched with intrigue and excitement.

And when he slammed his stiff erection against my wife, the gasp that came out of her mouth made my already hard cock leak from the tip. I didn't want them to stop. I wanted him to do it again.

Even now, I can't deny the visions that keep flashing through my mind. Imagining him up there, instead of hiding his arousal in his pants, letting it out, so he could slam it into her for real. The more I think about her face and the sounds she would make as he fucked her, the harder and more excited I get.

Before I get lost in the erotic spiral of those visions, I pull my hand out of the tub and say, "Seeing you all tied up in that rope turned me on."

"Oh yeah? So what are you going to do about it?" Isabel asks seductively as she sets her book to the side and rests her head against the back of the tub.

I bring my focus back to her, this goddess of a woman lying naked in front of me, waiting for me to pleasure her. And I want nothing more than to indulge her.

"Well, let me think…" I say as I unbutton the sleeve of my right wrist. She bites her lip as she watches me roll it up to my elbow. Once it's pushed out of the way, I touch her neck again, taking my time to graze every perfect inch, from her collarbone down to her right breast, squeezing it in a delicate pinch. She whimpers as I skate my touch over her belly, and she begins to squirm when I find the tiny triangular tuft of hair between her legs.

As I slide my finger through her folds, she arches her back and lets out a hungry moan. Slipping my finger back, I find her clit and massage it in teasing circles as she begins to writhe in the water, causing some of the bubbles to spill over.

"Tell me what you want, Red. Tell me how you like it."

"Yes," she moans, her fingers gripping the sides of the tub. "Keep doing that."

"This?" I ask as I increase the pressure on her sensitive nub.

"Yes," she says again.

Keeping my touch on her clit for a while, I try to memorize the look and sound of her pleasure as I take her as close to her climax as I can get before I slow my massaging.

"I want to be inside you, pretty girl. Can I be inside you?"

Biting her lip, she lets her head hang back as she nods. "Mm-hmm."

With that, I ease my middle finger down to her entrance, pressing into her in one slow intrusion.

"Oh God, Hunter…" she cries out, and I quickly use my other hand to cover her mouth. With one hand on her face and the other buried deep in her warm pussy, I thrust inside her, bringing her close to climax again.

"Remember the first time, Red? Your eighteenth birthday. When I made you come with my hand in your bedroom while your parents were downstairs? Remember that? It was just like this, wasn't it?"

"Yes," she replies, her voice muffled by my hand.

"I had my hand up your skirt, and you soaked my fingers. Remember that, baby?"

"Oh, Hunter, yes," she cries, and I can tell by the way her thighs hug my hand tightly that she's at the height of her orgasm.

"That was the best day of my life, Red. The first time I felt you come. That was the day my life began. You know that, right?"

"Yes, yes, yes," she says with a long hum as I pull my hand away, so she can cry out loudly this time.

Unable to control myself, I slam my mouth against hers, tasting the warmth of her tongue against mine, a familiar friction. This woman has had a hold on me ever since I met her ten years ago.

And somewhere in the back of my mind, I know the reason I let her cry out is because I want him to hear it. Not because I'm showing off but because, in some way, I feel like he should be involved too.

He always is, where she and I are concerned.

Rule #6: When your friends won't let you leave the trip early, take it as a good sign they actually want you around.

Drake

"I HAVE EIGHT MONTHS LEFT ON MY LEASE. THIS IS FUCKING bullshit," I bellow into my phone. We're somewhere off the freeway at one of those roadside attraction rest stops, and while I'd like to be enjoying whatever *The Thing* is, the dismal phone call from my landlord is more important.

"I'm aware but the clause in your lease clearly states that the building owner reserves the right to terminate the contract in the case of massive renovations." The man on the line has a nasally voice and an uptight attitude and I'd like to sock him in the jaw right about now.

"So where the fuck am I supposed to go?"

"That's not our concern, Mr. Nielson. I'm very sorry for the inconvenience. You have until the end of the month to vacate the premises."

With that, the line goes dead, and I resist the urge to toss my phone into the desert.

"Ugh!" I growl as I pace the grease-stained concrete outside, waiting for Isabel and Hunter to come out.

When I glance up and see Isabel emerging with a bright green alien stuffed animal under one arm and a cup of coffee larger than her tiny head in her hand, my dark mood begins to crumble.

"What is that?" I laugh.

"You looked like you could use some cheering up." She hands me the alien, and I am physically unable to keep the scowl on my face, letting my expression morph into a smile just for her.

"Thank you," I reply. "So, what was *The Thing*?"

She shrugs. "I don't actually know. Might have been a dinosaur bone? Or an alien? They weren't exactly clear in their description."

I laugh, looking down at the green alien plush. "Sorry I missed it."

"Everything okay?"

"No. I'm being evicted," I mutter angrily.

"What? Why? Are you struggling—"

"No," I snap, cutting her off. "I make every payment on time, but these assholes decided they want to turn my apartment building into a parking garage."

"Oh my God!"

"Yeah. So I have until the end of the month to get out."

"Can they do that?" she asks, her hand over her chest. Oh, sweet, naive little Isabel. So pure she can't even wrap her head around how dickheads work. I love that about her.

"Apparently."

"So what are you going to do?"

"Probably going to have to catch a flight home from Austin. I need to find a new place to live."

Now, I could be imagining things or just seeing what I want to see, but I swear there's devastation in her expression.

"No! You can't do that."

And here I thought I was the annoying third wheel. Surely, she'd enjoy a nice road trip with her husband alone.

"I have to. I need to find an apartment and move out of my old one in the next three weeks."

When her hand lands on my arm, squeezing my bicep in a comforting grasp, I have to will my heart not to beat its way out of my chest. Every touch with Isabel after last night feels different. I can still remember what it felt like to hold her in my arms, her legs squeezed around my waist and her ass in my hands. I dreamt I was tying her up again; this time, she was naked and I was naked and I kept winding and winding and winding rope around her until her body became *our* bodies and I was tying them together.

In my dream, I was inside her, no longer pretending with layers of clothes between us, but I was buried deep in the same way we were simulating last night. When I woke up this morning, I couldn't move for over thirty minutes because the raging hard-on in my boxers taunted me with my own shame. I would never *ever* lay a hand on my best friend's girl like that, and tugging on my cock with the memory of her still fresh in my mind doesn't feel any better.

Now, there's a new tension between us, and I can't stand it.

Isabel has always been as much my friend as Hunter is. I love her…like a sister—nope. I can't even say that in my head without it feeling weird. Because even though I would never touch her like that, it doesn't change the fact that my body clearly wants to. So saying she's like a sister to me is the hardest nope of nopes.

"Drake, just stay with us," she says in a sweet, pleading tone.

"Like I said, I wish I could—"

"No. I mean…stay with us. At the house. I mean…you built the damn thing. I'm not going to let you rush into finding a new apartment. Put your stuff in storage and just take the extra room at our place until you get something more permanent. And for God's sake, buy this time."

I let out a huff, my shoulders sagging as I smile at her. "I can't do that, Isabel. I'm up Hunter's ass enough as it is."

The bell on the front door chimes as it opens, and we both look up to see the dark curls and tan skin of the devil himself as he emerges from the shop. "What's up?" He immediately notices our serious expressions.

"Tell Drake to stay with us."

Hunter freezes. "Okay...Drake, stay with us," he says, obeying his wife without question.

"His landlord is evicting him *this* month to turn his apartment into a parking garage," she adds.

"Seriously?"

I nod, letting out a heavy sigh. "They want me out by the end of the month. I need to cut my trip short. I'll fly out of Austin."

If I wanted Isabel to look disappointed at the news of me leaving, it was nothing compared to how good it feels to see Hunter's immediately gutted response at the news. Then, in true Hunter fashion, he takes control of the situation.

"No. You can't leave early. I need your help. You're looking at club infrastructures, remember? I don't know shit about that. So you have to stay on the trip."

"Dude, I have three weeks to move out and find a new place to live."

"Isabel's right. Just stay with us. You'll have a week to move your stuff into storage after we get home. You practically live at our place as it is. So enjoy the rest of the road trip with us and worry about your apartment when we get back."

My jaw clenches as I realize I've been cornered. There is no arguing with Hunter. He's always been like this. The leader, decision-maker, commander-in-chief of our friendship, and I'd be lying if I said it bothered me. The truth is, it's always given me a strange sense of comfort, knowing that everything is in his hands. Even, sometimes, my life.

"Besides, all you own is a bed and a couch. You don't even have a TV in that apartment. It'll take us less than an hour to move it all out. So just relax."

He bumps my shoulder as he passes by, throwing an arm around Isabel and leading her to the car.

I'm not sure why this is bothering me so much. If I love handing over control, then why is this one time troubling me so much? Maybe because Hunter has no idea just how much it scares me to live with them. It has nothing to do with sharing a space with them. I mean, obviously. We're on this two-week road trip together, sharing rental houses and the car, and like he said, I stay over at their place all the time. And I've lived with them before.

But something about *living* with them now, even if it's temporary, is making me anxious. What if I don't find a place right away? What if I get used to being there? Drinking coffee with Isabel every morning. Staying up late with Hunter every night. Sharing meals and doing laundry together. It's so fucking domestic, and something about that makes my skin crawl.

I love Hunter and Isabel, but their happy little married life is not for me. Sleeping with the same person every night and waking up with the same person every morning. The monotony of it sounds so draining.

And what about bringing home women? I can't possibly bring a hookup into their house. I've never done it before and it's clearly different from a vacation rental. That's their home.

I guess it's a good thing I have the club.

Fuck, between work and Salacious, I doubt I'd ever be at their house anyway.

And I do hate the idea of cutting this trip short, even after the awkward stage moment last night.

"Fine," I mutter from the back seat of Hunter's Durango as we pull out of the gas station.

Isabel turns toward me with excitement. "You'll do it? You'll stay?"

A smirk tugs on the corner of my mouth. "Yeah. I'll stay. But only for a week or two. Until I find a better place."

"Of course," she says, a beaming smile spreading across her cheeks.

Our eyes meet, and the excitement in her expression morphs into something else, something more loaded than just eagerness.

I'd give my right arm to know what she's thinking right now, to know how excited she really is and why.

"You can stay as long as you want," Hunter says, glancing at me through the rearview mirror, and I quickly avert my eyes from both of their gazes.

"Thanks. You guys are too good to me."

When I feel Isabel's hand against my leg, I flinch, something I've never done before. And she notices, but she doesn't move her hand away. "You don't need to thank us, Drake. You're family. We would do anything for you."

I know what she's saying is true. They *would* do anything, but that's the problem. Hunter and Isabel hold me on a short leash… and they don't even know they do it. It's like an emotional boundary I can't cross, never letting me get too far away from them. And that's my fault—because I've indulged them repeatedly over the past ten years.

I've been a third wheel in their lives for so long, I don't know how to be without them, and I know they'll grow sick of me before long. This little triad has to come to an end eventually. A thought that doesn't feel good when I think about it because it's not about my feelings for Isabel or for Hunter…it's about them with a capital T.

I care about the two of them more than anyone else in the world.

Rule #7: There's a kink for everyone.

Hunter

IT'S A LONG DRIVE FROM PHOENIX TO AUSTIN. DRAKE AND I TAKE turns driving, and he took over in El Paso. Isabel is sleeping peacefully with her head in my lap in the back seat, while Drake has his music on, which means a lot of time for me to think. And the only place my mind wants to reside anymore is on that demonstration in the club last night.

At first, it was strange how *not* angry I was at seeing my wife's legs wrapped around my best friend. But it's even more alarming that every time I think about it, I get a buzz of excitement, and I have to adjust myself in my pants.

Now, I just have to admit it, at least to myself—thinking about them together in a sexual way turns me on.

I've been in the kink business for seven years now. I know that the shit that gets us excited doesn't have to be something we're ashamed of—assuming it involves consent, of course. So I'm not going to bother being embarrassed by this new revelation. I'm a human, like anyone else, and I have no more control over my kinks than Garrett, the voyeur, or Emerson, the Dom.

But why haven't I noticed this one before?

When we started the Salacious dating app, which is still running without a hitch, thanks to our development team, I was in charge of that department. I found the guys who made the technical stuff happen, but it also meant I was the guy responsible for organizing the whole damn thing. I had to explain to a group of code-writing virgins what each of these kinky designations meant and how to set an algorithm that would filter the app subscribers into their proper kinky groups.

So I know probably more than any other owner of the club when it comes to kinks.

Which means I know exactly what cuckolding is—known more recently as *hotwifing*. Not something I knew existed seven years ago, but apparently, there are a whole lot of people out there who want to watch someone fuck their significant other. It's grown in popularity over the last few years and was ranked in the top five of our categories, which meant our members were more into cuckolding than being whipped and paddled—which came in at number seven.

Number one was submission, for what it's worth. Turns out a good Dom is hard to find.

What's really weird to me is all that time, when I was helping the team develop the algorithm and putting together the entire *Find Your Kink* quiz new members had to take, I had no clue that I had one myself.

But cuckolding is based on humiliation and degradation, and I sure as fuck don't want to be humiliated. I want to be aroused. Does that make my kink more *hotwife*—just a guy who wants to share his beautiful woman with someone else? Who the fuck knows and who cares about terms? The point is…the idea of them gets me aroused and I want to know why.

The idea of being turned on by watching someone else touch Isabel never crossed my mind. Not until I saw the way Drake hoisted her into his arms, one hand planted firmly on her ass and the other holding the harness wrapped around her torso. And my body immediately reacted with a visceral response screaming *mine*.

But it was that instinctive possessiveness that turned me on in the first place. Because she's mine, I wanted to see him touch her. Because she's mine, I wanted to watch him experience just how perfect she is. And seeing him touch what is mine only made me more desperate to claim her again.

It awoke something primal and territorial in me.

So powerful, in fact, that I want to see them touching again. I know that's insane, but I can't help it. Even now, with her head resting on my leg, just thinking about her on Drake's cock has mine stirring.

I glance up at the rearview mirror, but Drake's eyes are focused on the road as he bops his head to the classic rock blasting through the speakers. Watching him, I briefly wonder…is it only Drake I want to see with Isabel?

What if it were Garrett? Or Emerson?

The image is uncomfortable and ill-fitting. It doesn't have nearly the same effect that picturing my best friend does.

But would he do it? No. I know that answer without a second thought. There is no one on earth more loyal than Drake, and from the moment I claimed Isabel as mine, he threw his hands up in surrender, never bringing up how beautiful he thought she was that day we saw her walking by.

Drake and I don't have an origin story. I don't remember a moment in my life he wasn't there. We grew up as neighbors on a completely different side of the tracks than Isabel did, and when the world gave us less than nothing, we always had each other.

When my dad laid into me on his extra drunk and angry days, it was Drake's basement I hid in. When his mother brought home yet another faceless, nameless boyfriend, with no sense of respect for her own son, it was my room he escaped to. Through the years, we had each other's backs through it all, which meant some less than questionable decisions in our teens, but when I decided to clean up my future for Isabel, I brought Drake with me. Lent him the money he needed to get his contracting license and the startup for his own company, never giving him a choice about it either. I wasn't leaving him behind. Not ever.

So would he do this if I asked him to? Without question, no. And not because he has trouble refusing me, but because he's just that loyal.

Would she?

That one is a little more of a tricky question. And it's one I don't like thinking about too much. She would if I asked her because that's what Isabel does. She makes me happy, no matter the personal cost. But would she want to? That's the real question.

I'm not blind. I know Drake is more attractive than me. Taller, more built, fewer tattoos, and a face created for smiles instead of scowls. If anything, he's a better fit for my demure Isabel, if not for his relentless promiscuity.

Of course, all of these thoughts are purely hypothetical. I couldn't bring myself to actually ask for this—could I?

No, it's ridiculous. Asking two people to forfeit their own values for my personal pleasure. I couldn't do that to them. What on earth would they get out of it? Aside from sex, of course.

And if I could tell anything by that little display on the stage, it's that these two clearly have some chemistry and want each other. If I ask them to have sex and let me watch, isn't that just me giving them permission to do what they already want?

Isabel has *only* been with me. Maybe being with someone else would give her more perspective. She could see what sex is like with someone else, even at the risk of her liking it so much she wants more. That's a risk I'd have to take.

Rule #8: If you're going to ask your best friend and wife to sleep together, breakfast isn't really the time to do it.

Hunter

"Oh, there's a brunch place down the street that does mimosa flights," Isabel says, staring down at her phone. Fresh out of the shower, with her wet hair cascading down her back, she's curled up on one of the dining room chairs, scrolling through the best places to eat in Austin.

"That sounds good," Drake replies groggily over his mug. "Coffee first, though."

"I wonder if they're still even doing brunch," she adds.

It was the middle of the night when we finally pulled into the Austin hotel we're staying at for the next two nights. This time we got an actual hotel, but this one is a suite, so we're still in the same room, but not sharing spaces. It has a big living room and a giant window that overlooks the city.

The first thought to assault my mind when I open my eyes is that little idea I had before going to sleep last night. I can't stop thinking about it. I'm obsessed, and until I say something to them, the idea is going to keep hounding me.

And as I watch them casually chatter back and forth about

brunch and mimosas, the invasive thoughts about them together don't ease up. If anything, they get worse.

Our plan today is to explore the city a little before hitting the club tonight. The club we're seeing is another female-owned club, but the theme here is a little more like Salacious. Kinks and variety and lots of opportunity to mingle.

But I can't think that far yet. My brain is like a hamster on a wheel with this cuckolding shit.

Isabel laughs at something Drake says, and I lean back in my chair, watching them. God, I want this so bad. Somehow in the past twenty-four hours, I've grown obsessed with this idea.

"What do you think, babe?" Isabel asks, looking at me.

"Huh?"

"Do you want brunch? They have Bloody Marys."

She's staring at me with those sweet green eyes, brows raised and a gentle smile on her lips. And I can't help myself. I've lost my fucking mind because if I don't get this out now, I might fucking lose it.

"Do you know what cuckolding is?" I ask, and she freezes, her face stuck with the same waiting expression she wore after asking me about brunch.

"What the fuck are you talking about?" Drake replies when Isabel doesn't.

"Cuckolding. It's a kink. Isabel, do you know what it means?" I ask, my eyes not leaving her.

She finally moves, clearing her throat and averting her eyes from my face. "Yeah, isn't that…like being cheated on or something?"

"Why are you asking about that?" Drake interjects. His knuckles are visibly tighter around his mug.

"It's not quite cheating because everything is consensual. Some people just like seeing their partner with someone else," I explain.

She's fidgeting uncomfortably when she gazes back up at me. "Oh. Okay. Why do you ask?"

Here goes nothing.

"I think I'd like that."

Drake lets out a loud scoff and an uncomfortable laugh. "No, you wouldn't."

Isabel is tense, frozen in her seat as her eyes dance back and forth from my face to her hands.

"Yeah, I think I would," I reply, staring at her. "Is that wrong?"

"It's a form of humiliation," Drake argues. "That's not you at all."

"It *can* be a form of humiliation, yes. But it doesn't have to be," I reply.

"Why are you bringing this up?" she asks.

"Because I can't stop thinking about it. And we own a sex club, where everyone gets to explore their fantasies, and I think I just found mine. What? Am I not allowed to express what I want?"

"You want me…to cheat on you?"

"Not cheat, baby. I want to watch you with someone else. That's all."

She laughs. "That's all?"

Suddenly, Drake stands up, the legs of his chair scraping against the floor as he walks to the sink. "You've lost your damn mind, Hunt. I'm not kink-shaming anyone, but sharing your woman…that's not exactly a kink. It's just plain crazy."

"Not if it's with someone you trust," I reply, and he freezes, his mug halfway to the sink.

The tension in the air grows thick as we drown in silence, and part of me wants to take it back. This was an insane idea, but it's too late now.

Drake sets his mug down and slowly turns toward me. His brows are furrowed, pinched with a deep wrinkle between the two. He's giving me a skeptical expression as if he's trying to discern if I'm kidding or not.

I'm not.

There's a long moment of silence, very *awkward* silence, before he finally lets out a heavy breath. "I need a drink. I think I saw a bar on the way in. I'll walk. You guys have fun in the city and I'll meet up with you tonight."

His heavy footsteps carry him across the hotel room before the door opens and closes slowly as he disappears in a rush. Feeling defeated, I melt into the chair and stare across the table at Isabel. It's a long time before she speaks, her sweet voice gentle and polite.

"That was really awkward," she murmurs.

I reply with a laugh. "Think so?"

"Why did you say that, Hunter?"

"Because I can't stop thinking about it. I figured there might not have been a better time or place to bring it up, but—"

"Wait," she stammers, leaning forward. "You're being serious?"

"You don't think I'm that bad at making jokes, do you?"

"Hunter!" she yelps, covering her mouth with her hand. "How can you ask that?"

When I reach for her, she bolts backward, standing from her chair as she stares down at me in shock. Seeing the horror on my wife's face has me instantly regretting everything. I thought there was no harm in asking, but now I'm afraid there was a lot of harm in asking. What if this thing lives between us forever, implanting doubt and betrayal that she never truly sheds after I've asked her to fuck someone else?

"Baby, I'm sorry. It was just…"

"You don't want me anymore," she replies, tears filling her eyes.

My face falls and my blood runs cold. "Isabel Scott, don't you say that. Of course, I want you. I will always fucking want you."

"Then, why would you want me to be with someone else?"

"I don't know," I reply, the tone of my voice growing louder as I throw my hands up. "I wish I did! All I know is that seeing you onstage with Drake, seeing him…touch you…it did something to me."

"Oh God," she wails, dropping her face to her hands. "This is about that night. Of course it is! It meant nothing—"

"I know it meant nothing," I say. "That's my point, baby. The thought of it being more than nothing...turns me on."

When she pulls her face out of her hands, she looks back up at me with her mouth hanging open and her eyes soft and wet from approaching tears. "Really?"

"Really. Izzy, I would *never* ask you to do something you don't want to do. If you say no, then I'll never ask again for as long as I live."

"No," she snaps without hesitation, and the air in my lungs flies out in a disappointed whoosh.

That's the end of that, then.

It takes me a moment to close my jaw and round the table to pull her into my arms. She collapses easily against my chest as I kiss the top of her head.

"I'm so sorry, baby. That was stupid of me to ask. I know. I just...I can't help what turns me on."

"It's okay," she mumbles against my neck. "I only want you, Hunter. You're the *only* one I've ever wanted." When she lifts her chin and gazes up into my eyes, I lean down and press my lips to hers.

"I don't deserve you," I reply, and I feel like a monster for what I just admitted. "Izzy, if I ever made you feel one time in our marriage like I didn't want you, I'm a fool, and I didn't mean to."

"Then, why would you want this?"

The last twenty-four hours I've been asking myself that same exact thing, and I wish I could understand the psychology behind why I want this, but none of it makes any sense. It's not a way of thinking...it's a way of feeling.

Running my thumb along her jawline, I tilt her head up toward me again. Those emerald-green eyes are even brighter when she's on the verge of tears, and as beautiful as it is, I hate her tears. Seeing Isabel cry feels like a knife to my heart. She waits with those tear-soaked irises aimed at me, and I owe her as much of an answer as I can find.

"If anything, Red, it's because I *do* want you. My whole life has been a struggle, but lately, it's been so easy. Loving you is easy. Being with you is *so* easy. My job is easy. My friendship with Drake is easy. I miss the fight. I want to fight for you again. And I think seeing you with someone else would wake up that fight in me."

She gives me a contemplative expression. "There has to be another way," she replies.

And I kiss her again. "I'm sure there is."

"I mean…what if it makes you crazy with jealousy? What if you can never forget it and it ruins our entire marriage? What if—"

I quiet her worries with another kiss. "Red, forget about it. I won't ask about it again."

"Hunter, I can't risk losing you."

"I know, baby. But nothing in the world would ruin our marriage, understand? Nothing."

The feel of her warm body in my arms brings me enough comfort to ease the anxiety I felt a moment ago.

"Are you going to talk to him?" she mumbles after a moment.

"I probably should."

"Go," she replies, pulling out of my arms.

"No, we have plans today," I reply. "You wanted a mimosa flight."

"There is time later for mimosas, Hunter. Go talk to him before he books a *flight* home."

"Are you sure?"

She leans up on her tiptoes and presses her lips to mine. "Yes. I'm going to shower. Don't drink too much. We still have to tour the club tonight."

"I love you," I murmur against her kiss.

"I know you do. Now go," she says, pushing me toward the

door. Pocketing my cell phone and grabbing the hotel key off the table, I glance back at her before disappearing through the door in search of my best friend…to apologize for basically asking him to fuck my wife.

Rule #9: Don't make bets with a gambling man.

Drake

BRIGHT LIGHT BATHES THE DARK CORNERS OF THIS SEEDY BAR every time someone walks in, and every time that happens, I glance up, expecting it to be Hunter. Because I know he's coming. Eventually, he's going to walk through that door and want to talk about what just happened back at the hotel.

And every time the bright Texas sun infiltrates my corner of the bar and it *isn't* my best friend silhouetted in the doorway, I breathe a sigh of relief. I'm not ready.

I've rehearsed my argument over and over, replayed every moment of that short and awkward conversation, twisting and bending his words in hopes of finding the part where I misheard him. But no matter how I try to translate it, it comes out the same.

And I'm pretty fucking sure this is a test. No, I'm one hundred percent sure this is a test. After that rope bondage thing the other day, Hunter is feeling insecure and nervous, so he's hooking me up to the machine to test my loyalty. To see if I would ever touch his woman. And he should know, I would *fucking* never.

The real problem is, I don't know how to respond to this. Because the more I keep trying to say *no, no, no* in my head, it all sounds so forced and fake.

Probably because it *is* forced and fake.

I'm forcing myself to say "no, I will not fuck Isabel" because Hunter *cannot* know just how badly I want to. How I've dreamt about fucking her two nights in a row, and before this trip, I've casually dreamt about it for the past ten years.

Again, I would *never*. But the brain does some tricky shit even when you tell it not to. And the only part of me that listens worse than my horny brain is my horny dick. Both of them have conspired against me.

So when he does walk through that door, I have to be ready. I have to make it sound like I genuinely do not want to sleep with that beautiful woman, without it coming across as insulting to her. I'm going to pass this fucking test of his, and then I'm never going to touch Isabel again for as long as I live.

I'm on my second beer, at only noon, when the front door opens again, revealing a familiar crop of curly hair and broad shoulders. He's not in his usual suit and tie for work. In vacation mode, Hunter has on a short-sleeve Henley, tight enough to reveal the shape of his hard pecs and bulging biceps, and I consider it an honor that he will let me see him like this since he's always hiding his tattoos from his *work friends*.

His dark eyes find me across the bar in a heartbeat, without even having to look for long. I mean, I am six three and hard to miss, but Hunter's always had the uncanny ability to seek me out of any crowd like a homing beacon. A lifelong friendship has given us a natural sense of connection. I can just sense when Hunter is in a room, as if his presence changes the air around me. As if it's easier to breathe when he's there.

My hand tightens around my glass as he crosses the dingy, dark bar to take the barstool next to mine. I keep my eyes focused forward as he orders his own beer, and I wait for him to speak first.

Except, he doesn't. It's quiet for too long. The bartender drops the beer on the counter. Hunter takes a sip. Then he lets out a heavy sigh, and I keep waiting for him to say something, but he doesn't. Why the fuck is he so bad at this? Why can't he just speak? At least to me.

My patience runs out as I mutter in his direction, "I know you're testing me."

"I'm not testing you," he replies plainly.

"Yes, you are, and I don't blame you, but—"

"Drake, I'm not fucking testing you," he barks in response.

My eyes widen. "So you're telling me that was serious?"

"Yes." The cool confidence in his expression is infuriating. How can he be so calm about this? It makes me want to knock him right off his seat.

Hiding my frustration, I turn away from him, facing my beer again. "That club is going to your head."

He laughs. "My sex club, you mean?"

"Yeah. You've changed. All this kinky shit is going too far."

Leaning forward, he glares at me. "You mean the same sex club *you're* at every night? It's changing *me*?"

"Yes, Hunter. I've always been the way I am, but the man I knew ten years ago would never say what you said this morning."

"Oh, come on, Drake. It was one fucking idea. Isabel said no, so I dropped it. It's over."

My brows pinch together in disgust as I turn toward him. "How could you ask her that? I get it if you want to put me to the test, but her?"

"I asked *her* because I'm not the kind of guy who asks my best friend to fuck my wife without letting her in on the request."

My beer glass slams so hard against the lacquered bartop, it silences everyone around us. I have to cool myself down before I get myself kicked out, but my temper is rising. I honestly have no clue why I'm reacting so viscerally to this. But it's Hunter's nonchalance that really makes me irritable.

This means so little to him. It couldn't possibly mean more to me.

"Stop saying that," I grit through my teeth.

"I'm not going to be ashamed of what I want. Even if I can't have it. I have never passed judgment on you for your sexual activity or the things you like, so I don't understand why you're being so dramatic over mine."

"Maybe because *I'm* involved."

"You're only *involved*," he replies, leaning closer so no one else can overhear us, "because my little fantasy involves watching someone with my wife, and you're literally the only person on earth I would trust enough to do that."

"Do you hear yourself?" I reply in a low whisper, leaning closer. "You're asking me to sleep with Isabel."

Then, point-blank with his stoic eyes focused on mine, he asks, "Do you want to?"

And I'm rendered speechless. All the rehearsals I did in my head for how I would answer this, without sounding fake or forced, are useless now because it's written clear as day on my face.

Instead of answering, I stare slack-jawed at him, and it's enough of a confirmation for him. I quickly pull away, grabbing my beer and guzzling the rest of it down.

"You think I'm mad because you want her?" he asks, but I ignore him, nodding at the bartender, so he knows to refill my empty glass. He walks over, giving Hunter a skeptical side-eye as he takes my glass and carries it over to the tap.

Hunter continues, "Drake, I'm not surprised you want her. Who wouldn't? If anything, the fact that you do want her and haven't made a move proves to me more than anything how good of a friend you are."

"So this *is* a test?"

"No," he barks.

"It's not normal," I mutter as the bartender returns my glass, foaming at the top, and I quickly take a long drink.

"Define normal," Hunter replies.

"You are my best friend, and that is just a line you don't cross."

"I'm asking you to cross it."

"When you got married, I stood at the altar next to you. I was there when you made those vows, and I took them very fucking seriously."

"I'm not breaking vows, Drake. It's just sex."

I don't know if I'm losing my patience because he won't give up or because he's starting to wear me down. Or because I know Hunter always gets what he wants. I know, deep down, that if this is really what he wants, he's going to get it. Even if I say no. Even if Isabel already did. Hunter will somehow get us to say yes and he'll get what he wants because he always does.

Turning toward him, I give him a scathing glare. "My parents were never married. I never even met my dad. The only marriage I know is yours, and it's sacred, maybe not to you, but to me. I would rather die before I did anything to jeopardize that. Please don't ask me to do this."

I feel the curious stares of the people at the bar now, but the only pair of eyes I see are the dark brown ones staring back at me. There's heavy emotion in his features, telling me that he's listening. That he feels something about what I'm saying, but I'm afraid it's still not enough.

Then he leans closer to me, his jeans brushing against mine as his knee squeezes between my legs, and I have to force myself to swallow because Hunter doesn't see touches like that the same way I do. They don't affect him the way they affect me, so I bite my tongue and keep quiet.

"Maybe the reason my marriage is so sacred to you is because you've always been a part of it. And maybe what I'm asking you isn't so crazy after all."

I'm frozen in place as he drops a twenty on the bar and gets up from his seat. Even as he walks out of the bar, I'm stuck in a state of shock.

What the fuck was that supposed to mean?

When I get back to the hotel, four tall beers later, I find it empty and quiet. They must have gone sightseeing after all.

We're supposed to check out another club tonight, and normally, I'd be all for that, but right now, the idea is turning me off. The only thing I want to do right now is take a piss, sleep off this beer buzz, and pretend this morning didn't happen.

Groggily, I wander down the hall toward the bathroom, and charge through the closed door, heading straight for the toilet. But I don't make it to the toilet. Instead, the feminine gasp and the sight of pale, freckled flesh in front of me halts my movement.

The beer has my brain moving a little slowly because, instead of bolting out of the bathroom like I should when my eyes land on a naked Isabel, I stand and stare like the dumb asshole I am.

"Oh shit," I say in a breathy mumble as my gaze focuses on her small, perky breasts, cascading downward until I'm just staring at the tiny triangle patch of curly, copper pubic hair.

She doesn't cover up. Her hand does not slide over her private parts like they should when your husband's best friend barges through a clearly closed door, like the ogre he is, and although I'm probably standing there staring for only a split second, it feels like so much longer. That one long second might as well be ten minutes of me gawking at her naked body, memorizing every tiny freckle, the curve of her collarbones, the way her hip bones jut out from her delicate frame, looking so fragile she could break.

In that one split second, I commit all of Isabel to memory, a memory I have no rights to and definitely don't deserve.

But like I said, my brain is a horny, fickle asshole who doesn't behave.

When the world starts spinning again, I crash backward, out

of the bathroom and bolt toward the living room. A moment later, she's behind me, a soft hand on my shoulder as I stumble toward the fridge for a bottle of water.

"Drake, stop," she commands, and I keep my eyes averted, even when she puts herself in front of me. To my relief, she's covered herself, wrapping a white towel around her body.

"I'm sorry. I didn't know you were home. Where's Hunter?" I ask, looking around for him.

"He went out to get something to eat. We decided to stay home since you were gone."

"You didn't have to do that," I reply. "Why were you naked?"

"I went down to the gym while you guys were gone. I just showered again."

I'm anxious, feeling cornered by her in the hotel room because, at any moment, Hunter is going to walk through that door and see me standing here with his almost-naked wife and normally, that wouldn't freak me out, but after how bizarre this whole fucking week has been, being alone with Isabel has a whole new significance.

"Are you okay?" she asks.

Finally, I meet her gaze to see that she's just as unnerved as I am. "I'm okay. Are you okay?"

Instead of saying yes, she shrugs. "We should talk about this."

"About what?" I ask, even though I know full well what we're supposed to be talking about.

"About what he said this morning."

"I told him no, Isabel. You told him no. I know Hunter can be relentless, but this is up to us, and as long as you say no, that won't change."

Her lips press into a thin line as a look of uncertainty colors her features. *Oh no, Isabel. Please don't waver. Please, please, please.*

"What's that look for?" I ask, feeling myself deflate.

"Are you saying no because you don't want to...or because you think it's wrong?"

Holy shit. If the earth could just swallow me up right now, that'd be fucking great.

"Does it matter?" I ask.

"Yes. It matters to me." She's so perfect, so gracious and delicate and wonderful, and it would be too easy for a man to take advantage of Isabel, a thought that makes me see red because she's the last person on earth to deserve that. So admitting to her how badly I want her feels just as harmful as lying and saying that I don't.

But something is calling me to tell her how I really feel, to make sure she knows that my resistance to this ridiculous idea has nothing to do with her.

Hunter put me in this position, and I hate him for it.

"Isabel, I'm saying no to Hunter because jeopardizing our friendship and your marriage is the last thing on earth I'd ever want to do." I take a big inhale, sealing my fate to hell as I continue, "But if you're asking if I'd ever want what he's asking for, the answer is unconditionally, enthusiastically…yes."

Her breath hitches as she gazes up at me, wide green eyes and gentle lips parted. I shouldn't be this close to her or even talking to her like this, but Hunter did this. Hunter brought it up and forced us into this conversation.

"Really?" she whispers.

I take a small step forward until the knuckles of her hand holding up her towel are brushed up against my abs as I lean down until my mouth is closer to her ear. "Really."

Maybe I'm more drunk than I thought. Because I would never do this. I would *never* do this. But I still have the image of her perfect body in my head, and I need her to know that I'm not going to agree to this, but it's not because she doesn't turn me on.

Drifting a hand to her lower back, pressing gently against the fabric of the towel, I pull her closer until the aching stiffness in my pants is wedged between us, so she can *feel* how true my words are.

It's a violation. I know that. But again…it's Hunter's fault. He opened Pandora's box, and this relationship between Isabel and me was purely platonic and innocent until he flipped the lock open and unleashed it all, so now we're swimming in evil, sexual tension and possibility.

She gasps at the feel of my erection against her stomach, leaning in just enough for me to know she's not cowering in fear.

Then we both pull away. And that's the end of it. Turning away from each other, we both take a moment to catch our breaths and steady our beating hearts.

With her back to me, she mumbles, "I know you're afraid of jeopardizing our friendship, but I'm afraid if we *don't* do this, I'm jeopardizing my marriage."

"Isabel, you should never feel pressured into doing something—"

"I'm not pressured, Drake. I feel…the same way you do."

I turn away again. That wasn't exactly something I needed to know. Now I have to live with that knowledge and I have a feeling it's going to haunt me for a while.

"But I'm also afraid that my husband wants something I can't give him."

"Then, say no," I argue, turning back and finding space between us again as I lean against the counter, fighting the urge to go to her like before.

"That's not— It's not important. My point is that it's just sex. I trust you, and I don't think Hunter is asking for anything we wouldn't all benefit from."

Benefit from? Is she serious? I'm not looking to *benefit* from anything. I feel like I'm the only sane person in the group right now. And I really can't believe I'm about to be the only one turning down sex.

"What if it drives him crazy? What if he sees me with you and hates me forever? What if he takes it out on you?"

Her shoulders soften as she gazes up at me. "That won't

happen. You know Hunter as well as I do, and he doesn't do things on impulse. He's looked out for me since the day we met and he's looked after you even longer."

"I can't believe you're considering this. Isabel, think about this."

"I have, Drake. I know it will change everything between us, but...what if things between us are ready for a change?"

She's not making any sense. But I don't have any more time to argue because a moment later, the hotel door opens, and Hunter enters with two big bags of food. He pauses a few steps in, when he sees me standing in the kitchen opposite his wife in nothing but a towel.

Moving slowly, he sets the bags down on the table. "I assume you two were talking..."

"Yes," she replies.

My jaw clenches as I stare at the floor. I can't explain my anger, but it's still boiling inside me.

"And..."

She lets out a sigh. "And...nothing. We're just talking." It actually sounds like she's on his side. That didn't take much.

So maybe *it is* just me. Maybe these two are so fucking reckless that they're willing to bet everything on Hunter's stupid fantasy. Well, I'm not. He'll see me touch Isabel once, and not like the way I did at the demonstration, but more. Kissing her or something, and he'll snap. He'll realize how fucking wrong this is and regret everything.

Then, an idea pops into my head.

"Trial run...tonight," I blurt out, the half-thought-out plan just slipping through my lips without a second thought.

"What?" she asks.

"At the club tonight, Isabel can go with me. You can watch—no sex," I add, clearing that up real fast. "But we'll see how it feels before we commit to anything else. I bet you anything just seeing her on my arm will have you changing your mind."

"What are you willing to bet that on?" he replies, staring back at me with a smug expression.

"If you keep your cool tonight, and you really still want it, then I'll agree to it. But if you freak out at all, even a little, it's off. Forever."

"Deal," he replies.

The room is bathed in silence as we stare at each other. The beer buzz is officially gone, so I can't blame this on being drunk, but it doesn't exactly clear things up.

What the fuck did I just agree to?

Rule #10: It's okay to want what you want.

Isabel

EVERYTHING IN HERE IS PINK. IT'S SORT OF GENIUS, ACTUALLY. Keeping the design feminine is very empowering. And for a club filled with horny, straight men, I love it.

Drake and I are lingering by the door as we wait in line to enter. I'm filled with anxious energy with my arm looped through his. If this, whatever Drake has planned, works out, tonight is sure to be interesting. And if Hunter keeps his cool, then that means we're doing this.

I'm going to have sex with Drake.

While my husband watches.

My belly tingles with heat and excitement every time I think about it. But I have no doubt Drake isn't going to make this easy on Hunter. He's going to do everything he can to trigger my husband into backing out of the deal. It's like a sexy game of chicken, and I'm in the middle.

Hunter is already in the club. He came an hour early to meet with the owner, so just knowing that he's somewhere in this building, ready to watch, has me on edge.

"You okay?" Drake whispers, and I smile up at him.

"Yep."

When we reach the front, the woman takes our names, checks our reservation, goes over some rules, confiscates our phones, and ushers us inside. Based on the lobby, the inside is…not what I expected. For one thing, there are far more women here than men, it's far too bright, and there are quite a few people walking around almost completely naked.

Unlike Salacious, where the public displays are kept strictly in the VIP and voyeur hall, that's not the case here. There is a woman openly groping another woman…at the bar.

"Um…wow," Drake mutters as he freezes two steps inside the club.

A feeling of disappointment washes over me. I really, really wanted to love this club, but even this is a little too openly sexual for me. Silently, I summon my inner Mia—the girl who doesn't bat an eye at masturbating in public, since she literally does it every day—and I pull Drake farther into the club.

"Do you see him?" I ask, looking around without obviously searching for him.

"No, but I'm too distracted to see him anyway. This place is a little…in your face."

At that moment, a completely topless woman approaches us with a tray balanced on one hand. "Welcome to Pink," she says with a smile as if she's the hostess at a Chili's. "If you have any questions, feel free to ask. Any open table is yours, and I'll be around to take your drink order."

"Um, thanks," Drake replies as he drags me to an open table. They are bar height with four chairs at each. He pulls out my chair and waits as I climb up, feeling far more uncomfortable than I wanted to. That's when my eyes dance upward and I notice there's a second floor I didn't see before. At first, I thought it was just mirrors, but when I look again, I can faintly make out the lights on the other side. Which means they can see us from up there.

"He's up there," I mutter to Drake, and he quickly glances at the ceiling, noticing the two-way glass.

"Yep. I bet he is."

After he takes a seat, the half-naked waitress comes back and we put in an order for two vodka tonics, both of us grateful for the alcohol. Drake is tense. I can tell. He keeps fidgeting with his hair, a telltale sign that he's nervous.

"Relax," I tell him after we get our drinks.

"I can't," he replies, squeezing the glass between his hands.

"Just act like you would if I were any other woman."

When he laughs, I can't help but smile. "What's so funny?"

His sexy blue eyes land on my face, and my body starts to relax in his gaze. "Isabel, if I treated you like I treat other women, we'd be fucking by now."

Well, okay, then. "Good point," I mutter before taking a sip of my drink.

"How do we know he's really watching?" he asks, glancing up at the mirrors again. "Can't exactly text him."

"He's watching," I reply. "This is Hunter we're talking about. He's never late and always shows up."

"True," he replies.

"So just stop thinking about him and try to relax." Drake has so much confidence around women and I hate to see him so uptight and uncomfortable with me.

"You're right," he says, jumping out of his seat. When he swallows the distance between us, I tense up. "I'm just going to... stand close to you, okay?"

"You literally rubbed your erection on me today, Drake. I can handle you standing close."

He doesn't laugh at my joke, and the second he crowds me on my stool, he steps away again. "I can't do this. It feels so wrong."

Reaching out a hand, I set it on his, feeling the tremble under his skin. "Drake, just kiss me."

"What?" he stammers, staring at me with a look of shock.

"Kiss me. I think it might make things feel more natural."

His chest is heaving as he stares at me, his eyes leveled on my lips.

"You want to freak him out, and yet the only one freaking out right now is you," I add.

"I think I need to get out of here. I don't like this place," he replies, and I feel my shoulders deflate in disappointment. It wasn't supposed to be like this. Drake made a bet with Hunter, and those two don't make bets they're not willing to pay up for, but if Drake doesn't get out of his head, then this is about to get so much more uncomfortable.

But he's right. This club is terrible and not the right vibe at all.

"Okay, come on. Let's go," I say, standing and reaching a hand out toward him, which he takes, before I lead him toward the exit. But when I try to take the short way to the left, Drake nudges me to the right, around the bar, and I assume he just wants to see the far side of the room. The lights are a little dimmer here, and it's not as congested with people.

I take one glance back up at the mirrors on the second level when I hear Drake whisper my name.

"Iz."

I glance back at him quickly before his hands are on my waist and I'm being pressed into the pink wall. I gasp, my mouth open as I stare up at Drake, and he takes the opportunity to capture my lips in his. Then, he's kissing me. Drake is kissing me, and not some awkward pressing of our lips but a ravenous, overwhelming kiss.

A short murmur slips through before his tongue is in my mouth, not invading or forcing but softly exploring. Our tongues glide together as he hums, a deep gravelly earthquake of sound that makes my knees weak and my panties wet.

Drake is so much taller than me so being crowded between him and the wall feels a lot like being swallowed up by him, and I love it. His hands are still frozen on my waist, but with every lap of our tongues, he squeezes, like he's sending me a silent signal of desire.

My hands, which were glued to his chest a moment ago, relax and begin to roam, exploring the hard surface of his pecs before gliding upward to wrap around his neck, giving him even more access to my body as it curves eagerly against him.

When his hands lower, wandering over my ass and squeezing one whole cheek in the palm of his hand, heat strikes my core. And when he lowers his touch even farther, gathering up the back of my dress as his hands move, my heart beats even faster.

In his aroused hunger, he brings my dress up far enough to expose my ass and puts his palm against my flesh, squeezing again, this time with another low growl. With his body pressed to mine, I feel the erection in his pants, grinding against me like a promise. I ache to touch it.

Then, he pulls away from our kiss, both of us breathless with his hand still on my ass, his large fingers dangerously close to something else entirely. Our foreheads are pressed together as we both try to catch our breaths, eyes closed and tense.

His fingers squeeze again, this time nudging them closer to the warmth of my moist panties. And I gasp. Ever so subtly, he rubs the tip of his finger against the fabric, before pushing it aside and finding the sensitive folds underneath.

My eyes open as I stare up at him.

"Is this okay?" he whispers.

My cheeks are hot. My neck is hot. My chest and stomach and arms are all so hot I am nothing but a blazing inferno of desire and indecision.

Is this okay?

This is what we came to do, right? This is why we're here, but then again, it's not like Hunter can see that Drake's finger is delicately prodding the entrance of my eager pussy.

And the fact that I *do* want this—I want it badly—doesn't exactly make me feel better. It makes me feel worse.

"You're so wet, Isabel," he whispers, and I nearly melt to the floor. "Are you going to tell him how close I was? Are you going to tell him how I'm touching you right now? My hand up your dress. Playing with your pussy. Almost inside you."

I whimper.

I know he's asking me questions, but my brain isn't working well enough to answer them. I don't know. I don't know anything right now. All I know is that a man, who is not my husband, is touching me and this is what Hunter wanted…

But Hunter wanted to watch. And right now, we're in a dim corner, pressed intimately against the wall. Can he even see this? Panic starts to race up my spine.

This is wrong. It wasn't supposed to be like this, and I wasn't supposed to want it this much.

Oh God. What are we doing?

"Drake," I whisper, about to push him from me, when I sense a figure in my periphery. I turn my head, my eyes landing on Hunter, standing a few feet away, staring at us. His chest is heaving and his mouth is closed tightly, and the sudden sensation that I've been caught washes over me.

Drake pulls his hand out from under my dress, taking a step back, just as my husband charges forward. Before I know what's happening, the room flips upside down and I'm being hoisted over his shoulder.

"What are you doing?" I shriek as Hunter carries me across the room. I can't see where we're going, only the back of his suit. Suddenly, it's quieter than in the main room and a door closes behind us. We're in a small room, but I don't have a chance to get my bearings when he drops me on a counter and wraps his hand around my throat, pulling me toward him to kiss me hard on the mouth.

"Hunter," I cry out against his lips.

"Take my cock out, Isabel."

My hands are clenched around the lapels of his suit jacket,

frozen in place. My mind is still in a frenzy, and while he doesn't seem mad, I'm still in a state of shock and I just need to see his face to know for sure. So I push him away to look at him.

His eyes are wild but not with anger. I've never seen him like this before, so overwhelmed with lust. The grip on my throat tightens as he pulls my face closer to his.

"Did he touch you?" he asks.

I nod.

His fingers tighten. "Did you like it?"

My heartbeat picks up speed as I nod again.

Pulling me even closer, he takes my bottom lip between his teeth, biting enough to make it hurt, and I whimper against his mouth.

"Then be a good little slut and take out my cock, Isabel."

Sudden arousal lances my belly, making me not just ready for it but *needy* for it. I'm fumbling quickly with his belt, unfastening his pants in a daze, eagerly reaching into his boxers to hold his cock in my hand like it's the only thing that will bring me comfort.

The moment his hard length is out, he lets go of my neck, yanks me by my legs to the edge of the counter and wedges himself between my legs, rubbing the head of his cock against my moist panties. It is rough and unhinged, and I want it so badly I'm feral for it. He drags my thong to the side and thrusts himself inside me with force, and I have to latch my arms around his neck to stay upright.

He slams into me again, lighting my body up like fireworks, and I let out a cry. "Harder."

His heavy grunts are in my ear as he fucks me in this tiny, dim room. "That was so fucking hot, Red. Watching him touch you like that. I can feel how wet you were for him," he mutters between savage grunts.

"Hunter," I say, calling his name like an oath. "I'm yours."

"Fuck right you're mine." He groans. His thrusts pick up

speed until I'm barely even touching the counter anymore, levitating in his arms until my body tenses in overwhelming pleasure. It hits me so hard I scream, my nails digging into his jacket and my thighs clenching around his waist.

A moment later, his orgasm follows, and he slams my body against his so tight, his hip bones are sure to bruise my legs. Then I feel his cock flinch inside me as he comes with a roar.

I'm held so tightly against him, I never want to let him go. The grip of his fingers on my legs is hard and aggressive, his way of making me feel safe and desired.

It's a long time before we loosen our hold on each other, but when we finally pull our chests apart, I kiss his lips, needing to taste the familiarity of him.

"I love you," I whisper against his mouth.

"Oh, Red." Pulling away, he holds my jaw in his hands, gazing into my eyes. "I didn't hurt you, did I?"

"Hunter, you could never hurt me. I like when you're rough."

"I know," he replies, still buried inside me. "But I lost control. I've never felt like that before."

"And that was just from watching me kiss him. Are you sure you want to watch me—"

"I'm sure," he answers without hesitation. "More than ever before. I want this."

Just hearing him say that makes it hard to breathe. He really wants me and Drake…to sleep together. This feels impossible and insane, but he's so sure.

"Do you?" he asks. "Want this?"

My heart is still hammering in my chest, and it feels like it hasn't stopped since Drake cornered me against the wall. I can still feel his lips against mine. He didn't seem nervous anymore. He was confident and hungry for me, and it felt so right. I want that again.

And I realize, at this moment, that I've been feeling bad for how much I want Drake, but Hunter *wants* me to want him. He would never ask me to do something I didn't want, so my desire is what makes it so much hotter for him.

So with a bite of my bottom lip and my legs wrapped around his waist, I nod. "I do."

Rule #11: If you can't join 'em, get drunk.

Drake

THERE'S NO TWO-DRINK LIMIT AT THIS CLUB. THERE PROBABLY should be because Hunter and Isabel have been gone for almost an hour, and I've been sucking down vodka tonics like they're nothing.

I touched Isabel. That's the thought that's currently playing on repeat in my head. I touched her, kissed her, felt the soft cushion of her ass, grazed the pooling arousal of her pussy with my fingers, and tasted the sweetness of her lips.

This might come as quite a shock, but I don't actually kiss women—or men, for that matter—very often. It's usually a couple quick, soulless kisses and then we're naked and our mouths are elsewhere.

Truth be told, I actually enjoy kissing men more. You can be rougher with a man, and the growing scruff of facial hair adds a little bit of texture to the act.

But I didn't want to be rough with Isabel. I wanted to savor her. I wanted to let my mouth celebrate the softness that was her. It was the most intimate kiss of my life, and the only one I'm ever going to get, so I'm glad it's permanently etched in my memory.

On the bright side, Hunter flipped out, which I knew he would, so the deal is off.

Hallelujah.

I should be so happy right now. Instead, I'm drunk. And alone. And I'm sure he's in some room somewhere, fucking her senseless to undo everything I did...even if she was slick with the arousal I gave her.

Jesus fucking Christ, what is wrong with me?

"Another," I mutter, grabbing the attention of the bartender, who brings it over with a reluctant, tight-lipped smile.

"This is your last one," he replies. "And I'm making it weak."

I shrug. It's irresponsible to serve alcohol in a sex club anyway, but lucky for them, I'm a complete gentleman.

"Let's go," a soft voice murmurs in my ear, and I turn to see a flush-faced Isabel running her hand softly against my back.

"I just ordered a drink," I reply, turning back to my watered-down tonic.

"We have drinks at the hotel."

I'm filled with bitterness. I know I shouldn't be. I signed up for this, and I did what I came here to do. I scared this idea right out of Hunter's head, but at what cost? Now I've had a taste of the one woman I can't have, and I have to deal with that forever. So she can let me have this drink.

"I'll meet you there. Where's Hunter?"

"Saying goodbye to the owner. Come with us," she pleads.

"No. Just because you two don't have to go home alone doesn't mean I should. I'm going to try and find someone for the night. I'll see you later." Before turning back to my drink, I catch the expression of devastation on her face.

"Seriously?" she argues.

"Seriously," I mutter.

As she turns to walk away from me, someone blocks her path. At first, I register it as Hunter, so I don't react. But then I hear a stranger's voice in a low, husky tone.

"If he won't go with you, I will."

The hairs on the back of my neck stand up and chills run down my spine.

"No, thank you," Isabel replies, trying to move around him, but he blocks her again.

"Come on, sweetheart."

"She said no, motherfucker," I growl.

When his hands wrap around her waist, hauling her to his side against her will, I see red. There's no bar, no club, no rules or decorum. There is only his hands on her and the look of helplessness and disgust on her face as she tries to pry herself out of his grasp.

I don't remember standing up or marching toward him. All I know is one second I hear her scream and the next moment, he's on the floor and my fist is throbbing.

"Drake!" she yelps, and I don't know if she's mad or scared, but suddenly, chaos ensues.

Security guards are hauling me toward the door, but I can't see Isabel anymore, and it has me panicking. So I fight against their hold to get to her, which only makes them more aggressive. I'm not a small man by any means, and these three bouncers aren't big enough to handle me in desperation mode. What starts as a couple arms around mine, as they try to drag me to the exit, quickly turns into a choke hold with my face pressed against the floor and a knee in my back.

"Get your fucking hands off of him," a deep, familiar voice growls, and I lift my head just enough to see Hunter snarling in the face of one of the security guards.

"Tell him to calm the fuck down and we will," the man argues.

"He was clearly defending me!" Isabel shrieks. I hate the terror in her voice. This is all my fault.

"Lady, back the fuck up," one of the guards snaps at her, and there's a scuffle again. This time, I have enough room to fight my way off the floor, and I jump up in time to see Hunter fighting with one of the men in all black.

God, when was the last time the two of us were in a brawl? A long, fucking time, that's how long. And definitely before Isabel.

I know how desperate *I* am to get her out of here. I can guarantee Hunter is even more so. So as much as I'd like to help him put these handsy guards in their place, my first objective is to get her the hell out of here.

I grab Isabel by the hand and latch a fist on Hunter's collar as I drag both of them toward the bright red exit sign.

Hunter is still yelling threats at the bouncers as we make our way out into the warm night air, where it's instantly quiet and muggy, the only sound being our own heavy breathing.

"Fuck that place!" Hunter barks.

"Are you okay?" I ask Isabel.

"I'm fine."

"You're shaking," Hunter notices as he pulls her into his arms. I stifle the rising feeling of jealousy at the sight.

"Let's just go, please," she replies.

The hotel is only a few blocks away, and we walked here, so we head out on foot toward the hotel. We're all still fuming about the altercation at the club.

"I'm sorry. I shouldn't have drunk that much," I say, breaking the silence first.

"It's not your fault," Isabel replies, placing a hand on my arm.

"They need a two-drink limit," Hunter grumbles. "And to vet their members better. That shit would never happen at Salacious."

"Never," I reply.

The *click-click* of Isabel's heels draw my attention to her feet. She's wearing black stilettos and they do not look comfortable for a three-block walk. Grabbing her arm, I stop her.

"You can't walk all this way in those."

She glances down at her feet. "I'm fine. They're comfortable."

I tilt my head to the side and glare at her.

"What?" she argues. "Are you going to give me your shoes?"

"Come on, I'll carry you." Turning around, I kneel, so she can reach my back, and I wait for her to climb on.

"Drake, you can't carry me all the way back."

"Remember when you twisted your ankle on our ski trip and I had to carry you all the way down the mountain? That was nothing, and this time, you don't have ten pounds of ski gear on. Just quit arguing with me and climb on."

She lets out a long sigh. Then she slips each shoe off, hands them to Hunter, and quickly climbs onto my back. My hands grasp onto her thighs that are squeezing around my waist as we start our walk again. I can't help but notice Hunter is wearing a crooked smirk on his face.

"This is hardly the dress to wear for piggyback rides," she says, her voice just next to my ear.

"Your underwear isn't showing," Hunter replies from behind us.

"Barely," she adds, and we all chuckle as we walk.

Up ahead, there are colorful lights shining on the side of the road next to what looks like another bar. As we get closer, we see people crowded around a food truck and the aroma of grilled meat fills the air.

"Ooh, tacos," Isabel says with a hum. "I'm starving."

"Yes, ma'am," I reply, heading toward the food truck.

"Damn, those smell good," Hunter adds.

Fifteen minutes later, the three of us are sitting on a curb in the heart of the city, scarfing down street tacos and drinking beer. Hunter has shed his jacket, letting Isabel sit on it, and I have my hair pulled into a bun to keep it out of my carne asada.

This is us. More than fancy suits and exclusive clubs. It's moments like this one that feels most like us, where we came from. Hunter and I were never cut out for the fancy shit. We spent the first half of our lives clawing our way out of the slums and even now, doing as well as we are, I need gentle reminders like this that we're still us.

And as fun and relaxing as this is, there's still an awkward conversation to be had. It's still us, but it's also not entirely us because everything between the three of us has changed, and I'm not sure it will ever be the same again.

I kissed my best friend's wife. And he looked pissed about it.

That's not something we just move on from and assume it won't ever come back and haunt us. And since I know Hunter will be the last person to ever start a tough conversation, and Isabel will avoid confrontation at all costs, it's on me to bring this one up.

Crumpling up my napkin and chugging back the rest of my Mexican lager, I brace myself for what I'm about to say. "I just want to know that we can put this whole thing behind us."

"The fight?" Isabel replies, looking at me with confusion on her face.

"No. Not the fight. What happened before the fight."

Her expression morphs into understanding with a soft "Oh."

"Why would we put it behind us?" Hunter asks. "We made a deal."

"Don't you remember losing your shit and throwing your wife over your shoulder as you stormed off?"

"I didn't lose my shit," he argues.

My jaw falls open. "You're joking, right? Hunter, I've never seen you look so angry in all my life."

"I wasn't angry. I was…"

"You were what?" I ask, because he's fucking delusional if he thinks that the way he reacted to seeing me with my hand up Isabel's dress wasn't pure, unadulterated rage.

"I was…" He's stumbling over his words, clearly worked up again.

"Hunter, let it go, man. It's not worth it. I know you were jealous. We could all see that, so I don't know why you're pressing this issue when it could blow up in all of our faces."

"I wasn't jealous, Drake. I was turned on."

Those dark brown eyes of his are staring at me intensely, and I feel like I've lost the ability to breathe. Is he joking right now? He was turned on by seeing me almost fingering his wife?

Why?

"Turned on?" I ask.

He averts his eyes, staring across the street with a furrow in his brow. "I'm not going to try and explain it. Fuck, I don't even understand it myself. I just know that I liked it." With a huff, he bolts up to standing and walks toward the garbage can, tossing his trash.

I glance sideways at Isabel, who's biting her bottom lip.

I know I sound like an idiot arguing about this. It's probably the one thing I've wanted more than anything, to be with the woman of my dreams, but I wonder if Hunter is really thinking this through. There's so much at stake here. Our friendship. Their marriage. Not to mention my fucking heart.

Rule #12: Who needs two beds? Sometimes one is plenty.

Hunter

"THERE SHOULD BE TWO ROOMS."

The man behind the counter types on his keyboard again, but reluctantly shakes his head when he doesn't have any good news to give me.

"I'm sorry, Mr. Scott. There's only one king room on this reservation."

"Everything else is booked," Isabel adds from next to me. "Not even the seedy hotels have rooms available."

"There's a jazz fest this weekend and they've booked up all our hotels," the man explains. "It's busier than Mardi Gras."

"Is that why you gave away our second room?" I grumble, glaring at the concierge.

"Hunter…" Isabel says in warning.

We're just outside New Orleans, and after a long, awkward ride in the car all day, the last thing I need is to fight with the hotel staff. Drake has been uncharacteristically quiet since last night. I didn't want it to be this way. I'm not going to *make* him sleep with Isabel if he really doesn't want to, whether we made a deal or not—I'm not a monster. But I just wish he'd get on board with the idea. Because I know he wants it. I saw the look in his eyes last night when he was kissing her against the wall. I saw the fire between them, chemistry like I've never seen before, and it was hot as fuck.

The forbidden nature of it all makes it that much better. I can only imagine what his hand was doing up her dress, and maybe he's right. Maybe I should be more angry about another man being inside her, but I'm not. I'm fucking turned on as hell.

"Come on, honey. We can make it work."

"One bed for all three of us? Drake takes up a king-size bed by himself," I argue.

"The only other option is to skip the club tomorrow night and just move on to Nashville today."

I groan. "We've been in the car all day. I really don't want to drive more."

"So let's just take the room."

With a sigh and an eye roll, I look at the concierge as I say, "Fine. Give us the room."

He forces a tight smile and clicks on his computer. "Yes, sir."

Drake is sitting alone in the car, and I glance out the tall glass doors of the lobby and watch him. He looks nervous. Maybe sleeping in the same room will help loosen him up. I know once he lets go of all of his worry, he'll see how good this can be. He's done much crazier things.

After getting our key to the room, Isabel and I head back out to the car.

"Well…" I say as I drop into the passenger seat. "They only have one room."

He stares at me like he's waiting for me to explain.

"With one bed," Isabel adds.

"You're kidding," Drake replies.

"Sleepover," I say, trying to lighten the mood, but he doesn't look entertained. With a heavy sigh, he drives the car around to an empty parking space.

When we get into the room, Isabel goes straight for the shower, leaving me and Drake alone in our awkwardness. He doesn't even hesitate as he reaches for the bottle of tequila he packed in his bag.

I open the minibar and find some cold beers, so I grab one out and pop the top. It's funny to think I would have never paid twelve dollars for one hotel beer ten years ago, but we've come a long way.

"Room service?" I ask, grabbing the menu.

"I'm not hungry," he mutters after swallowing down a shot without so much as a wince.

With a scoff, I toss the menu down in front of him. Isabel is still in the shower, so she can't hear us. If she could, I wouldn't be so hard on him because she's always trying to protect him or go easy on him, but right now, I'm done with his attitude.

"All right, fine…" I mumble.

"What?"

"Deal's off. If you're going to keep brooding about it, then we can pretend I never said anything. Okay?"

With a scowl, he pours another glass. "I wish I could forget it, Hunt."

"What is your problem? There's no damage done."

"What about last night?" he asks, looking offended.

"What? One kiss?"

He takes the second shot and stalks over to the fridge to take out the other cold beer.

"Drake, just fucking talk to me."

When he finally turns toward me, I'm surprised to see the hurt in his eyes. "You assume that I just fuck anyone, anytime, and my feelings don't get involved."

I flinch. "What? I don't think that—"

"Yes, you do. You think it means nothing to me, that I'll just sleep with Isabel so you can get off on it, and then I'll walk away like nothing happened. Is that how you think it will go?"

Jesus. Is that what I thought would happen?

"Drake, I didn't—"

"It's fine, Hunter. Just drop it, okay?"

As he cracks open his beer, I let his words sink in. Peeling the label off my bottle, my eyes keep dancing up to his face, and I wish I could let this go, but I think he might have just opened up a whole new can of worms.

"I don't think that about you. I just…assumed that you were better at separating feelings from sex. I thought it would be easy for you."

"With other people, it would be."

"But not with Isabel?" I ask.

And when his eyes slide their way up to my face, it steals all of the air out of the room. "Not with *either* of you."

Just then, the bathroom door opens, and Isabel emerges from the steam in nothing but a towel wrapped around her slender frame.

"Forgot to grab my pajamas," she says lightheartedly before tiptoeing across the room to our suitcase. The room is still drenched in tension as Drake and I stare at each other, those words hanging heavy between us.

I don't know what he meant by that or if my imagination is getting away from me, but when he included me, he didn't mean *me* in a sexual way.

"You guys ready for bed?" Isabel asks after coming out a minute later in her flannel pants and tank top.

Without another word, Drake and I take turns in the bathroom, averting our gazes as we pass each other. Then we climb into the bed, putting Isabel in between us.

"This reminds me of the time we went camping and it was so cold we slept in the back of the SUV," Isabel says with a smile.

I hug her close, looking across the pillow at Drake, staring back. "That was a fun trip," I say.

"Yeah, it was," he adds.

With her pressed against my body, there's a sliver of space

between her backside and Drake's chest. And as the two of them reminisce, I think about what he said. About how sleeping with Isabel would put his heart at risk, making him more attached to her than he wants to be.

I'm ignoring the part where he included me because he clearly doesn't mean it in the same way he means Isabel.

And call me crazy because there's a part of me that wants him getting emotionally involved. I don't want Drake just having meaningless sex with Isabel. I want it to mean something. I mean, I know he can separate sex from emotions, but I don't think I want him to.

Is this cruel of me? To set my best friend up for heartbreak? Or do I know, deep down, I would never let that happen? That somehow, I can still protect him after all of this is said and done.

Clicking the lights off behind me, I bathe the room in darkness. With the small amount of light coming from the city through the window, I stare at Drake again. I'm an asshole for this, but I'm also a little bit drunk and I'm tired of playing around with this idea. I'm ready to make it happen.

Tugging Isabel closer, I press my mouth against her ear as I whisper, "Drake looks lonely over there. Why don't you cuddle with him?"

She pulls back and gazes up into my eyes, and I shoot her a warm smile, kiss her forehead, and give her a reassuring nod. After a moment, she does as I said. Slowly, she rolls out of my arms and nestles her body against his.

Without hesitation, he swallows her up in his arms. I can't get over how small she looks against him and how the moment he has her, she is the center of his focus. He's no longer glaring at me but gazing down at her. She's facing him as he runs a hand down her back, stroking her spine while she breathes into his neck. It's so intimate and perfect, and not an ounce of me is mad about it.

There's subtle movement between them, and when Drake

pulls his head away to look down at her, my heart beats faster in my chest. The look on his face is full of desire and anticipation.

And I'm holding my breath as I wait.

When Drake rubs a thumb over her jaw, her lips part. He stares at her for what feels like forever, their gazes locked in the dim light. He sends me a hesitant glance before turning back to her. Then he closes the distance between them, pressing his mouth to hers, and my body lights up with excitement.

Their mouths are fused as she bends against his body, running her fingers through his hair to pull him closer. There's a soft hum and the sound of heavy breathing as their kiss picks up speed.

"Is this okay?" he murmurs, and she barely lets him get the question out before she's pulling him back down.

"Yes," she cries out against his lips.

I feel like a fiend, wanting more, *needing* more. I've never felt anything so visceral in all my life. The energy between them and the sight of my two favorite people on earth devouring each other has me wanting to explode. I love it so, so much.

"Pull up her shirt," I whisper, and I see Drake's hand move toward the hem before pausing. He moves away again, looking down at her with hesitation before she nods emphatically.

"Yes," she says in a panting moan.

Then her shirt is up and her breasts are exposed, his large hand quickly covering one soft mound, squeezing and pinching the tight bud of her nipple. The more he massages her breast, the more I notice his hips grinding against her.

And the satisfaction I feel when he rolls on top of her, settling himself between her legs, is nuclear. I want him to fuck her so much it hurts. I know he probably won't do that tonight. I imagine they'll both want to take this slow, but the way they're consuming each other right now has me questioning that.

His mouth moves from hers, instantly covering her nipple with his lips. He's sucking and nibbling, moaning into her flesh, which I know drives her crazy. Her back arches and she lets out a loud hum of pleasure.

I'm just lying here on my side, watching this scene play out, and I feel like a lurker, intruding on a private moment between two people who desperately want each other.

My God, how long have they felt this? Have these feelings been lying dormant or is it the forbidden nature of it all that's driving this passion? Either way, I can't believe how good this feels to watch.

"You should taste her," I say. "You wouldn't believe how good she tastes, Drake."

Isabel lets out a small yelp, lifting her head to stare down at him.

"I want to taste her," he replies, his feral gaze on her face. "Is that okay?"

She nods again. But before he moves down between her legs, she grabs his face and pulls him up to her mouth to kiss him again. When he's had his fill of her mouth, he travels down her body, tugging down her pajama pants and taking her underwear with them, so she's bare for him. She's hesitant, I can tell. Wriggling her knees together as he runs his hands along her thighs.

"Spread your legs for him, baby," I whisper. "Let him see how beautiful you are."

Her knees finally fall apart as her breathing picks up. At the sight of her naked cunt, Drake lets out a growl.

"You're so fucking perfect, Isabel," he whispers as he tosses her clothes away and lowers himself between her legs. First, he plants a soft kiss against her belly, and I watch her tender flesh erupt in shivers and goose bumps. Then he presses his lips to the inside of each thigh, and Isabel pants and hums in anticipation.

When she turns her head to look at me, I smile, biting my lip as I lean in, taking her mouth in a bruising kiss. With her lips against mine, she lets out a loud whimper, and I glance down to see Drake's mouth buried between her legs. I pull away from her to watch as he licks at her pussy, lapping his tongue eagerly against her clit.

Isabel is squirming and clawing at the bed with her nails as he tongue-fucks her with vigor.

"Drake, yes!" she cries out. I can't help but touch her. I know I'm probably not supposed to be involved, but she's too delicious to abstain. I brush her hair back, running my hands down her throat, feeling the vibration of her noises against my fingers.

"Look at you, baby. So beautiful like this."

Drake growls against her cunt, gazing up at her as he thrusts his tongue between her folds. Her legs are squirming around him, her back arched, and her small breasts bouncing with the deep heaving of her breaths.

"Make her come, Drake. She's so beautiful when she comes."

Drake hums again. Then he pierces her with two fingers as he sucks eagerly on her clit, making her scream. Her panting is growing slower and deeper, a sign that I know means she's about to lose it.

She digs her fingers into his hair, latches her thighs around his head, and nearly flies off the bed. It's the greatest thing I've ever seen. I've made Isabel come more times than I can ever count, but I never had the chance to truly watch it. My eyes are feasting on the sight of her strong muscles contracting, her long neck exposed as she lets her head hang back. Her eyes are closed in a look of euphoric bliss, and her delicate lips are parted as she lets out a raspy cry.

Once her orgasm has faded, I kiss her again, brushing her fiery red, sweat-soaked hair out of her face.

"That was amazing," I whisper against her mouth.

Drake rises from his place between her legs, kneeling back on his knees, and my eyes instantly fall to the bulging length in his gym shorts. He catches me looking and trails his eyes down my body, landing on *my* matching erection.

Well, fuck. What now?

There are a few long moments of awkward silence before he grabs Isabel's pajamas and helps her slide her legs into them, pulling them into place. Then, she's looking at me, her bottom lip pinched between her teeth.

"What about—"

"That's enough, Red," I reply. "Let's get some sleep."

"Are you sure?"

I nod. "Yes, baby."

"Okay," she says with reluctance.

Without a word, Drake escapes to the bathroom, closing the door behind him. I'm not sure what he's doing in there, and I'm not going to ask. Isabel cuddles close to me, her hand drifting over my stiff cock. I take her gently by the wrist.

"Red…" I say in warning.

"Are you okay?" she asks, finally taking her hand away.

"I'm fucking great. Are you okay?"

Her green eyes gaze up at me as she nods. "I'm fucking great too," she whispers. The F-word rarely comes out of her mouth, but fuck me, it's so cute when it does.

"Good."

"Do you think he's okay?" she asks.

"Yeah. I don't think he would have done that if he didn't want to. But…"

"But what?" she replies. I curl her hair behind her ear and kiss her forehead.

"But when he gets into bed, would you be comfortable cuddling with him instead of me? I just want him to know that you want him for more than sex."

She lifts her head and gives me a puzzled look. "More than sex?"

"Yeah. I think it would make him feel better. To know you really care about him."

Her touch travels over my cheek as she takes a deep breath. "Are you sure you know what you're doing? I don't want anyone to get hurt."

"You care about him, don't you?"

"Don't you?" she replies.

More than she understands. Fuck, more than *I* understand, and I know what my wife is worried about, but everything in my gut is telling me this is right.

"Of course I do."

"Okay, because you keep saying *me* and how much I want him, but you want this too, Hunter, and I think he needs to know how much you care about him—as much as I do."

Sometimes I feel like Isabel can see into my thoughts. I swear she knows things I keep hidden in my head, even before I think them out loud, but that's just what makes us so perfect for each other. She is in my head as much as in my heart.

A few minutes later, Drake emerges from the bathroom, hits the light, and climbs back into bed behind Isabel. She stays cuddled against me for a moment, and I'm about to start worrying that she can't do it. That letting him eat her pussy was one thing but cuddling with him while they fall asleep is too much.

And I can't stop thinking about what he said to me earlier, about not wanting to get hurt. I just need him to know he's not just a quick fuck to either of us. That for some fucking reason, him getting attached to Isabel is exactly what I want.

Then, just when I start to lose hope, she kisses me quickly on the lips and rolls away, resting her head on Drake's outstretched arm. He hesitates for a moment, gazing at me through the darkness. But when I don't protest, he relaxes his body, laying his arm over her, and slowly falls asleep.

Rule #13: Establish the rules early on and never ever break them.

Isabel

THE HOTEL GYM IS EMPTY, WHICH IS NICE FOR A CHANGE BECAUSE I can't seem to get enough miles on the stationary bike.

My head is a mess. I just keep reliving last night and how absolutely *insane* that was. Letting another man go down on me while my husband watched. I must be crazy because this is not something normal twenty-seven-year-old women do—and enjoy, entirely too much.

I should be ashamed of the thoughts that are running rampant through my mind today. Like how Drake kisses differently than Hunter. How his mouth feels different with slightly poutier lips. How his mouth felt different *down there*. Not better or worse... just different.

How I haven't come that hard in a long time.

I would have never done that without Hunter literally telling us to—never. But God...I'm glad he did.

I'm rounding my eighth mile on the bike when the door to the gym opens and I do a double take when I notice it's Drake. Quickly, I pull out my earbuds and slow my pace on the bike.

"Hey," I mutter.

"Hey," he replies. "He's working, so I figured I'd get a workout in."

I nod with a tight smile. A week ago, I would have made an inappropriate joke to Drake, maybe something about how he gets plenty of workouts in, but I can't make those jokes now. After last night, I can't do or say anything around him now that doesn't feel awkward and loaded.

He's hovering awkwardly around the weights, and I try my best to act natural, but it's impossible. I hate this. I hate that we aren't us anymore, and I *loved* us.

Let's be real—Drake is my best friend too, even if we don't claim it the same way he and Hunter do. I don't have close girlfriends, just a few friendly acquaintances. Drake is the guy I want to hang out with on the weekends and invite to the movies and drink with and sit around with doing absolutely nothing—at least he was before it got awkward.

And as great as last night was, I'd rather have that friendship back than *this*.

He must feel it too because he quickly turns around to face me as he says, "Is it just me or are things super awkward now?"

I quickly shake my head. "Totally not just you, Drake. It's super awkward now."

"I hate it. Can we please just talk about it, so we can go back to the way things were?"

"Please," I agree.

"Okay…" he says, letting his voice drawl into silence.

I guess this is the part where we actually talk about the third base we rounded last night, but it's apparently not so easy.

"Are you sure you're okay with this?" he asks. His bright blue eyes are focused on my face with warmth and concern, and I just love him for this. How can such a sweet and sensitive man not be committed to anyone?

"I'm okay with this as long as it doesn't make things weird between us."

"Me too."

"So last night was okay?" I ask delicately, as if I need him to confirm that eating me out was everything he could have wished for. It feels ridiculous to even ask.

"Last night was amazing," he replies, and I feel a tingle of butterflies in my stomach.

"It was…"

"God, this is so weird," he adds, and I laugh.

"Probably not as weird as cuddling was," I reply, trying to break the thick, thick tension.

"Oh, come on," he jokes, shoving my shoulder. "You're an excellent cuddler."

"So are you! We should have been cuddling this whole time."

He laughs. "I'm not usually much of a cuddler."

"Well, it turns out those beefy biceps of yours make great pillows."

With a smile, he flexes, and I roll my eyes at him. "These pillows?"

"Stop it, you show off," I tease him, and just like that… we're us again. Well, mostly. The awkwardness is still there, but at least we can make jokes and work around the parts that make us uncomfortable, like the fact that he was literally prodding his tongue in my pussy last night. God, why did I just remind myself?

Thankfully, he moves over to the weights against the wall, and I'm able to hide my blush behind the redness of my cheeks from working out.

"You know…" he says as he picks up a barbell, "we should probably have some rules. Maybe that would help us separate everything, so it doesn't get too weird."

"That's a great idea," I reply. "What do you have in mind?"

"Well…" He thinks for a moment, curling the weights like they're nothing. "First, you and I can't do anything without Hunter around."

"Obviously," I reply.

"And everything has to be consensual. If you want it to stop, just say...namaste."

I laugh. "Is that supposed to be my safe word?"

"Yeah, why not?"

"That's literally the worst safe word I've ever heard."

"Good. Then you won't forget it." He sets the barbell back on the rack. "And I hope you never need to use it," he adds.

A smile tugs on my lips as I keep up the speed of my bike. Did he just admit that he hopes I *want* to have sex with him, and did he mean to say that?

After a long, tense moment, he turns toward me. "That's not what I meant. I just meant...I hope you never feel uncomfortable—"

"I know what you meant, Drake." I'm smiling now, which makes him smile, biting his lower lip as he turns away. It's a bright, toothy grin that stretches across his face, and it literally warms my belly. Drake has the best smile, one I'm sure drives the ladies crazy.

"We, uh, have to use protection. Every time."

"I'm on the—" I start, but he holds up a hand.

"I don't want this getting any more complicated than it needs to. I want to use protection."

I close my mouth. "If that's what you want, it's fine with me."

A few quiet minutes go by before I add, "And Hunter should just...watch, right? You don't want him...getting involved?"

Drake's head snaps up to stare at me, his brow arched. "I don't mind. Do you?"

My mouth falls open. "No, I don't mind. I just thought..."

"I don't think that needs to be a rule," he adds, going back to the weights. It almost looks like he's avoiding eye contact on purpose. Did that question make him uncomfortable? I just assumed that Hunter being his friend, and strictly wanting to do this because he wanted to watch, would make things easier if Drake said he couldn't join in at all. We're trying to avoid awkwardness, but Drake almost seems to...want Hunter involved.

I can't stop thinking about it as I finish my tenth mile on the bike. I know Drake sleeps with men from time to time, and Hunter has always been supportive of that, but I've noticed that he doesn't seem to *love* it. Whenever Drake would talk about a man he hooked up with, Hunter would clench his jaw and change the subject.

And I never noticed any signs of attraction between them. So why would he suddenly be encouraging Hunter to join in?

Drake is doing squats now with a long barbell draped over his shoulders. I notice the way he winces on each drop, shaking out his leg as he stands.

"You okay?" I ask.

"Yeah, my hamstrings are just tight as fuck." He sets the barbell back on the rack and rubs at the back of his leg.

"Let me help you stretch it." I hop off my bike and grab a mat from the corner, rolling it out on the floor between us.

"You don't have to do that," he replies, and I tilt my head toward him.

"It's literally my job. Come on."

With a sigh, he gets down on the mat, sitting with his legs extended.

"Lie down."

"Don't hurt me," he replies playfully.

"No promises."

Once he's lying on his back, I lift his right leg and hold it against my chest as I press it toward his body. He lets out a long groan, and I can tell immediately just how tight his muscles are.

"You need to stretch more. You're way too tight."

"I hate stretching."

I roll my eyes, pressing his leg a little farther to his body. "Don't be such a baby. I do this for Hunter all the time."

"Well, maybe if I were married to a beautiful yoga instructor, I wouldn't hate it so much."

I let out a giggle, pressing his leg even deeper into the stretch, but when neither of us say anything for a few minutes, it starts to grow tense again.

Our eyes meet, and it's a loaded gaze. I've looked Drake in the eye a million times before, but suddenly, any eye contact between us now feels different, as if our connection has been magnified, blown up to one million percent its original size, and I'm not sure how I get it back to the way it was. I'm not sure I even want to.

"Why haven't you ever settled down?" I ask carefully.

He swallows, gazing back up at the ceiling. When I push his leg a little closer to his body, he winces. "I don't know. I never felt what Hunter did."

"What do you mean?"

"I remember the day he saw you for the first time. When you were walking across the street in that emerald-green dress and those black sandals, he couldn't take his eyes off you. Then, he couldn't stop talking about you, and we started going back to that corner every day just to see you. It was a really big deal, and I just kept waiting to feel what he felt that day, but it never really happened."

"I remember that dress," I reply, distracted by the fact that Drake remembered what I was wearing that day ten years ago.

"I never saw you wearing it again after that day."

"You know…not everyone meets their spouse like that. It's not actually that normal to be as sure as Hunter was. Some people know their soul mates for years before realizing it."

"I know," he says, as I release his leg and move toward the other. "But that's what I want. I don't want to settle for less."

"You'll find someone," I say, feeling a hint of disappointment at the thought.

Heaving a sigh, he looks up at me. And just like that, the tension is back. He must feel it too because he immediately says, "Let's make a deal to always be open with each other. Whatever you're feeling, you have to tell me. I don't want to do anything to hurt you or Hunter."

"Me neither," I add.

"So we have to communicate everything. No matter how awkward or painful it is." There is such sincerity in his eyes.

"I know."

"Deal?" he asks.

"Deal," I reply.

Rule #14: Some people need to be tied up.

Hunter

DRAKE, ISABEL, AND I ARE GATHERED AROUND A TABLE IN THE back of the Crescent City Kink Club in the middle of a rope bondage workshop. The instructor is a beautiful woman named Silla, tall and slender with a soft voice and a beaming, bright smile. It's hard to focus on what she's teaching us and the dozen other couples and groups here to learn when she levels those dazzling hazel eyes on us.

Drake is having the same problem. I can tell by the way his eyes cascade down her body, licking his lips as his gaze settles on the shimmering dark flesh busting out of her thin white bra.

"Will you two pay attention, please?" Isabel whispers.

Drake and I both chuckle, hiding our shameless smiles, as Silla instructs us to pick up the long black rope. Each of us holds a strand as she walks us through some basic knots. Isabel picks it up easily while Drake and I fumble, causing more unintentional knots than what we're supposed to be creating.

Things between us have been surprisingly comfortable today. When they both came back from the gym this morning, they were wearing smiles and joking like they used to. They were both worried about nothing. It's still us. This changes nothing.

I don't want to rush things, but last night was so incredible that I can't wait to do it again. I need to see those two together as badly as I need Isabel for myself. We haven't even had sex today, which means I'm still a pent-up mess from last night.

"Now, I'd like for you to pick one person in your group to be the rigger and another to be the submissive." And when Drake and I stare at her blankly, she continues with a playful grin. "The rigger will be the person doing the tying. The submissive will be the one being tied up."

We look in unison at Isabel, who immediately shakes her head.

"Not it," she chirps. "I got tied up last time. I think one of you should try it tonight."

"Well, Drake got to tie you up last time. Isn't it my turn?" I ask.

"Nope. Why don't you tie him up tonight?"

My cheeks heat with a flush as I widen my gaze at her. Is she doing this on purpose?

When I look at Drake, he looks a little too comfortable for my taste. "I don't think we have much of a choice...unless you're open to being the submissive tonight?" Then he actually fucking winks at me, and I have to force my face not to give away the way my insides are exploding.

"Nice try," I mutter as I grab the rope.

"Come on. Be honest. You've always wanted to tie me up, haven't you?"

"To shut you up, yes, I have."

He chuckles just as Silla gives us our next instructions. "The submissive should be in as little clothing as possible, so the ropes lay against the skin to get the full effect. This is entirely up to you how much you choose to take off."

Drake is grinning now, and I'm struggling to keep my composure. Why was this so easy last night? Why all of a sudden am I nervous as fuck, especially as I see Drake peel off his tight T-shirt, revealing his hairless chest and chiseled abs?

Damn, that construction job of his does him good.

Then, he unbuttons his pants with his bright blue eyes on my face, and I avert my gaze as he drops his jeans to the floor, so he's standing in front of me in nothing but his tight black boxers, which leave nothing to the imagination.

"I'm ready, sir," he says in a teasing tone, and I bite back a laugh.

"Knock it off," I snap.

"Now I'm going to show you a basic box tie," she says, demonstrating on her partner how to place his forearms stacked behind him, which Drake does to mirror his actions. Isabel watches from the side with a mischievous smile on her face.

I fumble through the instructions, messing up the rope placement in front of everyone around me. She's not going too fast, and it's not that complicated, but I can't seem to think straight or function correctly as I touch my best friend's bare chest and back. I'm as straight as they come, so why the hell is there swelling in my pants? It's making it hard to focus.

"Need some help?" Silla asks as she approaches our table, clearly seeing me struggle.

"He's a lost cause," Drake jokes.

"Oh, surely not," she replies as she moves around to where I'm fighting with this current knot. I should have paid more attention when she was demonstrating.

"It's not that bad," she says, taking over and trying to show me where I've messed up. All I can seem to focus on is that she's touching him.

"I'm impressed you're willing to learn, Mr. Scott. You're just here to find an expert for your own club, right?"

"Yes," I reply. "But I'd still like to know a little more before I work with someone."

"And what exactly do you think of me?" she asks with a flirtatious smile.

"You're very knowledgeable," I reply.

She tugs tighter on the rope winding around Drake's arms, and he lets out a grunt as she pulls on it. Then I watch as she runs her long nails over the muscles of his arms and back.

"The rope is going to leave beautiful marks on your skin…"

"Drake," he replies, glancing back at her.

"Drake," she echoes in a sultry tone. Then she moves around to his front. "And what do you think? Should I come visit your club sometime?"

"Oh definitely. I'd be happy to give you a personal tour."

"I'd love that," she says, and my jaw clenches. Why the fuck must he flirt with everyone? I literally watched him with his head between my wife's legs last night, but seeing this other woman fawn over him has my blood boiling.

Stealing a glance at Isabel, I see a mirrored reaction on her face. Her lips are pressed together tightly as she stares at Silla, who still has her hands on Drake's half-naked body.

If I know Drake, and I do, he's not going to stop until he has her moaning his name in some private room at the club before the clock strikes midnight. But he wouldn't do that now, would he?

We should really discuss some ground rules. I can't have him banging some other girl and my wife in the same weekend. Isabel deserves better than that.

But am I really asking him to be exclusive…to us? And for how long? How many times am I going to let them sleep together? I really didn't think this through.

"There," Silla announces as she steps back to reveal her artwork. Drake's forearms are bound behind his back, ropes looping around his large biceps, the cord pressing into his flesh, and I'll be honest, it looks painful. But with the way he's *still* flirting with Silla, I hope it hurts.

"Looks great," Isabel replies with forced enthusiasm.

Without warning, Silla quickly unties everything she's done, and then she looks at me. "Now that you've seen me do it, I want you to try again. Rope bondage is all about the connection between you and your submissive. Zone out together. He's giving you his trust, and that's a gift. So I want you to try this again, but this time…focus on the man you're touching. Not the rope."

"Umm…" I stammer. "We're just friends."

She gives me an unimpressed expression. "Good. Then this should be easy. I assume he already trusts you."

Isabel clears her throat, and I brush off the nerves, squaring my shoulders and taking the rope from Silla.

"Don't wrap him too tight. A little loss of circulation is expected, but if it gets too uncomfortable, talk to your rigger. And don't stay in the bind for more than twenty minutes or you risk nerve damage. Understand?"

"Yes, ma'am," Drake replies with a wink.

"When you're done…I'll be happy to give you a tour," she says, smiling directly at him. My molars grind as I watch her gaze up into his eyes.

"That would be great!" Isabel chimes in, interrupting their little starry-eyed connection. Silla fakes a smile in my wife's direction before excusing herself to help the other tables.

Then, I heave a sigh as I attempt the harness again, trying to shut off every voice in my head. As the rope drapes over Drake's shoulders, I chance a look in his direction, our eyes meeting in a heated connection. With a cool expression, I pull the cord a little tighter, and he lets out a nearly silent grunt, still staring at me.

Then with another tug and his chest surrounded by black knots, the air leaves his lungs in a satisfied exhalation. He submits to the binding with a lazy sublime look on his face.

When I've finished, Drake appears almost sleepy, and I notice my binds are tighter than Silla's. I step back and stand next to Isabel as we assess my work.

"It looks so good," she mutters quietly.

It does. It looks so fucking good.

"Someone gonna untie me?" Drake asks after a moment, and

I shake myself out of the hypnosis I'm suddenly under. What the fuck has gotten into me?

"I should leave you like that," I grumble before walking away. I don't have the patience to try and keep calm right now, and as badly as I want to tell him what a jerk he is for flirting with Silla right in front of us, I have no place telling Drake what to do. I know that, and yet…I want to. I want to dominate him, and that's a new feeling I'm not quite sure what to do with at this point.

With a laugh, he calls after me. "What did I do?" But I don't answer. I leave Isabel to untie him while I head to the bar for a drink.

Rule #15: Strangers are great people to confide in.

Drake

I WISH HUNTER WOULD JUST SAY WHAT'S ON HIS MIND. HE'S always been like this, sulking and brooding in silence until he just walks away, without ever really expressing himself. It makes me want to push his buttons, which is exactly what I'm doing now. I know what's got him so pissed off, but if he's not going to talk about it like an adult, then I'm going to make him suffer for it.

"I should go check on him," Isabel says after we've pulled off all of my ropes and piled them on the table. I pull up my pants, but leave my shirt off for a moment. My skin is still feeling a little sensitive from the rope, and I'm fighting the urge to itch.

"I'll meet you over there," I reply. She sends me a tense smile before disappearing into the next room, where the bar is. This club is pretty similar to Salacious. There's a main room, lots of smaller rooms, and a large one at the end, where they must hold their workshops and shows. It's making me brainstorm ways we can add a space like this to our club.

I turned the main room into a giant voyeur hallway, so I could easily manage this.

"Oh, look at your rope marks. They're beautiful." Soft hands graze my arms and I turn to find Silla inspecting my skin like it's a piece of art.

"Thanks?" I say with a question.

"Not all skin marks the same from the ropes, but yours turned out perfect. Let me show you." She pulls out her phone and aims it at my back. When the flash goes off, she lets out a disgruntled noise. "The lighting in here is terrible. Here, come with me. I'll take you to a room with better lighting, so you can see it."

"My friends—"

"It'll just take a second. I need to get a good picture before they fade."

Letting out a sigh, I take one last glance toward the door before following her. My fingers run over the divots in my arms, where the rope was squeezing tightly against my muscles. It was painful but in a strangely satisfying way. I almost wanted them tighter. I liked feeling restrained and at Hunter's mercy. I loved being the center of his attention and so connected to every one of his movements that I could just lose myself in the rope in his hands.

"So, was that couple your…"

"My friends," I reply, answering her question because I know exactly what she's asking. Pretty funny that no one has asked that before. We're always together, and I guess we do sort of look like a throuple. I'm realizing now that a lot of people at the club proba-bly assume we are.

"Oh," Silla replies with a smile. "They're a beautiful couple."

"Yeah, they are."

"Here we go," she says when we reach the third door in the dark hallway. It opens to a dim room, and she hits one of the lights on the wall. It's not exactly bright, definitely no brighter than the other room. It's ornately decorated with a large bed on one side and a sizeable chair on the other, almost as if it's made for watching. And there are mirrors along each wall, ornate ones with elaborate brass designs.

"Come here," she says, dragging me to the wall. As she places my back toward the mirror, she pulls out her phone again, and this time takes a pic without the flash. "Perfect," she whispers. Holding her phone up to my face, I see the intricate designs across my back from the rope, but I'm not nearly as impressed by it as she is.

Then her fingers are on me again. I'm staring down at her thick, fluttering lashes and tight black curls. She's beautiful, and I realize that if I wanted to, I could fuck her right here, right now. I mean…that's why she brought me in here. I don't believe for one second it was about the lighting. She's playing her cards strong, and I've never had a woman have to try this hard.

Her eyes skate upward, landing on my face. "How about that tour?"

"You want to take me on a tour?" I ask.

"I'll show you whatever you want," she replies, her nails dragging across my pecs. Then she leans in to press her lips against my chest, and I curse my stupid, rotten luck. My head hangs back as I practically growl with frustration.

Placing my hands on her arms, I gently nudge her backward. "Fuck, I'm so sorry I have to do this."

"Then, don't," she replies, pushing back against me. Her fingers hang on to the waistband of my pants, and I grit my teeth.

"Silla, you are unbelievably beautiful, and I wish I could do this…but I'm sort of with someone."

"Where is she?"

"It's complicated," I reply, running my hands through my hair. "And I'll be honest, I don't even know what I'm doing or what we are, but I just can't be with anyone else right now."

Her shoulders sag. "Of course, you're a gentleman."

A laugh bursts from my lips. "Hardly. In fact, I'm a fucking scoundrel. I wish I could show you how much of one I am, but these people…this person…is important to me."

She's staring at my face with a gentle squint, and finally her eyes widen and her mouth forms an O shape. "Oh…it's them, isn't it? The couple."

I open my mouth to protest because it's not something I was prepared to own up to, but then I realize I don't know this woman. She doesn't know me or the club or anything, so she's actually the best person to confide in.

"Actually…yes."

She nods with a tight smile. "Both of them?"

"No…just her, sort of."

"Sort of?"

"Well…he wants to watch," I add with a grimace.

"Oh, kinky," she replies with a laugh. "But that doesn't mean you belong to them."

"I know, I know. But I can't be sleeping with *her* and other people."

Silla's brow furrows. "For how long?"

"I guess that's the question."

"How long have you been sleeping with her?" she asks, and I wince.

"I haven't yet."

"I see…" she replies with an inquisitive expression, like she's trying to figure all of this out. Good luck…even I don't understand it. "So let me get this straight. It's just about sex, right?"

"Right."

"And you *want* to do this?"

"Of course," I answer.

"So…what's the problem?"

"The problem is that these are my best friends and I want this as much as they do, but what am I going to do when it's over? What if I lose them over this?"

She steps back and twists her lips in thought. "But what if you gain them?"

"Huh?"

With a sigh, she takes a seat on the end of the bed and stares at me. "If it's possible to lose them, then isn't it just as possible that you gain them?"

"We're already best friends. How could I gain them?"

"Ugh...don't be so dense. You know exactly what I mean!"

I do, but...that thought is so far from my mind. This is just sex. It's just a kinky thing Hunter wants. It's not like I'm going to join...or be in their relationship or whatever. I don't even know what that would be called.

"No," I reply, shaking my head. "These are my best friends. And what we're doing is just sex. We're not going to become a throuple or anything."

"You don't want that?" she asks. My eyes squint and stare up at the ceiling as I think about it.

No, I don't want that. I don't want to settle down...although if I did, it would be with someone like Isabel.

"It doesn't matter. He's not bisexual. How would that even work? We'd both be with her?"

She shrugs. "Sure."

"But that's *his* wife."

"Who he's asking *you* to fuck."

Touché. "See, this is what I'm talking about. It's complicated, and the sex I usually have is *not* complicated. It's simple. No attachments. No strings. Fuck, half the time I don't even get their name. And that's how I like it. This shit has too many moving parts and things to worry about."

"But you're still doing it," she replies.

With a sigh, I say, "Yeah."

I keep waiting for her to ask why, but instead, she's nodding her head with a knowing smile. And I guess there's not really any question why I'm doing this. I'm doing it because I want to. Because I want them.

"Come on. Your kinky couple is probably looking for you," she says, pulling me toward the door.

With her arm linked through mine, I smile down at her. "I like you. I'm going to put in a good word and get you at Salacious."

"I've never been to California," she replies.

"It's expensive and crowded, but we have great beaches," I reply.
"And great men."

"Obviously," I say, and we both laugh as she opens the door.
I'm in a much better mood than I was a few minutes ago. Until we
peer down the hallway and find *my kinky couple*, as she calls them,
waiting for me with irritable expressions on their faces.

Hunter's eyes dance between me and Silla while Isabel waits,
nervously chewing on her lip.

"Let's go. We're leaving," he grunts before storming away.

"Wait," I call, chasing after him. Turning back to Silla, I send
her a helpless glance. "I'll see you later, okay?"

"Go, go, go," she replies. "But wait!" She grabs my arm and
slides a card into my hand. "In case you want to bring them back
here," she says, nodding her head toward the room we just walked
out of.

"Thanks," I mutter, looking down at the matte black card in
my hand.

Isabel is watching us, a notch of concern in her brow. Putting a
hand on her back, I lead her toward where Hunter just disappeared.
He's already halfway out the door when we catch up to him.

"Will you slow down?" I snap, grabbing his arm.

"Deal's off." He grunts, pulling away.

"What?" Isabel and I reply in unison.

"Drake, you can't be playing the field while we do this. It's
not fair to her."

"I didn't—"

"We both saw the way you were flirting with her. It was
obvious."

"I flirt with everyone, Hunter," I argue. Why do I suddenly
feel like I'm arguing with a jealous boyfriend instead of my best
friend? "I didn't sleep with anyone. I'm not that much of a whore."

"I didn't say you were a—" He's struggling with his words
now, clearly worked up, and I feel the card in my hand, squeezed
so tightly, it's left marks in my palm.

Forcing myself to swallow, I remember how perfect that room was. It had a chair in the corner and it was classy, not some sleazy hotel bed. And I'm really committed to this crazy idea, so here we go. No better time than the present.

I hold the card out to him. "She gave us a room. I haven't done anything in it except talk to her. You can trust me. So…do we want to use it or not?"

Hunter's eyes focus on the card I'm holding between us. Then, I glance sideways at Isabel, who's standing silently next to her husband. She's staring at the card too, like it's going to explode or something.

It's her who speaks first. "I'm ready."

My heart beats a little faster. "I'm ready too."

Then, she and I both stare at Hunter as we wait. And I watch as his jaw relaxes, his shoulders fall away from his ears, and the wrinkle between his eyebrows dissipates. Finally, he looks me in the eye as he responds, "I'm ready."

There's still tension between us as I open the door to the room Silla and I were just in. Isabel walks in, tentatively glancing around and taking in the decor of the place, as if she's trying to decide whether or not this is the kind of place she wants to have sex with just the second man in her entire life.

"It's nice," she whispers, looking around, and honestly, this is all a little too uncomfortable for me. Awkward sexual encounters really aren't my style. If I were with a normal girl, I would just make things physical quickly to snuff out any of those pre-sex jitters. But that's not exactly an option for us right now.

Hunter wants to watch, and in a way, I know he wants to sort of orchestrate it too. Or at least that's what I gathered from last night. If we're going to do this, it has to be on his terms. And to some degree Isabel's. And then to a lesser degree, mine.

I'm *still* shirtless from when Silla dragged me in here, so I toss my shirt on the dresser as I face Hunter. "What should we do now?"

He doesn't answer as he continues to explore the room, opening drawers and cabinets to inspect what they have to offer. I notice the usual, condoms and lube and some basic toys like cuffs and pillows.

Then, he pulls open a cabinet and I'm surprised to see what looks like a stereo receiver. Even Hunter shares my expression of surprise. Then I realize that's why it's so awkward in here. We can't hear the music from the main room, so it's basically silent.

Hunter tries a couple knobs and buttons, and a moment later, music begins to play through the ceiling's speakers. It takes me a few minutes to place the song, but when the singer chimes in, I immediately recognize it as "Stand by Me." It's a classic, romantic and sultry, and I glance at Isabel, who's hovering nervously by the bed.

Hunter loosens his tie and then rolls up the sleeves of his shirt. Chin lifted, he watches me through his thick lashes as he says his next words as a command.

"Dance with my wife."

Arousal goes off like an explosion inside me as I glance in Isabel's direction. Without a word, I hold out a hand toward her.

A smile creeps across her face. Then she places her hand in mine and lets me pull her against my body. My hand slides down her back as we begin to sway side to side, the music carrying us. And when it breaks into the instrumental bridge, the lights grow dimmer. Hunter leans casually against the cabinet and watches us as I hold her close in my arms, gazing down into her eyes. And when the music begins to fade, it settles into another song. This time something from Marvin Gaye.

"Kiss her," a voice from the side of the room chimes in, and I'm already leaning my mouth down toward hers. She closes the distance, lifting onto her toes to capture my mouth with her own.

And the moment we're touching, all of the tension melts away. Her mouth is eager and warm, her tongue sliding against mine, and I realize this is only the third time we've really kissed, but it already feels so natural, as if we're made to do this. My hands slide down her back, stopping at her waist as I tug her closer, so she can feel the thickness in my pants. I want her to know what she does to me.

"Take off his clothes, Red," Hunter commands, and I glance over her head to see him now relaxing in the large chair, watching us through a lust-filled, hooded gaze. Isabel doesn't hesitate. Her fingers are already fumbling for the button on my pants, and I bite my bottom lip as I watch her.

I've known this beautiful woman for ten years. I've had her in my life almost every single day, and while I admired her for every moment of it, I never looked at her like this, never once expecting we'd get here and I'd want it so goddamn bad.

Each breath feels like a struggle as her fingers graze my abdomen. When my zipper is down, her gaze lifts to my face. Soft, innocent green eyes gaze up at me, and then over at her husband, as if she's waiting for his permission. He gives her a quick nod, licking his lips as he watches her reach into my pants. My face winces with surprise as she wraps her hand around my hard cock, nudging my pants down my legs to give her more access.

She squeezes it tighter than I expected her to; sweet, quiet Isabel has a firm grip, and she tugs mercilessly on the head, making me grunt due to the mix of pain and pleasure. And with her eyes still locked with mine, she lets go of my cock, lifts her hand to her face and licks a wet line across her palm, slicking it up before returning it to my length.

"Fuck," I groan as she slides her hand from base to tip with more ease.

"Is he hard, Red?"

"Yes," she replies in a sultry tone.

After a few strokes, she starts to look anxious, as if she wants to do something else. Finally, she turns her head and glances over her shoulder at her husband sitting in the chair.

"You know what to do, baby," he says, and my heart starts to beat harder. Without hesitation, she lowers to the floor before me, barely coming up to my dick when she's on her knees, so she has to reach. I brush her hair out of her face, so I can watch as she swirls her tongue around the head of my cock.

My mouth hangs open as she elicits each groan and grunt from my chest with the movement of her tongue. When she drags me into her mouth, welcoming me into the warmth of her throat, I make the mistake of looking up.

And I find him not watching Isabel but watching me. Our eyes meet for a long-drawn-out moment, and I notice the way he forces himself to swallow, then bites his bottom lip. Isabel sucks hard, stealing my attention, and I look back down at her, those soft pink lips wrapped around my fat cock. It's the most beautiful thing I've ever fucking seen.

"Fuck, you're so good at that, Isabel. I want to come down your pretty little throat."

"Not yet," Hunter barks from the chair.

So I quickly pull my dick out of her mouth because I was a lot fucking closer than he realized. Even now, cum leaks out of the tip, no matter how hard I try to stop it.

"Get on the bed, Isabel. On all fours and face me." His simple commands make everything we do so much more sensual. We obey and we get rewarded.

She quickly stands, leaving me on the edge of my orgasm with my saliva-coated cock. Hunter and I both follow her with our eyes as she does as he said, climbing onto the bed on her hands and knees. Turns out sweet little book-loving Isabel is a fucking vixen.

"Now lift your dress for him," Hunter says, leaning forward as he gives her instructions, slowly and deliberately, with a subtle huskiness to his voice.

When Isabel lifts her dress for me, exposing her pale ass, my mouth goes dry. I don't need instructions, but I wait for them anyway. Glancing his way, I realize he looks as if he's going to come undone. Still confident and dominant but with a hint of excitement too.

"Go to her," he says, his voice so raspy now it sounds like it's difficult to speak.

In a rush, I shuck off my pants and boxers and walk to the side table to grab a condom. I'm enjoying the filthy view of her wet cunt as I slide on the rubber. Then, I move into place behind her. She has a thin pair of panties on that I easily slide down her legs.

I'm then nudging the head of my cock against her pussy, but I don't enter her, not yet. Not until he tells me to. And he's dragging it out to torture me, I can tell.

So after a long wait, I lift my gaze up to his face. My dick is inching its way into his wife as he and I stare each other down. The eye contact between us is intense and new, nothing like I've ever felt looking into Hunter's eyes before, but considering the current situation, it makes sense that this would be different. There's also something in his expression that has me feeling excited.

My blood is pumping loud in my ears as I bathe in his wanton gaze. And I imagine for a moment that it's not just this experience he wants but me. And when he finally mumbles a guttural, "Fuck her," I swear it's not only Isabel I'm eagerly sinking into.

Rule #16: Two orgasms are better than one.

Isabel

MY FINGERS CLAW AGAINST THE SHEETS AS DRAKE ENTERS ME with force. And just like that...Drake and I are having sex. How did this happen? And when he slams in again at an angle that makes my toes curl and my next breath leave my body in a raspy moan, I wonder...why didn't we do this sooner?

When I lift my gaze again, my eyes find Hunter, watching from a perched position on the chair. He looks anything but relaxed as he watches, and I wonder if this is what he wanted. Are we giving him the high he was chasing? Right now, he looks like he might fly out of that seat at any moment, but his hooded gaze and heavy breathing seem to signify that he's enjoying this. There is a wildness in his eyes, and they are dancing between my face and Drake's.

Every rational thought in my head is blown away as Drake violently pounds into me, the walls of my pussy clenching around him. A raw, guttural moan claws its way out of my chest as my forehead falls to the mattress.

"More," I cry out, so he slows his thrusts, making each one

a violent pounding that practically rattles my bones, but God… does it feel good. I let out another groan, each one a mixture of pleasure and pain.

"You can be rough with her," Hunter says from his place across the room. "She likes it."

"Oh yeah?" Drake replies, and then there's a fist in my hair and he yanks me upright, so his mouth is against my cheek. He's still buried deep as he whispers, "This is the best pussy I've ever fucked, you know that?" He thrusts again. "The best."

Winding my arm back, I loop it around his neck and pull his lips to mine, desperate for a taste of his mouth—dying for a taste of those sweet words. And he kisses me with fervor, tugging my bottom lip between his teeth, humming against my mouth as he thrusts inside me. For a moment, as we are entangled in our lust, I almost forget my husband is watching. It's just us—me and Drake—and it doesn't feel wrong or weird. It feels right.

Then I feel Hunter's eyes on us and a new bolt of electric excitement courses through me. I love knowing he's here, almost as if he's a part of this too.

Without warning, Drake's thrusts are gone, and I'm being flipped onto my back, then tugged closer by my legs, as Drake lays his body over mine and enters me again. My legs wrap around him as he moves, and I gaze up into his eyes, loving the ability to see his face while he fucks me. I still can't believe this is happening, but it's everything I never knew I needed.

His large body engulfs mine as he drives his hips relentlessly: hard, bruising thrusts that set my body on fire.

"Don't stop," I cry out as the muscles in my legs begin to seize.

"I don't ever want to stop," he mumbles quietly, so quietly Hunter probably doesn't hear.

Reaching up, I touch his face, running my fingers through his thick, shoulder-length hair draped over his face, as he finds a fast rhythm. When our eyes meet, electricity soars between us, a connection so intense, my heart splinters and cracks at the intensity. I realize just how much I care about this man—as more than just a friend. Feelings I never allowed myself to feel before. Feelings I never gave a name to before.

With that, I'm soaring. My body seizes up around him, pleasure rippling through every vein. He keeps up this cadence, clearly struggling to hold out long enough to let me finish as I moan my way through an earth-shattering orgasm.

Once my limbs relax around him, he pounds into me one last time before shuddering out one long groan and filling the condom between us. When he relaxes, resting his chest against mine, I feel his heart beating quickly as he tries to steady his own rapid breaths.

I'm on a cloud somewhere in the heavens. No longer on earth.

My husband's voice drags me back to the surface. "Bring her to me."

Opening my eyes, I gaze up at Drake as he pulls his warm body away from mine and lifts me deftly off the bed and carries me over to my waiting husband. He's still in his chair, pants unzipped and hard cock out and waiting for me.

The craving to be in his arms is visceral. I *need* him, but I also don't want to lose Drake's tender touch either. I take one last kiss from Drake's lips before I'm straddling Hunter. He takes my mouth hungrily as if he's trying to kiss his friend's taste from my lips. His grasp is fierce as he holds me, and I do the same, clawing at his neck, trying to deepen our embrace as I lower myself onto his hard length.

The moment he slides inside me, we groan in unison. Then, I rest there, holding him inside me as we devour each other's mouths.

"I love you so fucking much," he growls into our kiss.

"I love you," I reply.

I want his pleasure, the comfort and familiarity of his touch, the sense of home and safety I feel when I'm in this man's arms. I want Hunter inside my body and my soul because that is where he belongs. He is as much a part of me as my own heart is. And I know by the way he grips me tightly, staring ardently into my eyes with so much love, that he feels the same. Not a moment in our ten-year relationship have I ever felt an ounce of anything missing. Not love or attention or lust or desire. Hunter signed over his entire soul to me the day we got married, and I hold it dearly, like it's my own.

"It was so hot watching him fuck you, Red," he mumbles against my mouth as I slide up and down on his cock. His words light a fire inside me and I pick up speed. "I want him to see how good my girl is. How perfect this pussy is."

I let out a moan as I slam down on his lap a little harder. His fingers dig into my hips as he moves me faster until I feel myself starting to rev up again, pleasure lighting its way up my spine.

Our lips barely leave each other's as his cock starts to tremor and flinch inside me, and I scream through my second orgasm, grinding my hips hard against him to chase the rapture of another violent climax.

My bones feel like they've turned to mush by the time Hunter and I have caught our breaths. When I finally lift up, his eyes are grazing the room, and I turn to see what he's looking at, but before it registers, I already know.

Drake is gone.

Rule #17: No one likes a lurker.

Drake

IF THEY THOUGHT I WAS GOING TO STICK AROUND FOR THEIR heartfelt *I love yous*, they're wrong. I need a minute to think. And a drink. Thank God for bars and drink limits. This place does it right.

I'm not mad. I'm not bitter or upset or jealous.

I'm just...confused. And to be honest, a little nervous. Because that was good. Very fucking good. Like the best I've ever had good. And I have a lot to compare it to. I've just never felt so much during sex like I felt with Isabel. Her hands on my face and the feel of her perfect body in my arms. I can't remember the last time I've slept with someone and immediately wanted to sleep with them again.

I'd resigned myself to that lifestyle a long time ago. Like mother, like son. There was practically a revolving door on our house, and I saw so many men come and go, I stopped being surprised when I woke up to find yet another stranger drinking coffee in the kitchen when I'd get ready for school.

There were times I had the dumb sense to get attached to one or two of them. A few of them actually came back for an encore and I'd talk them into taking me out for burgers or letting me ride with them when they'd go pick up beer and smokes. Then, they'd disappear like the rest, and when I'd ask my mom when Hank or Steve or Brent were coming back, she'd laugh in my face. Give me some line about what a crappy lay they were.

So when Hunter met Isabel, I knew that he was waltzing right into the life he was meant to live and I was waltzing right into mine. He was the married-life kind of guy. The one content with loving the same woman forever. Confident enough to know he'd always be enough for her. Bold enough to get attached to her without the fear of her walking out of his life.

And I can't help but think about what Silla said before she gave me the room key. About *being* with them. That's not really an option. We're not like that. I could never insert myself into their relationship because before too long, the jealousy would drive Hunter crazy. I'm not sure it hasn't already driven him crazy. I mean…he just watched me fuck his wife, but it was also so much more than that.

Isabel and I weren't supposed to…connect so much. It wasn't supposed to be that intimate. We should have just stuck to some basic carnal fucking, without all the sweet talk and touchy-feelies.

"Hey," his familiar voice mutters as I feel him approaching to sit in the seat next to me at the bar. As he takes his seat, I glance at him for a quick moment, but he's wearing that calm and collected expression he always has. Well, except for when he was sitting in that chair watching us. He was anything but calm. He looked downright feral.

"Hey," I reply.

"You didn't have to run," he says, and I brush it off with a shrug.

"Didn't want to intrude on your moment. I figured my part was done."

"Your part? Drake…"

"You know what I mean, man. I'm fine. We're cool, right?"

"We're cool," he replies as he waves down the bartender for a drink.

"Where's Isabel?"

"Still in the room. She wanted me to come find you by myself."

"Ah," I reply, a crooked smirk on my face as I glance sideways at him. From this angle, I catch the glint of light in his dark brown irises, and I quickly look away, so I'm not caught staring.

"Yeah, I think she wants us to...talk."

"I bet you were excited about that," I joke.

He lets out a heavy sigh as the bartender places a bourbon on ice in front of him. "Ecstatic," he mutters before taking a big sip.

"How are you feeling?" I ask. "About what happened."

I turn to see his jaw click as he clenches his teeth. I almost feel bad for him because he really does hate talking about anything, but he literally brought this on himself. It's a miracle in itself that he even had the nerve to ask for this in the first place.

"I'm feeling great, Drake. It was exactly what I wanted."

Nodding my head, I face forward and stifle the strange mixture of disappointment and excitement I feel at hearing him say that. On one hand, I almost wanted him to say he didn't like it. Then I would have no choice and things would go back to the way they were. And if he loved it, then I would likely have the opportunity to be with Isabel again, which would also make me happy.

I've never been more torn in my life.

"If you didn't like it, then we don't have to do it again—"

My head snaps in his direction. "Who said I didn't like it?"

"You look awfully...conflicted about it. You bolted out of there like a marathon runner as soon as it was over. I just get the feeling that you're not really into this."

"I'm into it. I did like it. No...I fucking loved it. I only left because I didn't want to feel like an intruder in your marriage."

"Drake, I told you already...you're not intruding. You're *never* intruding."

"I know, but I am—"

"No, you're not."

"Hunter—"

He turns, placing a firm hand on my shoulder, his fingers dangerously close to my neck, pressing in just enough to make my cock jump in my pants. Just once, I wish this fucker knew what he was doing to me when he did stuff like this. But he's so fucking straight; he doesn't see how touching my neck or breathing into my ear or gazing into my eyes while I fuck his wife can be dangerous for me. He'll never see it.

I clench my molars as I look at him. There's sincerity in those dark eyes, haunting me with how deep they are, as if I could lose myself in them.

"I don't think you understand what I'm saying, Drake. We *want* you to stay. Next time, please…stay."

My brow furrows as I glare at him. He wants me to stay to watch *him* have sex with Isabel? It doesn't make any sense. I thought for sure he'd appreciate me leaving, so this is not the reaction I expected at all.

"Next time?" I ask, watching his expression.

His hand is still on my shoulder, his fingers still pressing into my neck, and he squeezes gently as he lets out a sigh. "Tell me you want to do that again."

There's something loaded in his request, something more I'm not totally grasping, but I'm too eager to answer his question before he thinks I'm hesitating and rescinds his offer. "I want to do it again," I reply.

Finally, he pulls his hand away, and my shoulders deflate. I don't let it show as I turn toward my drink and pick it up. He's swirling what's left of his bourbon in the ice-filled glass. "That wasn't weird to you? Seeing me with her?"

"Strangely…no."

"Or hearing me say how much I liked it. How much I liked her."

He chuckles. "Stop trying to scare me away, Drake. It didn't bother me."

"I don't get it, man. If I thought about another man touching her…" My fists clench just thinking about it.

"But you're not just another man."

"You know she and I talked about some rules today," I say, glancing at him.

"She told me."

"And we're never going to do anything when you're not around."

"I know."

He turns toward me again, but this time, his hand stays away from my shoulder. "Drake, it's not about you being with her. It's about me watching. That part didn't bother you?"

I think it over for a moment, but it's an easy answer. I'm not quite sure if he's ready to hear it, though. Oh well…fuck it. "It didn't bother me at all. I really fucking liked you watching."

He swallows, his eyes staying on my face. "Good."

It's true. I loved him watching, but what I can't say is that I wish he'd do more than watch. He's definitely not ready for that. Because once he gets involved, then it's not just a simple fantasy fulfilled anymore. Then it's something else entirely.

Rule #18: The good ones always remember the coconuts.

Isabel

"WHERE ARE WE?" I ASK GROGGILY AS I WAKE UP FROM A NAP, stretched across the back seat, using Hunter's sweatshirt as a makeshift pillow.

"Somewhere in Mississippi," Drake replies. Hunter is behind the wheel, which is funny because he was definitely in the passenger seat when I fell asleep. I must have really been out of it. Sleeping with two men really takes it out of you, I guess.

Who am I?

If my parents could see me now, I think with a laugh, blushing for the tenth time today as I relive the memory of last night. I didn't even know I was the two-guys-in-one-night kind of girl. Or is that just how people perceive me? Was I just conditioned to think of myself as modest and quiet because that's how I was raised?

My parents were modest upper-middle-class accountants, and I was their only child. But I think even I was a regretful incident because my childhood was spent feeling mostly ignored and brushed off. Without overly affectionate or attentive parents, I found my role models of love and affection in novels. What started as *Little Women* and *Emma* quickly became *Flowers in the Attic* and *The Claiming of Sleeping Beauty*. Every wicked curiosity and dirty thought I had stayed buried deep inside me and the space between my bed and my mattress hid more smutty romance novels than I can count.

Everyone thought I was so knowledgeable and astute because of my countless trips to the library and secondhand bookstores, but only the librarian knew the truth. Oh, I was knowledgeable all right. Knowledgeable in the many eclectic terms used to describe an erect penis.

On the day I passed Hunter and Drake for the first time, I was returning books three through seven of a popular romance series in hopes they would have any of books eight through sixteen. I was like an addict in desperate need of a hit.

Then, I met my own alpha. A man who could show me everything I had ever wanted to explore while never making me feel like a deviant for what I wanted. Even if he did act annoyingly like a gentleman in the early days. I was only seventeen when we met and although he started talking to me at that time, he made me wait the four months between then and my eighteenth birthday before he would touch me.

And then another six months before he would have sex with me. I was a fiend for him. And I think he liked making me wait as a form of torture. Hunter doesn't always like to inflict pain, but he does like to be in control.

A lot of that came from his childhood. I know his home life was not nearly as comfortable as mine. He's told me about his abusive father. Hunter and I were desperate for a stable, loving home and not for entirely different reasons. We were lucky to find each other, so we could share the love and attention we both craved growing up.

But I notice things. I'd be blind not to. The way he glances at Drake sometimes. The way his jaw clenches when Drake mentions being with another man. For so long, I brushed it off as being a little uncomfortable with his friend's open sexuality, but I'm seeing things differently now. This whole arrangement has me itching to point out to my husband that perhaps that irritation doesn't come from judgment but from jealousy.

Jealous of Drake for being able to live so freely. Or even jealous of the men who get a piece of his best friend he can never have.

What if Hunter has been putting on a facade this entire time? Stifling these feelings to protect me. He can't exactly explore his sexuality if he's married.

But I want him to. I mean…I had sex with his best friend, for goodness' sake.

If there was ever a time to open this door, even to just peek through, now's the time.

Drake says something that makes Hunter laugh, and they share a quick glance, but Hunter's eyes linger on Drake's face—as they often do.

"Oh look, two beds," Drake jokes as he disappears into the second bedroom of our rental in Nashville. We opted out of the hotels for the rest of the trip, since renting an apartment seems to be the better choice. Although if you ask me…sleeping sandwiched between those two wasn't so bad at all.

"I'm exhausted," Hunter replies as he drops onto the plush sofa and reclines his head against the arm.

"I'm not," I reply eagerly.

"Of course you're not. You slept the whole way here."

Only because you two gave me quite the workout last night…is what I *want* to say. But I don't. We're not really talking about what happened so casually just yet. Besides, saying stuff like that makes it feel normal, like we do it all the time, which we don't. This isn't a relationship. It's a fantasy.

But as I stare out the window of this second-floor apartment in the city, I fantasize for a moment about what that would look like. Drake in our marriage. No more waking up next to just Hunter, but waking up next to both of them. Every night and every day, it could be the three of us.

"Let's go do something fun. I'm bored," I whine as I approach a half-awake Hunter on the couch.

He drapes an arm over his face and lets out a low groan, but I know exactly how to perk him up, so I straddle his hips and grind down just a little.

"What are you doing?" he mutters from under his arm.

"Trying to wake you up."

A low hum rumbles up from his chest as I grind a little harder this time.

"Are you ever not in the mood?" he asks.

I lean down and bury my face in his neck. "Nope." He finally pulls his arm away from his face and runs his hands along my backside.

Then we hear a door slam in the bedroom where Drake disappeared to. "What the fuck?" he barks.

I sit up in a rush, staring in fear at the bedroom. My worst fears involve cockroaches or hidden cameras, but to my surprise, Hunter only laughs.

My head snaps back in his direction. "What's so funny?"

Drake finally appears in the doorway with wide eyes and his mouth hanging open. "What the fuck did you do?" he asks, staring at Hunter.

Hunter's laughter only escalates. "What did you find, Drake?"

My head is dancing between the two of them as I wait for clarification.

"Oh nothing...just happened to notice the strange hooks on the wall and a *very* interesting bench."

Hunter's practically howling now, and I jolt up from the couch, running to Drake's room. Sure enough, there's a large leather bench in the corner with a high part in the middle and a lower ledge on either side.

"Go ahead and open that cabinet," Drake says, and I practically sprint across the room to the large cabinet against the wall. It looks like something from IKEA, white and modern with a pretty floral-patterned paper covering the frosted glass. Definitely not something you'd expect to be housing a plethora of whips, ropes, and cuffs.

"Hunter, did you rent a sex dungeon?" Drake asks, and my cheeks instantly flush bright red at the sight. And at the very same time, my thighs clench together at the realization that I'm spending the next two nights here…with those two men.

"Dungeon?" I ask, meeting them in the living room. "It doesn't look like a dungeon. It's so pretty."

"Yeah, I thought you'd like that," Hunter replies once he's stopped laughing. He rises from the couch and approaches me with a hand around my waist. "I couldn't help myself. I saw the listing and figured this might be good for business…research."

"Research," I echo him with a quizzical smile.

"Aw, you guys have a swing!" Drake calls out from the master bedroom, and I quickly jolt down the hall to see. There is a large black sex swing dangling in the middle of the room. There's also a St. Andrew's cross mounted to the wall and a small seat in the corner with a hole in it.

Suddenly, I'm noticing things about this apartment I didn't notice when we walked in. The chaise longue in the living room clearly wasn't made for reading in, and the fancy hooks on the walls aren't decorative.

Salacious has only been open for a few months now and not much can make me blush anymore, but suddenly standing in a quiet room with these two…my blood might as well be boiling.

The three of us stand together in silence, gawking at the well-stocked and expertly designed sex dungeon, and it all feels a little too much.

"What are the chances we can get some food…and maybe some alcohol before we start…researching?" I ask, and Hunter replies with a smile. Pulling me against his chest, he kisses my temple.

"Let's get some dinner, Red. You'll need the energy later."

We send Drake for takeout, and Hunter falls asleep on the couch, which it turns out is just a regular one, no sexual modifications. I busy myself with poking around the apartment. I didn't even know kinky Airbnbs existed. I can already see a Salacious B and B in the company's future. A whole kinky resort full of rooms like these, where couples can come for a week, instead of an hour.

I'm in the middle of browsing through the various ropes they have in the drawer when the front door opens. I smell the Indian food in Drake's arms before he even sets it down on the table. There's another bag in his hand that looks suspiciously like booze.

"I'm starving," I say as I open the bag of warm, delicious-smelling takeout.

"There're three boxes. Just don't take the one with the *X* on it," he replies as he fishes out a bottle of tequila and a bottle of green margarita mix.

"Margarita mix?" I ask with a laugh.

"You don't like it straight. Is this not okay?" he replies, reading the bottle. "It's organic."

I fight back a grin as I take the bottle. "You got this for me?"

"Yeah," he says with a shrug. "Hunt and I will just have a couple shots."

"Thank you," I reply, trying to hide the sudden blush rising to my cheeks. Has Drake done stuff like this for me before? Am I just now noticing how considerate he is?

Whatever it is, it feels nice.

With a shameless smirk on my face, I make myself a margarita on ice, using the mix Drake picked up for me. Then, I grab a white Styrofoam container and a fork and start to dig in. I haven't eaten since breakfast and this curry smells divine.

But I don't even get the rice-covered forkful to my mouth before Drake is snatching it out of my hands. Rice flies all over the counter, and I gawk up at him in shock.

"What the hell was that for?" I shout.

"I said *not* the box with the *X*!" he replies angrily.

"Geez, I'm sorry," I stammer, feeling suddenly uncomfortable. He's never really yelled at me before and that happy grin I was wearing a moment ago has melted away. Behind me, I hear Hunter stirring from the couch.

"What's going on?" he asks.

"Iz, it has coconut milk in it," Drake says.

And instantly I pause, mid-reach to the non-*X* marked box. My eyes drift upward to Drake's.

"How did you know I have a coconut allergy?"

His expression morphs into a look like I've offended him. "I've always known. You told me that like the first time we ate together. I had to stop ordering the coconut cream pie from the diner because you would always steal the crust. Did you really think I forgot about that?"

I'm frozen in place, staring at him, and something suddenly starts to sting in my throat—and it's not an allergic reaction.

"I…I'm sorry," I stammer, quickly looking down at the safe-to-eat curry in front of me. "I guess I forgot that you knew about that."

It's tense for a moment, and I feel Hunter's hand on my back as he takes the other non-coconut dish. He sends me a quick, tight-lipped smile, but I can't seem to shake this feeling that something has been here all along…and I'm only now starting to see it clearly.

Rule #19: Sometimes joining is better than watching.

Hunter

I HAD THE SEX DUNGEON PLANNED LONG BEFORE I KNEW I'D BE instigating sex between my wife and best friend. I assumed when I booked it that Isabel and I would wear the master bedroom out while Drake found himself some company for the spare bedroom, like he so often does.

Now I'm picturing her cuffed to the spanking bench with his cock down her throat, and I'm not sure what the fuck is wrong with me...because that image is amazing. It's the only reason I don't have an appetite for food and keep glancing back and forth between them and waiting for the moment when I can appropriately tell them to take their clothes off and start fucking.

But things are strangely loaded between them now. Not in a bad way, in more of a serious way. I don't know why Isabel wouldn't have known Drake would remember her coconut allergy. Maybe that comes from a childhood of being mostly forgotten and ignored. I've spent the last decade drilling it into her head— the ones who love you show it.

And still, she acts so surprised that the guy who's been around her as much as I have in the past ten years remembers that she has a food allergy. I bet she'd be shocked to learn that he also knows her favorite movie is *Empire Records*. Her favorite song is "Hallelujah" and her favorite flavor of ice cream is butter pecan.

Drake knows almost as much about her as I do. And as of this week, he knows her as intimately as I do too.

I notice Isabel is picking at her food now, paying more attention to her margarita than her dinner, which means she's trying to loosen up as well. I glance up at the clock and see it's a little after nine.

"I need a shower," Drake announces after his food is gone.

"Me too," she replies, putting her uneaten takeout in the fridge. A slow, evil smirk stretches across my face.

"Well, this place might have two beds…but it only has one shower."

Drake pauses midway to the bathroom and stares at me. "Oh really?"

I nod. "Afraid so."

Isabel is biting her lip, staring back and forth between me and Drake.

"Well, okay then. What do you say, coconuts? Want to get clean before we get dirty?"

"Umm…" she barely gets a response out before he's hoisting her out of her chair, throwing her over his shoulder and carting her to the bathroom off the hallway. In no hurry, I pour myself a shot of tequila and take one slow sip after another until it's gone, allowing the liquid to burn its way down my throat. I like the idea of letting them get warmed up before the good stuff.

"This thing is huge!" Isabel calls, letting out a giggle after the words leave her mouth, and I smile, imagining what Drake might be doing to make her laugh. I love her tipsy giggles. My girl's no lightweight, but after just one drink, her smile and her laughter take on a new cuteness that is both sweet and sexy at the same time.

"I assume you're talking about the shower," I reply with a smile, pouring myself a second shot.

"I was," she calls.

I hear the water running, muffling the sounds of their voices, so I can't make out what they're saying. Until she calls out again, "Big enough for three…" She draws out the word in a sultry sing-songy tone, like a siren calling me to the depths of the ocean.

I'm frozen in place as I stare down at the amber liquid in the glass in my hand. Should I join them? Do I want to? Assuming it's just a shower…is that crossing a line with Drake? We are still just friends, and it would be very out of character to shower together.

But maybe we're not just friends anymore. I've watched him fuck my wife. I've laid in bed with him and seen him naked—and erect. I mean…I know I wouldn't feel weird being naked in a shower with him, but would he feel the same? I have to be careful with his emotions, as much as I have to be careful with Isabel's. I'm the one making requests of them, and I'm not going to do anything to hurt either one.

"Was that an invitation?" I reply after the bathroom grows quiet.

"You're quick," Drake replies in a sarcastic tone, and I roll my eyes before gulping down the second glass of tequila.

"Listen," I say as I stand from my seat and head toward the bathroom. "There are too many paddles and whips in this apartment for you to be getting snarky with me—" The moment I reach the bathroom, I freeze, the words falling from my lips as I stare through the steam at a fully naked Drake, leaning against the tiles of the giant shower, stroking his quickly growing cock as he stares at Isabel, who is standing under the spray of water.

My eyes rake over his body, watching the water from the showerhead on his side cascade over the muscles of his broad frame. He's so tall, he almost has to duck his head. But my eyes aren't on his head. They're on the languid strokes of his hand.

"You comin'?" he asks, looking at me as if this is completely normal. He's staring at me…and his hand is still moving.

Suddenly, my cock is twitching in my pants, throbbing as it fills and presses painfully against my zipper.

"Yeah…I guess," I stutter, pulling off my shirt and draping it neatly over the rim of the sink. Next, I ease down the zipper of my jeans, wondering if he notices how hard I am already, just from watching him stroke himself.

Anyone would get hard from that, right?

Of course…not everyone secretly wonders how nice it might be to reach out and touch it. How another man's cock feels in your own hand. How it tastes.

Fuck—a lightning strike hits the base of my spine and my cock twitches at the thought.

As I step toward the shower, Drake steps aside, pressing Isabel between us as I move under the hot spray of water. It's truly a big enough shower for three people to stand in here without touching, but where's the fun in that?

As I rinse my hair, trying to stay as composed as possible, no longer bothering to hide the hard length jutting out from my hips, Drake runs his hands over Isabel's wet body. She hums as he tweaks her nipples. With their eyes on me, both of them fondle and caress each other, not doing anything other than touching—and driving me insane.

Is it weird to feel like the third wheel when it's your best friend and wife?

"All right, you two. Dry off and get out. Meet me in the spare bedroom."

Isabel bites her lip as she smiles at me. Then, I step out of the shower, grab a towel, and resist the urge to stroke myself as I dry off. We have a potentially long night ahead of us…if I can keep it together.

After a quick dry-off, I leave them in the shower and head down the hall toward the spare bedroom—with a quick detour to the tequila bottle, of course. In the room, I browse through the cabinets and drawers. I know what I have in mind tonight, but I don't know if they will be into it. It's not really Drake's style.

So I pick out a few of the easier toys. No need to go crazy this time around. A red leather paddle with a lot of flex. A soft leather flogger for sensation. My experience with these things goes about as far as the research for the club. This isn't something Isabel and I have tried yet, mostly because I don't have it in me to hurt her. Too much trauma in my history, but Drake could—if she wants it.

I'm holding the paddle when they finally walk in, still naked. Isabel is behind him with her hands on his waist, stroking his bare skin with intimacy, and something strange strikes me at that moment. Something I can't define.

This whole time I've been more turned on than jealous at the sight of them touching each other, but suddenly, seeing just how comfortable they are together, the feeling has changed. Just a little but the shift from arousal to envy is there.

Shrugging off the hesitation, I move silently across the room. Pulling Isabel from behind Drake, I lead her toward the bench. With her cheeks flushed red from the shower and a sheen of sweat across her forehead, she's so breathtaking, I can't help myself as I pull her in for a kiss. On instinct, she melts into my arms.

"Do you know what this is, baby?"

Her eyes dance over the bench, the four cuffs attached to the head and foot on each side, and I spot the twinkle of curiosity in her expression. Lips parted, she nods.

"Drake is going to strap you to this bench and spank you for all the dirty things you've done. How does that sound?" I mutter lowly in her ear.

There's a slight hitch in her breath.

"While you watch?" she asks, her round green eyes finding mine.

"Yes, baby. I'll be in that chair, watching him make you scream."

The corner of her mouth lifts as her hand unexpectedly takes a hold of my cock. I let out a grunt as my knees go weak. She tugs a long stroke of my dick, pulling me closer to her as she says, "Don't touch yourself while you watch. I want you to hold out for me."

With a growl, I cover her hand with mine. "My filthy girl. You're getting an extra stroke for that."

As Isabel and I pull away from each other, I look at Drake, who's touching his lips as he stares at her, pinching the bottom one and rolling it in a way that makes me feel something I shouldn't.

"What do you think? Is this a good plan for you?" I ask him.

Suddenly, his arm is around Isabel, tugging her closer as he buries his face in her neck. She lets out a yelp as his giant body engulfs her tiny one.

"Punish this dirty girl while you watch? It would be my pleasure."

"You'll need a safe word, Red," I say, but she cuts me off before I have a chance to suggest one.

"Namaste."

My head tilts to the side as Drake lets out a light chuckle.

"Okay, then." By the time I sit in the chair across the room, Isabel is already climbing up onto the bench. With her belly and chest against the high part, she easily rests her knees and hands against the lower ledges, and Drake takes his time cuffing her wrists and ankles. There's a look of eager anticipation on her face as she squirms with each lock of the cuffs.

I keep glancing back at the small dish on the dresser labeled *Spanking Bench Keys*, as if they're going to magically float away and my wife will forever be stuck to this sex device.

She's facing me on the bench, so I don't get a good look at her backside, but this view is enough. Her head and ass are in prime locations for access and she has little to no mobility, something I'd say she's enjoying by the salacious gleam in her eye.

"How does that feel, baby?" I ask from the chair.

"It feels good," she replies, squirming against the bench, her voice going a little deeper and quieter than normal. She's ready.

"How many?" Drake asks as if he already knows I call the shots.

"Let's start with six on each side."

I watch Isabel's fists clench on either side of the bench as Drake readies himself. He massages her ass a little before rearing back and laying one back-handed smack with the paddle against her left cheek. She lets out a high-pitched hum as her eyes lift up to gaze at me.

Drake rubs the other cheek with the face of the paddle before rearing back and smacking again. She squeals again, squirming even more.

"That's one, baby," I say, my voice starting to strain with the need to touch myself.

Drake smacks her again on each side for number two, and her reactions stay the same, but I notice the new color in her cheeks and chest.

"I think she can take it a little harder," I say, and he looks down at her and then at me as he strokes a soft hand down her spine.

"Does this dirty girl want it a little harder?" he asks.

She nods without hesitation. "Yes, please," she whispers in a low, raspy tone.

When Drake lays into her for the next round, smacking her so hard I see a flash of fear in her eyes before she lets out a long, guttural cry, I find it painstakingly hard to keep my hand off my cock. It's leaking at the tip, throbbing a little more, as he spanks her hard again for number three.

"That's my girl." I groan, gripping the arm of the chair.

"I think she wants it hard again," Drake says, reaching all the way across her body to dig his fingers in her hair. She yelps as he pulls. "Don't you?"

"Yes," she cries out.

And he does, the sound of the paddle hitting her flesh making me wince. She cries louder this time, her legs starting to tremble with each hard smack. When he does the other side, my cock leaks a dot of cum from the tip, and I watch it slide down the head.

The next two rounds go by in a blur, and I can focus on

nothing but her face, the expression of pain mixed with lust and
need, a look of feral craving that I've never seen before. And just
when he gets to six, I'm about to tell him to stop, that I can't take
anymore, but I realize he's done when he tosses the paddle on the
bed and massages her ass cheeks with his bare hands.

She flinches and yelps as he grabs her sore flesh in his tight
grip, but I can tell by the look on her face when he runs his fingers
along a spot she likes.

"She must have liked that. She's practically dripping."

"Then, I think she earned an orgasm. Make her come, Drake."

He smiles wickedly at me as he drops to his knees behind her,
running his tongue along the length of her, from her clit to her
asshole. She cries out, fighting against the restraints now.

She watches me as he licks her pussy, sucking on her clit and
thrusting his tongue inside her. But I can tell by the restless way
she fidgets, that it's not what she wants.

"What is it, baby? What do you want Drake to do?"

Biting her lip and trying to hide her blush, she stares at me
and meekly cries, "Fuck me."

I smile, watching as he rises to a standing position. "Your girl
has a dirty fucking mouth."

"Yes, she does. Fucking filthy," I reply.

She squirms some more, as if she's trying to find his dick.

"I mean, look at her," Drake says, teasing her with his hands
around her backside. "Cuffed to this bench like a little slut,
begging for dick."

I lick my lips, his dirty talk going straight to my cock.

And as he continues, I nearly lose my breath. "She almost
sounds like she needs two cocks."

Isabel immediately hums in response.

"You liked the sound of that, didn't you?" he asks.

"Yes," she begs, looking straight at me.

As Drake reaches behind him to the drawer of condoms, I rise
from my seat and move toward her. She smiles up at me, looking

wicked as sin as I take her hair in my hand, leaning down so I can kiss her on the lips before I move her mouth toward my waiting cock.

"Is this what you want?"

"Yes," she cries.

Her right hand barely hangs over the edge of the bench and I gently place my leg where she can feel it. While Drake gets himself situated, I lean down and kiss her again.

"Tap my leg if it's too much, okay?"

She gives me a secret smile, squeezing my thigh between her fingers as she agrees.

Looking up at Drake, I watch as he aligns his cock at the same time that I move mine past the ring of her lips, both of us plunging inside her. She squeals, her voice muffled by my dick.

It's an obscene sight, this beautiful woman, taking two dicks at once. I wasn't supposed to do this. I was supposed to be watching Drake fuck her, but now…as I see her strapped to this bench, I wonder if I didn't subconsciously have this planned all along.

Her mouth is like heaven, tongue out and lips parted as I fuck her throat. When she gags, I pull back, stroking her chin. Her hand still rests with assurance against my leg.

"Jesus, Red. Look at you," I mutter, staring at the way Drake is thrusting hard into her from behind. "You look fucking beautiful like this, taking our cocks like the dirty girl you are."

"She's *our* dirty girl," Drake replies, his voice strained from the exertion. And I look down at Isabel as he says that. Did she hear it? That she's *ours*, not just mine. Because she is ours, and I want her to be ours.

I could stay like this forever, sharing this moment with the two people I love the most. Drake's eyes are on me, his fingers digging into her soft hips as he makes her scream around my cock. We are relentless and so in sync, and there's something fucking surreal about finding your pleasure in not just one but two other people. And knowing they're finding theirs too.

It could be the euphoria of this moment or being on vacation and far from reality, but I suddenly realize that I do want her to be ours. His as much as mine.

Maybe she always has been.

His thrusts pick up speed, so I match his tempo, intent on timing my release with his. And I can tell by the way his eyes close and his grip tightens that he's close. But I don't make it.

With that thought, I lose control, shooting everything down the back of her throat, emptying my cock onto her tongue as she stares up at me. With tears streaming down her cheeks, she swallows, and I wipe away the bit that drips down her chin. Behind her, Drake still thrusts slowly.

Pulling away from her mouth, I stroke her cheek, admiring the fact that I have the most amazing fucking girl in the world. And I want my best friend to have that too.

Rule #20: There's no hurt in trying.

Drake

I SUDDENLY UNDERSTAND WHAT ALL THE FUSS IS ABOUT. WATCHING Hunter unload in Isabel's mouth lights a fire inside me, like a fucking inferno in my groin.

I've been in threesomes before. Fuck, I've been in foursomes, and one time…an awkward fivesome, but the point is that none of those times ever felt as explosive as this. Everything with these two just hits different.

And seeing her tied to this bench is fucking filthy. I always knew Isabel had a hidden kinky side, but I had no idea it was *this* kinky. I love how adventurous she is. It makes me want to do everything I can with her.

Hold up…pump the fuckin' brakes. I'm not supposed to be getting attached or wanting more. It's just a vacation full of kinky, wild fucking and then when we get back to Briar Point, it's back to reality.

Except I'll be living with them.

Just down the hall. With the memory of this moment—and every other one—swimming through my head. How the hell am

I supposed to go back to how things were in those conditions? What is going to stop me from bending her over the dining room table Hunter is eating at? Or crawling into their bed to lick her pussy while he sleeps, making her scream loud enough to wake him up? The temptation will be unbearable.

Speaking of, Isabel lets out a loud whimper as her legs begin to shake, and I realize I literally lost myself in fucking her. I'm on the brink of my climax, but I'm not ready to be done yet. Now that I've accepted just how terminal this arrangement is, I want to make every time last.

Hunter is back in his chair across the room, stroking his spent cock back to life as he watches us. And I get an idea.

He wants to watch me fuck his wife...well, then maybe he wants a closer view.

When I pull out of Isabel, she lets out a loud, needy cry. But I move fast, grabbing the keys from the bowl on the dresser and quickly undoing her restraints. The moment her hands and legs are free, she's on me, kissing me and wrapping her legs around me. And I'm just as eager to hold her.

This is only our second time together, but I'm already noticing the way Isabel and I fit together. Like we were made for each other. Every move she makes, I anticipate. Every touch, every kiss, every moment is perfect.

Who the fuck am I?

I'm a scoundrel, not some pussy-whipped, clingy boyfriend type. And I intend to prove it as I carry her over to her husband, who immediately sits up when he sees that I'm about to deposit her on his lap.

"Hold her," I say as I lay her down on him, spreading her knees open for me. Then, I drop to my knees in front of her, align my cock with her warm cunt, looking down at the place where I'm about to enter her. I pause here, teasing her as she squirms and waits, but before I thrust inside, I spit, my saliva landing against her clit. With my fingers, I moisten her folds, and she keens and squirms even more. God, I love how much she wants it.

Hunter takes her wrists in one hand, holding them above her as she rests her head against his shoulder. With her legs draped over his, she is completely at our mercy again, succumbing to our dirty desires with so much trust. I rake a hand over her chest just to feel her heart beating wildly beneath my touch.

Then, after I've made her wait long enough, I thrust inside her. She yelps, then groans, her back arching against Hunter's naked body. My hips brush against the inside of his thighs, but it's too late to ask if this is too much for him. If he was uncomfortable with this close contact, he would stop it. I trust that he's controlling enough to tell me if it's too much.

I'm watching her face as I fuck her. The carnal expression and the light sheen of sweat on her red-flushed skin is so goddamn beautiful.

But I force myself to look away from her intense eye contact because I'm trying not to get attached, but where do my eyes wander? Straight to Hunter's face. Probably because he's watching me. And as I thrust between *his* legs, brushing up against *his* thighs, I realize how much it looks and feels as if I'm fucking *him*. Did I do this on purpose?

He's not looking away. He's just staring at me, looking turned on as hell as I fuck his wife on his lap. Still with his gaze glued to my face, he reaches down and strums at her clit. She shrieks and howls, urging him on, so he can take her to the orgasm she's so clearly earned.

Suddenly, I'm feeling bold. My left hand, currently on her thigh, starts to drift. I have to look away from him as I do it, but I pretend it's from the jostling of my thrusts, and I nudge my hold inward until I'm gripping his thigh. And I wait.

When he doesn't react, I look up at his face again. He's breathing heavily, his mouth slightly parted as his licks his lower lip, pulling it between his teeth.

This feels…like something powerful. Am I imagining this? I'm holding his leg and he's biting his lip as he stares at me.

Then…his fingers move. They drift from her clit downward until I feel the light brush of his touch against my cock. He's holding her pussy, exploring this place where she and I are connected, and in doing so…he's basically stroking my cock.

Fuck, I'm gonna come.

His lust-filled gaze is still on my face and this is all too fucking much.

"I'm almost there…don't stop," Isabel calls out, and I feel a wave of shame that I've been so focused on him, I barely considered her pleasure. So I keep up my cadence exactly the way it is, and Hunter's hand remains, two fingers on either side of my cock, when Isabel finally clenches up in his arms. With a high-pitched moan, she trembles her way through a climax that looks as if she's being possessed. Her naked, sweaty body seizes up, and the urge to fill her up is unbearable.

Of course, instead of really filling her up, I fill the condom hugging my dick, but it's still earth-shattering nonetheless. My orgasm rips a long grunt out of my chest as my grasp on Hunter's thigh tightens.

When I finally pull away from them, I don't make it far. After quickly pulling the used condom off and tossing it into the trash, I collapse against the bed. When I look over at Hunter and Isabel, I half expect them to be so focused on each other that I'll feel like a third wheel again. Instead, I'm almost pleased to find they're both looking at me.

It's almost three in the morning when I find myself standing alone in the kitchen, sitting in dark silence with only a bottle of water for company. Hunter and Isabel finally peeled themselves off the bed in my room, and he carried her to their own, where I'm sure he spoiled her with aftercare, and she quickly drifted off to sleep. I haven't seen them since.

But I can't sleep.

I seem to have woken up in the twilight zone or something because, all of a sudden, I don't recognize my own life. I don't have any regrets about what we're doing—and I think that's the problem. The sex is amazing. This whole trip has been amazing. But I haven't been doing any of the regular stuff that I used to do.

I wake up and think of them. Every second of my day, I'm thinking of them. At night…it's them.

And not just Isabel.

I'm a fucking idiot—that's all it comes down to. I've muted this little infatuation with my best friend since I was old enough to realize that I liked Hunter *a lot*. I liked his company, but I also liked his body. His attention. The way his eyes crinkle when he smiles and the darkness of his eyes. I liked being one of the only people in the world who knows the real Hunter, who sees the tattoos and knows the dark secrets of his past.

Then my dumb ass had to go and agree to fuck his wife. Thinking for one damn second that I could separate the two. That I could do this without letting my stupid fucking heart get its hopes up.

Like tonight, for example. I pushed his limits. I put him in a situation he might not have been comfortable with because, apparently, I like to play with fire.

And he played back, which did not help my situation at all.

I've always been known to look into things a little too much. As a bisexual man, I have to know how to read people really, really well, because misjudging someone's interest can end very badly for me. So I'm always careful.

And what happened tonight felt like a pretty fucking clear sign. It was a giant billboard on the freeway. Lit up. With flashing lights.

He touched my cock, for fuck's sake. He stared at me while biting his lip, letting me grip his leg while he touched my cock. Am I reading this situation correctly?

Is Hunter…into this? Into *me*?

Nope. It was just the heat of the moment. He probably barely even noticed me touching his leg, and he wasn't intentionally touching my cock; he was just holding his wife's pussy.

Pack up your hopes and dreams, Drake, you fucking idiot. He's still as straight as they come, and that's not going to change. It's not anyone's fault… It's just the way it is.

A door opens down the hall, and I freeze. When I hear footsteps, I can tell by the heavy way they travel that it's Hunter, and I immediately tense up.

"Hey," he says groggily, when he notices me sitting in the dark like a villain waiting to attack.

"Hey," I reply. "Can't sleep?"

"I drifted off for a little bit, but then I woke up and realized I needed some water. What about you?"

I shrug. "Just enjoying the quiet for a minute."

"Everything okay?" he asks, watching me skeptically.

"Yeah," I reply quickly. "Everything okay with you?"

He nods. "Everything's great."

"And Isabel?"

He chuckles as he takes a swig from the water bottle. "She's in there snoring, probably still smiling. I think she had more fun than anyone tonight."

"You made sure she drank something before falling asleep, right? Gave her some time to relax after everything?"

He holds up a hand. "I took care of her, I promise."

"Good," I say with a slow nod, looking away toward the city lights through the large living room window.

"You know…maybe next time, you could be there for the aftercare. If it would make you feel better."

I try not to read into that too much. He's just being considerate. I'm not much of an aftercare kind of guy, but I can't deny that taking care of Isabel does sound nice. "Sure," I say with a shrug.

It's quiet as he leans against the counter next to where I'm sitting on the barstool. In nothing but a pair of tight boxers, I struggle to keep my eyes forward and not let them cascade across the dark designs all over his abs to his chest.

He won't break the silence, so I do it first.

"If I overstep, you'll tell me, right?"

His head turns in my direction. "Of course."

"I mean…" God, this is uncomfortable. "Between you and me."

"Oh," he replies, and I wait for him to finally express how tonight was probably too much for him and how I definitely shouldn't get that close during sex ever again. "You won't overstep, Drake. It's fine."

I force myself to swallow. Is this a joke to him? Because he can't actually mean that. For once, I'd like him to just be honest and tackle the awkward conversations, so we don't land in a place we can't come back from. Instead, he's forcing me to.

"No…I definitely *could* overstep, Hunter. You're a straight man, and I'm not. If we're going to keep…doing whatever we're doing, you have to be up-front with me."

He turns toward me. "Are you referring to what happened tonight? Drake, it was fine. It didn't bother me."

"I don't want it to just *not bother* you. From now on…I'll just keep my hands to myself," I reply, wishing this painful conversation could have just never happened at all.

Silence stretches between us before he finally replies, "But I didn't keep my hands to myself either."

And my mouth goes dry. He just admitted it. He literally owned up to touching my cock on purpose and I have no idea where to go from here.

To my surprise, Hunter fills the quiet first. "Yeah, I'm straight, but I've known you my whole life, Drake. Touching you doesn't fucking bother me."

I stand for some reason. I'm too unsettled by this conversation, and it feels wrong to be sitting. He's being too nonchalant about this and I'm afraid now that he's being too compensating. He's giving me what I want because I'm the one fulfilling his fantasy. And the more I think about that, the more I can't stand it.

"That's the problem, Hunt. There's a big difference between liking something and not being bothered by it. And I've known you my whole fucking life too, long enough to know when something is up—and something is definitely up with you. I think you're more bothered by it than you're going to tell me, and I'm telling you…you don't have to do that for me."

"Come on, Drake. All this for a little touching? What is wrong with you?"

"Right now, it's touching, but what happens when it's more? How am I supposed to know you're cool with it if you won't—"

"Jesus Christ. Here," he mutters, and then I'm struck silent because his hands are on my face and he's pressing his soft lips against mine.

Hunter is kissing me.

My hands are hanging down by my sides because I did not see this coming and I'm too stunned to move. Why is he kissing me?

At first, it's just lips pressed against lips, meant to prove a point. He's perfectly happy touching me—I get it. But the seconds tick by and his mouth is still lingering on mine.

Ever so slowly, he pulls back, putting enough space between our mouths so he can look me in the eye, but his lips linger an inch from mine.

"I just want to try something," he whispers, his breath brushing against my face, and the weight of those words land like a tidal wave. Because I know what's coming next.

He's kissing me again. But instead of the awkward, brief kiss before, his lips part, and I feel his tongue gliding against the seam of my mouth. I don't hesitate to let him in. The moment our tongues collide, I swear the apartment trembles. Or maybe the earth quakes or the universe implodes. I don't know, but something cosmic as fuck takes place because my best friend and I are now officially making out in the kitchen in the middle of the night.

His hand glides around to cup the back of my head, pulling

me down a few inches, as he deepens our kiss. His tongue finds its way farther into my mouth, the sensation both rough and soft against my own tongue, and when he licks his way out, his teeth pinch my lower lip before diving in again.

Holy fuck. He wanted to try something all right.

My hands are still hanging useless by my sides because, suddenly, I don't know what the fuck to do with them. Where do I normally put my hands when I'm kissing someone...or being mouth-fucked, which would apparently be the case now?

Finally deciding on what to do with them, I touch his sides, sliding my fingers up his bare rib cage and around to his back, hooking them around his body to pull him in closer.

I'm hard, because of course I'm fucking hard, but I'm more than a little curious to know if he is too.

When he finally shifts a little closer, I get my answer. There's a certified chub against my hip, and it's growing less chubby and more hard by the second.

Is this what he wanted to know when he did this? Is he pleased with the result or mortified? Why the fuck am I so in my head right now? Maybe because this is Hunter, the one person I have trained my body to ignore. But now he's kissing me, and all of the feelings I've sedated for so long are finally starting to resurrect.

The kiss only lasts less than a minute but time didn't seem to exist in that kiss. It felt like forever and no time at all, and as he pulls away, I already know I'm royally fucked.

He releases his hold on my head and my hands fall away from his back as we're bathed in silence again. I'm a little scared for what he's about to say, and I honestly would be just fine if he followed this up with a simple "Thanks. Good night."

But he doesn't. Instead, he stares at me. Then he licks his fucking lips. This asshole.

"So..." I say first with a crack in my voice. "Is that what you expected?"

"No," he replies solidly. "I'm sorry. I shouldn't have done that. You're not some sexuality lab rat for me to experiment on."

Um...yes, I am. Yes, the fuck, I am.

I don't say that because that would be lame, but I do quickly shake my head. "Don't apologize. It's fine. You're fine, Hunter. It's...um...I—"

"Yeah," he replies with a laugh. "That's how I feel too."

We both let out an awkward chuckle, but it doesn't do much to quell the tension. So I try for something reassuring. "It's been a crazy week. I wouldn't blame you for being a little confused. Don't sweat it, man. It's me. You never have to worry with me."

With a huff, he smiles. "Weren't you the one who was worried?"

Oh shit, I was. "Well...I'm not anymore."

"Good," he replies, and those dark eyes stay focused on my face. It might sound cheesy as fuck, but his eyes feel like home to me. Those dark abyss-like irises have been the only constant in my life, so when Hunter says everything's fine, then I know everything's fine.

Even if it does feel as if my entire world has been tilted off its axis.

"I should get some sleep," I say, taking a step from the kitchen. Separation feels like the only solid choice right now. Also, I'd like to do something with this brick shaft in my shorts before it goes away. And I know exactly what I'm going to think about when I do.

"Night, Drake," he mutters, watching me walk away.

"Night, Hunter," I reply.

Then, I carry the sound of his voice all the way to my bed, where I drift off some time later, constantly licking his taste off my lips as I do.

Rule #21: It's never just a kiss.

Hunter

I KISSED DRAKE.

I kissed a man…my best friend—Drake.

I'm still lying in bed, replaying the events of last night, *all* the events. Like the moment I realized I didn't want this temporary arrangement to be all that temporary. Because I want Drake to be with Isabel more. I want to *share* her.

Across the hall, Isabel is in the shower, and Drake escaped early this morning to the gym chain he has a membership to. Which leaves me here, alone, with my thoughts.

I really didn't mean to use my best friend as an experiment, but there's no one else I'd be willing to use to see if I have a taste for men. What's strange is that I haven't been attracted to another man in all my life. I can appreciate an attractive body and pretty face, but seeing a man naked has never interested me. The thought of fucking one has never whet my appetite before either.

But that kiss. That fucking kiss.

Maybe Drake is right. This week has been crazy and more sex-filled than even our day-to-day sex-club-owning lives are. Being oversexed has just gotten to my head. That's all.

When Isabel struts back into the room stark naked and drying her hair with a towel, I let out a growl at the sight. It erases every thought in my head as the sight of tits and ass commonly do. See…perfectly straight.

As she passes by, I snatch her by the wrist. "Bring that beautiful ass over here." I tug her onto my lap and she lets out a cute giggle as I kiss her neck.

"Not today, Mr. Scott."

I peek my head up and stare at her. Fuck, what's the date? The fifteenth…middle of the month. *Dammit.*

"Oh shit, your period started today, didn't it?"

"Yep," she replies with a grimace.

"How are you feeling?"

"Okay so far, but I know in a few hours, I'll feel like chewed-up gum on the highway."

"What do you need? Want me to get you some tea or soup or something?"

She cuddles against my lap. "No. But do you mind if I skip the club tonight? I think I'd rather spend the evening with Netflix and pizza."

"Of course, baby." I kiss her neck again, inhaling the familiar scent of her strawberry shampoo. Period sex doesn't bother me, but Isabel gets pretty sick on the first day of her cycle. So for one day a month, I am her humble servant.

Okay, let's be real. Every day of the month, I'm her humble servant, but more so between the fifteenth and the twentieth.

"What were you thinking about when I walked in? You looked like you have a lot on your mind."

I let out a heavy sigh. I want there to never be any secrets between me and Isabel. If she's going to be mad that I kissed someone else, I'd rather take her anger than keep it from her. So I just let it out.

"I have to tell you something."

She tenses, staring at me as she waits. So I don't waste time and just come out with it.

"I kissed Drake last night."

She bolts up and stares at me with wide eyes. "What? When?"

"Around three in the morning, I think." I'm wearing a grimace as I wait for her reaction.

"Can I ask why?"

"…an experiment," I reply slowly.

"And how did that experiment go?" Her tone lingers on each word as if she's being careful with them. It's not anger in her voice but curiosity.

My head falls back, hitting the headboard. "I don't know. I honestly don't."

"Okay, back up. What were you two doing before the kiss?"

"Just sitting in the kitchen talking. About what happened last night. He was all worried that he overstepped when he touched me during sex."

"But you touched him too," she replies.

Oh, she noticed that? I wasn't quite sure. It was all in the heat of the moment.

I don't respond; I simply shrug.

"So you told him it was okay…that he touched you during sex?"

"Yeah, I did, but he didn't believe me. So I proved it."

"By kissing him."

"Yep."

She doesn't say anything for a moment, only chews the inside of her lip as she scrutinizes me.

"You're not mad?"

She shakes her head. "Considering what I've done with him this week, it would be a little hypocritical of me."

"This was different, Iz."

"I know…but to be honest, I'm actually kind of glad you did."

"Glad? Why?"

"Because…" Her word drags out and I can tell how nervous she is to express whatever it is she's thinking.

"Just say it, babe. Whatever you're thinking."

"I'm just glad to see you exploring this…option."

"You mean men?"

"I mean Drake."

My eyes linger on her face for a moment while I quickly scan my memory for any instance in which I ever showed interest in my best friend, but I come up empty.

"I feel like I'm missing something," I mumble.

She leans in, touching my cheek. "I've only been around you two for ten years and you've been together for twice that long, so maybe that's why I see things you don't."

"Like what?"

She smiles. "Like the fact that Drake is head over heels for you."

"What?" I laugh. Then I laugh some more because this is ridiculous. "Isabel, just because he's into men doesn't mean he wants *every* man."

Her head tilts as she gives me a stern glare. "Hunter, I'm being serious. If you haven't noticed, it's probably because you've been around him so long, you've gotten used to it. But I see it. I'm sure everyone sees it."

"We're just friends…"

"Yeah, I know. But you can still be in love with your best friend."

"In love?" I reply in shock. "We're talking about the same Drake, right? The man sleeps with more people every year than there are days on the calendar. He has no interest in being tied down or matched up with anyone. Drake doesn't fall in love, Isabel. Come on…"

She doesn't bother arguing with me, but the expression on her face says enough. The tight-lipped grimace and soft eyes mean she's just waiting for me to hear myself.

Wait a fucking minute…is she right? Drake has feelings for me? And that's why he won't settle down with anyone else?

I let out another long sigh. "And I fucking kissed him! Oh my God…" I groan.

"Yeah…"

"Fuck."

"Which is why I asked…how did that little experiment go?"

She's asking if I liked kissing him. If I would do it again.

This is all too much. It was just supposed to be a kinky fantasy fulfilled, and now I'm thinking about asking my wife to open our marriage to my best friend and then thinking about my best friend in a sexual way, and I don't know which way is up at this point.

"Hunter?" she asks when I don't answer.

"I liked it," I stammer. "I really fucking liked it, and I got hard as hell and I was kinda disappointed when it was over."

She bites her bottom lip hard as she tries to stifle a smile.

"It was just a kiss," I add.

"I know. But maybe…"

Oh God. I don't like the mischievous look on her face. Can't she tell this is all a little too much for me, right now?

"Maybe when you're at the club tonight…you could see how you feel about more than just a kiss."

"No," I snap. "No. I can't even think about that. Plus…what if he gets the wrong idea? I don't want to hurt him."

She's staring at me again, as if she has all the answers, and let's be real, she probably does. But I'm afraid to know what they are.

"Baby, I'm not sure what the wrong idea is. And I don't think you do either."

I don't reply as I mull those words over in my head. Eventually, she crawls off my lap and fishes out the comfiest clothes in her suitcase, rolls her hair into a bun, and snatches the smutty romance novel off the side table to take with her out to the living room.

Meanwhile, I have to get ready to go to the club. Where I may or may not get to second base with my best friend.

Drake is being quiet again as we get out of the car. He didn't say a word on the entire drive over, and I know it's because of what happened last night. But even when things are tense between us, he's usually a chatterbox. I guess this is just a different kind of tension.

The club we're touring tonight is called Pitch, and no, it's not a baseball-themed sex club. The name refers to the lighting. Most of the club is saturated in pitch-black darkness.

I'm meeting with a man named Mario, who is part owner. Like us, this club is owned by a team of people, and out of all of the clubs we're touring this week, this is the one I'm most excited about. As we step inside, I notice the lobby is much like Salacious. Black curtains and a small space, where one woman stands ready to greet us.

"Welcome to Pitch. Are you members?"

I adjust my tie as I step up to her podium. "I have a meeting with Mario at ten."

"Hunter," a deep voice calls as a tall, handsome man appears through the black curtain. "I saw you coming in on the cameras."

"Mario," I reply, shaking his hand. Unlike some of the more uptight clubs we've been in, he's friendly and a little casual, enough to settle some of my nerves.

"This must be your...partner?" he asks, reaching a hand toward Drake.

"Drake Neilson is a friend of mine. He's head of construction at Salacious and has been touring clubs with me."

"So nice to meet you, Drake," Mario says, smiling at him with those bright white teeth, and I feel mine clench at the sight.

"Nice to meet you," Drake replies with a little less enthusiasm than he usually does. Drake has always been a people person, so I can tell something is up with him today.

"Come with me, and I'll give you guys a tour."

I spare one cautious glance back at Drake before we follow Mario into the club. The expression he gives in return is unreadable and a little too cold for my taste.

"Pitch is separated into four main areas: the main floor with the bar and some tables and plenty of lighting to see who you're talking to, and then we have three dark rooms."

The first room we enter is clearly the one he just mentioned, and again…it reminds me of Salacious. There's no stage or dance floor, and it's not nearly as big as our main room, but the sudden reminder of our club has me feeling a surge of unexpected homesickness.

Instead of a multitude of doors off the main room, there are only three. Each is guarded by an employee, and although the music plays in here, I can tell it plays even louder in there.

Mario walks us over to the doors. Without opening them, he gestures to each one. "The first room is for those who identify as female, the second for those who identify as male, and the third is for…all."

"And it's completely dark in there?" Drake asks, peering curiously at the doors.

"Light enough that you can find your way around, but dark enough that you can rely on anonymity. When you're in there, it's liberating. You can touch anyone, be touched by anyone, or just bask in the vibe."

Drake and I are just staring at the door in front of us, the one with two male icons on the center, my heart starting to race at the idea of what a room like that can hold.

Reading our hesitation, Mario adds, "It's amazing how much you can see in the dark, about yourself, I mean."

I force myself to swallow.

Mario kills the silence as he starts walking again, pulling us along with his conversation. "Now, you're probably wondering about safety. All members are required to use protection, show a negative test every month, and pass a rigorous background check. There are bouncers in each room, equipped with night-vision goggles to ensure everything is consensual as well as emergency alarms within reach almost everywhere. Not to mention, our bar is alcohol free. We take safety very seriously."

"I see that," I reply, but honestly, I was only partly listening. I'm still staring longingly at the rooms. I'm suddenly not in the mood to discuss work.

Rule #22: It's amazing how much you can see in the dark.

Drake

"WHY DON'T WE HEAD UP TO MY OFFICE TO TALK NUMBERS?" Mario says to Hunter, and I immediately halt in place.

"Uh, I think I'll just wait at the bar. Numbers aren't really my thing."

Hunter's expression has a hint of panic in it and I like that. I like that he doesn't want to let me out of his sight here.

"Feel free to have a look around. Get the full Pitch experience," Mario says with a suggestive bounce of his brow.

Hunter's expression of panic and concern only deepens.

"Sounds good. Meet you back here in an hour," I say, waving at Hunter as we part ways, him to the office and me to the bar. Of course, I'm not actually going to the bar. Why would I waste my time sitting alone drinking a Dr. Pepper when I could be checking out these fuck fests behind me?

I'm not going to touch anyone. I may not be the best guy, but I would never do anything to hurt Isabel or Hunter.

I'm just too fucking curious to pass this up. But as I head toward the rooms, I'm suddenly faced with three doors—well, technically two, since one is for women only. I don't know what leads me toward the men-only door, but maybe it's the promise that male sex tends to be a little more enthusiastic in my experience. It's likely to be a better time, even if I keep my hands and cock to myself. It's also going to be harder to keep those things to myself in here, since men are also a lot less subtle, but I can handle them.

The moment I pass through the doorway, I walk down a longish hallway until I meet the guard at the end. There's a door behind him and a door to the right labeled *locker room*.

"First time?" he asks.

"Is it that obvious?"

He smiles, then gestures to the door on his left. "Feel free to use the locker room before going in. You can wear whatever you want in the dark room, but condoms are mandatory and I will be checking."

My brows rise as I nod. "Yes, sir." I guess that means I'll be hitting up the locker room first…and getting myself hard while I'm at it, since I have to go in suited up. Shouldn't be too difficult. Even through the loud music, I can hear *everything* in the other room. It sounds exactly like what it is. Lots of people fucking.

There are bowls of condoms on the counter and men moving about the dimly lit space, some naked, some dressed. I grab a rubber and head over to a curtained stall to get myself ready. Some guys aren't shy about making themselves hard out in the open. I'll do just about anything, but I'll save jacking myself off in public for sexier scenarios.

As I peel open my jeans, I find my man already at half-staff. It's like he knows we're in a sex club, reacting the same way a dog might react to pulling up to the dog park. Ready to play.

Sorry, bud. We're just here to watch.

It only takes a simple reminder of the shit that went down last night to get my cock hard enough to roll on the condom. Isabel cuffed to that bench. Hunter coming down her throat. The look on his face as he climaxed. The way his abs contracted and his tattoos practically rippled with his orgasm.

All right, I should stop, or I'm going to blow early and miss my chance to experience the dark sex cave.

I've already decided I'm going to go into the room fully clothed. It'll help to keep a barrier between me and anyone with the wrong idea. So with my jeans still undone, I take my safely-sheathed cock out to the bouncer to show him that I'm ready to play...although I'm really ready to do absolutely nothing.

A waste of a condom, if you ask me.

The bouncer nods appreciatively at my cock and gives me a flirty wink before opening the door to let me in. "Have fun," he mutters before I disappear into the darkness.

True to its name, it's dark as fuck in here. Easing my way in, I watch the green glow-in-the-dark markers on the floor that lead me through the room, so I don't topple over people or furniture.

I hear grunting off to the side, and I pause for a moment, trying to see who or what made the noise, but I can't make out shit. There are more of the glow-in-the dark markers on the floor and a few on the walls with exclamation points stationed at various spots. Those must be the emergency buttons Mario told us about. And when I spot a green dot moving, I realize it's on a bouncer.

When someone touches my arm, I flinch. "Excuse me," the man mumbles before brushing past me. It's such an eerie feeling, knowing anyone in here could touch me. I could literally fuck someone in here and never know what they look like or what their name is. It's bizarre as hell when you think about it. But also... strangely liberating.

It doesn't matter what you look like here. It doesn't matter if you know them or even if you don't like them. It's all about chemistry and feeling.

For the first time since I walked in, I'm actually regretful that I can't do anything because it sounds fun as fuck. Playing the field without knowing who you're even playing with. Or if you've played with them before. Hell, I bet this would be a great way to date. No judgment or preconceived notions. Just two souls finding each other.

It's almost romantic, if you think about it.

The grunting to my right doesn't sound very romantic, though. Leaving them behind, I keep on walking through the green markers. I hear more sex on either side of me and as my eyes start to adjust, I meander away from the path and find an empty space to just be alone and observe—as much as I can when I can't see shit.

I feel someone watching me. It's too hard to make out for sure, but there's definitely a figure standing a few feet away, and I get the feeling that they're staring at me—if that's even possible. Glancing up at the ceiling, I spot the red blink of a security camera on each corner, which is reassuring. They really do try to keep shit safe in here.

I hear footsteps approach before I feel a set of small hands brush over my biceps. "Oh, hey," a soft voice says as he fondles the muscle through my shirt. He sounds young and he's definitely a lot smaller than me.

"Move along, kid," I say, pressing a hand gently against his arm, trying to lead him toward a more willing person in the room.

"I'll suck your dick," he says sweetly, still touching my arm.

"That's sweet, but no thanks."

"You waiting for someone? I love a party."

See? Never subtle.

"Have a good night," I reply, hoping he just gets the hint and takes off. His fingers linger, dragging a line across my abdomen as he walks away, and I let him have his moment. If all he wants is a little touch, then knock yourself out.

But his fingers are only gone for a moment before I'm ambushed by someone much larger and stronger. I panic, throwing up my arms as a firm hand grips the back of my neck and turns me away from the young guy, pushing me farther into the room. I stumble through the dark, afraid of walking into someone or over something. When I glance back at the man guiding me, I catch the subtle outline of something on his face and realize he's wearing the night-vision goggles the bouncers wear.

Am I in trouble for something?

I'm about to protest, but I'm suddenly slammed against a hard wall, and the goggles come off his face in a quick swipe. I know this because I hear them hit the floor. I still can't see him or anything, but there's no time to try because his mouth is suddenly on mine. With one hand firmly around the back of my neck, he kisses me hard. Delicate stubble around his lips scratches with mine, and when he pulls his tongue out of my mouth, he nibbles on my lower lip.

"Mine," he mutters darkly, and my cock stirs in response.

Hunter.

I've only kissed him once, but I know this move already. I memorized that first kiss. Every little playful swipe of his tongue, I know by heart. I feel for his chest, running my hands over the lapels of his jacket, up to his cotton undershirt and austere tie secured at the top. It smells like him and feels like him and tastes like him, but fuck, it's so dark in here, and it's messing with my head. Is he really in here? Would Hunter even do this? Last night was an experiment, and we haven't talked about it since, so I'm not quite sure if he's mentally there yet.

God, I want to believe it's him. And I need to know. So I gently pull away.

"Hunter?" I ask.

"Shut the fuck up," he snaps, and now I know. It's him.

I think.

His mouth takes mine again. Letting out a groan, he bites and nips at my entire mouth in a lust-filled fury. I'm drunk on this kiss, like I'm being carried away by a strong tide, and I'm powerless against it. His body is pressed to mine, and I can't get my hands on him enough, so my mind is overwhelmed as well as torn, not sure if I should be focusing on the feel of his mouth or the sensation of his hard body under my fingertips. Soon, my brain focuses on nothing, just drowning in sensation. Without sight, I am nothing but a pile of flesh and bone and this all-consuming *need*.

It feels like we've been kissing for so long. Another man more comfortable with gay sex might have moved on by now, but Hunter is still so uncertain. The hand on the back of my neck slides to the front, holding me by the throat as he presses me against the wall again.

Our lips part, and although I can't see him and he can't see me, it feels as if we're looking at each other. Then I feel his other hand drift down my chest, over my stomach, and finally into my still-open pants. When his hand wraps around my cock, I jolt and let out a grunt.

Hunter is holding my cock.

It's just a hand, but for some reason, this one feels better than all the rest. His warm, fierce grip creates a lightning strike all the way down my spine and I shift my hips to get more.

The darkness makes everything so much more visceral. I can't see anything, only feel, which makes the sensation of his stroking that much more intense. Desperate to show him just how good it feels, I reach for his cock, but I find that his pants are still buttoned up tight. So I use both hands to unfasten his belt, then the button and zipper. The whole time he's thrusting his hips toward me, seeking out my touch.

When I have his pants open, I dig my hand into his boxers, pulling out the steel heat inside.

He's not wearing a condom.

God, this better fucking be Hunter and not just some horny bouncer who caught me at a weak moment.

"Fuck yes," he growls when I stroke his cock, and I instantly feel better at the sound of his voice. I'd know that voice anywhere. His fingers around my throat tighten as we work each other, but I need more. For all I know, this could be the only time and place

Hunter is comfortable exploring this, so I'm not going to waste it on hand jobs.

It would seem my best friend is reading my mind because I feel a certain tug on my throat and I know he's trying to shove me down.

"Suck me off," he says, low and commanding, and I eagerly drop to my knees in front of him. I don't know why I look up, but I do. Even if I could see his face, he wouldn't give me a chance. With a hand on the back of my head, he guides his cock to my mouth, and I open for him, letting him slide his length across my tongue.

I let him go deep. Deep enough to feel my throat constrict around him.

"Oh fuck," he barks.

He thrusts into my mouth hard for a few strokes before I take the base of his cock in my hand and get to work on my own. Coating his dick in saliva, I suck hard on the head before swallowing him down again. His grip on my hair tightens.

"God...Drake." He moans, and the sound of my name on his lips like this urges me on. It feels so natural, like we should have been doing this all along. He's incoherent, mumbling and groaning and barely breathing as I keep up the motion of my mouth around him.

"Need to come," he grunts, and I suck the head again, ready for him. My hands clutch him hard around his ass, pulling him deeper, hoping he feels it, hoping he knows this is my way of saying *I want you. I need you.* The hand on the back of head is joined by the other, both of them drifting down to my neck as Hunter curls himself around me. It's intimate and sexy as fuck, and I can feel my cock leaking beads of cum into the condom sheathed around it. I'm desperate to touch myself, but I don't want to let him go.

A moment later, he's shuddering and crying out as the warm, salty drops hit the back of my tongue. Once he's let it all out,

I swallow, lapping up his dick again, not quite ready to let this moment end.

But it does end, like all good things. Because a moment later, Hunter is zipping up his pants and pulling away. I don't see him leave. Well, I can't see shit, but when I reach out for him, he's already gone.

I kneel in the darkness for a while. I consider jacking off, but the devastation of being so impersonally used and discarded has my dick deflating.

And the entire time I sit there, I try to put myself in Hunter's shoes. This was his first sexual encounter with someone of the same sex. That had to be pretty intense. Maybe a little scary. He obviously liked it, and I'm sure he's off somewhere questioning everything about himself.

But that fucker left me on the floor. On the goddamn floor. And I can't imagine a scenario in which I would do that to him.

I didn't force his dick down my throat. If anything, it was the opposite.

After a while, I decide that my self-loathing pity party would be better spent somewhere with alcohol. So I pick my sad ass off the floor, find the exit, discard the unused condom, and text Hunter.

I'm going to a bar. I'll order a ride back to the apartment later.

I'm marching through the main room, staring down at my phone, when I hear him call my name.

"Drake," he barks, putting himself in my path. "Where are you going?"

"Did you get my text?" My eyes skim over his suit, remembering the way it felt in my hands, the lapels, the shirt, the tie... the belt. I could argue with him right now, but I don't want to. I'm mad, but I'm more in the mood to stew about it than fight.

"I'll come with you," he replies, and I look at his face for the first time. His expression is chaotic and unsure, but I hope he reads the emotion in mine. *You left me on the fucking floor.*

"I'll meet you at the apartment," I reply, and without another word, I leave.

He doesn't follow me or call me or argue. He just lets me go.

There's a dive bar down the street from the club and it's perfect for what I need. I'm on a mission to get drunk fast, so I don't talk to anyone, flirt, or converse. I just drink. It takes roughly three hours before I'm good and wasted. I still feel sad, but my inebriated brain can no longer form self-deprecating thoughts to accompany all the gloom.

Rule #23: Fuck the rules.

Isabel

I'M HALF-ASLEEP ON THE COUCH WHEN I HEAR WHAT SOUNDS LIKE a grizzly bear entering the apartment. A drunk grizzly bear.

"Drake?" I whisper, just as he loses his footing and stumbles into the doorframe of his room. He lets out a groan as he melts onto the floor.

"Go to bed," he mutters.

"Come on. Get up." My tiny frame is nothing against his giant drunk one. But he finally manages to get back on his feet and shuffle to his bed, where he lands against the mattress. I watch him struggle to pull off his shoes, but he's clearly a lost cause, so I swat his hand away to help him.

"Stop. Don't be nice to me," he says with a harsh expression on his face.

"I'll be as nice to you as I want." I pull one of his shoes off and drop it onto the hardwood. Then I work on the other. I think for a moment that he's fallen asleep, but as I pull the second shoe off and gaze up at his face, I see him staring back at me.

"Where have you been?"

"I had to get drunk."

"Why?" I ask.

"Because…your husband is an asshole."

Well, shit. Despair gnaws away at my gut as I move to unbuckle Drake's pants. When Hunter came home, he didn't say much, but I could tell something was up. He's usually so open with me, and after the talk we had this morning, I was anxious for him to report back. Clearly, whatever went down at the club between him and Drake didn't end well.

"Lift," I tell him as I shimmy his jeans down his hips. Tugging them off each leg, I discard his jeans on the floor and climb over his body to help him pull off his shirt. His hands slide up my thighs as I do, but I glare at him. "No funny ideas, mister. You know the rules. Plus…I'm on my period and no living thing is allowed near this." I gesture toward my cramping, aching belly.

"I'll make you feel better," he says in a teasing tone, and I just shake my head.

"I think you want to have sex with me to get back at Hunter for whatever he did."

"I would never do that to you," he grumbles. He pulls me down until I'm lying in his arms and my heart aches a little as I snuggle against his chest. I've wanted this for so long, but now I'm afraid everything we do is crossing a line that's going to get us all hurt. But this familiarity between us is too pure and good to ignore.

"Tell me what happened at the club," I say.

He moans. "I can't."

"Why?"

"Because you'll be mad at me. And him."

"He already told me about the kiss, Drake. And I gave him permission to do anything he wanted at the club—with you, of course."

There's a delay in his reaction because of the alcohol, but he does eventually lift his head to glare at me. "You did?"

I nod.

"You guys have the weirdest fucking marriage."

"I know…" I reply.

"What did he say about the kiss?" he asks.

"Not much. But he liked it. And he's just really confused."

"Yeah, well…me fucking too."

"So tell me what happened."

When he finally relents to talking to me, he shifts to his side and pulls me closer. It's intimate and making me want so much more with him. In true Drake fashion, his hands never stay in one place. He's constantly rubbing my back, my hip, my cheek. He does not rest, ever.

"I sucked his dick."

Gotta love how blunt and shameless Drake is. But I keep quiet for a moment because I need to explore my own reaction first. At first…it's shock. Maybe a touch of jealousy. And then I imagine it. Drake and Hunter in a club together…Drake's mouth around Hunter's dick. I can't help the way that image makes me feel—hot and excited and very, very turned on.

"Isabel…" he says, gauging my reaction.

"I just need a minute. This is all so hard to get used to."

After a few minutes of letting this new information sink in, giving myself enough time to check in with how this is all making me feel, I tap Drake's chest.

"Okay…" I reply. "What happened after the blow job?"

"He barely put his cock away before ditching me there. On the fucking floor."

Goddammit, Hunter. My emotionally stunted husband can be the most affectionate, tenderhearted sap sometimes, but then other times…he's so flighty and irrational, it makes me crazy.

"I'm sorry," I whisper. Tilting my head, I gaze up at Drake. I realize in this moment that Hunter and I are just a blip on the radar of Drake's love life. Soon, he will be back to his old ways, living his life as freely as he wishes and doing it mostly alone.

His eyes find mine, and he touches my cheek, stroking softly before finally pulling my face up to his for a tender kiss. He's playing with my heart when he does this, making me think I can have things that I know I can't. Like him.

After a soft pressing of our lips, he pulls away and kisses the tip of my nose. "Don't apologize, Iz. It's not your fault."

"I know, but I don't want you fighting with him either. He needs to apologize, but I also think you have to remember…Hunter's father was a cruel bigot who ingrained some nasty stuff in Hunter's head. Obviously, he knows it's all bullshit now, but those cruel voices are still there. He just has to overcome them, and he will."

Suddenly, he lifts up and stares at me as if he's surprised by something. "How are you not mad, Isabel? Your husband got a blow job from someone else—and don't say it's okay because you and I have been having sex because he's there for that, and you know this is different."

I stare up at him, searching for the words to describe how I'm feeling. I am a little jealous, but not because he cheated on me, but because I wasn't involved.

Finally, I force out an answer that I hope makes sense. "It's not cheating to me, Drake. Not when it's you."

"That doesn't make any sense," he mutters, his drunkenness peeking through.

"None of this makes any sense…but also, being *with* you like this makes more sense to me than the way we were before."

"What?" His face contorts, as if trying to wrap his head around that notion actually hurts his brain. I let out a little laugh as I pull him down for a kiss.

"Never mind. My point is…if it had been anyone but you, I'd be out of my mind with anger and jealousy."

He takes my lips again, shifting his weight, so he's half on top of me and half beside me. "I know how you can get him back for it," he whispers against my mouth. His hand is drifting toward my panties, but I quickly snatch his wrist.

"Just kiss me," I say, placing his large hand against my lower back instead. And he does kiss me. He kisses me for so long I think he's starting to sober up. We take our sweet time with each other; like teenagers making out for the first time, we lie there, exploring this new thing between us.

I briefly wonder as he massages my back and hums against my lips if he shows all the girls he's with this much passion and attention. I want to be someone special to Drake. I don't want to be just another girl he's hooked up with.

With his thick erection pressed up against my hip, a flash of heat is shot to my belly every time he grinds it on me. And although I said we'd only kiss, I can't take it anymore. It feels like torture to do this to him, especially after what Hunter did to him tonight.

So I rub the thick mound through his shorts and he lets out a heavy groan into my neck. He doesn't ask me to, but I know he wants me to touch it, so I reach under the elastic band and wrap my hand around his smooth, rock-hard length. It's so hard it feels like it must hurt.

"Isn't this against the rules?" he whispers.

"Fuck the rules," I reply as I start to stroke him.

He groans loudly again, and I almost hope he wakes up Hunter. Let him see us like this. Let him see me finish what he started.

Drake's hips jolt and shudder, and I know it won't take him long.

"Get on top of me," I whisper, rolling him so he's between my legs. I quickly lift my shirt, exposing my breasts as I continue to work his length, moving faster and faster, reading his expression until I see he's about to come. And I aim the head at my chest, letting him cover me with it.

"Oh, Isabel," he grunts as he watches the cum paint my breasts. Then he just sits there for a moment, staring at the mess he's made. Reaching out a hand, he massages one side, seemingly rubbing it into my skin.

"I love this," he whispers. "Seeing you covered in my cum." When he leans over me to plant a long kiss on my mouth, butterflies erupt in my stomach. "You really are the best. You know that?"

I don't reply, but I give him a tight-lipped smile and kiss him back.

He reaches over to the side table to grab a handful of tissues and takes his time cleaning me up. When he's done, he collapses next to me, pulling out the covers and burying us both beneath them. I curl up against his chest, and we lie like that for a while. Just when I think he's asleep, he starts talking.

"Hunter doesn't remember that green dress, but I do. And you looked at me."

"I looked at you?"

"Yeah, you looked at me first," he replies carefully, as if it's hard to admit.

I remember that, and I've never told Hunter that. When he asks, I tell him I don't remember him standing there staring at me, but I do remember part of that day. I remember Drake. But Drake never pursued me. He barely even looked at me once Hunter started talking to me.

Tears prick my eyes at the memory. But the next words out of Drake's mouth cut me like a knife.

"I thought you were the most beautiful girl I'd ever seen, but I would have never gone after you. Not because of Hunter, but because I didn't go for girls like you."

"Girls like me?" I ask, keeping my voice steady.

"Too good for me. Too smart and pretty and nice."

"Drake," I say, looking up at him with tears filling my lashes.

"I'm glad he did. I'm proud of him for doing right by you."

I believe his words, but I see a pain behind his eyes as he whispers them. And I don't know what to say. I want to tell him that I love him—that I've always loved him, just as much as I love Hunter and in the same way, but I'm not sure that admission would help anything right now.

"I know you think I'm just a man whore who never wants to settle down, but I've always wanted a wife like you, Isabel. And recently, I've realized that I just want *you*."

Another tear rolls down the side of my face, landing on his arm. I'm still speechless as I gaze into his eyes. It's clear there are no words left to say, so he kisses my forehead and closes his eyes, drifting off to sleep quickly as I lie there and let his drunk confessions seep in, committing them to memory, where I will keep them forever.

Rule #24: Wake up.

Hunter

MY DREAMS ARE WARPED AND RESTLESS. FIRST, I'M FEELING around the darkness for him, but my hands keep finding the wrong people. It's all foreign flesh under my fingertips when all I want to find is the one my body knows by heart. Every time I think I've found him, he slips away.

Then, when I do get my hands on him in the pitch-black room, I feel the rope against his skin, but it's wound around him too tight. It's restricting his movement and his breathing, and I begin to panic as I struggle to find the end of the rope to untie him. He's whispering my name, asking for me.

Hunter, is that you?

Hunter, get me out of this thing.

Hunter, help me.

But I can't help him. No matter how much I try, I'm useless. The only thing holding me back is my own stupid pride and fear. Why didn't I pay better attention during those workshops? Why was I always slipping away to do business? I should have been there.

Now Isabel is untying him and it's not so dark anymore. She's undoing his knots like it's the simplest thing. Why couldn't I do that? She's staring at me with gentle impatience on her face—not anger because she understands it's not my fault. But how long will she make this easy for me? How long will she allow me to fuck up before she's had enough?

When she gets Drake untied, he goes to her. They cling to each other while I watch, but it's not like before, when watching them got me excited. Now I just feel alone.

Someone jerks me away from them. It's the asshole from the club in Austin and he's pummeling his fist against my face. He just keeps punching me until he's not that man anymore—now, he's my father.

And I know why he's punching me. He *knows*. He found out what Drake and I did in the dark room of that club and the sneer on his face is full of disgust and hatred. And I'm drowning in his disappointment. He never really liked me anyway, and maybe this is why. Maybe he's always known.

His punches are accompanied by words like weapons—*faggot, queer, pussy*. I just let him hit me. I don't fight or try to stop him. Just like the words, I let him berate me with the things that are supposed to hurt me, his fists and his insults.

But as he pummels me into the ground, until I'm nothing but a clump of broken flesh on the floor, I realize I don't feel anything. The punches don't hurt. And neither do the names.

They slide through me as if I'm being beaten by a ghost. Because he *is* a ghost. Even beyond the grave, this sad old man, who drank himself to death years ago, is trying to hurt me. But he can't, not anymore.

And just like that, he's gone. I'm lying on the floor of the ornate room in New Orleans where everything changed, and their faces come into my vision. They're urging me to get up. They are naked and so am I, but I'm too paralyzed by the damage my father's done to me that I can't move. Even if there's not a drop of blood on my face, I lie there as if I'm bleeding out.

Get up, baby. Come to bed with us.

Her voice sounds so real, my eyes pop open in surprise. Lifting my head from the pillow, I look around for her, but the room is empty. And so is my bed. Grabbing my phone off the nightstand, I check the time: 8:22 a.m.

Getting out of bed to find her, I discover the living room and kitchen empty. And when I realize where she is, I pause. What will I find if I go to his room and how will I feel about it?

I have no goddamn right to be mad if I find them naked, that's for fucking sure. I've toyed with their emotions, forced them together for my own enjoyment, opened Pandora's box. So I better be fucking ready for what comes out.

When I reach his door, I glance in hesitantly. My breath comes out in a quick exhale. They are sleeping in their underwear, their bodies entangled. Her head is on his arm and her leg is draped over him, the same way she sometimes sleeps with me. For a guy who almost never lets women sleep over, he looks pretty content with this one.

Seeing Drake is like being punched in the face again. I was an asshole to him last night. I'm fully aware of that. And I'm also aware that being an asshole in general sucks, but being an asshole to your best friend, who trusts you to *not* be an asshole, is an all-time low. I owe him the biggest of apologies and then I need to figure out what the actual fuck is wrong with me.

That blow job in the club was the best blow job of my life—sorry, Isabel. Although I'm sure she'd understand. Having his mouth on me and not a single thought in my head other than *finally* was euphoric. The dark room was exactly how I imagined it would be. Liberating, encouraging, sexy. For the first time in my life, I could have him in my hands and I didn't have to think about what that meant or what would happen next.

Drake was perfect. *We* were perfect.

But somewhere on the downhill slope of my orgasm, my father's voice chimed in to remind me that there's something wrong with me. I didn't know *how* to face Drake after that. I was afraid he'd want me to reciprocate and I panicked. I figured he'd assume I was just playing the part—anonymous sex, no strings attached, but even I knew that was wishful thinking. I left him kneeling on the floor like the fucking coward I am.

And I don't blame him for ditching me after that. I would have ditched me too. He chose to get drunk at a bar. I got drunk on the tequila left over from the night before. I avoided my wife, lied about Drake, and got hammered.

I don't know what draws me to his bed, but I figure I have a choice. I can play *poor me* and go back to bed alone, sulking and grumpy. Or I can take a step in the right direction with my tail between my legs.

As I crawl into bed behind Isabel, sandwiching her between us, I briefly wonder how the hell we're going to go back to normal after this week. This was supposed to be temporary, but the way these two are cuddling right now proves that even they know there's nothing really temporary about this now. We opened a door and it's not going to close as easily as we thought.

And frankly, I'm not sure I want it to.

I join them under the covers, and I stare at Drake. His hair is draped over his face, so I gently reach across and brush it aside, softly curling it around his ear. My touch rouses him, and he blinks his eyes open. When he sees me, his expression tenses before he closes them again as if going back to sleep is his way of giving me the cold shoulder.

"Drake," I whisper. He doesn't open his eyes, but I know he can hear me. "I'm sorry. I was an asshole and I have no excuse for the way I treated you."

He waits a few long seconds before responding. "Then, why did you?"

"Because I'm fucked in the head. I just panicked. I'm sorry."

Finally, he opens his eyes and stares at me. "You never liked the fact that I was with guys."

He's cornering me into a conversation I'm not ready for, but ready or not, I have shit to own up to.

"It was never because I was judging you," I say, not ready to give him more than that yet.

"What now?" he asks, his voice still laced with impatience.

"We start our drive back home tomorrow. I don't know what will happen when we get back to Briar Point. That's up to you and Iz."

"What do *you* want?"

This whole trip has been about what *I* want. But if he's asking, then I'll tell him. "I don't want this to end." I force myself to swallow. This is so fucking uncomfortable to say out loud, but I'm going to royally fuck this up if I don't try to express myself. "And I want a second chance."

His eyes find mine again as his clenched jaw relaxes. But as soon as the hard look is gone, it comes back. "I don't think that's a good idea," he whispers.

Everything in me shatters and I feel like that lump of broken flesh on the floor again, just like I was in my dream. Then, Drake stares at me as he tugs Isabel a little closer. "But I agree. I don't want this to be over either."

I know he's talking about Isabel, and maybe I should feel territorial, snatch her back into my arms, and remind him who she belongs to, but I brought this on myself. Plus, I'm holding on to hope that if he still wants her, there's a chance he still wants me too.

Rule #25: Sometimes you have to take the long way home.

Isabel

THERE ARE TWO THOUSAND MILES BETWEEN NASHVILLE AND Briar Point. And so far, every single one is awkward and quiet. After the first day of driving, we stopped for the night in a hotel, but Drake insisted on his own room.

On the second day of our long drive, I sensed a hesitation in our traveling. We made more frequent stops. More detours, and I think Hunter drove slower than he usually does. What should have taken two twelve-hour driving days is quickly turning into three.

No one wants to return to reality. No one wants this fantasy to end, but we're also too hesitant to talk about it or touch each other.

By the morning of the third day, my period is gone, and I'm starting to feel like a feral cat in heat, and I can't take another second of this insufferable tension. We stop for gas in northern Arizona, and while I'm waiting by the pump and the guys are inside, I see a road sign ahead that makes me pause.

Los Angeles, 318 miles.

Las Vegas, 107 miles.

I've never been to Vegas. The idea plants itself in my head, and I keep brushing it away. We have to go back home at some point. We can't keep avoiding reality. No matter how many detours we take or stops we make, the impending reality is waiting for us, no matter what we do.

"You driving?" Drake asks as he returns from the gas station and hands me my energy drink.

"Yep," I reply, eagerly jumping into the driver's seat. Hunter returns a moment later to find Drake and me in the front seat. With a shrug, he climbs in the back.

"Thanks, babe. We're only about four hours away."

"Mh-hm," I mumble.

But that idea is still implemented in my mind, and once I get an idea, it's impossible to get it out until I just do it. So as we get back on the freeway, I'm faced with that fork in the road—literally.

West...or north?

It's the memory of the night handcuffed to the bench that turns the steering wheel on the car. It's the feeling that we've only scratched the surface of something. And I'm too afraid that we won't ever go down this road again once we get back home. So I'm putting all my chips on the table now.

"Hey, Red...where are you going?" Hunter asks from the back seat when he notices me taking the wrong exit.

"I'm going to Vegas," I answer with a shrug.

"But we don't live in Vegas," he replies.

"I know that." I glance over at Drake, who's staying quiet through this, chewing on his bottom lip in contemplation. "But we have everything worked out with Drake's apartment. We don't need to go back to work until Friday. And I'm just not ready to go home yet."

There's a subtle weight in the car now. Because everyone knows exactly what it is I'm not ready to go back to. After a few minutes of driving toward Sin City, Drake finally jumps in.

"I'll look up a hotel," he says as he pulls out his phone.

I do a silent little dance of excitement in my seat. And I hope, this time, he actually does find *one* room.

———————

Drake finds us a hotel on the strip for two nights. It's a double room with two beds, and it's perfect. After checking in, I jump in the shower to get cleaned up and send the guys down to the bar after they get dressed. I'm a woman on a mission.

I brought a long black gown on our trip, in case we had a formal event to go to. It's hanging safely in the garment bag in the hotel room. And after I curl my hair, apply the makeup that's sat mostly unused all week—except for the essentials: mascara and lip gloss—I slip the sleek black fabric over my body. It hugs my chest, low cut enough to show off my barely there cleavage.

Once I'm dolled up and ready, I head for the elevator with a subtle pulse of nerves just under my skin. I squeeze my clutch close to my body, and when the elevator pings on the casino floor, the doors open to reveal Hunter and Drake waiting in their all-black suits. *My men.*

They were always my men, weren't they? I may be married to Hunter, but Drake has been more present than not, and in the past week, he and I have crossed a line we've both wanted to cross for a long time. It was always meant to be this way. What started as a kinky fantasy has shown us what we really mean to each other. I love them *both*, and they both love me.

Now, they just need to figure out what they are to each other. And it's up to me to help them along.

I notice Drake silently mouth the words, *holy shit.* Hunter is smiling at me appreciatively, and my stomach is assaulted by butterflies.

As I approach them, my husband grabs me around the waist, pulling me toward him, so he can kiss my cheek. "I'm half tempted to take you right back up to that hotel room."

"I'm down with that idea," Drake replies. His eyes rove over my body, then to my face hungrily.

"Boys, we're in Sin City. Let's go see what kind of trouble we can find first."

"I think we found it," Drake says to Hunter as I lead them through the casino floor.

We meander our way down the busy strip, and I have the two of them walking behind me like sentinels, scowling at anyone who dares to walk too close to me or look at me too long. It's almost comical, but it's also clear I need to get some alcohol in them, stat. They need to relax.

When I see a sign for a rooftop nightclub, I take both of their hands and guide them toward the signs that lead us up a special elevator. As we reach the door, one of the bouncers eyes me appreciatively as Hunter steps in front, squeezing me between him and Drake. After we enter the club, he takes us straight to the bar.

Drake is staying close behind me, and I feel his hand brush my waist, almost as if he wants to show me affection in public too. It's funny to think just a few days ago we were nervous about even kissing, but now we can barely keep our hands off each other.

After two rounds of shots, they both seem so much more relaxed. The club isn't too crowded, but the dance floor is a gyrating mass of bodies moving to the heavy beat of the music.

"I want to dance," I announce, grabbing both of their hands and dragging them into the throng. I can feel their hesitation, and I didn't exactly plan this, but I couldn't just take one and leave the other. Either one of them would be mauled alive by these women, if I left them unattended, and tonight, I'm feeling just as territorial as they are.

I pull them deep into the crowd, the alcohol already starting to make me more fearless. As I start to dance, I loop my arms around Hunter's neck and grind my body against his to the beat. He stares into my eyes as we dance, and I feel Drake's body lightly touching mine. Pulling one arm away from my husband, I reach for the man behind me, tugging him closer until I'm swallowed up by their bodies.

We dance for so long, I lose track of time. I only feel their touch and the music until I'm lost in the sensation of them. Hunter pulls me in for a hot kiss, his hand around my lower back as he grinds against me. I feel how hard he is for me and I pull myself even closer. The anticipation for what's to come is overwhelming.

When I pull away from his kiss, I feel Drake's presence behind me. Turning my head, I find his lips next. He kisses me the same way, hot and needy, as he presses his arousal against my back.

They have me squeezed so tightly between them I can hardly breathe.

Across the dance floor, I feel more than one pair of eyes scrutinizing us. I'm sure they're thinking some pretty deplorable things about me, but I don't care. Maybe being around the girls at the club, like Mia and Eden, has finally gone to my head. A past version of myself might have been embarrassed by strangers labeling me a whore or a slut, but I don't care. In fact, I like it. I like the idea of people knowing that both of these men are mine. That I didn't have to choose—and neither do they.

"Let's get the fuck out of here." Hunter growls into my ear, and then his eyes find Drake's and they stare at each other for a long, heavy moment.

Suddenly I'm being whisked away, and I don't even fight it. I want what they want just as badly. The walk back to our own hotel goes by in a blur until we're in the hotel elevator headed up to our room. And I don't want to wait anymore.

The moment the elevator door closes us in, I'm in Drake's arms. Pulling his face down to mine, I latch on to his lips, and he growls in response, his hands going down to my ass, squeezing it hard as he drags my body roughly against his.

Hunter crowds me from behind, taking a handful of my hair and pulling me away from Drake's kiss, stealing my mouth with his own. Pain lances through me from his grip on my scalp, but it only intensifies the pleasure. Just as the elevator comes to a stop, he mutters darkly against my lips, "Let's get one thing clear. I'm not interested in watching tonight."

My eyes widen as I stare at him. Does this mean…he wants me to himself? The idea fills me with dread. Not that I don't love my husband and want to be with him, but my heart is so attached to the thought of having them both.

Then as the doors open, he stares at Drake as he says, "Let's go."

And I'm filled with relief as he drags me off the elevator to the front door. Hunter pulls out his key card, and Drake is behind me, kissing my neck and shoulder. We are a tangle of hands and bodies and mouths as the three of us stumble into our room.

My mouth is on Hunter's as Drake tears off his own shirt and begins unbuckling his pants. I'm quickly undoing each of Hunter's buttons as he starts on his own pants. As soon as they are in just their boxers, they both reach for the hem of my dress.

In all of their frenzy, I feel the pop of a stitch. "The zipper! The zipper!" I yell, pointing to the back. This might have been my *fuck me* dress, but I love it too much to let it be destroyed by our passion. Slowly, Drake eases down the zipper at the back, kneeling as he does, letting his lips meet every vertebra of my spine on his way down.

Then, I'm standing in only my black panties and lace bra. Drake is still peppering my lower half with delicate kisses as Hunter focuses solely on my mouth. I reach into Hunter's boxers, desperate to have his arousal in my hands. He hums a deep and gravelly sound of approval as I stroke him. Behind me, Drake works his way up my body, and I reach for him with my other hand.

As my hand wraps around his cock, I remember just how insane this is; I keep going back and forth from this being totally natural and normal and it being wrong in every way.

Drake puts a hand on the back of my neck and steers my mouth toward his, stealing my mouth in a rough kiss. Their fingers roam my body until I don't know whose are whose. My bra comes off while I'm back to kissing Drake, then someone pinches the tight bud of my nipple, sending a blast of arousal to my core.

I *need* them.

With each of their cocks still in my hands, I drop to my knees between them. One at a time, I slip their boxers all the way down and continue stroking their impressive lengths. Gazing up at their hungry expressions, I pull Hunter to my mouth first. Keeping the other hand moving on Drake, I lick a wet circle around the head of my husband's cock before swallowing him down until he reaches the back of my throat and I start to gag. Leaving his shaft nice and wet, I jump over to Drake's and do the same.

Their filthy groans fill the hotel room as I go back and forth between them, teasing them and keeping them wanting more. Then, looking back up again, I pull their cocks toward each other's, and I hear one of them gasp as they slide together, slick with my saliva.

I know Drake is still mad at Hunter, and I don't want to force him into anything he doesn't want to do, but I also know it's a delicate balance right now, and one little move might be enough to push these two over the edge and past their respective hang-ups.

Apparently, that one little touch of their cocks was enough because when I look back up, Drake's hand is on Hunter's hip. It's enough to have those butterflies in my belly going wild.

I pull them both toward my mouth again, fitting the heads of their cocks against my tongue and trying to fit them both in as much as I can. Their groans get louder, and I feel someone's hands in my hair.

"Goddamn, Red. You look so fucking good taking our cocks like that," Hunter says in a low, raspy growl.

"She likes two cocks. Don't you, baby?" Drake asks.

"She *needs* two cocks," my husband replies.

I nod as I suck them each down again. I can't get enough of their pleasure. But when I notice Drake's hand pull away from

Hunter, I do what I can to bring them back together. Releasing my lips from their cocks, I coat them each again, so they're perfectly slick, and I point their cocks upward as I slide them together again. I wrap my hands around them both, so they're so close, they're practically chest to chest, leaving almost no room for me.

Slowly their gazes travel from me to each other, and I hold my breath in anticipation. I keep up my stroking as I notice the erratic movement of their chests. As the moments stretch, I wait.

Finally, it's Hunter who makes the first move. Maybe it's his way of showing that he's sorry, but I knew it would never be Drake to make it. He needed Hunter to do it for him.

Hunter grabs him by the back of the neck and crashes their mouths together. Drake's eyes squeeze closed as he holds the back of Hunter's head. I let out an uncontrollable whimper as I watch them kiss. It's so hot and carnal, like they can't get enough of each other. My body is on fire with desire just from watching this one kiss.

When they finally break apart, their chests are now heaving, and I rise to my feet, eager to kiss the lips that were just fused together. I reach for Hunter's first, sliding my tongue against his, wanting to tell him just how much I love him and how incredibly hot that was. My husband just kissed someone else while I watched…and it was amazing. This all feels like a dream.

Moving from Hunter's mouth, I go to Drake's, tugging his bottom lip between my teeth. Hooking his hands around my thighs, he pulls me easily into his arms, and I wrap my legs around him.

"I think she's ready for us," Hunter says as Drake carries me to the bed.

"I'm ready," I cry out in a needy whine. Drake drops me onto the mattress and runs his hands down my body, tugging my underwear off in a quick swipe. Then he places his hands on my thighs, parting them wide as he leans down and places a warm kiss against my clit, first with just his lips and then with his tongue.

I cry out, digging my fingers in his long hair and grinding him against me. He kisses me three more times before rising up and leaving me writhing alone on the bed. When I glance up, I notice him rifling through his bag, and I assume he's coming back with a condom, which he does. But he has something else too.

As he returns, he has a devious expression on his beautiful face. "Want to know the best part of being your husband's best friend? I know everything he's ever done to you. *Everything.*" Drake crawls back over my body, hooking an arm under my knee and pulling it up to expose every part of me. Then he draws a line with his finger down the back of my thigh, straight to my ass. I tense as he starts rubbing circles over the tight hole. He leans his face in close, pressing his lips to my ear. "I know he's fucked you here. I know all about how you begged for it, how you soaked your bed because you came so hard, how you used a toy on yourself while he fucked your ass."

I gasp, turning toward Hunter, who is watching us lazily while he strokes himself and waits. I'm not really *surprised* he told Drake about all of the sex we've had. I'm just a little surprised by the amount of detail he went into. I'm almost flattered to know they talk about it so much.

"And that's why I'll be the one fucking you here tonight."

Suddenly, Drake's finger breaches my tight hole and I gasp even louder, tilting my hips for him, giving him even more access to this dirty, forbidden part of me. He lifts up, uncapping a bottle of lube in his other hand and dripping it on the finger pressed inside me. Then he begins to prep me, easily sliding in and out, and I can barely take it. It's exquisite torture.

Gripping the sheets on the bed, I squeeze them tight in my fists as he reaches deeper and deeper, teasing me to the point of agony. He adds another finger, and I moan and writhe like a cat in heat.

"Oh my God, Drake, please. Fuck me."

"What do you think, Hunt?" he asks, staring down at me like

a predator ready to devour its prey. "Do you think she's ready for me?"

"I already told you she likes it rough. She's always ready," he replies in a husky tone. He's leaning against the dresser, watching us with languid strokes of his cock.

I whimper when Drake pulls his fingers out of me. While he fixes himself with a condom, Hunter stalks closer, climbing onto the bed next to me. In a quick motion, he flips me on top of him and then kisses the air out of my lungs. His tongue tangles with mine as I feel Drake settle his weight behind me.

"I want to hold you while he fucks you again," Hunter mumbles into my mouth. A moment later, I feel the head of Drake's cock against my back entrance. He's slick—he must have lubed up while Hunter was kissing me into a stupor.

I rest my forehead against my husband's shoulder as Drake slips his cock past the tight ring of muscle. It's such a foreign feeling; nothing compares to it. I love how different it feels, how wrong and taboo. It makes this usually demure and polite girl feel like a sensual, sexy vixen, and I love it.

"More," I call with a guttural hum as I try to catch my breath.

Drake growls in response. "Baby, I'm all the way in." He slides out then back in again, filling me so much, it makes the walls of my pussy throb.

"God damn," Drake says with a grunt. "Hunter, you were right. Her ass takes a cock so well."

"That's my girl," Hunter whispers against my ear.

His hands are all over my body, on my back, my breasts, my hips, and then finally on my clit, rubbing fierce circles and driving me crazy. My legs begin to shake as Drake picks up speed, and I feel so overwhelmed with sensation I'm about to explode.

And I do. My climax rolls over me like a truck. I let out a scream into Hunter's neck as I'm blinded by the sensations.

"You're so wet for me, Red. I need to be inside you so bad. Are you ready?"

I'm still catching my breath, a sheen of sweat covering my body and making my hair stick to my face as I lift up and kiss Hunter, needing the familiar taste of him, the feel of his mouth against mine.

"Yes," I whisper, and Drake stops his thrusting for a moment.

With a little shifting, I feel Hunter there, and he was right. I am slick because he slides in easily. With both of them buried to the hilt, no one moves as I adjust and savor this feeling of overwhelming fullness. It's intense and unbelievable, not just sexually but emotionally too. They're both claiming me, using me, loving me, and tears spring to my eyes as Drake folds himself over me, kissing my back and affectionately wiping my hair from my face.

"I can feel him inside you," Hunter whispers as I look into his eyes. He grips my hand in his, intertwining our fingers. The other hand goes to my back and I feel his fingers graze Drake's.

And we stay like that for a moment, the three of us as one.

"Rock your hips, Red."

I look down into my husband's eyes as I begin to rock, slowly at first, and then faster, and the sensation is incredible.

"Oh fuck," Drake says with a moan.

"God, you feel so good," Hunter replies, and I don't know if he's talking to me or his friend because, at the moment, I'm not sure where one of us ends and the others begin. We are melted together into a pile of heat and pleasure and carnal cries of lust.

I'm pistoning my hips now, throwing myself back, impaling myself on their cocks. This time, my orgasm comes on slowly, like an approaching storm, and it lasts longer than ever, until it becomes a part of me. I'm no longer fucking them but dancing with this orgasm, my body riding out the climax.

"Yes, yes, yes," one of them howls, and I recognize the sensation of one cock throbbing and shuddering inside me. Or maybe it's both.

I collapse onto Hunter's chest, waiting for the tingling in my body to stop. Someone brushes my hair away again, and by the time he's kissing my cheek, I realize Drake must have pulled out of me.

Sitting up, I stare down at Hunter, who gently strokes my cheek with a smile. Then I turn to see Drake lying next to him. "You are so fucking amazing, Isabel."

I smile in return before falling into the narrow space between their bodies. I cuddle into this familiar position as Drake curls up to spoon me. With an exhausted and satisfied grin, I reply, "No. We're fucking amazing."

Rule #26: If your heart won't get over them, let your dick do it for you.

Drake

WHEN I WAKE UP, I'M NO LONGER ON THE OUTSIDE OF THIS LITTLE sandwich. Instead, I'm the little piece of meat squeezed between two pretty pieces of very naked and sexy bread. Isabel must have gotten up sometime in the middle of the night and crawled back in on the end, pushing me toward her husband.

Whether she did this out of convenience or because she thinks by pushing us together, it's going to make Hunter get over all of his bisexual hang-ups or me get over my stubborn anti-relationship hang-ups, then she bit off a little more than she can chew.

I mean…I'm not mad about the warm, muscled body pressed up against my back. And I'm definitely not mad that I get her all to myself with the way she's curled up in my arms like my own personal teddy bear, but I am a little annoyed by how much I don't hate this.

I never sleep with the people I screw. But these two are different, and I'm starting to forget why. They're different because they're my friends…yeah, that's it. They're different because these are the two most important people in my life. My family. The only two people I love...wait, fuck.

Hunter stirs, and it's obvious he doesn't realize I'm the inside of this spoon when he stretches his naked body and drapes an arm over my waist. Once he feels my six-three frame, instead of Isabel's petite five-foot-one, he tenses. Oh God, this is awkward. His... dick is against my ass. His morning wood hasn't quite kicked in yet because he's still soft, and I don't know if that's a good thing or not.

Hunter and I might be toying with this weird new dynamic to our relationship, but we're definitely not at the...rub your hard cock on my ass phase yet.

He lifts his head and looks at me through one half-open eye. I glance over my shoulder and since this is a double instead of a king, there's not a lot of room for me to give him.

"Morning," I mutter.

"Morning," he grumbles. Then, as expected, he quickly rolls out of the bed. It makes me wonder if he was actually ready to wake up or if forcing himself out of bed was worth not having to be pressed up naked against me.

I do happen to catch a glimpse of him as he bolts to the bathroom, and I can't be certain if that was morning wood or the effects of our sleeping arrangement that had him suddenly sporting a hard-on that wasn't there a moment ago.

"What time is it?" Isabel mumbles, barely moving against my chest.

"Time doesn't matter here. We're in Vegas, baby."

"Breakfast..." she moans.

I smile down at her, remembering just how much energy she exerted last night. I've never seen her like that before, wild and ravenous. I really did mean what I said before...Isabel is the best. I hate myself for the way I feel about her, my best friend's wife, but she makes everything easy and fun. I never have a single complaint when I'm with her and the sex is always out of this world. I may not be a settling down kind of guy, but I swear if I had a chance to settle down with this one, I'd be a fucking idiot to pass that up.

Thirty minutes later, the three of us manage to drag our tired asses down to the breakfast buffet. We eat and laugh and talk and everything feels so normal...that it's actually strange. Like we're just us again, but not the same us we used to be because now... we fuck.

After breakfast, Isabel drags us through the city, seeing every hotel, every sight, every stupid tourist shop, and I can't fucking help myself, but I'm happy.

She's wearing a long plastic cup filled with green margarita strapped around her neck as we meander through the Venetian. I catch myself reaching for her, holding her hand, and she lets me nuzzle her under my arm. My eyes cast in Hunter's direction, but when he catches us cuddling and her making me take a sip of her giant drink, he smiles. This part definitely wasn't in his plan. He just wanted to watch us fuck...so when did it turn into this? When did we become part of a relationship? And how do I feel about this?

I mean, I don't hate it. Isabel fits so nicely under my arm, her head not even reaching my shoulder. I never really got off on this alpha/*mine* thing with other people, but when Isabel tucks herself against me, something primal wakes up inside me, and it feels good. I actually imagine myself protecting her, laying out some asshole who dares to touch her—like the incident in Austin. I want to be the guy responsible for keeping her safe.

"We should go to the real Venice. I bet it's even prettier," she says while we wait in line for the gondola ride.

"I bet it's crowded and touristy," Hunter replies. "But if you wanna go, Red. We can go."

Then she glances up at me. "You in?"

I can't help myself. I lean down, pressing my lips to her temple. "I'm in."

To be fair, I would have always been down for a vacation with them. It was hard enough getting them to go on a honeymoon without me, and that was before Hunter made the big bucks, so it was just a small trip to the beach, but every other trip, they've dragged me along.

When we reach the front of the line, I start to pull away. "You two go."

Isabel looks up at me in shock. "Nice try, big guy. Three's company." Oh yeah, she's drunk already. Her words slur a little, and it's adorable.

"Actually, the saying goes, 'Two's company; three's a crowd.'"

She scoffs. "That's a dumb saying."

And she doesn't let go of my hand. She somehow hauls both of us onto that gondola and it does not go unnoticed by the gondola guy or the crowd around us that she's holding both of our hands, rubbing both of our legs, and by the end of the ride, she's had her lips on each of ours.

I can tell Hunter is tensing up a bit, but I don't care. I love it. This is the first time I've really felt like I wasn't the third wheel, like I'm really *part* of their relationship. It's not bad.

The entire day is actually pretty fucking awesome, but there's a looming uncertainty in the air because tomorrow we really do go home. Tomorrow, the fantasy ends. Vacation over and this threesome vacation version of us over along with the trip.

Maybe that's why tonight feels different.

After dinner, Isabel's margarita buzz has worn off and we wander together toward our room. I don't even know what time it is—three a.m., maybe.

In the elevator up, the mood is a good deal more somber than it was last night. We don't make out this time. She takes both of our hands and pulls us close, then she drags us slowly toward the room.

Instead of the wild fucking we got into last night, tonight we do what would likely be considered making love instead of fucking. Cuddled up in one bed, Isabel comes first by my mouth and again by Hunter's hands. Then she rides my cock while he watches before falling into his arms and letting him take her sensually from behind while I cover her face with kisses. Our pleasure melts into one, so we feel every orgasm together as if they belong to us all. It's slow and sensual with a sense of finality and foreboding.

Because this is it. This is the last time we're ever going to be like this. And we all know it.

"That's the last one," I say, dropping the final box in the storage container and pulling the bay door closed. It's depressing how quickly we were able to pack up my possessions in the apartment. It took less than a day to load up my couch, bed, and some random boxes onto the truck and haul it over here. Now I'm left with nothing but a suitcase and a guest room at my best friend's house.

We got home yesterday morning and everything has been a whirlwind since. The only saving grace of the whole being evicted situation is that it's distracted us from how weird this is now. We were so busy yesterday with recovering from this long trip that I didn't even bother to worry about sleeping arrangements or awkwardness. I crashed in the guest room. They slept silently in their bed, and that was that.

Back to normal.

I should be happy. This is what I wanted. But when I woke up alone this morning…I didn't feel happy.

"I'm headed to the club," Hunter says as we climb back in his car. "We have a meeting at seven, but I can drop you off at the house if you don't want to come."

"Have you figured out what you're going to propose?" I ask. Hunter has been busy spinning his wheels all week, and I know he's trying to think of ways to impress his partners with the new ideas he's gleaned from this trip.

"Shibari demonstration, for sure. I'm thinking about asking that Silla girl from New Orleans to come. I liked her."

"I liked her too," I reply, remembering the deep conversation we had at the club that night and how I felt comfortable confiding in her since she was always going to remain an outsider. Now I'm frantically trying to remember just how much I told this woman before she shows up at my doorstep armed with my secrets.

"I definitely liked Pitch," he adds, and I swallow down the thrill that tries to creep up with those words. I don't respond to that because what the fuck would I even say? He loved it. I loved it. Those aren't secrets. That dark room was fucking amazing— right along with everything we did in it. Right up to the moment he ditched me there.

"I'm sure they'll love any ideas you bring," I say finally.

"Thanks," he mutters. "Does that mean you'll come?"

Deciding whether or not to come to the board meetings isn't usually something I dwell on so much. It really boils down to how badly I want to get on Emerson Grant's nerves that day—I mean, it's pretty fucking clear he's not my biggest fan. He and I are just too different. He's a control freak, who doesn't like to share, and I'm...well, the opposite. Now if I dare to even breathe in his girlfriend's direction, I risk losing my contract with the company. And possibly my head.

But now...the decision to join the board meetings is more complicated. Obviously, none of the other owners know about what's gone down between Hunter and Isabel and me, but what if they can tell? What if they can sense that I'm not the same ladies' man I was two weeks ago? I just don't think I'm ready for close proximity to people I know right now.

"Maybe," I reply. "I really need to spend my time searching for a new place."

"No rush, Drake. I'm serious. You don't need to hurry out of our house. You're always welcome there."

There's something about the way he says it that feels heavier than it should. As if he's trying to convey how much he doesn't want me to leave.

I just wish time would pass quickly, so we can all get over

this awkwardness. Maybe I need to just fuck someone else. That would help get them out of my system. I've just been with them for so long now that they've literally fucked me senseless. I can find a girl at the club to help get Isabel out of my head.

But that thought quickly sours. I don't want another woman. I want that petite, freckle-faced, fiery redhead with a dirty side and a sweet smile. Fuck.

I knew this was a bad idea. But I never would have thought I'd get so attached so fast. Of course, I never want to commit to a woman, but the first one I do want, I can't have.

Maybe I'll find a guy at the club then… Nope. For some reason, that thought feels even worse.

"Drake?" Hunter asks, pulling me from my deep thoughts. "Club or home?" We're sitting at an intersection, and I have to quickly decide what I'm going to do. I know what I want and I know what I can have, and unfortunately, they're not the same.

"Club," I mutter with hardly any enthusiasm.

———————

We're at Salacious an hour before the meeting, so we head to the bar first. It's good to be back. After seeing so many clubs, I find it such a relief to be back in ours. God, it's good to be home.

"Hey, guys. Welcome back," Geo, the bartender, says with a greeting and a wide smile.

"Thanks," Hunter and I reply in unison. He orders a whiskey sour and I go with a beer. And we drink them in silence. I watch as Hunter pulls out his phone, responding to a text from Isabel, and I wince with the sudden envy that hits me.

I really need to get over this fast because this shit sucks. While he texts, I glance around the main hall. It's early, so it's quiet, just a few regulars lingering around. Newbies won't show up until it's crowded and they have other bodies to hide among. That means I've either already slept with the people here or am not interested in them for one reason or another.

I nod toward Ronan Kade, the filthy rich silver fox sitting at a bartop with Eden. They're having a casual conversation that doesn't look much like flirting, but I'm fairly certain those two have either fucked so much they don't even have to try anymore or have never fucked and are truly *just friends*. A phrase that makes me laugh a little now.

Hunter and I are *just friends*.

Isabel and I are *just friends*.

And look at how well that worked out.

Goddammit, brain, stop thinking about them. Move the fuck on.

The main floor is disappointing, so I turn back toward the bar. That's when my gaze meets a familiar pair of green eyes, and I catch them staring at me with a certain twinkle, and I know what that means.

I pause, staring at Geo, who quickly diverts his attention once I've caught him checking me out. As he helps another bar patron, I let my eyes roam over him. Geo is attractive—*very* attractive—and I'm not sure why I haven't noticed it before. He's slender with an athletic figure and tan biceps that look smooth to the touch. I bet he surfs or runs, both visions of him working up a sweat outside give my groin a slight stirring. Nothing major but it's potential.

Suddenly, I'm drinking my beer faster, hoping it means he'll come over to refill it. Finally, he does, and I swear he's smiling at me differently now.

"Want another one?" he asks, taking the empty bottle from in front of me.

I lean forward, placing my forearms on the bar as I smile at him. With a wink, I reply, "Yes, please." I feel like myself again.

Geo bites his lip in response. Then he turns toward the ice chest to grab my beer. Before he returns, I feel Hunter's attention suddenly on me. He's wearing a scrutinizing expression as he watches me take the cold bottle from Geo and lift it to my lips while holding his gaze.

"So how was your trip?" Geo asks, leaning against the bar.

"Long," I reply, and I swear I notice Hunter's jaw clench in my periphery.

"See any good clubs?"

"Nothing as good as this one, but we saw some interesting places."

"Oh yeah?" Geo asks with a flirtatious lift of his brow. "You'll have to share some of the stories with me sometime. I'm intrigued."

Hunter's drink slams against the bar with a clunk so loud I'm surprised his glass doesn't break. "We have a meeting. Let's go," he barks as he stands from his seat.

And I almost get up. I almost follow him because that's what I've always done. He leads, I follow. He says jump, and I say "how high." Or rather…he says "fuck my wife" and I say "yes, sir." But that's what got me in this situation. And now my heart is a fucking mess. My head is a mess. I'm not the same person I was before this trip, and I can't risk losing their friendship even more than we already have. So I can't just follow Hunter anymore.

For his own good, I keep my ass on this barstool, and I force a tough swallow. "I don't need to go to the meeting. If you have any construction questions for me, we'll meet up after. But you go. I'm gonna stay here."

My eyes lift up to meet his and the intensity of his expression literally hurts. It's a punch to the gut. Because I'm drawing that line back in the sand. And I swear it looks like he has something to say, but in true Hunter fashion, he swallows it down.

"Fine," he mutters. Then he glances ominously at Geo before looking back at me. "Just remember our club has a two-drink limit."

"Yep," I reply, trying not to let those words hurt the way he wants them to.

And with that, he turns and walks away. I recognize the anger in his gait, but I don't dwell on it. Turning back to Geo, I smile. I need to get back to myself, and there's only one way to do it.

If my heart isn't going to get over Hunter and Isabel, my dick will.

Rule #27: Get your story straight.

Hunter

I'm early for the meeting, and I hate being early. Not even Emerson is here yet, and he's always the first one in the room.

I drop into a chair with a scowl on my face and stare at the wood grain of the conference table. I'm stewing like the stubborn asshole I am. I'm mad at Drake for ditching me, obviously flirting, and I'm proactively angry at him for what I'm pretty sure he's about to do with the bartender.

What the fuck is wrong with him? He goes straight from our trip to trying to fuck someone else. How could he do that to Isabel? Why can't he just keep his dick in his pants for one fucking second?

It seemed pretty clear to me this past week that the three of us have a bond. Did he not see it that way? No. It was just fucking to him and we mean nothing. And to think I wanted to make this relationship work among the three of us. I actually considered bringing him into my marriage long-term, but of course, he doesn't want that. That would require not sticking his dick in the first person that walks by.

"What's wrong with you?" Garrett, one of my co-owners, says with a furrowed brow as he enters the room. He's not exactly the kind of friend you confide in. Garrett is great for a laugh and a good time, but if I unloaded every detail of the past two weeks on him, his head would explode from trying to take it seriously. I force my chest to take a deep breath as I glance up at him.

"I'm fine," I lie.

Garrett laughs. "Sure. Judging by the angry scowl on your face, you're either not too happy to be back or didn't have any fun on your trip at all."

"Nah. The trip was great, and I'm happy to be back." One truth and one lie. The trip *was* great and I wish it never ended.

"You didn't lose Drake in the sex clubs, did you?"

"He's here. At the bar," I mumble.

"I bet he had a good time. I was half expecting him to not come back at all."

I don't respond. A minute later, the rest of the team start filing in. Emerson and Charlie, her walking in front of him with his hand pressed gently against the small of her back. Maggie typing away at something on her phone like she usually is.

They all greet me, smiling and asking about my trip, and I try to keep my smile as natural as possible. Then, of course, they all inquire about Drake and my fake smile gets harder to hold.

"All right, Hunter. Tell us everything. I'm sure you have a lot of thoughts and ideas." Emerson leans back in his chair, staring at me thoughtfully as he waits. I do have a lot of thoughts and tons of ideas, but a certain giant blond asshole won't get out of my brain and let me think.

"Yeah..." I stammer, "I didn't get a chance to put together a presentation yet. We had to move Drake out of his apartment yesterday, but I can whip something—"

"It's fine," Emerson says with a crooked smile. "We don't need a presentation, Hunter. Just tell us about your trip."

I let out a heavy sigh. *Think, Hunter. Think.* But there are no clear thoughts, just images and memories and nothing I could possibly share with them. Like the moment I watched Drake tie up my wife for the first time...during that... "Shibari demonstrations," I blurt out, suddenly using the memory of them as my muse. "We saw some pretty amazing demos that I'd love to bring here." I sit upright in my chair. "Once a month, let the members learn how to do it themselves."

"Perfect. That would go well with our other kink demos. Anything else?"

It was at Fire Palace that the owner reminded me that we might not be doing enough to make things discreet for our members, especially the women. "We should be doing more to protect our members' privacy, especially the women who don't feel comfortable just walking around our club. Maybe a masquerade evening once a month."

A few people at the table perk up in interest. Emerson nods as I move on.

I scan through my memory of the trip...landing on the moment I watched Drake and Isabel kiss for the first time and how I felt after that, stealing her away because I had to have her at that moment. "Quickie rooms," I say. "We were at a club, and they had these stalls that you didn't have to rent, but you could use...for a quickie." A grin starts to tug on the corner of my mouth as I remember that night. I notice Charlie, Emerson's girlfriend, biting her lip as she blushes and quickly types what I'm saying on her laptop.

"Quickie rooms...I love it," Emerson replies. "And Drake?"

My head snaps up to stare at him. "No, I was with Isabel," I say quickly to correct him, my cheeks starting to suddenly burn.

Emerson smiles. "I mean...can Drake build us something like that?"

Fuck me. I can't believe I just thought he was asking if I fucked Drake in a quickie room. I'm now fighting the urge to bolt from this room like a coward.

"Oh," I reply, clearing my throat and feeling the eyes of everyone in the room on me. "Yeah, easily."

"Great," he says, and I could be imagining it, but I swear he's watching me with more scrutiny than usual. I squirm in my seat. "Anything else?"

The next one is easy, but I feel a lot less excited and proud of the memory as I say, "Dark rooms."

"Dark rooms?" Garrett asks.

"Yeah. Pitch-black. Completely anonymous. Anyone in there can do anything they want...with anyone they want." I swear they can all read my mind as I remember that night. It plays on repeat in my mind.

The club owner had offered to let me see the room with the goggles on, and the next thing I knew, I saw Drake standing there with his jeans unzipped and a kid barely old enough to drink touching his chest. All of the years of watching Drake flirt with men, kiss them and go to bed with them, I'd finally snapped.

"Interesting..." Emerson replies.

"Where's the fun in that?" Garrett adds with a laugh. Being the voyeur he is, of course he hates that idea.

"And it's safe?" Maggie asks.

"Very. The rooms all had cameras, bouncers with special goggles to see in the dark, and condoms were mandatory. I felt very safe there. It was really liberating actually."

"You used it?" someone asks, and I don't even catch who it was. I was too caught in the memory, and I probably shouldn't have let that last part slip.

"Um...yeah. I went in there. Drake and I both did." Jesus, why am I still talking?

The table nods collectively, and I wish I knew what they're thinking. Could they possibly suspect what really happened during our trip? Surely not all of it. Not me asking Drake and Isabel to sleep together because just the thought of it turned me on. Or Drake going down on me in a dark club. Or the three of us fucking like animals in Vegas. Or falling in love with my best friend. They definitely didn't see that one coming.

"Sounds fun," Emerson says after a long, awkward silence. "The dark rooms might be a little harder to create with our limited available space. Not unless Drake wants to build another level on the club. Where is he anyway?"

Garrett answers before I get the chance. "Hunter must have been a real cockblock all week because Drake's out there laying the moves on Geo, probably getting his dick wet as we speak."

My jaw clenches. I don't blame Garrett because these are the jokes we make all the time. This is what we do, but now it grates on my nerves like never before.

"You'll meet with him at some point and get a quote for some of these renovations?" Emerson asks, his face set in a serious expression.

"Of course," I reply.

"If he has any ideas for the dark rooms, I'd love to hear them."

"I'll let him know," I say.

Then Emerson just nods and I can't help but feel as if he's staring at me for a reason. Like he can read everything behind my eyes, and it makes me uncomfortable as hell. So I avert my gaze and write myself a couple notes on my notepad.

The rest of the meeting goes by without incident. After everything is done, I make a quick exit to avoid any unnecessary small talk or prodding questions. I'm too anxious to find Drake. What if he's not at the bar? What if he got a room with someone?

I squeeze my fists together at the thought as I march out toward the main hall. For Isabel's sake, that would be fucked up.

When I tear open the door from the staff hallway to the main room, I don't see him at first. Then, my gaze passes the bar and I see him, sitting in the same spot but now he's leaning over the surface, laughing with Geo, who is now leaning right back over in his space.

I'm storming toward the bar as I quickly remind myself to keep my cool. But honestly, what *the fuck* is he doing?

"Let's go," I say, my words coming out more like a growl than something a normal, civilized person would say. Geo stands upright and slowly backs away from Drake. Good call, kid.

Drake looks at me with alarm. "Everything okay?"

"Can I talk to you for a second?" I ask, feeling the anger boil.

"Sure," he replies, getting up and following me to a discreet corner. "What's wrong with you?" he asks.

"Me?" My eyes widen. "What's wrong with *you*? Geo thinks you're trying to take him home and fuck him, and honestly, so do I."

His shoulders shrug as he forces his eyes away. "So what if I am? All of a sudden you have a problem with me being with guys?"

"It has nothing to do with him being a guy," I snap before quickly reeling it back in. "What about Isabel?"

I watch as Drake composes himself before answering. "I thought everything that happened on our trip was just fun. We're back home now. Right?"

When his eyes meet mine again, I freeze. Is he asking me that? That was the deal, but if I really say that wasn't all it was, then would he really change his mind and come home with me? Is that what I want?

Drake is never going to settle down, not for long at least. If I draw this out, then Isabel is just going to get hurt in the long run, and I can't let that happen—to her. If this is how he's going to act, then it's best to just cut things off now.

"Right," I reply coolly.

"Hunter, I can't be the third wheel in your marriage forever. This trip was fun, but the sooner we get back to the way things were, the better."

My heart feels like a lead balloon in my chest. "So what are you going to do, Drake? Just go back to fucking random strangers? Do you really want to do that forever? Like your mom."

There's fire in his eyes as he glares at me. That was too harsh and if I could take it back, I would. "And all this time I've avoided comparing you to your father…" he replies.

We're not going back to the way things were at all. Right now, we're careening toward the opposite, and I feel helpless to stop it.

"I'm sorry," I say, as if that's enough to fix the damage of a fucking tsunami of insults.

"It's fine," he replies with a sigh. "For your information…I don't plan on just fucking random strangers. I was thinking… maybe it's time for me to date for real. Actually get to know someone and try to make it a long-term thing."

Why do I hate this idea more? "Then don't fuck him," I say, staring straight into those familiar blue irises.

"Okay," he replies, but it's not convincing.

"I'm serious, Drake. If you want to be in a real relationship, then don't fuck him right away. See if you can even do that."

He doesn't respond as I storm away, feeling like an asshole after slinging insults at my best friend, as if that's not half as bad as what he's doing to me—lying to me. Because no matter what he says about not sleeping with Geo, I know him too well, and I don't believe him for one fucking second.

Rule #28: If you love someone, let them go. (Easier said than done.)

Isabel

I KNOW SOMETHING IS UP WHEN MY HUSBAND WALKS THROUGH the front door—alone. He's wearing a scowl and barely says a word as he bounds up the stairs toward our master bedroom.

Coming home from that trip felt like the ultimate test—one that we failed. A little over twenty-four hours back in BP and we're already falling apart. I have a good idea why too.

I follow Hunter up the stairs and find him taking off his suit in the walk-in closet, hanging his jacket on the hanger and angrily yanking off his tie.

"What happened?" I ask.

"Nothing," he mutters.

I swallow down the rising emotion from hearing how frustrated he is. He doesn't say a word as he tears off his shirt, balls it up and tosses it into the hamper. As he starts on the button of his pants, he finally looks at me, and I notice the dam break inside him.

"I figured he'd go back eventually. I thought he might just take some time, but no. He's already at the club. He's probably already naked with the bartender, and I honestly don't know why I care. That's how he wants to live his life. That's up to him. I'm just sorry your emotions got involved…and I did this. I brought all of this on. I never should have asked you to do that…"

Honestly, I feared this more than I expected it, but I had a feeling that we wouldn't be able to keep him for long. I mean, what did we expect? To bring him into our marriage forever? It's not fair to anyone, least of all him.

And my husband knows that, but I'm afraid he's gotten himself even more emotionally involved than I have. And I'm nearly dying inside with how this feels, not to have Drake here. To know someone else gets his smile and his touch.

"Have you told him how you feel?" I ask.

Hunter freezes. "What? That I'm tired of him being a thirty-four-year-old man whore? Actually…yeah, I kind of did."

I wince. "No, Hunter. That's not what I meant."

He turns his back on me as he undoes his pants, pulling out his belt and hanging it on the hook. It's a long time before he responds. "What do you mean, Isabel?"

My throat stings for real now. "Did you tell Drake how *you* feel about him?"

His head snaps toward me. "I know what you're thinking, Iz, but it's not like that. Yeah, we fooled around a little, but there's nothing more there. We're just friends."

I bite the inside of my lip as I fight away the tears that want to come. I can't speak, but he continues for me, "Besides, I shouldn't have to. He should know…we are special. I thought *we* would have meant more. But he couldn't stick around for one fucking day."

"Stick around for what, Hunter? He's been here his entire adult life. You've sheltered him, protected him, given him a home and a family. Fuck, Hunter, you gave him your wife."

His nostrils flare as I say that, and he quickly looks away. But I draw his attention back. "You give him hell for never settling down and for being promiscuous, but you have kept him in a choke hold, tethered to *you* for his entire life. He's never had any room to grow."

He lets out an angry sounding huff. "What are you saying? I just let him go?"

"What choice do we have?"

That question lingers in the air between us, even as he storms out of the closet and gets into the shower. What choice do we have? None. Hunter and I chose each other, and we've kept Drake on a short leash this entire time.

And while the vacation was fun, we did the worst thing possible. We gave him a taste of the one thing he can't have. He turned the third wheel into the center of attention for a brief moment, and I know the idea of forming a full relationship between all three of us has crossed everyone's mind, but until those two get over whatever is keeping them stuck in their old ways, it will never happen. Hunter will have to be the one to bring it up first, and that's the most unlikely thing of all.

It's past midnight when I hear the front door open. Hunter is asleep fitfully next to me, tossing and turning every few minutes. So I ease myself out of bed without making a sound. I notice the light on in the kitchen as I make my way down the stairs. I'm in nothing but a pair of underwear and one of Hunter's T-shirts, but we're past modesty at this point.

I half expect Drake to be drunk again, like the last time I caught him sneaking in too late, but he's not this time. I see the sobriety in his eyes the moment our gazes meet each other's. He's not just sober—he's somber. And I think I know why.

"Did I wake you?" he asks.

I shake my head.

Awkward silence settles over the room. Finally, he says the words that I desperately needed to hear.

"I didn't sleep with him."

Thank God.

"Why not?" I'm gripping the kitchen island between us as if it's the only thing holding me up.

"I don't know…"

"What happened between us was just a fling, Drake. A crazy vacation, but it's over now," I reply, watching his expression for a sign that he agrees.

His brow furrows as he steps toward me. "Is that really what you think? You think it meant nothing?"

"Do you?"

We stare at each other for a long, tense moment before he scoffs and runs his hands angrily through his hair. "I think we're both at the mercy of the person upstairs. I think what he wants and what he's willing to admit he wants are two different things and until he fucking figures that out, we're both stuck like this."

I blink away the impending tears because I know deep down that what he wants will never happen. And if Hunter can't get over that, then Drake will never be happy. And if Drake can't have Hunter, then I can't have Drake.

Dread stabs my heart like a knife.

Brushing the pain aside, I move silently around the island, opening the cabinet next to Drake to retrieve a glass for water. As I close the door, I feel him standing closer. When I try to move around him to get to the fridge, he blocks my path.

The knife sinks in a little deeper.

"Drake," I whisper, unable to look him in the eye. His hand touches my waist as he steps closer, breathing against my neck.

"I've never been so addicted to another person in my life, Isabel. But I can't stop thinking about you." His lips touch my neck, and I close my eyes from the shame that washes over me. I don't move, but I don't stop him either.

"I still feel you in my hands. Every time I close my eyes, I hear the sounds you made when I was fucking you. I know your taste and your smell. I know I have to move on, but I don't know if I can." His voice is pained and sincere. So sincere it cracks my heart in two.

I want to fall into his big arms and feel that special comfort I only feel in Drake's embrace. And for a moment, I almost do. I don't know if doing that would be weak or brave, but I am neither.

Turning my head, I stare into his eyes, our mouths so close I can feel his breath. "We can't. Not anymore."

The pain that flashes in his eyes is worse than the knife currently lodged in my chest. Instead of kissing my lips, he rests his forehead against mine and we stay like that for a moment, breathing each other in as much as we can, expressing everything through our simple touches that we can't express with more.

Finally, I pull away, and he lets me. As I'm leaving the kitchen, feeling as if my body is heavier and slower than it was when I came down here, he says my name, so I stop and turn toward him.

"You know you've always been my girl, right?"

I bite back my emotions. Calmly, I nod.

"And no matter what, you'll always be my girl."

Tears prick my eyes and I force a smile. "Good night, Drake."

"Good night, Isabel."

Upstairs, I crawl into bed next to Hunter, but I fall asleep with my back to him, something I almost never do, but right now, I'm mad at him. He did this to us, played with our hearts like they were his toys, and now he's tearing us all apart. And if he's not careful, he's going to ruin more than just his friendship.

Rule #29: Love makes you an idiot.

Drake

I'M ON A DATE. A CERTIFIED DATE. MY FIRST, IF WE'RE BEING honest. I mean, I've met up with other people before, but it was always with the intention to fuck. This evening, I'm sitting at a restaurant with Geo, the bartender, with the intention to actually get to know him.

It's excruciating.

Not Geo—he's great. He's funny, down-to-earth, and likes to compliment me a lot. I could see us hanging out, getting drunk, watching a movie, waking up next to each other. I mean...the possibility is there, but the excitement? Not quite.

"So...you promised to share some stories from your trip. I want to hear all about those other clubs," he says with a flirtatious smile as he sips on his margarita.

"Eh..." I scratch the back of my neck. "I don't really want to talk about my trip, if that's okay."

He looks immediately apologetic. "Of course, that's okay. I'm sorry."

"Don't apologize. It's complicated, that's all."

"Because of Hunter…or because of Isabel?"

"Uhh…"

"I'm sorry. God, that was nosy of me," he replies with a laugh. "Please ignore me. I always put my foot in my mouth when I drink."

This time, I laugh, and it helps to ease some of the tension. "It's fine, really. But to answer your question simply…yes."

"Oh."

"Yeah…"

"Well," he says, lifting his glass toward me. I pick up my drink and tap it against his. "To rebounds and fresh starts."

I laugh again as I carry the glass to my lips. He studies me for a minute as he picks at his dinner. "Can I ask you a personal question?"

"Of course," I reply. That's what we're here for, isn't it?

"Have you ever dated a man before?"

"Um…Geo…I've never dated a person before."

"Damn," he replies with a chuckle. He really does have a cute smile, but I'm not feeling that intense chemistry I'm craving. Is this normal for dating? I mean…if we're compatible and we get along, the physical chemistry will come. Won't it?

I mean, I can imagine myself with him, his lips wrapped around my cock or his knees pressed to his chest while I bury myself inside him. But that's all my brain can imagine. It always goes back to sex. The attraction to Geo is there…but the desire to call him and see him after that? Not so much.

"Yeah, I just never saw myself as being boyfriend material. And I always had my best friend to do things with on holidays or birthdays or vacations, so I never really needed anyone else."

He nods, and I start to feel like I'm talking about Hunter too much. "But if you're wondering if I could see myself settling down with a man…" I shrug. "Yeah. I don't see why not."

"You wouldn't miss pussy?"

I nearly choke on my beer at his bluntness. As I wipe my face, I consider it. Would I?

"Umm…"

After a few minutes of contemplation, he smiles. "I'll take that as a yes."

"If it's any consolation, I think I would miss dick just as much if I settled down with a woman."

"Was that supposed to make me feel better?" he asks with a laugh, and now we're both chuckling so hard, our faces are red.

"Sorry. This is awkward," I say when our laughter dies down.

"Nah, you're doing great."

"Does this mean I get a second date?" I ask with a hopeful expression.

He drums his fingers against his glass as he thinks about it. "I don't know if it's a second date you need, Drake."

My shoulders deflate as he shuts me down. Fuck. I'm starting to accept my fate of getting old and dying alone when he reaches across the table and touches my hand. When his eyes lift up to my face, there's something sultry and inviting in his expression. And for the first time, I feel that spark of chemistry I so badly wanted. Suddenly, I'm thinking about taking him home and bending him over the back of his couch, so I can fuck him until he screams.

"And what is it I need?" I ask in a low murmur.

"I think you need a good fuck to get whatever happened on your trip out of your head."

"And you…can help me with that?"

He leans in, tugging his lower lip between his teeth. "Abso-fucking-lutely."

Perfect. Yes, I'm going to get laid tonight. This is what I need.

I smile as I lean back, but something sour and wrong settles over me. I didn't want this to be a one-night stand. I wanted this to be a real date, but maybe Hunter was right. I am just like my mother.

"Uh-oh," Geo says. "What's the look for?"

I force a crooked smile. "I don't think I've ever passed up sex before."

"Why start now?" he asks playfully.

"Because I'm a fucking idiot."

He lets out an easy laugh as he nods. "Love will do that to you."

———————

I said goodbye to Geo over an hour ago. I couldn't even give him the kiss I'm sure he was leaning in for. Now I'm sitting in my car in front of Isabel and Hunter's house, debating whether or not I want to go in. It's only nine. They will still be up, but I don't know if I can face them.

We've barely had to coexist in this house since we got back from our trip a few days ago. And I'm not really looking forward to the first time we will. So far, after only three days, things between us have not naturally fallen back into place like they were supposed to. I don't know if it's because we need more time together or more time apart, but this tension is going to be the death of me. I just want my friends back.

Finally gathering up some courage, I get out of the car and walk up to the front door with my spare key. As I step into the house, I smell the aroma of something sweet filling the space. There's music playing from a speaker somewhere and I stop on the doormat as I watch Isabel cross the brightly lit kitchen in nothing but a T-shirt and apron. She's sliding a muffin pan out of the oven as she sways her hips to the Sam Cooke song playing.

I scan the room for Hunter, and when I don't see him, I almost turn around and walk out of the house. Not today. I *cannot* handle this temptation today.

But she sees me first, and it's too late to bolt. "Hey!" she calls. "I'm baking cupcakes…" Her voice carries, and I know by the playfulness to it that she's drunk.

"You are?" I ask as I close the front door and head into the large kitchen.

"Yep. I got vanilla and strawberry." She reaches her finger into the batter, and holds it out to me. "Try it."

My mouth forms a crooked grin as I step closer. With my eyes on her, I close my mouth around her finger and lick it clean of the sweet mixture. She whimpers at me as I do.

Releasing her finger, I ask, "Where's Hunter?"

"Upstairs," she replies, her expression turning somber.

"Everything okay?"

She glances cautiously up at the stairs. Then in a low whisper, she replies, "We haven't been talking much the past couple days."

"I'm sorry."

She shrugs in return. Then she gets back to work on the cupcakes, scooping them out onto the cooling rack.

"What are you drinking?" I ask with a smile. Her face contorts in confusion as she stares at me.

"Drinking?" Then a moment later, realization dawns, and she giggles. "Oh, no. I'm not drinking. I took an edible. It helps me relax."

"Ah…" I reply. And then I swallow down the sudden wave of guilt that rises. I hate that she has to take anything to relax. I hate that I'm part of the reason she can't relax in the first place.

"Want one?" she asks. "They're not very strong. I'm just a lightweight." She giggles again, and I smile wide as I watch her laugh to herself.

"No thanks. I'm okay."

"Okay," she replies with another cute shrug.

Sitting on the barstool, I watch her bake. Every step is engrossing. Her nimble fingers measuring the ingredients, pouring them into the mixer, wiping the flour from her nose. It's everything I wish the date with Geo had been. If that date had been half as satisfying as watching Isabel bake, I would be busy fucking his brains out right now. But by no fault of his own, there was nothing between us—nothing close to this.

When I hear footsteps behind me, I tense. Hunter enters the room and stands next to me, watching Isabel too.

"She's high, isn't she?"

I laugh. "Yep."

"She only bakes when she's high."

"I am not high," she argues with a blush. "I had one cotton candy gummy bear an hour ago. Geez." Then, she flips on the mixer too high and the flour erupts from the bowl, covering her face. She bursts into laughter, suddenly unable to even breathe, and it's so fucking infectious that now I'm laughing. And when I look over at Hunter, he's grinning from ear to ear too, his shoulders shaking with his own amusement.

"Red, you're a mess."

Finally, she stops laughing and plants her hands against the counter. Glaring at Hunter with a slightly glossy stare and a wicked grin on her face, she reaches into the bowl and proceeds to fling a handful of flour at her husband.

He stands frozen, white powder covering his black button-up shirt, and we wait in anticipation for his reaction. Finally, his tongue peeks out from between his lips and licks up the bitter taste from his face. "Oh, you're a bad little girl. You better fucking run."

I watch with a smile when Isabel shrieks, beaming as she takes off, bolting into a run from her side of the kitchen. He rounds the island to catch her, but even stoned, she's too fast. They're both covered in baking ingredients and laughing as they run circles around the island, both laughing and smiling.

This is what I missed. This is definitely something we would have done before the whole threesome complicated everything. Call it wishful thinking, but it feels like we can finally move on and get back to the way things were.

"Save me, Drake!" Isabel screams as she crouches behind me.

"Get behind me." I laugh, but before I can stand and block her from the threat of Hunter holding a bottle of chocolate syrup, I'm assaulted by a handful of vanilla frosting to the face.

Isabel squeals in laughter as she wipes it all over me, from my chin up to my hair. I don't know how I missed her grabbing that in her dash around the counter. I'm sitting here in shock, and when she tries to run away, I snatch her by the waist and drag her toward me.

"I was going to help you," I say in an ominous tone. "But now you're screwed."

Once I have her against me, I pin both of her hands behind her back and hold tight. "Get her," I say to Hunter, who smiles wickedly as he douses her with chocolate. She's laughing and fighting against my grip as he pours it all over her head and face.

"Here you go, Drake. I made you a sundae. Have a taste." Hunter says these words in a playful tone. A moment ago, I thought things had finally gotten back to normal, but I can't help myself. This is definitely *not* normal. All of her fidgeting and fighting against my body has my cock twitching in my pants, and I do want a taste. So I drag her closer and lick a long line along the side of her face, and as I do so, she slows her struggling.

"Mmm…she tastes good," I whisper in her ear.

"Take off her shirt," Hunter commands, and I do. Releasing her hands, I hold her by the waist as I untie her apron and drag her shirt over her head. I'm holding her like a prisoner, even though I know well and good that she wouldn't go anywhere now. Her smile is fading and in its place is a lustful expression aimed at her husband.

In nothing but her panties, she stands and waits as Hunter dribbles chocolate sauce across each of her nipples. She lets out a sweet little moan and he instantly takes the right one in his mouth and I take the left. Her cries grow louder as she reaches up to hold our heads there, lapping chocolate off her breasts.

When Hunter pulls his mouth away, he stares at her as he dribbles the sauce on her stomach, watching it drip down to the waistband of her pink cotton briefs.

I want to be the one to lick that chocolate away so bad, but I want to watch him doing it just as much. We're being reckless and doing exactly what we know we shouldn't right now. Any one of us could easily break up this sexy little food fight, but we don't because like Geo said, love makes you a fucking idiot.

"Go ahead," I say as I wrap an arm around her waist and hold her against me. Hunter drops to his knees and kisses his way down her stomach, covering his mouth with chocolate as he goes until he finally reaches her panties. Tugging them down, he doesn't hesitate before he plants a warm, wet kiss between her legs.

She moans and writhes in my arms as he sucks on her clit, and my dick throbs as I watch them. I can't keep my mouth off her, licking the sweet taste off her neck and finding her mouth so I can devour those sounds of pleasure.

He stares up at us as he fucks her with his tongue, my cock leaking as he slides his finger inside her. She's trembling now, fidgeting and fighting against me as her orgasm approaches.

"I'm gonna...gonna..." She whimpers breathlessly. I pinch the chocolate-covered bud of her nipple as I kiss her neck and her body seizes up in my arms. "Yes, yes, yes," she moans.

When her muscles finally turn soft and she relaxes against me, I assume it's over. But she gives Hunter a devious look as she snatches the whipped cream can off the counter and glares at him.

"My turn," she says wickedly, and he responds with an *I dare you* expression.

I watch curiously as she turns toward me. With her bottom lip pinched between her teeth, she drops a dot of cream against my neck. I feel it seeping down into the collar of my shirt as I stare at her. Then she looks at Hunter, her brows raised as she steps out of the way.

I freeze, eyes wide as I stare at her. Then it dawns on me what she's doing.

We're playing *that* game.

It's silent as we wait for him to make up his mind. This is huge for him. The pressure to finally fess up to what he wants, no matter if he's really ready for that or not. And maybe he doesn't want that anymore. Maybe what happened in Nashville was a one-time thing and he decided he doesn't like being with men.

The problem is that Hunter doesn't back down. He's too proud, too stubborn, and just like the bet we made in Austin, he *never* loses.

My heart picks up speed as he closes the distance between us and he spares me one last glance before he attacks my neck with his lips. I don't even have the brain cells left to try and talk him out of this or make sure it's really what he wants because his lips on my neck feel *too fucking good.* Goose bumps erupt over every inch of my body as he sucks the tender flesh where Isabel put the sweet cream. I find my hands reaching for him as he licks and nibbles on my neck, my dick twitching in my boxers.

As Hunter pulls away, I feel as if my legs might give out beneath me. He's staring at me with a hungry gaze, but before he moves toward me again, Isabel steps closer.

"You're a mess, Drake," she says in a sweet tone. "Let's take this off." Suddenly, my shirt is being pulled over my head, and she's squirting cream all over my chest.

I let out a grunt as Hunter quickly licks it up, kissing his way across my pecs and then down my abs. He stays on his feet as he devours every inch of my chest and stomach, and I feel as if I might be dying. It doesn't feel like he's being dared to do this anymore. It feels like he wants to.

"Goddamn," I mutter as his tongue traces a line above the top of my jeans. I'm going to fucking blow in my pants. Isabel watches, her lips parted as she takes long, heavy breaths, clearly aroused by her husband licking another man.

When Hunter rises to his feet, he turns to kiss her, hard and passionately, and it gives me a moment to catch my breath. I should walk away now. We are stumbling into dangerous territory, but I might as well be drunk on his touch because there's no righting this collision course we're on now.

As Isabel kisses her husband, he begins taking off his own

clothes, unbuttoning his flour-drenched shirt and chocolate-soaked pants. And when her carnal gaze meets mine, I take it as my cue to do the same.

I barely even register taking my boxers off because I'm too focused on this moment. The three of us naked together—again. And I reach for her, but she pushes my hand away. Pulling from Hunter's kiss, she faces me. With a fierce sort of courage I've never seen on Isabel before, she places the whip cream can against my hard, jutting cock and draws a long line of soft white cream from the base to the tip.

And I expect *her* to lick it off. But she looks at him, and I freeze. She can't be serious. He's not ready for that.

"Isabel…" I say, but her eyes don't leave his face.

He barely, just *barely*, hesitates. I figured he'd put up more of a fight and I don't know if he's kneeling in front of me because she basically dared him to or because he really wants to, but the vision of Hunter kneeling in front of my hard cock and staring at it hungrily has me feeling dizzy.

Then he looks up at me and I feel more tethered to him than I've ever felt before. This is us. The same us we've always been. The us we were always meant to be, and for this one perfect moment, he's not caught up in his head or hearing his father's scornful voice. It's just me and him.

As he runs his tongue around the head of my cock, I suck in a breath through my teeth. My body is on fire as I watch him lick the cream off, a little clumsy at first, but suddenly ravenous after he gets his first taste. Then he opens his mouth and pulls me in, keeping his lips tight around me as he reaches as far back as he can.

I have to resist the urge to come already. This is too much—too fucking much. He's stubbornly trying to take me deeper with each stroke of my cock down his throat. When he finally gags, I grab his hair to pull him off. I'm not ready to come yet, but if he doesn't stop doing that I'm definitely going to blow.

"Fuck," I say in a long, drawn-out groan.

I hear the can of whip cream hit the floor as Isabel jumps into my arms, kissing my face before pulling my lips to hers. Then Hunter stands and joins our kiss, devouring her mouth and then mine until we are a tangle of tongues and lips and heat.

Hunter's body is pressed against mine, and when I feel Isabel squeeze our cocks together, stroking them as one, I growl into her mouth.

"I want you both inside me," she mumbles sweetly against my lips. "Like this." Her bold green eyes stare at me, and I pause.

Goddamn...this woman. From the stories Hunter told me, I knew she was freakier than her sweet, shy personality led everyone to believe, but this? I did not expect this.

She strokes us together, and the heat from his cock against mine is so intense and inviting, how could I possibly say no? Hunter and I glance at each other, but we're both so lost to the lust of the moment that we are useless to protest against anything.

Letting go of our cocks, she wraps her hands around my neck, and I pull her into my arms, her legs wrapping around my waist. Hunter squeezes her between us until I feel him wrap his hand around our cocks. She's tense in my arms, and for a moment I'm worried this won't work. I don't want to hurt her, and just as her wet cunt touches the head of my dick, I pull her away.

"Wait," I stammer. "Condom."

Her shoulders melt away from her ears as she smiles and leans her forehead against my temple. "Drake, I trust you." Then, she pulls her lips to mine.

"We both do," Hunter adds. "You've never had a positive test result and she's on the pill."

His fingers graze my hip, just below Isabel's legs, and I get chills from his touch.

"She's so wet and ready for us," he says, and she whimpers as he runs his fingers through her folds. Then he's gripping our cocks again, and I lower her body down until I feel just how wet she is.

She squirms and gasps as we work our way inside her, slowly to allow her body to accommodate our sizes. But once we slide just a few inches in, Isabel lets out a breathy cry of pleasure.

"Tell me how that feels, baby," Hunter whispers against her cheek.

"It's so tight, so…full."

Her arms are clutched around my neck as I slowly start to bounce her on our cocks. She hums in my ear.

"Yes. More."

"I don't want to hurt you," I reply, my voice strained by the overall sensation of this. I feel them both so closely, we are practically one.

"You won't. I promise. Just fuck me."

Her sexy plea is enough to drive me wild. Holding her under her knees, I bounce her harder on us, letting the sound of her cries guide me. Hunter is grunting with each thrust, his lips so close to mine, I feel his breath on my face.

And just when I least expect it, he leans his head forward to kiss me, another rough, carnal kiss.

"Oh God, yes," Isabel cries out. "More. Harder."

I have to pull away from Hunter's mouth to slam her down on our cocks even harder, and she lets out a guttural cry as I do.

"I'm gonna fucking come," Hunter mumbles, barely keeping it together.

"Me too," I grunt.

"Please don't stop," she begs. "It's so good." It's not easy, but we hold our orgasms at bay long enough to feel her spasm and tremble in our arms.

But when I feel Hunter's cock start to twitch inside her, I lose it. It's too fucking hot and filthy. Soon, we're both filling her up as she slumps in my arms.

I want this moment to last forever, the three of us in a tight embrace with Isabel's petite body swelled between us. It doesn't matter that my face is starting to itch where the frosting has crusted or that Isabel is covered in chocolate, or that the kitchen is a disaster. I never feel as whole as I do when I'm with them.

The three of us are gasping for air together as Hunter and I pull out of her. He takes her from me, never letting her feet touch the floor as he carries her in a cradle hold toward the stairs. Just when I think I'm going to get left behind again, he turns toward me.

"Come shower with us," he says, and I hate my stupid fucking heart for the way it beats faster at those words.

"I'm coming," I reply, following closely behind him. Because that's what I do.

That's what I always do.

Rule #30: If it sounds like an invitation, it probably is.

Hunter

WE SHUT DOWN SALACIOUS FOR TWO NIGHTS THIS WEEK FOR renovations. One of those renovations is the addition of *quickie closets* as Garrett has deemed them. There's one on either side of the club, toward the back, so they're not obvious but just discreet enough. Of course, for the purpose of red tape and city codes, they are officially classified as changing stalls...like a dressing room.

What they really are is enough space for a little action, without having to reserve a room or change any sheets. A clever idea to boost membership, honestly.

The other renovation is turning the back two rooms into an interchangeable workshop room, and Drake is being obstinately resistant to this one. Maybe because we're only giving him two days to work on it when he fought Emerson for more. Maybe because the mention of workshops brings back too many tense memories.

It's kept Drake's mood a little grumpy lately, and I can't help but feel like that it's partly on me. So when he doesn't come home...I mean, back to the house, one night, I decide to pay him a visit. Isabel is teaching a class at the studio, and I hate being home alone.

It's past seven when I show up at the club. All the trucks are gone, and it's quiet inside. For a moment, I start to worry that he's not here. That maybe he's on another date.

After our little rendezvous in the kitchen last week, I sort of figured he was done with dating for a while. As far as I know, things with Geo didn't go well.

If he can just avoid seeing other people, stay at the house with Isabel and me, and we don't have to define this or make anything official, it would be perfect. Seamless and easy for everyone.

Yeah right.

Even I know how unfair and unlikely that is.

I just never expected all of this to get so complicated. Everything is a mess, and it's only a matter of time before our flimsy little arrangement implodes. As far as what happened last week with Drake, I'm not really mentally acknowledging that right now.

As I enter the club from the staff entrance at the back, I hear music coming from somewhere down the hall. It's a heavy rock beat, and it's blaring through the empty club. I walk cautiously down the hall toward the two back rooms, where the bulk of the renovations are happening.

Once I reach the doorway, I pause, blood pumping its way up to my cheeks, making me blush as I stare with my mouth slack. Drake is shirtless and sweaty as he lays planks of wood on the floor, pounding in each piece. He's completely oblivious to my presence, and I keep it that way as I let my eyes rake over the rippling muscles across his back and shoulders with each piece of wood he installs.

Have I always been this attracted to him or is it just happening now that I've finally allowed myself to act on it? I've always known that Drake is good-looking. He gets the attention of every girl in every bar we walk into. I'm not much shorter than him and

I don't consider myself that much uglier, but I don't have those long blond locks or charming blue eyes.

What really finishes off his attractiveness is the way he flirts, smiles bright, and gives whoever he's talking to the whole of his attention, as if they are the only person in the world who exists. I watch it, night after night, work its magic, and it's maddening.

And until last week, I never felt that charm directed at me. Until we were standing toe to toe, naked and aroused.

Suddenly, I'm remembering the taste of his neck as I kissed him. And the way those abs felt against my tongue. My dick has begun to stir in my pants. Then I remember exactly how it felt to wrap my lips around him, the swell of his cock down my throat and how badly I wanted his pleasure.

My own cock is doing a lot more than stirring now—it's throbbing and trying to talk me into walking across this room to get another taste.

So yeah, I guess that answers my question. I'm definitely fucking attracted to Drake.

Adjusting myself, so I'm not showing off a major hard-on, I cross the space and walk into his line of sight; he looks startled for a moment as he glances up at me.

"Hey!" he shouts, grabbing his phone out of his pocket to lower the music. Once it's low enough to hear each other, he kneels back on his boots and waits for me to explain why I'm here.

Why *am* I here?

"Something wrong?" he asks.

"No. You just didn't come back to the house…so I figured I'd check on you."

"Oh, yeah, I just need to get this flooring laid today, so we can finish tomorrow," he replies.

"You've got a lot of work to do. Can I help?"

His brows dance upward. "You don't have to do that."

I unbutton my shirt and peel it off my body as I avoid his gaze. "You think I'm too soft now, don't you?" I ask with a smirk.

"When's the last time you lifted a hammer, Mr. Business?" He's grinning now, a flash of white teeth making my blood pump a little faster. *There's that fucking magic.*

"Don't you worry about me."

"All right, here," he replies. "Help me lay these planks."

He tosses me a long piece of wood—the double meaning not lost on me, and I kneel next to him. Together, we make quick work of the new wood flooring. He does the cuts while I continue locking each board in place, working in comfortable silence. It takes a couple more hours, and by the end, we're both sweating.

After the floor is finished, he and I both slouch against the floor, downing the water I grabbed from the bar.

"Where's Isabel?" he asks.

"She was teaching tonight. But I'm sure she's home now."

He nods. The silence between us has grown awkward with the mention of her. It's not like we're talking about the intense threesome we had in the kitchen or how I gave him a blow job before that. I keep waiting for him to bring it up and want to talk about it, but he doesn't.

It's like a delicate explosive. We don't touch it or talk about it or even look at it because, once we do, it's going to take us all out. Instead…we keep relighting the flame.

He stands up and looks down at me with an austere expression. "I'm going to grab a shower here before heading home." Then he lingers for a moment too long, as if he's waiting for me to respond.

"Okay," I stutter, my voice coming out in a weak attempt at sounding normal. Then he shoots me one quick, loaded glance before disappearing from the room.

Suddenly, I'm overcome with nerves.

I sit on the floor for too long, playing that last moment over again and again. My mind is like a tennis court, jumping back and forth between reason and desire.

Did he really need a shower? Or was that an invitation?

No. Not everything he says to me is a come-on. How many showers has he taken in our entire friendship that meant nothing? Thousands? This is the same.

But this isn't the same. He's definitely leaving the ball in my court.

And even if he did mean for that to be an invitation, am I ready for that?

Do I want it to be an invitation? Yes.

Do I want to take it? Yes.

But what if I go in there and it's all too much, too soon, and I freak out? What will that do to him?

Then again, it won't be too much. That's just my ingrained fear talking. And the longer I sit here and play this decision over and over in my head, the lower my chances of finding out are.

If I'm wrong and it wasn't his way of asking me to come and get naked with him, then I can play it off without anything awkward happening. But there's only one way to know for sure.

In a rush, I hop off the floor and practically run to the men's locker room. To my relief, the water is still running when my shoes click against the tile floor. It's steamy as hell in here, and I shed my pants, shoes, and socks in a rush.

As I peel my boxers off, I feel a nervous shake in my hands. I can't believe I'm doing this. I can't believe this is happening. What if I'm wrong? What if I'm not ready?

This is my best friend—which means it's safe. There's no one I'd be more comfortable finding out with.

With a deep breath, I shut my brain off and step into the large shower area. He's facing the wall as the water streams over his back, and I stare for a moment at his perfect, long body, sculpted over time by muscle and manual labor. I wait for one second to see if he's going to speak, but something tells me he's holding out for me.

So…here goes nothing.

My cock is jutting straight out, hard and excited, and just as nervous as I am. Holding it in my hand, I stalk closer to him, waiting for the moment he asks what I'm doing or tells me he doesn't want me to touch him.

But that doesn't come. I reach his tall frame, extending out my hand to slide it against his wet skin. He hisses as I glide my fingers over his shoulder and around his neck. When I ease my grasp around his throat and pull his hard body against mine, wedging my hard cock between us, he smiles.

"What took you so long?"

And I distantly realize that he could mean tonight, just now in the shower, or he could mean our entire friendship.

The moment I have Drake in my grasp, my brain silences, and my body takes over. Rutting my cock against his back, I hold one of my hands around his throat as the other travels to the front to wrap around his impressive length.

We groan in unison as our cocks receive the mutual attention they crave. Drake's hands are planted against the wall as I grind myself against him. I wish I knew what it was about his body that feels so fucking good. And I've only experienced the tip of the iceberg, but with every touch, the craving for more gets even more unbearable.

"What are you doing to me?" I ask, my lips exploring the back of his neck and shoulder.

Suddenly, he spins and drags me against him, so our chests are touching as he crashes his mouth on mine. His kiss is warm and brutal as we stumble against the wall. I shove myself hard against him. It feels impossible to satisfy this need, as if I can't get enough of his skin against mine. I desperately need more.

Our kisses don't stop as we grind against each other, and it's all happening so fast. His taste, his smell, his touch, it's a kaleidoscope of bliss—him and me together—and it's making me crazy.

Grabbing the back of his neck, I growl into the space between us. "You make me fucking crazy."

"Then go fucking crazy," he replies in a low, breathless whisper, his voice like a dare.

I hook an arm under his leg, lifting it up so I can grind even closer, our cocks rubbing together in an exquisite sensation of scorching heat and delicate friction.

This is my best friend—my best fucking friend—and I want to fuck his brains out right now.

"I'm gonna come," I grunt before looking at him. "Then I'm going to take you home and fuck you while my wife watches."

He lets out a shaky breath, a long groan following as he fills the crevices between our bodies with his cum. I take his lips between mine as I unload too.

We are falling down the hill on a train with no brakes. There is nothing we can do to stop this, except for crash at the bottom. And I know, eventually, that's exactly what's going to happen.

Rule #31: Just because you're letting them have their moment, doesn't mean you should have to miss out.

Isabel

THE SOUND OF THE FRONT DOOR CLOSING DOWNSTAIRS JERKS ME out of my sleep as the romance novel I was reading hits the floor. My eyes pop open and I reach for my phone to check the time. It's late, so it must be Hunter or Drake…or both. The distant sound of muffled voices and grunts carries up the stairs. At first, I panic, thinking it's a scuffle. Especially when I hear a body slam into the wall.

Then I hear my husband's low growling command, "Get your ass upstairs."

My belly warms and my thighs clench together. I know that tone, and I know what it means when he talks like that. With a gulp, I climb out of bed and peek out through the door.

I almost let out an audible gasp at the sight. They are fused at the lips, Drake grinding Hunter into the wall midway up the stairs. There's a tussle, and then Hunter gains control. Flipping Drake around, he bends him over on the stairs, rutting against his backside, and Drake lets out a painful-sounding groan.

"Go to the guest room…now," Hunter growls. "Get yourself ready for me."

Then he shoves Drake away as they both continue their walk up the stairs. I don't know why, but something about this doesn't involve me and I don't think I want it to. In a silent rush, I run back to my bed and collapse against the pillow, closing my eyes and feigning sleep, just as Hunter walks into the room.

His footsteps pause at the door, and he stalls there for a moment. *Please don't wake me up*, I silently pray. *Just be with him alone.*

It's strange how badly I want my husband to sleep with someone else without me. But the idea of him and Drake together appeals to me so much more than the idea of being involved. Not every time, of course, but right now…I feel as if this could be the straw that breaks the camel's back. This could be the moment everything shifts. Hunter will finally accept this about himself and, with that, accept Drake fully into our relationship—where he belongs.

As Hunter steps closer to me, I force myself to look asleep. Eyes closed. Breathing even. Face relaxed.

Please don't wake me up. Please don't wake me up.

He leans down and presses his lips to my forehead. "I love you," he whispers. Then he turns off the bedside lamp and quietly disappears from the room.

My heart is hammering in my chest. I wait a few moments before opening my eyes. The room is dark and Hunter is gone. Down the hall, I hear more muffled voices, but I can't make out what they're saying.

As quiet as I can, I get out of bed and creep down the hall toward the guest room. Stopping outside the door, I listen.

"I need you," Hunter mumbles quietly.

"Then what, Hunt?"

"What do you mean then what? Since when are you worried about what happens after sex?"

Drake sighs. "Since I started fucking your wife. Since you kissed me in a dark club. Suddenly, it fucking matters a hell of a lot."

It's quiet for a while, and I close my eyes, willing them to get past this. To finally talk about it. Get over whatever is keeping all of us from the life we truly deserve—together. And part of me really wants to burst in there and tell them exactly what they need to do to get over it, but I can't. They need to do this themselves. Hunter needs to prove to Drake that he's not letting his father's voice stop him anymore. And Drake needs to prove he's ready to commit.

When it's quiet for so long I get curious, I carefully peek around the corner, catching a glimpse of them lying on the bed together. They are naked, Hunter stretched out on Drake's body, perched on his arms as he stares down at him.

"What do you want me to say?" Hunter whispers.

Another long, tense silence stretches in the darkness. Finally, Drake says in a low, husky whisper, "Nothing. Just fuck me."

I almost let out a whimper at the sound, my body growing hotter by the second. I clamp my hand over my mouth as I listen to them. Their groans, curses, gasps, and grunts. As much as I want them to talk it out, this is too hot to stop.

I peek my head back into the room and watch in the dim moonlight as Hunter crawls down Drake's body and eases Drake's cock down his own throat. Drake lets out a deep, guttural sound as he clamps a hand around Hunter's black curls and thrusts his hips upward until I hear my husband gagging.

Dipping back into the hallway, I press my back against the wall as I listen to them. It's nothing like I've ever heard before, and my body is on fire with arousal from the sound. I can't believe myself as I lower my hand to my cotton panties, slipping my fingers inside to touch myself, if only to ease some of the pain from this acute need.

With the other hand clamped around my mouth, I draw circles around my clit as I listen to the filthy noises of Hunter's wet mouth around Drake's cock.

When I hear the bed creak with their movement, I peek in

again. Again, it sounds more like a struggle than sex, grunting and movement and a fight for control. Hunter is lying on Drake again, the moonlight catching the blond in his hair as it's fanned out around him. Kneeling between his spread legs, Hunter opens a small bottle and everything is quiet for a moment until I hear Drake moan.

"You like that?" Hunter whispers.

"More," Drake replies.

"Fuck, you're so tight."

"More, Hunter."

I can hardly breathe. My skin is burning hot as I listen to whatever it is they're doing. I assume by the way Hunter is kneeling between Drake's legs that he's prepping him, and the idea of something so intimate, so…new for him is driving me wild.

"I'm ready," Drake says quietly, and I watch from the dark hallway as Drake lifts his knees and Hunter aligns his cock with Drake's tight hole and eases himself in. He does so with a long, breathless groan, and I can't help the tiny squeak that slips through my lips.

Quickly dodging the doorway, I keep my back to the wall and my hand down my panties as I wait to be caught. But I'm not. Instead, I listen as Hunter moans again, his cries mingled with his best friend's, and I know the moment he's inside him as far as he can go because Drake lets out a strangled, "Fuck."

"Goddamn, that's good," Hunter replies. His inhales are rapid and desperate sounding as if the air is being choked out of his body. "Fuck, that's so good, Drake."

"It is, isn't it? Just keep moving."

I'm losing it. This feels so wrong of me to even be listening, let alone pleasuring myself to the sound, but I can't help it. Those men are mine, both of them, and I didn't think there could be anything as good as having them both, but I was wrong. Because watching them have each other is far, far better.

The bed creaks, the headboard slamming into the wall as

Hunter fucks him with fire and passion now, thrusting to a heavy beat. And if they thought I was going to sleep through this, they are crazy.

"Stroke my cock while you fuck me," Drake commands, and I assume Hunter listens because the next thing I hear is Drake muttering broken words and phrases: *like that, yes, good, perfect, oh God.*

"I'm gonna come," someone says in a breathy exhale, and I don't know who it was because I'm too lost in my own orgasm. My head hangs back, my spine slick with sweat, as I soar toward my climax, blinded by pleasure.

When the hearing returns to my ears and my eyes finally open again, I make out the sound of their kisses and what sounds like a tender moment of whispers that I can't quite distinguish. After everything, it sounds like a private moment, so once I've caught my breath, I slink back down the hall and straight into my bathroom.

Standing at the sink after I've washed my hands and doused my face with cold water, I stare at my reflection. The girl staring back is momentarily happy, but I quickly cure her peace with all the fears and thoughts I've been keeping pushed away.

Like, what is going to happen to us if this all falls apart? What if Drake doesn't want to commit and leaves us? What if Hunter can't come to terms with his sexuality? What if losing Drake breaks our marriage because I'm not enough?

They're stupid worries, really, but I can't help myself. I'm barely used to one person loving me so much. What are the odds the three of us actually make this work and end up together? It's too good to be true. There are too many complications to worry about. Too much at stake.

I want to crawl into bed with them, lie between them and let their nearness scare away all of the worries, but I can't. Instead, I climb into bed with my own fear and fall asleep, alone.

———————

When I wake, I'm no longer alone. I hear the buzz of Hunter's electric razor as I peel my eyes open.

"Morning," he chimes with a bright smile.

Well, aren't you chipper this morning?

"Morning," I reply with a stretch. Climbing out of bed, I walk into the master bathroom and we go through our usual morning routine, like everything isn't so strange right now. After washing my hands and brushing my teeth, I pause and lean against the counter, staring at him through the mirror.

Hunter will try and stay silent through everything. He doesn't want to talk about it because talking about it means facing the truth and having to make a decision. It means change, and change is scary. But I'm not going to let my husband live in silence anymore.

"You didn't come to bed last night."

He pauses, the playful grin melting off his face. "I slept in the guest room with Drake."

I bite my lip as I stare at his reflection. Then that wicked grin tugs on the corner of his mouth again as he steps closer to me, crowding me against the sink. Staring back at me through the mirror, he leans in and kisses the side of my neck.

"But you knew that already, didn't you, Red?"

So he did hear me in the hallway.

"Maybe," I reply, my lips pressed together.

His arms snake their way around my waist, pulling me closer. "And did you like what you saw?"

"Did you?" I reply, staring at him and fighting the urge to melt to the floor. I want to hear him say it. My husband had sex with a man last night, a pretty big deal that I'm not going to let him just avoid facing.

He pauses in his attempt to make this about me watching him. Then his gaze lifts to my face in the mirror. Sincerity washes over his expression as his brow furrows and his mouth sets in a thin line. "Yes."

"What does this mean?" I ask carefully.

"It doesn't mean anything. We got carried away and—"

"Hunter," I snap, cutting him off.

He swallows, looking more nervous than confident at the moment. I turn to look at him, touching his face. The fear in his eyes guts me to my core. "This doesn't change anything about who you are. If anything, I think it just makes you more *you*."

"What about us?" he asks with trepidation in his eyes.

"I think we need to start acknowledging that there's a new *us*."

He takes a deep breath, letting his shoulders slide down away from his ears. "Is that what you want?"

I bite my lip. "Yes."

Hesitation burrows itself back into his expression as he pulls away. "I don't know, Red. I just don't know how long that can last. It's too complicated."

"So what...you want to just keep having sex with him and keeping him tethered to our marriage? Is that fair?" I ask. Distantly, I wonder if Drake is still here. Can he hear us from the guest room?

"How do we know he even wants to be in a relationship? He's literally never been in one before," he argues, and I feel him putting up a fight before he even bothers to open up to let in the truth.

"Because he's been in our relationship the entire time," I say.

"Not like this," he says, his voice getting a little too loud. "The sex is great, babe, but what if that's all it is?"

"It's not and you know it," I reply in a whisper. Moving away from Hunter, I walk toward the door.

Before I disappear from the room, he adds, "I'll think about it, okay?"

And for Hunter, that's enough. For now, at least.

Rule #32: If you don't even recognize yourself anymore, chances are you've got it bad.

Drake

"Hey, I recognize that giant, sexy blond hunk."

There's something oddly familiar about the voice behind me as I walk through the lobby of the club. So I pause and spin to see the feisty and adorable, sable-haired beauty from New Orleans.

"Silla?" I say with a smile, opening my arms for a hug.

She walks into my embrace and squeezes me tight around the middle. After pulling away, she cocks her head in my direction. "Let me guess—your boyfriend didn't tell you he invited me."

I laugh. "Okay, first of all…of course, he did. I just wasn't expecting you today. And…he's not my boyfriend."

She winks. "Sure. The three of you had a good time in that room *I* rented."

"You gave me the key," I reply enthusiastically.

"I know. I know. I'm a good influence."

I place an arm behind her back. "Come on. I'll take you to the workshop space. We finished it this week." Waving to the hostess, I guide Silla through the curtain into the main room and then off to the right hallway, where the back two rooms have been joined as one large room, something we can flip between rentable rooms and space for classes.

"Oh, very impressive," Silla says with a smile as I show her the space. We erected a small stage at the front and enough space for tables, which is how it's set up tonight. She walks up to the low platform to check out the ropes we hung for the demonstration.

"Look at you, Mr. Construction Man. So…have you been practicing Shibari with your boyfriend since our class?"

I blush. "Again, not my boyfriend. And no, we have not."

"Oh, come on…" she whines, her head hanging back. "You guys were so good!"

With a laugh, I shake my head. "We weren't that good."

"Babe, I could watch him tie you up all day. That shit was hot. Or better yet," she says, looking excited. "You tie him up."

"I don't think he would enjoy that," I reply, leaning against one of the tables.

"Oh, he *needs* to be tied up," she says with a laugh. I like Silla. It's just easy being around her. It's not often I'm in the company of people I'm not actively trying to fuck…or who aren't trying to fuck me. Of course, she was at first, but the moment we established that I was sort of entangled, she let off.

"So…" she says in a light tone.

"So…?" I reply.

"So did you end up losing…or did you end up gaining?"

My brow furrows quizzically as I stare at her. "I don't follow."

"Last time we talked, you were too afraid to get your sexy bits all tangled up with your friends because you were afraid of losing them, and *I* told you that you were just as likely to gain them. And you may not know this about me, but I'm very wise…"

My light chuckle echoes through the empty room as she smiles that big bright smile at me.

"Clearly," I joke.

"So which one was it?"

My smile starts to wane as I think about it. Which one is it? I didn't exactly lose them, but have I gained them? As I think back to everything that's happened since I first met Silla, it's a little daunting to believe.

"Oh…I know what that face means. Spill."

It feels pointless putting up a fight, so I give in and I tell her everything. Crazy that this woman just walked in the club and I've known her for all of like two hours total, but she's easy to talk to and I need *someone* to talk to about this stuff.

By the end, her eyes are wide, and she's staring at me for a long time before finally saying something. "So…do you want to be with them? In a committed, poly relationship with both of them?"

"Yeah." The answer slips out of my mouth easily. As easily as breathing. Because I do. And I thought the idea of committing would be daunting and scary, but with them, it's not. It feels seamless. I'm not losing anything and gaining everything.

"Do you think she does?"

"Yeah," I say, unable to hold back the slight grin that stretches across my face. Isabel and I have bonded in a way we can't undo now. I need her in a way I can't walk away from. I can't go back.

"But does he?"

That answer doesn't fall out of my mouth so easily. It's more complicated with Hunter. It's not that he doesn't want to be with me. It's that he has so many more mountains to climb before he can rightfully claim that he wants *both* of us. And until he does, we're stuck where we are.

"Okay…follow-up question. How long are you willing to wait for him to decide?"

"I don't know," I mutter.

"It sounds to me like he needs an ultimatum because, right now, you're giving him everything he wants without asking for anything in return. One of you is going to have to make him decide because neither of you deserve to wait for someone to admit to loving you."

Well, damn. The girl has a point.

And I wish it were that easy, but I'm too afraid that if we push Hunter, he'll fly off. Like approaching a bird you're trying to catch. Move too fast and it's gone.

What would that mean for Isabel? It's not exactly a risk I'm willing to take.

God, listen to me, trying to talk someone into a committed relationship. Who am I? Because I *used to be* a scoundrel. I used to only want to fuck, but now I want more. Because these two are the exception. They've always been the exception.

Noticing me deep in thought, Silla approaches me and places a hand on my arm. "I'm going to leave you with those big questions swirling around in that beautiful head of yours. But you know…if it doesn't work out, we could always use you at the Crescent City Club. Just a thought."

I give her a tense smile and nod. "Thanks."

With that, she heads toward the door. In the distance, I hear Hunter as he finds her with a warm, business greeting. I hear them say my name, but I stay in the room alone for a few minutes.

I just need some more time to think.

———————

Every Thursday night, the owners of the Salacious Players' Club meet up at the bar for a little downtime, no business allowed. I always tag along because…of course I do.

Tonight, I'm sitting between Hunter and Isabel at the table, staring at my beer with too many thoughts in my head. Everyone around me is laughing and smiling, and I hate that I'm not myself.

Across from me, I can feel Garrett's fiancée, Mia, staring at me in concern. After she and I got over the awkwardness of finding out Garrett used my name to catfish her on her cam girl app, thus making our first encounter a little…tense, we've actually become pretty good friends. Mostly because she's become the resident crazy-idea girl at the club. Which means I'm the first person she comes to when she has an idea she needs brought to life.

Drake, can we put a hot tub in the VIP room?

Drake, can you make one of the rooms look like an outdoor hiking trail?

Drake, can you build me rafters to hang from so I can masturbate in midair?

She's fucking crazy, but I like her. Except for right now, because she looks like she's reading my mind, and I don't like that.

Normally, I'd be at the bar, lingering around any single females who look like they need company, but, of course, I can't do that tonight. And I can't tell anyone why.

"Everything all right, Drake?" Garrett asks from across the table. His arm is draped around Mia's shoulders as she sips on her fruity red drink. "You're not usually sitting with us for this long." He smiles as he makes a joke, and I shrug it off with a forced laugh.

But what the fuck do I say? I may or may not be exclusively fucking my best friend and his wife. Although not *really* exclusive because we're just not talking about it.

Yeah…that response just rolls off the tongue.

"Guess I'm just not in the mood tonight," I reply, which makes not only him laugh but the others around us. Everyone except for Maggie, who's too engrossed in her phone to care.

Well, her and the couple sitting next to me, who are starting to look a bit too uncomfortable to join in the fun.

"Drake not in the mood?" Garrett laughs. "I call bullshit. My guess is you're seeing someone."

"A little birdie told me *someone* had a date with Geo last week," Charlie chimes in from the end of the table. She's wearing a cheeky smile as she leans on her elbows.

"Oooh," Mia replies.

Dammit. Now they're all looking at me.

"It was one date," I reply.

"Uh-huh…" Garrett adds.

I catch Hunter in my periphery and he's squeezing his glass so hard in his hand, it looks like he might shatter it.

"You two are being awfully quiet. What do you know?" Garrett asks, and Isabel replies with a shy smile and a shoulder shrug.

"We don't know anything," she says, and suddenly, I realize just how awkward all of this is, and everyone can tell. We might as well be wearing giant *something is up* signs.

Now everyone is staring, but with crooked brows and scrutinizing eyes. There's a part of me that wants to just blurt out this confession inside me, but I can't.

Honestly, why are we even keeping this secret? This is literally a group of people who have some of the kinkiest lives. Garrett's fucking his stepsister. Emerson is in a very serious relationship with his son's ex-girlfriend. Not one of them would even bat an eye if we told them we're having dirty threesomes every night. Fuck, they probably assume we've been doing that this whole time. So why do I suddenly feel like a dirty secret? When the conversation finally changes and the squinting eyes shift away from me, I glance sideways at Hunter to find him watching me. I clench my jaw before I toss back the rest of my drink.

I suddenly need to be away from here. So I don't make an announcement as I set down my glass and rise from the table. Isabel watches me, though, with a look that cracks my tough exterior.

"I'm just going to the bathroom," I say gently as she smiles at me.

Seriously, if anyone was paying attention and saw the way she was just staring at me, the cat would be way the fuck out of that bag. But they're not and I'm still irritable, so I march with a scowl toward the restroom at the back of the bar.

The entire time I'm fuming...about what, I don't even know. Silla's words got into my head. Not to mention, Hunter and I fucked, like *really fucked*—*twice*—three days ago, but we're just not talking about it. So yeah...I might be a little irritable now.

Yeah, yeah, yeah...maybe this is a taste of my own medicine.

How many people have I fucked and avoided? Never called them, although they gave me their number. Blatantly flirted with *someone else* in front of them. Kept them waiting for a commitment I would never give them.

But I'm not just anybody to Hunter. I'm his best friend—which at this point sounds too trivial of a word for what we are. And what we did in the guest room that night was not a meaningless hookup. It can't even be categorized as fucking, really. It was... God, I hate myself for admitting this, or even thinking it, but what we did that night...was making love.

I've never been so close to another person in my life and the sex we had was in another league—no, on another planet, and not even close to being the same thing I've done hundreds of times with countless strangers.

The only thing that could have made that night better would have been having Isabel there with us. Instead of lurking silently in the hallway, which is clearly where she was.

I'm washing my hands when Hunter inevitably walks in, like I knew he would. And just like I knew he would, he flips the lock on the public bathroom door, buying us at least a minute before someone starts banging to get in.

"That was uncomfortable..." he mumbles as he closes the distance between us. He reaches for me, but I pull away and his playful smile quickly fades. "What did I do?"

"How long are we going to do this, Hunter?"

"Do what?" he asks, which makes me even angrier. How dare he even act like that's a question.

"This!" I snap. "This secret thing...this undefinable thing where we fuck each other and act like it's nothing."

"Oh, so you want to be done now? Then go ahead, Drake. Go pick up some chick at the bar if that's really what you want."

My eyes roll as I turn away. "That's not what I want."

"Then what do you want?" he snaps, somehow taking the reins of this conversation as if *I* owe him something.

"I want to talk about what happened the other night. I want you to admit that you're bisexual and that you're okay with that."

He scoffs, looking offended, as if I just accused him of being exactly what he is.

"I want you to tell me what the hell is going on, Hunter. If you want me to be with only you and Isabel, I will."

"Really? You'll be exclusive? No other people?"

An annoyed huff slips through my lips. "Yeah, believe it or not, but I can stop being such a man whore for you."

"You know I didn't mean it like that."

"Yes, you did, but it's okay. Because for our entire lives, I've followed you. I've stayed by your side, never gave *anyone* more of my time because that's what I wanted. So, now that you've really got me...*all* of me, what are you going to do?"

His nostrils flare as he stares at me, looking both nervous and frustrated, too many demons inside him to let him be.

"You realize this is more complicated than that, right, Drake? Isabel and I are married. It's not like we can just..."

I laugh. "Just what? Start fucking your best friend and expect him to commit only to you without anything in return."

"Drake, stop."

"No. This is fucking bullshit. I get it. You don't want me screwing other people and screwing your wife at the same time, but that doesn't mean I belong to you either." My blood is boiling, and I feel ready to explode. I feel myself getting cornered in a scenario that leaves me feeling as if I'm somehow wrong for being angry in the first place.

"Then tell me what to do," he says, looking like he might surrender. And for a moment, I start to feel bad for him, my broken, scared friend. When Hunter struggles, he fights. I know this about him, but right now, what I need him to fight for is me.

I don't answer for a minute because...I shouldn't have to tell him. Isabel is so much better at this than me. She knows exactly what to say and how to get him to meet her halfway, but I don't.

"Tell me what to do, Drake," he says a little louder this time.

Looking down, I let the realization wash over me. I could give Hunter exact instructions and put the words in his mouth for him, but then what? He's not going to change if I do it for him.

I hate what this means. It fucking *kills* me. But Silla was right. Hunter is living behind a wall, one that keeps him safe without being vulnerable. And until he comes out from behind that wall, he's never going to make room for me in his life. Not like that.

I've gone from being his best friend to his fuck buddy.

There's a bang on the door. If we're not careful, we're going to draw suspicion. So I unbolt the door as I stare at Hunter. He's still waiting for an answer, but I have nothing for him. This part is on him.

"I don't know," I say as I open the door, and a man we don't know passes me. "Just fix this."

And with that, I leave the bathroom. Then, with a quick goodbye to the table—and a worried-looking Isabel—I leave the bar.

But it's not far enough. Something tells me even getting a new apartment and a new job still wouldn't be far enough to escape the damage we've done.

Rule #33: Fix it.

Hunter

THE WORKSHOP IS FULL. IT FILLED UP IN MINUTES ACTUALLY, AND we already have requests for more, which is great, but as I stand at the back of the room and watch Drake talking to Silla, I find it hard to focus on the workshop. Instead, I'm brooding, wondering if I can offer Silla a place here at Salacious full-time, even if it means I have to watch her flirt with and befriend the man I love.

I know that even though he's wearing that bright, flirtatious smile, he's not happy. Not really.

Isabel keeps glancing my way. She's watching my reaction. I don't know, maybe she's waiting for me to break.

Fuck, maybe I'm waiting for me to break.

Ever since the little fight in the bathroom on Thursday, Drake hasn't spoken to me much. Nothing aside from work-related conversations about the workshop tonight.

Isabel hasn't spoken to me much either. I'm single-handedly fucking up the two most important relationships in my life and I don't know how to fix it. He just said *fix it* as if it's that easy. As if I know what the hell to do now. He wants me to come out as bisexual. Okay, will that really make things better? Isn't that big step for me to decide? Am I really bisexual, though, because so far, he's the only man I've ever wanted to put my mouth on. So what does it matter to him if I come out?

Except, I know that it matters. It matters because until I accept who I am, I can't accept him. Until I can undo all the hateful, ignorant shit my father ingrained in me, Drake will never truly trust me.

Isabel glances my way again as if she can read my mind.

"Hey, Iz, come here," Drake calls, pulling her attention away from me. She crosses the room, quietly discussing something with the other two while the room continues to fill up and the patrons start taking their places at the tables. The workshop is set to begin in just a few minutes.

Every few minutes, Isabel glances my way cautiously, then back to them to continue their conversation. With a tight-lipped expression, she nods. I stand stoically as she leaves their conversation and heads toward me.

"Silla wants me to help demonstrate," she whispers carefully.

"With Drake?"

She nods, watching me with a sheepish look in her eyes.

"Sure. I think that's a great idea," I lie. As if watching them onstage again, is going to make this already tense situation any better.

"Okay." Staying glued in her spot for a moment, I notice the way she chews her lip and watches me, as if she's waiting for me to say more. "You know…if you want to come up there instead of Drake…"

"No," I cut her off. "I'm terrible at it. Drake's better."

"It's okay that you're bad at it. We're supposed to be learning."

"You two look better together anyway," I reply, and her breath hitches as she stares at me.

"Isabel, you ready?" Silla calls, but it takes my wife a few long moments to tear her eyes away from me. Finally, she rushes to the stage with Silla and Drake and plasters on the same fake smile that Drake is wearing.

From the back of the room, I stand silently, staring with a vacant expression. Unlike the last time, watching Drake and Isabel touch each other does nothing but make me feel empty. They're not excluding me. I'm excluding myself.

In the midst of my internal pity party, a deep voice whispers from behind me, "I'd call this a success." I turn to find Emerson Grant surveying the crowd. A sense of pride swells in my chest at his words.

"Yeah. People are asking for more too."

"I bet they are. You somehow managed to put this together quickly. You should be proud, Hunter."

"I am," I reply, turning toward him, my words coming out flat.

"Then why are you sulking?"

"I'm not." Even I hear how quickly I answered that.

He turns his attention to Isabel and Drake, giving her a quick, warm smile, which she politely returns from the front of the room. Then, he looks at me.

"Why is he up there and not you?"

"He's better at it," I reply.

With a nod, Emerson frowns, a crease forming between his brows. "Well, they do look good together."

I force myself to swallow, seething jealousy and profound attraction warring inside me. "Yes, they do."

"I'd lose my mind if Charlotte were that intimate with someone else—especially Drake."

I flinch, my head spinning toward them. "Emerson," I snap. The couple closest to us turns our way, but Emerson just smiles at them, and they lose interest in our quiet conversation.

"There's nothing going on between them if that's what you're implying," I whisper in an almost-silent, seething tone.

But he doesn't even bother to look skeptical because the look on his face says it all—he knows. With a flat, unimpressed roll of his eyes, he pulls me into the hallway. I expect him to argue, but he doesn't. "Drake said something strange to me this morning," he says, adjusting his tie, and I tense. "He asked if I had any other projects for the club that needed to be completed before the end of the month."

I force myself to swallow without looking surprised or worried—both of which I am.

"Do you know if he has plans of leaving or taking on another contract?" he asks when I don't respond.

"No."

A round of applause accompanied by *oohs* and *aahs* fill the room behind me, and I turn in time to see Isabel, once again, wrapped around Drake; this time, her hands bound above her head. They're smiling at each other, intensity coursing between their stares.

"I'd hate to lose him," Emerson says quietly, and I turn to face him with a furrow in my brow. He cracks a smile. "I know you all think I'm not the biggest Drake fan, but that's only because he tends to push my buttons more often than not, but he does good work. And I like having him around. Even if I'm the asshole who doesn't say it enough. I should do a better job of making it known."

With that, he just…walks away, and I'm left here standing speechless. I'm sure he has no idea why those words hit so hard, but I can't help but be annoyed at just how right he sounds.

Walking back into the room, I watch the rest of the demonstration, and Silla comes around to each table, instructing the various couples and groups. Isabel and Drake do the same, their eyes finding each other more often than not, and I don't see the same tension in their faces that I did before. The same tension I feel now.

I wish I could erase all of the stubborn demons making this so hard on me. I wish I could be exactly what they need, a man able to accept who he is without struggles, a man unafraid to tell the world he loves two people and wants them both. But what they don't understand is that my flaws aren't my choice; they are ingrained in the DNA of my very existence. The things that keep us apart are woven into who I am as a person and if I unravel those things, I don't know what will be left of me.

And just like that, the solution hits me.

It slams into me like a tidal wave, knocking me to the bottom of the ocean. Because now I know how to fix this, and it means removing myself from the equation.

I asked Drake to drive Isabel home, feigning a headache. She offered to come with me, but they were smiling and having fun with Silla and the rest of the team, and I couldn't bear the idea of ending that. Plus, I needed to get home first. It would be easier this way.

As I'm standing in my closet, I think about my dad. And a really distinct memory pops into my head. I was somewhere between childhood and adulthood, maybe twelve. It was almost a good day, when he was a little more sober than the rest of the days and both he and my mother could stand the sight of each other. They took me to the beach on my first day of summer vacation, and I remember thinking that that was the day everything was going to be better. If I just didn't make him mad, he wouldn't have any reason to hit me. If my mom could just keep smiling, they wouldn't split, and she wouldn't leave. If everything stayed the way it was *that* day, then everything would be fine.

We splashed in the waves, and I smiled as I watched them kissing in the water. It was a moment of perfect peace.

In the distance, a couple parked a pair of towels on the sand, not too far from ours. And the moment they unpacked their umbrella, a sense of doom settled over my heart. I mentally begged them not to do *anything*. Don't touch each other. Don't talk too comfortably. And definitely, *please don't kiss.*

Those two men had no idea they were about to ruin the perfection of my day. Although I guess my father was the one who ruined it—I realize that now. But to my prepubescent brain, it was their fault.

One look at them, and my father knew. It was enough to have him barking at us to pack up our things. Enough to make him mutter something ugly in their direction before leaving. Enough to make me promise myself at that moment, no matter what, I will *never ever* let myself be like those men.

I choked on that promise every day of my life. Even after he died twelve years ago. Even after that perfect day turned into another daily nightmare with his beer breath and belt bruises. That stupid fucking promise became my curse.

My stupid childhood perception stayed with me as I aged, like an ill-fitting suit that imbedded itself into my psyche. I can't just un-feel the way I felt as a child. But I can fix it now.

Because I do love Drake. Even if I can't say it out loud yet. I love that man as much as I love my wife, and I should have been telling him that all along. Instead, I've held him prisoner to my love—but that ends now.

I don't even know what time it is when they finally walk through the door, but I greet them in the living room with my bags packed. Isabel freezes on the doormat and stares at me with wide eyes when she notices the duffel bag at my feet.

Drake takes a moment longer to realize what's going on.

My throat aches with the emotion I've spent so long stifling. But it's one look at her face that finally makes it sting so bad, I nearly break.

"Where are you going?" she murmurs, tears already filling her beautiful green eyes.

All right. Here goes nothing.

"I'm going to stay at Maggie's for a while. She has a guest room for me."

Isabel's face contorts into shock and confusion, those sweet freckles on her cheeks lost to the blush of anger. "What? Why?"

Drake stands stoically behind her, a vacant stare in his eyes as he waits for my answer.

"You told me to fix it," I say to him. "And I realized that

the only part that's broken is me. I'm the one with shit to work through and demons to fight, and until I can do that, I can't give either of you what you need from me."

Isabel's nostrils are flaring at me now as she fights the urge to cry. "So you're just going to leave?"

"I don't think I can do this while we're together. I want you two to just be happy together and give me the time I need to figure this out."

"Are we…separating?" she asks with a whimper.

The fear in her voice guts me. "No, Red. We're not separating. I'm coming back."

"Fuck that," Drake snaps, stepping farther into the house, starting to pace as he throws a finger in my direction. "This isn't fixing it."

"Yes, it is, Drake."

"No, it's not, dammit," he barks. "You're running away."

"I'm running away? Tell me the truth," I reply, glaring at him. "Were you thinking of leaving Salacious? Were you thinking of going to another club? Another state?"

When he doesn't answer, it's pretty obvious.

Isabel replies with a gasp. "What?"

"Emerson told me you talked to him this morning. I bet Silla offered you a job in New Orleans. I know you better than you know yourself, Drake."

"You're leaving?" she whispers.

He shoots her a sympathetic expression, shoulders slumped and mouth turned down. "No. I'm not leaving."

She lets it all go and lets out one gentle gasp before the anguish takes over and she begins to cry in earnest. Walking into the kitchen, she keeps her back to me as she sobs into her hands, and it hurts so much that I hate myself for all the damage I've done.

I can't touch her. If I do, I'll crumble. Right now, she needs me to be strong. "I'm doing this so I can be better for you. Both of you. I had no idea when I asked for what I did that it would come to this, but I can't undo it and we can't pretend it never happened. So either I can figure myself out and come back to give you both what you deserve, or we can keep going the way we are and you two end up being the ones hurt."

She sobs again, grabbing a tissue from the counter and pressing it into her eyes. Drake is watching her, too, from the living room, and I give him one pleading glance. Which he immediately understands because, a moment later, he's going to her. Placing a hand on her back, he comforts her. She doesn't move into his arms or acknowledge him. She just cries.

"How long?" Drake asks.

"A couple months. Maggie said I could stay as long as I need to."

Isabel cries louder.

There's nothing else I can say. I've already said everything I need to, but now, I need to make good on my promise to fix this. Which means I need to leave.

Rule #34: When all you're left with is memories, memories will do.

Isabel

LONG AFTER THE FRONT DOOR CLOSES, I STAND IN THE KITCHEN and let the devastation settle in like a drug. I really shouldn't be surprised. I knew we couldn't keep going like this. Hunter avoided so much for so long. We couldn't keep going the way we were.

But I never saw this coming. I never expected him to leave us.

Drake stands behind me for a while, but then he finally pulls away to pour himself a drink.

I can't bring myself to stand here any longer, so I drag myself up the stairs. Numbly, I remove my clothes, and I stare at his shirt, a T-shirt he must have worn this morning. With tears brimming, I pull it over my head and let his scent engulf me. Then, I crawl into my empty bed, sticking to my side as the tears continue to fall, staining my pillow.

I replay every moment that led to this one. From all the way back to ten years ago when Hunter approached me in the library. I insert myself in that memory, trying to remember exactly how I felt in that moment.

"How is it?" his dark voice whispers through the shelves. I'm leaning against the wall, already halfway through the book I pulled from the shelf an hour ago. It's not the one I wanted to find, but it's similar and just as good.

"What?" I reply. His dark brown eyes are watching over the top of a row of romance novels. He looks like trouble with those dark circles and gaunt cheekbones. I tense as he continues down the aisle, coming out to stand in front of me. I've seen this guy. He lingers around the corner a lot with that tall, cute boy, but there's no sign of his friend now.

Every day, they say hello to me. And I keep waiting for one of them to make a move.

"How's your book? I've never seen someone so invested in a book before."

"You don't come to the library much, do you?" I ask.

The smile that stretches across his face scares me. It's the kind of smile that I'd do very bad things for. A smile that shines like a warning. But as it fades and his gaze settles on my face, I feel as if I'm swimming in his attention. It's not predatory or frightening. It's more like awe and appreciation.

"No, I don't come here often, but now I'm thinking I should."

"To pick up girls?" I reply, trying not to blush.

"To talk to you."

"That's a bad plan," I reply.

He looks shocked for a moment as he fidgets in his stance. "Why?"

"Because I come here to read, and if you bother me while I'm reading—no matter how cute you are—I'm going to really dislike you."

He bites his bottom lip as he grins again. "You think I'm cute?"

I let out a giggle, and one of the librarians glances sternly our way.

"So let's go somewhere else," he says, and I roll my eyes. If he's trying to just get into my pants, I'm going to be disappointed. I mean…I get it. He's a guy in his twenties. Of course he wants in my pants. But is it too much to ask that he also be interested in me as a person?

"No thanks," I reply, pulling my book back up to my face.

"Okay, fine. Then, pick out a book for me."

I giggle again—what has gotten into me? "For what?"

"For me to read…of course. I won't bother you anymore. I'm just going to sit over here and enjoy a good book."

"You're relentless, aren't you?"

"I generally get what I want."

I heave a sigh. "If I give you my number, will you let me finish this book?"

"Gladly."

"Here," I mutter, pulling out my phone. "Give me your number." When he does, I send him a quick text with nothing but a red heart emoji and a stack of books.

"I'm gonna save you in here as Red, but can I have your actual name?"

"Isabel."

"Isabel…" he says, trying it out on his tongue.

"And yours?" I ask.

"Hunter, your future boyfriend. No…your future husband."

This time I laugh so loud, I get an angry shh from the librarian, so I cover my mouth.

"Why are you laughing?"

"It's a bit overkill, don't you think?"

"No," he replies, looking offended. Then he leans in and changes my perception of everything. Drowning out everything around me, he whispers, "I don't normally do this. I don't talk to women or hit on random girls in libraries. I don't even like to start conversations, but I would do all of that just to get to know you. I would do anything to get to know you. That's not overkill. That's fate."

I'm yanked from the memory by the sound of Drake ascending the stairs. As he passes by my open door, I call out to him.

"Sleep in here. Please."

His steps freeze in the hallway. A moment later, the light goes off as he presses open the bedroom door. Quietly, he creeps into the room.

"Are you sure?" he whispers.

I don't answer. I just reach for him.

Without a word, he slips off his clothes and crawls into my bed next to me. I press myself against him, using his arm as a pillow and breathing in his familiar scent. It's not Hunter, but it's literally the closest thing I have at the moment. It's enough to make the tears dry up.

"He's coming back," he whispers. "He couldn't stay away from you if he tried."

"What if he doesn't?" I ask, my voice shaking.

"That's impossible, Isabel. You are his entire world. You never saw the way he changed for you, but I did. He did *everything* he could to deserve you."

"And now he's doing this to deserve you," I reply quietly into the space between his neck and shoulder. Drake stiffens.

"I never should have complicated things. This is all my fault."

My head snaps back as I stare up at him. "You only did what he asked you to."

"I pushed him. I did certain things…just to make him jealous. I knew what I was doing, and I knew he wasn't ready."

"Don't blame yourself."

"I guess while you were his whole world…he was mine."

My heart splinters as I stare at him. My sweet, open-hearted Drake. He has spent his entire life loving a man obsessed with someone else—someone *I've* had. How does he not hate me?

Because this is just who Drake is. He might be too giving with his body and his attention, but his heart has always been loyal.

With absolutely no motive in mind, I wrap my hand around the back of his neck and pull his mouth to mine, a simple, closed-mouth kiss, just so I can breathe him in. When our mouths part, he kisses my forehead and pulls me closer. We lie like that until sleep takes us, and my dreams pick up where my memory in the library left off.

Rule #35: Don't be afraid of change. It usually grows back.

Two months later
Drake

I THINK MY DICK MIGHT ACTUALLY FALL OFF. HOW LONG CAN ONE person go without sex before that becomes a real concern? I'm being dramatic, I know, but these past two months have been rough. And not just because I have not stuck my dick into anything other than my fist, but because a little piece of my life is missing.

Okay, a big piece.

Isabel and I have fallen into a comfortable routine. For the most part, I think she's doing okay. I work all day, finishing up jobs to fill the time between when Salacious needs me. She teaches each night. The only time we really see each other is when she walks in the door at nine after she's closed up her studio.

We make small talk, eat something together, and then crawl into her bed, where I hold her against me until she falls asleep—sometimes crying, although not as much anymore.

I've only seen Hunter twice at the club, and we didn't speak to each other. It was in passing as I was fixing the lock on one of the doors. I can only imagine the whole Salacious crew is onto us, although if they're curious, they haven't asked me.

And from what I know, he's only been checking in with Isabel over the phone. She hasn't seen him at all.

I know how hard his absence is on me—I can only imagine how much harder it is on her. The holidays are quickly approaching, and our patience is running thin. He needs to make a move soon, before we all lose our minds.

It's a late Sunday afternoon when I come in from the gym, tossing my duffel bag at the bottom of the stairs and heading toward the kitchen, when I hear sniffling upstairs. I pause, my hand on the banister as I listen in the silence to see if my ears were playing tricks on me. Then, I hear it again.

Fuck.

Taking two steps at a time, I bound up the stairs and follow the sound until I'm standing in the doorway of the master bathroom. My mouth is hanging open as I stare at Isabel. She's standing in front of the mirror, tears streaming over her cheeks, and her hair about two feet shorter than it was this morning.

"I just wanted a change, but I hate it," she sobs.

Her normally long, bright copper hair is now stacked in loose waves around her shoulders. I'll admit the change is jarring, and it's taking some getting used to, but it's still fucking gorgeous.

"Umm…" I stammer, and her face squeezes in anguish as she starts to cry again. Fuck, I'm bad at this. I've never been in a long-term relationship in my life. And suddenly, I was thrust into one two months ago.

I wasn't ready for all of this domesticity. I used to kick girls out before dawn, and now my towel is hanging from the hook next to hers and my clothes are no longer sitting alone in their own closet. This whole thing is very new to me.

"Don't cry…" I say, going toward her with open arms. "You look beautiful, Iz."

She lets me hold her, but her heart's not into it. "You're just saying that. You hate it."

"What?" I snap. Then I spin her so she can see herself. "Look at that stunning woman. Yes, the change is different, but you're fucking crazy if you think you don't look hot as fuck right now."

Her shoulders slump. "What if he hates it? What if he misses my long hair?"

The pain in her voice radiates, slicing through me. I can't stand it. I need to fix it.

Leaning down, I open the bottom drawer, rifling through the random things Hunter left behind until I find what I'm looking for. I knew he had one. Quickly, I pull it out, along with its long black cord. As I plug it in, she watches me curiously.

Checking the settings, I set them to something in the middle—not *too* short. Then, I quickly flip it on and run the clippers along the middle of my head.

Isabel lets out an ear-piercing shriek. "Drake! What are you doing?" she cries as most of my golden-blond locks fall to the floor.

"It's just hair, babe. And I just decided that I need a change too. So…let's both look different when he comes back."

Her hand is pressed over her gaping mouth as she watches me buzz the length from my head. I can't remember the last time my hair was this short. It was before Isabel was around, so this is all she knows. It's not buzzed down to the scalp; I left a few inches. And I love the way it feels as I run my hand over it. Refreshing and light.

It only takes me a few minutes to get it all, and when I have as much as I can, she helps me with the back. Finally, we're left with a mess on the floor and two entirely new people staring at their reflections.

Her tears have dried, and I catch her actually cracking a smile. "I like it," she says.

Looking in the mirror, I assess the damage. Not bad. I think I like the longer hair more, but the change feels good.

"Yeah, me too."

Our smiles begin to fade as we stare at each other, and as her expression grows in hunger, I try to stifle down the lust that's starting to build inside me. I won't cross that line with Isabel, not without him.

But with the way she's looking at me right now…

Without warning, she turns toward me, grabbing my face and pulling me down for a hungry kiss. Gathering her up by the waist, I kiss her back, my tongue sliding between her lips and rubbing softly against hers. She hums breathlessly into my mouth.

"Drake," she gasps, and I quickly lift her by her thighs, placing her on the bathroom counter. Her legs wrap around my waist, rubbing herself against the already stiff erection in my gym shorts. My fingers tangle in her now shorter hair as I kiss her deeply, her hands running along my sides.

When our lips part, she reaches for the hem of my shirt, and I stiffen. "Baby…we can't."

"Yes, we can," she whispers.

God, who am I? Talking a woman out of sex? A woman I want more than anything.

She's grinding herself against me, moaning from the friction, clearly as horny and needy as I'm feeling. Fuck, I'm not strong enough for this.

"Isabel…" I groan, trying to pull away.

Suddenly, she takes my face in her hands and pulls me closer, so we are inches apart. "We matter, Drake. You and me. He left me with you for a reason, and it's not because he trusts you *not* to fuck me."

"I don't want to be the kind of guy who fucks his best friend's girl," I reply.

She pulls away and stares at me with a hint of surprise on her face. "I thought you said I was *your* girl."

"You are…" And suddenly it all makes sense. My entire life I've told myself what a scoundrel I am, and it was a self-fulfilled prophecy, living my life between the sheets because that's what I thought I deserved. But how long have I wanted these two people and I *never* acted on it. Never.

And suddenly, I don't want Isabel for the same reasons I did a second ago. It's not for the sex, but for so much more.

Closing the space between us, I pull her face up to mine, pressing my forehead to hers as I look her in the eye. "I love you, Isabel."

She lets out a tiny gasp as her grip tightens around me. Then, her eyes gather moisture as she nods and whispers in return, "I love you too."

My mouth finds hers again, hungry for the connection, and she answers my kiss with one of her own, potent and heavy with emotion. This time, when she tugs on my shirt, I let her slide it over my body, breaking our kiss only as long as we have to, to take our clothes off.

When she reaches for the waistband of my shorts, I let her tug them down, and I quickly lift her enough to slide hers off until we're naked together. And it's not about sex or being horny or even about my dick. As I slide between her legs, pressing into the slick heat, it's about so much more than sex.

It's about us, like she said. Our bodies connecting because our souls are aching for it. I slide easily inside Isabel, letting her moans of pleasure fill me with satisfaction.

"God, I love you so much." I moan against her mouth.

"Baby," she cries, wrapping her arms around my neck and holding me close. Hooking an arm under her knee, I move even farther inside her. Surrendering myself to her, I let her take me as far as I can go, sliding into the depths of more than just her body. And I stay there, buried in her warmth with her heartbeat pounding against mine.

Then, I ease out and slam back in again, hard enough to make her squeal and writhe like a cat in heat, desperate for more.

Taking my jaw in her hands again, she levels her hard eyes on my face. "Fuck me, and don't stop."

So I do. Like riding a wave together, I pound into her at a rapid cadence that has us both moaning and growling into each other's mouths. We are coursing down a river as one. Our muffled cries echo against every surface of this bathroom, and I wish I could fuck her forever, but holding this rhythm is going to be impossible.

Before I lose it, I pull away from her kiss to gaze down at where her beautiful body is taking mine. She leans back, watching me stare at where my cock disappears inside her.

"I want to come inside you so fucking bad," I say in a needy grunt.

"Fill me up, Drake. Mark me as yours."

Goddamn. A thrill runs up my spine at her words, and my hips start working on their own, thrusting so hard, she nearly hits her head on the mirror. With one hand planted on the counter, she uses the other to rub nimble circles around her clit. The movement of her fingers sends me over the edge.

"You are mine," I bellow, fucking her wildly as she screams. "My girl."

I know the moment her orgasm hits because her spine goes rigid and her thighs squeeze like a vise grip on my hips. And the sounds coming out of her mouth are a jumbled mess of sounds and grunts.

I bury my cock in her one more time before it begins to pulse, pleasure gutting me as I spill myself inside her, throbbing for so long, I'm afraid it will never stop.

We're left panting and sweating, and I stay sheathed for as long as I can. I never want to leave her body, but I smile against her shoulder, knowing that I've officially marked her now. I'm not taking my friend's girl. I'm taking mine—no, *ours*.

Rule #36: It's never as hard as you think it's going to be.

Hunter

RAY THOMAS SCOTT
FATHER—HUSBAND—BROTHER
DIED, AGE 62

ACCORDING TO HIS HEADSTONE, HE WAS JUST A FATHER—NO signifiers to elaborate on what kind. I sure as fuck hope mine at least calls me a loving one.

Maggie suggested I come here, for closure, I think. She suggested I write him a letter or say a few words to express what it is that I would say to him if he were alive. But to be honest, I have a hard enough time opening up to living people, so the idea of speaking to a piece of stone placed over a rotting corpse and some dirt is a little bit much for me.

So just sitting here will do. Sitting here and thinking.

Thinking about how I was crazy to assume two months would be enough to undo all the damage this man has done. It was a start, though. Enough of a break to make me realize that I can't live like this anymore.

But this time alone *did* help. It gave me time to reflect, to feel what my life is like without them, and to force myself out of the mental funk I was in. And more than anything, it makes me realize one very important thing.

I can't live without them, and I don't intend to.

But I'm not going back to them empty-handed. I want to show them progress because that's what they deserve. Which means, I need to suck it up and get over my fear of expressing myself, and stop letting this man—this *dead* man—control my life anymore.

So I'm here to say goodbye. But I feel the itch to say something else.

"I'm bisexual," I blurt out loud, surprising even myself.

Oh fuck, that felt good.

"What do you think about that, asshole? I'm bisexual *and* I'm in love with a man." A laugh rolls off my lips as I stare at the word engraved in stone. Moss and decay have already begun to show themselves. Weeds sprout along the bottom because he was too much of an asshole to ensure people would care for his grave after he's gone.

I won't make the same mistake.

"God, I hope you're rolling around in your grave right now. Damn, I wish I would have said that to you when you were alive. I bet you would have been *so* pissed. I can only imagine the things you would have called me. You might have even tried to punch me for it. But you would have been too sick and weak to overpower me, and it would have felt really good to watch you try."

Damn...okay, I guess I can talk to a grave. I quickly turn to make sure I'm really alone, which I am, so I don't feel like such a weirdo for doing this. I feel lighter, like something has been lifted from my chest.

"Maybe if you weren't such an asshole and took better care of yourself, you could have met them. Maybe you would have been proud of me. I have a beautiful wife, and a fucking awesome...

boyfriend? I don't know what I'm calling him right now, but either way, I'm lucky enough to have two amazing people, who want to be with me, and I really fucking hope I didn't blow it because of *you*."

A breeze blows through the small cemetery, rustling the leaves that have fallen around sparse headstones. And suddenly, this feeling of being lighter is replaced by a sudden anxiousness. As if losing this burden has triggered my response to go back to them, to go *home*.

"All right," I mutter, looking down. Bending over, I grab the weeds that have laid roots around his grave. I yank a few out and toss them to the side. Then, I brush off the top of the gray stone. "Well, that's all I have to say. So…fuck off, old man."

And with that, I turn and head out of the cemetery, anxious to get to my car, to get to the club, to get back to the people I love.

There are two places where all of the owners of Salacious are in the same place at the same time—the bar and board meetings. Now that it's like a well-oiled machine with a staff of floor managers to contact us if anything goes wrong, we can actually *all* meet at the bar, just like old times. And since the bar has alcohol (as most bars do) where I can try and drown out my nerves, I decide Thursday night is the place to do this.

Drake and Isabel aren't here. I don't know where they are or what they're doing, which is how it's been for the last two months, and exactly how I want it to be. I talk to my wife over the phone from time to time to check in, but we don't talk about anything heavy, and she doesn't pester me with uncomfortable questions. My too-good-for-words wife understands that I have to do this soul-search alone.

And this is one of the milestones I definitely need to do alone.

We're on our second round when I clear my throat. "I have something to say."

Everyone freezes and looks my way. Those five words don't come out of my mouth often, and even they can tell how rare it is by how rapt their attention suddenly is.

Fuck, this is uncomfortable. And terrifying. And I'm thirty-three. How do kids do this?

"I'm sure you've all noticed..." I stammer. "That I haven't been living at home, and Isabel and Drake haven't been around much."

Maggie bites her lip next to me. Then I feel her hand rest against my back. Seeing as how I've taken up residence in her guest bedroom, she obviously knows everything about my situation. She's been my unofficial counselor this whole time, letting me unload everything on her.

I'm sure most of them assume something happened between Isabel and Drake, maybe that she cheated on me with him, but I let them believe what they wanted. I knew the moment would come when I would clear it all up.

"Well, the truth is that the three of us..."

I look up to find Charlie clinging to Emerson's arm, a hopeful expression on her face. Mia is staring wide-eyed at me, and Garrett is biting back a grin.

Inside, I'm screaming. These are my friends. No, this is my family. We've been in business together for over seven years. We raised and nurtured our company together like parents, and all of that bullshit about not going into business with your friends seems wrong. Because your friends are the only ones who won't steal from you or exploit you. This team has always had each other's back, and right now, I can feel just how much they have mine.

"The three of us are together. In a relationship. Even Drake and I. I...uh, I'm bisexual."

As those words bleed out of me, all of the weight and sickness I felt from holding them in bleeds out too. Across from me, Charlie is beaming. Mia is tearing up as she reaches a hand out for me, and at the end of the table, Emerson is wearing an expression of pride.

When no one says anything for a while, I let out a heavy breath. "You all knew that already, didn't you?"

The table breaks out in mumbled responses, confirming my suspicion. They knew this whole damn time.

"Why didn't you guys say anything?"

"It was none of our business," Emerson states.

"To be honest, I thought you three had been banging this whole time," Garrett replies, and Mia rolls her eyes at him.

"It just makes sense, Hunter. The chemistry between you guys is more than just friends," she adds.

"I'm just glad you finally got here," Maggie says, rubbing my back again.

"So…" Garrett says with his brow furrowed. "Why did you move out?"

"I just needed to figure some shit out before someone got hurt."

He nods, his eyes focused on me with a light, hopeful expression.

"What now? Are you going home?" Charlie asks.

"I think so."

She bites her lip in excitement.

"It's not fair," Mia whines, pushing her bottom lip out in a pout. "Isabel gets two. I only got *one*."

As she turns her grumpy features toward the man sitting next to her, his expression hardens as he snatches a pinch of her hip.

"You little brat."

"One? I have zero, so don't complain," Maggie adds as she scowls into her wineglass.

"That's because you work too much, Mags. And you're always with us. There are no more single guys here," I reply.

"I don't want any of you anyway," she replies. "You guys are too kinky and rich and full of yourselves."

The three of us stare at her, taking offense.

"Too kinky?" Emerson asks.

"Since when do we act rich?" Garrett adds.

And I can't help but laugh. I mean...we are full of ourselves, so that one doesn't even deserve an argument.

"Not even going to respond," she says astutely. You gotta love Maggie. She works hard, and she's surprisingly sweet and shy for a woman who's kept the three of us in check for almost a decade. But she never takes the time for herself that she deserves. Since I've been living there, I've noticed that she does nothing but work. Until her comment to Mia about not having a man, I honestly didn't know she even wanted one.

She's never dated anyone that we know of. Never *used* the club for anything. Never flirted or hooked up. She's an enigma to us all, but we love her all the same.

The table is busy arguing about her accusations of the way we act, and I'm thankful for the attention being taken away from me. And it was just that easy. I dropped the biggest bomb of my life, and my friends barely flinched. Because, to them, nothing really changed. I'm still me. Drake and Isabel and I are the same three people we've always been.

And to think I was afraid this would be hard.

Rule #37: Once you have him back, don't let go.

Isabel

It's past nine when I finally close the studio, ushering out the last person from my advanced aerial class. They usually like to stick around the longest to chitchat, and tonight was the first night in a long time where I actually felt up to making small talk.

After that little moment with Drake in the bathroom, I'm starting to feel like myself again. What happened between us was progress, finally able to let go of the grief of him leaving and the guilt of being together. But I know that is what Hunter wanted us to do. Maybe because finally being with him means that Hunter is making progress too, hence coming home soon.

I know in my heart that Hunter wanted Drake and I to be together. Because, deep down, it was never really about cuckolding or *hotwifing* or any kink, really. It was about finding the relationship we were always supposed to be in.

After locking the front door, I head into the back, so I can close out the books for the day, do some last-minute picking up, and throw the towels into the hamper to take home and wash.

Just as I shut the computer off, I hear the bell of the front door chime, and I freeze.

I locked it, didn't I? I swear I locked it.

The only other people with a key are my receptionist and…

Slowly, I walk toward the front, peering into the lobby from the staff room, when I see a man standing near the door with a bouquet of flowers in his hands. It doesn't matter that the lights are still on and I can see him clear as day. My brain doesn't compute right away and so I stare in shock at my husband, who I haven't laid eyes on in two whole months—fifty-seven days, to be exact.

A scream flies from my mouth as I sprint across the room, eating up every inch of space between us in desperation. The flowers he's holding are crushed between our bodies as I soar into his arms, crashing against him.

The relief is visceral. His scent, his presence, even the warmth of his breath against my neck is familiar. Every minute of the fifty-seven days we spent apart, I survived. But it truly was just surviving, and it was a struggle. But now…he's here, and I can finally breathe and let myself feel again.

"Oh, Red," he whispers against my temple as I bury my face in his neck, and the sound of his voice sends me over the edge. I let out the sob I've been holding in.

"Please don't go again," I beg. "Please, please, please."

His dark chuckle vibrates through me. "I'm not going anywhere. I'm done being away from you."

When I pull away from his embrace, I stare at him through my tears. "You are?"

He brushes my hair out of my face, his eyes raking over the new shorter length, without any real reaction. "Yes. I'm coming home."

More tears pool in my eyes, and I've never felt such gratitude in my life.

"If I can come home…" he adds.

"Yes, yes, yes," I cry, as I pull his mouth to mine, devouring the taste of his lips that I've missed so much.

He slowly crumbles to the floor, dropping the flowers to the side as he sits down in the middle of the lobby and holds me in his arms. We stay that way for a while. I just want to savor his nearness, without talking.

"What about him? Will he want me to come home?" he murmurs quietly, breaking the silence.

I force myself to swallow. "Yes, of course he does."

"I've been doing a lot of thinking, Isabel. And I realized that the night I watched you two together, I saw something I should have seen a long time ago. It wasn't about jealousy—it was about watching the two people I love, together. I do love you both."

Emotion builds in my throat, stinging as I try to swallow again. "I love you both too," I whisper.

"I also realized…that if I can't have you both…" His voice trails as he takes a heavy inhale, preparing himself to say whatever is weighing on his mind. I brace myself for the rest. "If I can't have you both, I'd rather you have each other."

"Hunter…" I whisper.

"I do hope you two have used this time to be happy together, Isabel. I just hope…there's still room for me."

I grab his face, kissing him fiercely on the lips. "There will always be room for you. We are nothing without you, and I know Drake feels the same. He wants to see you accept yourself as much as he wants to see you accept him."

"I came out to the team," he says, and I pause, staring at him in shock.

"Umm…how did it go?"

He laughs. "Fine. They didn't even seem surprised."

"Because loving Drake doesn't make you any different, Hunter. You've always loved him, but now you're just expressing it differently."

"We really should have done this sooner, shouldn't we?" he asks, and I feel myself melting again. I forgot how natural it felt in his arms.

"Yeah…that would have saved us both a lot of jealousy, always watching him go home with different strangers every night."

As Hunter runs a hand through my hair, he pulls me closer, kissing me again, as if he's just as desperate for my touch as I am for his. When our mouths part, he stares into my eyes.

"I am yours, Red. I'm sorry for leaving, but I needed to be the perfect man for you. Even if it kills me. Even if it drives me crazy. I would do anything for you."

"I understand," I whisper. "I missed you like crazy, but I'm proud of you. And I don't need you to be perfect. I just need you to be here."

"I still have a lot of work to do. It's not over yet, but I'm ready to start this crazy relationship…if you're both ready too."

I love this new version of my husband, where he expresses himself and speaks from the heart. And seeing the raw emotion in his eyes is more than enough for me.

"So, now what?" I ask, kissing him again.

After a long, hungry embrace that leaves us both breathless and desperate for each other, he pulls away and gives me a serious expression. "Now, we go find Drake."

––––––––––––––––

I happen to know exactly where Drake is tonight. Being it's Friday night, he's at the club, the only day every week that he spends there. And not for the same reasons he used to. Three months ago, you could find Drake at the club every night, with a different person.

But now, he only goes once a week for one person.

Silla has taken up semipermanent residency at Salacious since her one-week event turned into a two-week, then a two-month, and now…I don't think she's ever going back. So now she teaches her Shibari demo every Friday night with a certain blond hunk by her side. The two of them have gotten really good, actually.

And as Hunter and I slip into the back of the room undetected, we're met with the *ooh*s and *aah*s of the crowd as Silla hangs, suspended in midair, tied up into a little round ball. The apple-red cord against her dark, tawny skin is even more stunning than the rope bondage usually is. She looks exquisite as the crowd and Drake look on in awe.

But when Hunter gasps next to me, I have a feeling it has more to do with Drake's appearance than the feat of the woman floating in the air held by nothing but thin rope.

"What did he do to his hair?" Hunter whispers.

"There was no stopping him. He wanted us both to look different for you."

Glancing at my husband, I can't help but notice the expression of attraction on his face as his gaze absorbs the man onstage.

"I like it," he whispers.

I'm admiring how handsome Drake is with his new buzz cut, which somehow makes his smile look brighter and his frame appear taller—because he wasn't beautiful enough before—when I spot the moment he notices Hunter standing in the back of the room.

It's a little unfair now that I think about it. When Hunter showed up at my studio, I was alone, and nothing stopped me from running into his arms. Drake is busy spotting Silla and ensuring her safety, so he's stuck onstage with her. And you can tell by the way he's fidgeting and how his wide-eyed expression keeps drifting toward us that he's anxiously awaiting the moment to do the same.

Not even a minute later, he's helping her down, undoing her ropes carefully, so she doesn't fall. The crowd claps for them, and Drake doesn't waste a second.

Bounding off the stage, he bolts across the room toward us. His arms go wide to bring Hunter in for a hug, but Hunter doesn't take the hug. Instead, he grabs for Drake's neck, and fiercely pulls him in for a rough kiss. Their mouths fuse together, and I notice the brief look of shock on Drake's face before he melts into the kiss, pressing Hunter against the wall, letting his body express just how much he missed him.

Rule #38: Distance makes the heart grow fonder—and hornier.

Hunter

I don't want to talk. Isabel and I already talked enough. I know we *should* talk. I know that Drake probably needs to hear me say a lot of things, but talking isn't really my strong suit. I'd rather show him.

Our kiss lasts longer than I intend it to. The point of the kiss was meant to prove that I've made progress. I'm not done...but I am better. And I'm not afraid to show anyone how much I want this man.

Now it seems the kiss is turning into something else entirely. His tongue glides against mine as we taste and explore each other's mouths. In a way, it almost feels like our first kiss.

We're both panting by the time we tear our lips apart.

"I made some modifications to room twelve," he mumbles against my mouth, and I pull back to look into his bright blue eyes.

"You did?" *Why didn't I know about this?* I might have been doing most of my work from Maggie's house these past two months, but surely, I would have known about room changes.

Room twelve is basic with an extra-large bed, made mostly for parties of three or four. It's roomy but basic. Not equipped with anything extra, so I'm curious to know what sort of modifications he could have made.

"Yeah, I told the team not to tell you. I wanted it to be a surprise."

The deep timbre of his voice is so familiar to me, but not having heard it for two months means that now it's sending shock waves of warmth and excitement through my body. How did I go so long avoiding this attraction? It wasn't Pandora's box we opened. It was like breaking a dam. Now that these feelings are flowing, they will never be put back. Never be hidden. Never be ignored again.

"Well, I'd like to see it," I reply, a slight shake to my voice. It's hard to hide the emotion from this moment. He should be furious with me, and I expect him to rage at me for leaving, but he's not. He's as happy to see me as she was, and to think I was ready to grovel. I want him to make me pay, but it turns out, he just wants me.

"Come on," he replies, pulling me out of the room. Room twelve is only two rooms down. The light above the door is off, which means it's not in use, and Drake is faster with his master key than I am.

When he opens the door, I'm anxiously waiting to see what changes he's made, but as we step in, I try my best to hide my disappointment. My eyes search the room for anything, but I can't seem to find a single thing that's different.

The door closes behind us, Isabel at my side. She takes my hand as I turn toward Drake.

"What—" I ask, but my voice is cut off as the room goes dark. In fact, it's pitch-black. I'm struck speechless by the bright green spots scattered throughout the darkness. Two lines lead a pathway around the room. The hard edges of the furniture are all glowing so that the only thing we can see is what was in this room to begin with, but we can't see each other at all.

My mouth hangs open as Isabel's fingers wind with mine. The loud music from the main room carries into this one, through speakers installed in the ceiling, to muffle the noises from the other rooms, and it's so surreal, I can hardly move.

Drake's hand touches my back and I lean into it.

"We still have plans to do something bigger, like a whole section of the club like this, but for now...I thought you'd appreciate this," he says.

Flanked on both sides by these two people, I'm hit with a sudden emotion that I didn't see coming. "I don't deserve you," I murmur, and his hands feel their way up to my face, pulling me closer until our mouths meet. Isabel's fingers slide up my spine until she digs them into my hair.

"Shut the fuck up," Drake mutters into my mouth. "That's bullshit and you know it. You always think you need to make yourself better for us, and I get it. We were both born into shitty situations, but that doesn't make us any less worthy, Hunter. You are not your father, and I'm not my mother."

Something about hearing those words in the darkness, without seeing his face, makes them hit even harder.

"You can decide right now who you are and what you want," Isabel whispers from behind me, placing warm kisses along my back, her lips against my shirt.

"I think it's pretty clear what I want," Drake replies, and with that, he grinds himself against me, making me feel his rock-hard length through his pants. "And what do you want?" he asks, his voice thick and raspy with need.

"I want this," I growl, grabbing his cock through his pants. "And this," I add, snaking an arm around Isabel to pull her between us, moving my mouth to hers. She hums in delight as I stroke her through the fabric of her yoga pants.

My patience has worn thin, and I need them *now*. In a rush, I undo the buckle on my pants. "Get naked," I command as we lose the rest of our clothes in a hazy mess of limbs and lips.

Drake guides us to the bed, the three of us never letting go of each other. When I feel Isabel's sports bra slide over her head, I find her breasts in the darkness, running my tongue in tight circles around the sensitive bud of her nipple. She clasps onto my head, pulling me closer. I lay her on her back as my mouth continues to explore her body.

As I tug her pants down, I feel Drake's weight settle behind me. His lips travel down my spine, one vertebra at a time. In the darkness, our senses are heightened and everything feels more intense.

When I have my wife's naked body in my hands, it's like everything makes sense again. Quickly, I flip her onto her stomach, pulling her up to her knees as I bury my face in the heat between her legs. She lets out a loud moan of pleasure as I thrust my tongue inside her. Her scent and taste are so familiar to me, I devour her, erasing every moment of our time apart.

"God, I missed this," I growl into her heat. She hums in response.

Drake is behind me, his hands roaming my back and reaching around to my front, stroking my cock. A part of me tenses with him behind me. Am I ready for this?

But there's a resounding voice there too, reminding me of everything these two have given me. I can give just as easily as I can take. And I *want* to give.

Drake's strokes pick up speed, and I have to force myself not to come already.

"Drake," I groan, pulling my mouth away from Isabel.

"Yeah?" he replies with a grunt.

I lean up to my knees as I turn to him and say, "I want you to fuck me."

Isabel freezes in my hands, and Drake doesn't respond. Just grabs hold of the back of my neck and steers my mouth to his, tasting her on my lips.

"Good," he groans, "because I want to fuck you."

With that, he forces me forward, and I return to Isabel, kissing my way down to her warm cunt. She writhes and moans with her ass in the air for me as I slide a finger inside her, which only makes her moan louder.

"That's my girl," I mutter against the soft skin of her ass. "Come for me, Red."

I curl my finger inside her, and her breathing picks up speed. She screams, but the pillows muffle her voice.

When I feel the mattress dip behind me, I realize Drake has returned. I was so focused on Isabel, I hadn't even realized he left. Glancing back, I see the glow in the dark, green markings of something in his hands. Then I hear the click of a cap.

Well, fuck. They even put glowing paint on the lube bottles. Clever.

When I feel the warm liquid seep down my backside, I let out a moan into Isabel's skin. I pull my finger out of her heat to kiss her clit and bury my face in her again. She presses her hips back against my face, and when I feel Drake press his thumb against my ass, I stop breathing.

"Relax for me, Hunter." He groans as he rubs a little harder, slowly easing his finger inside. I try to relax to let him pass, but I'm too overcome with the sensation. As he finally breaches the tight ring of muscle, I growl low and loud into Isabel's wet pussy.

"Yeah? You like that, don't you?" Drake says, sounding pleased. "You're so fucking tight. I can't wait to be inside you."

I'm thrusting my hips back and forth now, eager for more, *desperate* for it.

"More…" I grunt.

"You want more? I'm so fucking ready to give you more." His voice is like gravel, sweet friction to my soul, and I need every word.

Isabel is still panting into the pillows as she purrs and pleads for me. I need to make her come before I'm too distracted to get her there. So I kiss and lick her sweet cunt, rubbing tight circles around her clit.

"Yes," she cries. "Right there."

I don't stop, and neither does Drake. He's working in a second digit when Isabel finally unfurls in my hands, letting out another squeal into the pillow. I'm too enthralled by her orgasm to notice that Drake's fingers are gone, and in their place…the blunt head of his cock.

Slowly, he thrusts. I'm bent at the hips and clinging to Isabel as he eases his way in. The sensation is jarring at first, the feeling of being so full and tight. I'm letting him into my body. I want him to have it. Take me, use me, fuck me. Make it hurt or feel good and last forever, I don't care. I just need this and I need more of it—this indescribable thing that breaks me apart and makes me whole all at the same time.

"How are you?" he asks, a large hand skating its way up my spine. I realize he's buried as far in as he can go, his hip bones pressed against my cheeks.

"I'm…" My voice trails. I don't know what I am right now, but if he's asking how I feel then I don't have the words to answer that. I'm both lost and found. In agony and ecstasy. Nothing and everything all at once. "I'm perfect," I reply.

"I need to fuck you now," he says, and my cock twitches. It's hanging heavy and hard beneath my body, and as Drake pulls back and pounds back in, hitting a spot that makes my cock leak at the tip, I drag Isabel to me.

Before Drake starts fucking me hard, I pull Isabel's body to mine, lining up my own cock so that on his next pistoning thrust, his movement pushes me into her. I'm physically connected to both of them. We are one. With each violent jolt from Drake, I'm shoved into Isabel. She leans back against my chest, letting me find her mouth with my own as I kiss the life out of her.

The darkness swallows me whole as I let their touch and embrace be the only things I feel. Her mouth, his hands, her cunt, his cock. I'm not quite sure when my orgasm starts or if it's been here this entire time, but as the pleasure brings me to life, I hold tight to them. We are moaning and breathing as one.

The feel of Drake's cock pulsing inside me is my salvation. His voice echoes like a boom against the walls as he comes, taking his pleasure from my body. And there is no shame or fear in this moment—only love.

When our climaxes have both crescendoed and calmed, I feel his warm lips against my back. And I realize something that might sound cheesy or ridiculous, but this man is my soul mate. If soul mate means a person whose heart mirrors mine, a twin flame, so compatible that one cannot fully exist without the other, then without a doubt, he is mine.

And I've known that all along, but we called it something else before. We've always been best friends, but maybe that's what best friends are—soul mates in disguise.

I guess that means a person can have more than one soul mate, because these two are so crucial to my happiness that I'd live a miserable existence without them. But I'm done thinking I don't deserve them. As long as I give them all of me, then I deserve them, and I always have.

There's not a drop of light in the room for our eyes to adjust to, but for the first time in my life, I see things very clearly.

Rule #39: You know you've done well if you can shock Madame Kink.

Isabel

"They didn't say anything?" Drake asks, turning his head toward Hunter, his now buzz-cut head leaning against the headboard.

"Not really." Hunter shrugs. "Garrett had some questions, but other than that, they just sort of…moved on."

"Wow," I say, running my fingers through Hunter's dark curls against my bare leg. The lights are back on now, which means I can drink them in, both of these gorgeous men, somehow all mine.

"They probably figured we were fucking the whole time," Drake adds, and the three of us laugh together.

"They did," Hunter replies.

"How did that feel? Coming out to them, I mean," Drake asks.

"It felt good." He seems so at peace now, as if he breathes a little easier and is more present than before. Hunter has always lived in a state of constant anxiety, always on edge and desperate to make the right decision and do the right thing. Never for himself, of course.

But now, he just looks freer than I've ever seen him.

"You know, I never came out, not officially."

Hunter and I both look at Drake with our brows furrowed. "What?" I ask.

"I just never actually *told* anyone my sexual orientation. I mean…I remember the look on your face when I told you I kissed a guy," he says with a laugh, looking at Hunter. "But you never really asked me to elaborate or gave me shit about it. You just… accepted it."

Hunter is wearing a heavy expression as if he has something on his mind. "I used to hate people who could express themselves so openly. My father taught me that. He made me hate what he hated, and I realized, over time, that I didn't hate anyone but him. I was jealous of people like you, Drake. People who could live without fear."

Drake's hand lands on Hunter's shoulder, giving it a reaffirming squeeze.

"I think you deserve a proper coming out," Hunter adds. "So go ahead."

Drake laughs. "I just fucked you and you want me to come out *now*?"

"Yep. You deserve to say it out loud."

With a proud grin plastered on his face, Drake states with confidence, "I'm bisexual."

Tears spring to my eyes as I clutch his arm harder. I don't think I've ever been so happy in all of my life.

"Hey, me too," Hunter replies, and the three of us laugh again. It's ridiculous and touching all at the same time. But that's how we've always been. We never stopped being *us* and we never will. Sex doesn't change that because we loved each other then and we love each other now.

With my head on Drake's shoulder and Hunter's head in my lap, I let out a long yawn.

"We should get home. You've had a long day," Drake says, and I notice Hunter watching us for a moment before anyone moves.

Something about the way his friend said that, as if he knows the kind of day I've had, like he knows my work schedule—which he does—makes this slightly uncomfortable.

"Let's just get this awkward conversation over with," Hunter blurts out as he sits up to face us.

I feel my eyes widen. "You want to talk about it?" I try not to put too much emphasis on the word *you*, but it's there. Hunter never wants to talk about the awkward stuff—never.

"Yes, if I've learned anything, it's that getting the tough conversations out of the way now prevents a lot of bullshit later. Plus, I've been reading up on poly relationships and the number one thing they say over and over is to have open communication, so if I want you both, I need to just get used to it."

Drake and I are staring in shock at Hunter. After a moment, I bite my lip to stifle the smile I feel growing across my face.

"Well…" Drake starts.

"Wait. Let me preface this by saying…I left you two alone on purpose. I wanted you to get closer. I don't want you thinking you can only fuck when I'm there to watch, like you're a couple of performing monkeys or something."

"Okay…" Drake replies.

Hunter is reading his expression. "Did you not have sex this whole time?"

"Almost the whole time…" I add.

"Seriously?" Hunter asks, staring at Drake in confusion.

"Well, it's not like we had any rules to follow. I didn't know."

Finally, Hunter laughs. "Well, that's your fucking fault."

"Great," Drake says, throwing his hands up. "Two months I kept my dick to myself, and now you're saying I wasn't supposed to?"

"Don't worry," Hunter adds. "You'll be making up for it soon. I love watching you two fuck."

As we start to get our clothes back on, I can't help but wonder if it's supposed to be harder than this. It really shouldn't be this easy; I keep waiting for the other shoe to drop.

Once we're dressed and ready to go, the three of us move toward the door and pause.

"What if someone is out there?" Drake asks, looking at both of us.

"Well…we just made out in front of a room full of people so…what are you worried about?"

Drake responds with a shrug as he pulls open the door, and sure enough…Eden St. Claire is standing on the other side. She's coming out of a room of her own alone, but her eyes instantly freeze on us as she assesses the damage—my messy hair, Drake's wrinkled clothes, Hunter's smug expression.

As Salacious's resident Madame and the embodiment of female sexual prowess, Eden doesn't shock easily. But as she stares at us for a few long seconds, I can't help but notice the curiosity in her eyes.

"Don't look so shocked, Eden," Hunter replies as he holds open the door for us.

"Oh, I'm *not* surprised. I'm actually a little relieved. I was waiting for this to happen."

"I have a feeling we're going to get that a lot," Drake replies.

I feel her arm loop through mine as she smiles at me. With her dark black hair pulled into a ponytail, she smiles at me wickedly. "Seems only fair that you add another girl to the mix to even things out."

"Get away from my wife, Eden," Hunter says in warning.

"Why does everyone say that to me?" she asks, and we all laugh. I have no interest in being with a woman, but no one can resist the appeal of Madame Kink herself.

The four of us continue down the long hallway toward the exit. Eden is still clutching my arm as Hunter watches with annoyance and Drake with playful interest.

"You're a lucky girl, Isabel," she mumbles quietly before planting a sweet kiss on my cheek. Then she pulls away and heads in the opposite direction. "Have fun, guys."

With a smile, I reach for Drake's hand and loop my arm through Hunter's.

"I personally think that is a fantastic idea," Drake says, and a laugh slips through my lips. It feels ridiculous to be this happy, but I am. And even though I really don't see myself taking Eden up on her offer, I know what she said is right.

I am one lucky girl.

Rule #40: Be flexible.

Hunter

"HOW CAN YOU LISTEN TO THIS CRAP?"

"Easy. I have taste," I reply coolly as we pull into the studio's parking lot. Drake switches the radio station, and I roll my eyes before turning it back, using the controls on the back of the steering wheel.

He scoffs. "Seriously, what kind of thirty-three-year-old man listens to Taylor Swift?"

"Thirty-*four*," I correct him.

"Even worse, my friend."

"She just gets me," I reply, turning it up so loud he winces. "I mean…listen to these lyrics. Straight from the heart."

As soon as I put the SUV into park, he jumps out, but I keep it running, singing the song loudly with the windows down. Pretty soon, I spot the door of the yoga studio open and see Isabel peek her head out, wondering what all the noise is about. Drake leaves me in the car to greet her.

I cut the engine in time to hear him say, "Fix your husband."

"He's a lost cause," she replies as he leans down to plant a casual kiss on her mouth. I love the little thrill I still get from their affection, and just that little kiss gives me an idea.

It *is* my birthday, after all.

"I've got everything just about shut down. Where do you guys want to go to eat?" she asks.

"Birthday boy gets to pick," Drake replies.

As I get out of the car and see them clinging to each other, I suddenly can't seem to think about food. I can only think about one thing.

I lock the car and approach them, stopping a few feet away. "I'm not hungry."

Isabel's eyes squint at me as she pulls her bottom lip between her teeth. "Oh really?"

"Really."

"What exactly do you have in mind?" Drake asks.

We could go home, but I'm not ready to go home just yet. We could go to the club, but there are so many people there, and it being my birthday, they're going to want to hang out, and I'd rather keep this just us.

"Inside, both of you," I say in a command. Both of them perk up as if the tone of my voice says it all.

"In my studio?" Isabel asks.

"You heard the man." Drake hoists her up with his arms around her waist and carries her into the studio. Following behind them, I lock the door and smile as I hear Drake gasp because I know exactly what he must have found.

"Can we use these?" he begs, sounding like a kid in a toy store, instead of a grown man in an aerial yoga studio. As I enter the class space, I bite back my grin. But it's hard not to laugh at the sight of him swinging in one of the silk loops draped from the ceiling.

"These are for my classes. They are *not* sex swings," she states, trying to pull him from the fabric seat.

"We won't get them dirty," he whines.

I creep up behind her and press my lips to her ear. "It's my birthday."

She softens against me with a sigh, and I can't help but smile.

"What did you have in mind?" Drake asks. "Get her naked in one of these silks and fuck her from both ends?"

"Drake, geez," she mumbles with a blush as she covers her cheeks.

"Actually, I'm going to watch tonight," I reply, kissing the spot where her neck meets her shoulder. She lets out the tiniest squeak as I do. "Is that okay with you, Red? Can I watch my best friend fuck you?"

She squeaks louder this time. When she doesn't reply, I pull her face to mine. "Give me an answer, baby."

"Yes," she gasps. Then I take her mouth in a harsh kiss, and as I tug on her bottom lip and overwhelm her mouth with mine, I feel her weight settle into my arms as if her legs have lost the ability to hold her up.

When I finally pull away, she sways in her spot.

"Come here, babe," Drake calls for her, and she floats toward him like a cloud. While he picks up where I left off, I go into the office to find a chair. On my way back, I dim the lights and close the door. By the time I find a place to sit down, they are both down to their underwear. Isabel is topless, and Drake is sporting an erection so hard, it's poking out the top of his boxers.

His mouth is devouring her breast as she hums with her fingers against his buzz cut. Normally, I like to give them directions, but I like the idea of letting them take the lead this time, so I sit back in silence and watch. My cock is throbbing in my pants, but I don't reach for it. I'd rather drag it out. Make the need turn almost painful before I let myself have what I want. Because, when they're done, everyone knows it's going to be my turn, and I'm going to take what I want.

Drake hooks his hands around Isabel's thighs and lifts her into the air. "Sit down, baby," he says as he deposits her onto one of the silk loops. She holds tightly onto the two sides as he kneels in front of her. "Lift up," he says, tugging her underwear down.

Then he kisses his way up her thighs, draping each one over his shoulders as his mouth finds the center, growling against her cunt. With each lick, she squirms and moans, her back arching until she's almost hanging horizontally in the silks.

"God, you taste so fucking good," he mutters, sucking intently on her clit. "Tell me how this feels, baby."

"It feels so good," she whispers.

"Yeah? What about when I do this?"

I bite my bottom lip in anticipation as he slides two fingers inside her, both of us watching her reaction as he does. I swear my cock twitches in my pants with the way she cries out.

"Yes," she gasps. "More."

"Keep doing that," I mutter from my seat, and Drake obeys, thrusting his fingers. His lips never leave her clit until she's finally screaming, her thighs tight around his ears and her back arched so much, she's now almost upside down. It's such a beautiful fucking sight.

I wish I knew why this feels so good to watch. Maybe because, even now, it still feels forbidden. Or because I really do love these two so much it hurts. And I don't even know if this is still considered a kink, since the three of us are in a poly relationship, but what I do know is that I really enjoy watching him fuck my wife. Almost as much as I like doing it myself.

Drake doesn't waste any time. Before she's even caught her breath or lifted herself out of her contorted position, he's tearing off his boxers and standing up, so his cock is aligned with her pussy.

I lean forward, desperate for the moment he finally penetrates her. With her thighs locked in his grip, he jerks her onto his cock. Their mingled moans fill the studio, and I turn to find their reflection in the giant mirror at the front of the room, enjoying the view from this angle.

He fucks her slowly but in hard, punishing thrusts, and I can't take my eyes off the way his muscles contract with every movement. I love the way his jaw hangs open as he slams into her and the way he dominates her, so connected to her pleasure as much as his own. My cock starts to leak in my boxers at the sight of his cock disappearing into her, the cadence starting to pick up.

Isabel lifts herself up, so she's no longer hanging, and she reaches up to his mouth for a kiss. I lose myself in the rhythm of their fucking as I start to undress myself. I want to be ready by the time they're done.

"Fuck!" he bellows, and I think for a moment that he's coming, but he quickly pulls out of her, letting his cock hang free as he composes himself, clearly closer to coming than he'd like to be.

Next thing I know, I'm stroking myself slowly as I watch him kiss her hard on the mouth again.

"Turn over," he mutters against her mouth, and in one fluid movement, he flips her onto her stomach so her hips are lying against the silk. Her fingers barely touch the floor, but she's clearly seasoned enough in these positions that she makes it look easy.

When Drake slams his fat cock into her again, she screams. With her body hanging from the fabric, she's at his mercy. With his hands on her hips, he brings her body to his in rapid, hard strokes.

I'm waiting with torturous anticipation for my turn. I don't know if I'll make it. My cock is dying to feel them—which one, I'm not quite sure.

"Harder, Drake," she cries out. His hips pick up intensity, pounding so hard against her backside, the sound echoes throughout the room. Finally, her toes curl and her moans go silent as she comes, and I don't have to be the one buried inside her to know what Drake is feeling right now. Her pussy pulsing around his cock, squeezing him so hard he won't be able to hold on much longer. So it's no surprise that a moment later, he lets out a grunt and stops his thrusts as he comes too.

I'm out of my seat in a heartbeat, going to him first. Standing behind him, I pull his mouth to mine for a kiss. He's breathless in my mouth as I reach around to feel where he's buried into my wife. Slowly, I pull him out, sliding my fingers through the cum already seeping out of her. With my eyes on him, I lift my soaked fingers to my mouth and lick them clean. His gaze grows in intensity.

"Remember that day in Austin when I found you two kissing, and it drove me so crazy, I had to fuck her in the other room?"

With his eyes on me, he nods.

I grab fiercely onto the back of his neck and pull him down until he's kneeling in front of me. "I felt the same way about you, you know. And now I finally get to act on it." Then I guide his mouth to my waiting cock, and he doesn't hesitate to pull me far down his throat.

I'm overwhelmed by warmth and pleasure. My hips thrust ever so slightly as I hold on to the back of his head.

"Your fucking mouth," I groan. He's bobbing eagerly on my cock as Isabel rises up from her position tangled in the silks. Motioning for her, I reach a hand out, and she takes it, letting me pull her in for a kiss. When our mouths finally part, I have to pull Drake off my cock before I come down his throat.

I look at Isabel. "Do you have any massage oils?"

She barely replies before running naked toward the supply closet at the back of the room. In a rush, she comes back with a golden bottle and hands it to me.

"Turn around," I tell Drake, grabbing as much of his short hair as I can in my fingers. He spins, without hesitation, until he's facing the mirror. Leaking oil on his ass, I feel a growl rise up out of my chest. His ass does things to me, things I never fucking expected. "I want to prep you, Drake, but I need to fuck you so bad."

"Just do it," he mutters in response.

Isabel kneels on the other side of Drake, pulling his lips to hers for a rough kiss. As I press my cock past the tight ring of his ass, he groans loudly into her mouth. I'm lost to the sensation of his body as he takes me all the way in. I can hardly breathe from the tightness of him. Like he was made for me.

In the mirror, we find each other, our gazes locked as my thrusts pick up speed. Isabel watches with desire in her eyes and my gaze drifts from Drake to her. And as she watches me fuck my best friend, I realize how damn lucky I am to have them both. What are the odds that we would end up this way? What are the odds I would find *two* loves of my life? Tenderly, I reach down and stroke her cheek, and she leans into my fingers.

With my eyes on her and his on me, I finally lose control. I'm blinded by pleasure as my orgasm cascades through my body. Holding both of them in my hands, I let my heartbeat slow to a normal rhythm.

"Happy birthday, Hunter," she whispers.

And I can't help but smile as I lean against Drake's broad frame. Another year older, and it doesn't scare me one bit. I have no idea what the future holds or where the three of us will go from here, but I know for certain it can't throw anything at us that we can't handle together.

Rule #41: Ready or not…

Epilogue—Six months later
Drake

"IT'S DONE!"

Two pairs of footsteps echo through the house as they come to see my handiwork. I'm pretty proud of this one, to be honest. It wasn't easy, but it had to be done. As much as Isabel loves being sandwiched between us, two six-foot-plus men cannot comfortably share a king-size bed with a girl in between, at least not for any prolonged length of time.

And sleeping in the guest room was out of the question. I tried it one night, and they lost their fucking minds. It had them thinking I was pulling out of the relationship, wanting my space, and regretting the decision to make this thing real.

I wasn't doing any of those things. I was just looking for a good night's sleep, without worrying about smothering Isabel in her sleep.

Besides, the guest bedroom is under renovations now anyway.

As they walk into the room, Isabel's eyes widen. "It's perfect!"

"It's a good thing you built us a giant master bedroom," Hunter replies.

"Yeah, maybe you saw this coming." Isabel is smiling as she walks over to the now giant bed. "So this is two kings?"

"Yep."

"That's way too big," she replies with a laugh, arching her back like she's trying to stretch muscles she can't reach anymore.

"Well, we need big," Hunter adds, walking over to rub her round belly and kiss her on the temple.

"Oh, hell no." I drop the drill in my tool bag before glaring at them. "I didn't build this bed to fit them too. I'm building them cribs, remember. They can sleep in those."

Isabel is biting her lip as she leans against Hunter, both of them looking too fucking smug as if they know I'm probably going to cave and let those two little brats take up my precious bed space. I'm thirty-five years old and I got this far never sharing a bed with anyone. Now I'm expected to share it with not just two, but *four* people.

Okay two people and two perfect little babies.

My babies.

Well...*my* in the loose, nontechnical way. We have a theory about who got her pregnant. Isabel swears she was supposed to get her period after that day she and I shared in the bathroom, and she definitely had it before... But then again, we did have a *lot* of sex after Hunter came home, so who's to say, really. And we're not playing any of that *we don't want to know because it doesn't matter* crap. Isabel wants to find out for sure, so if they are mine, she and Hunter can try after these two are out. Or vice versa, if they're his.

More than two kids...wonderful. Not exactly what I had planned for my future. I was a scoundrel, and I was okay with that. I had it all mapped out to work at Salacious as long as I could, maybe help build a whole new club somewhere, enjoy as much sex as physically possible, and never be tied down to anyone.

I was okay with that.

But this...this I'm more than okay with. I still work at Salacious. There's already talk of building a whole new club. I have way more sex than I ever thought physically possible, and I'm tied down to the two people who make life worth living.

"So...can we get a mattress on this thing?" Isabel asks, waddling her giant belly toward her beloved yoga ball where she sits, a sudden expression of relief morphing her features. She only has three months left, but I have no idea where she's going to put it. She already looks ridiculous with her tiny frame and protruding stomach. And yet...no woman has ever looked more beautiful to me.

"You get *two* mattresses," I reply. "They're still rolled up in the garage. They're those fancy new foam ones that are supposed to be good for you. You're going to love them. I'll go grab them."

"I'll help," Hunter replies, quickly following me down the stairs. Once we reach the garage, I bend over to flip open the first box, and not surprisingly, Hunter is there, grinding himself against my ass. I smile as I thrust it back against him. In turn, he digs his hands in my hair, now finally long enough to grip, as he pulls me up and slides the other hand around my throat.

"God, I love watching you bend over."

"I can tell," I reply with a wicked smile. He kisses my neck and my body starts to rev up in response. "We don't have time for this." The fight in me is gone as the hand at my throat slides down to my waiting cock, stroking it to life.

"Get hard for me. We only have a minute."

"You're getting me hard right now," I reply breathlessly.

Quickly, I spin around and shove him against the wall, stealing his mouth with mine as he works in a rush to get our cocks out. I growl into his mouth as he wraps his large hand around both of them together, stroking them between us.

Shoving his hand aside, I press him tighter against the wall, squeezing our cocks between our bodies and grinding hard to get the pressure we're craving. He lets out a loud sound that I know Isabel must have heard. I slam my hand over his mouth as I grind harder and faster.

We don't sneak around because she doesn't like us being together, but times like these, when we should definitely be doing something *other* than making each other come, we figure it's best not to flaunt the fact that we are.

"Harder," he grunts, so I give him what he wants, biting his bottom lip as I do.

Without warning, he explodes between us, warm cum staining my dark blue V-neck. I have no right to complain because I'm right behind him, making the mess even bigger until we don't know whose cum stain is whose. We're panting into each other's mouths as he mumbles, "We're going to get in trouble for that."

"Worth it."

With a laugh, we finally pull away. My shirt comes off in a quick swipe, and I toss it at Hunter, who quickly takes it to the laundry room as I finish getting these mattresses ready. We carry them upstairs while they're still rolled up, and we find Isabel glaring at us from her exercise ball.

"That took a while," she says with a grimace.

"He started it," I say with a smile as I lean down to kiss her perfectly freckled cheek.

"I believe you," she replies, turning her attention to Hunter, who only shrugs in response as if that's the best defense he has. "You owe me."

"Deal."

Getting the mattresses unrolled and on the bed is easy, but we reward ourselves by lying flat on them together as Isabel browses through the baby name book Mia bought her the second she found out.

"What about Austin?" she asks, when I feel myself dozing off. I screw up my face as I glare at her.

"They're both girls."

Isabel shrugs. "So? We had our first kiss in Austin."

Hunter seems to let the idea settle for a moment before responding. "I like Austin."

"Austin and Phoenix." The names roll off my tongue comfortably, striking a sudden pang of something in my chest. Like visiting a place you've never been that instantly feels like home.

I know it won't feel real until they're here. And maybe even then it probably won't feel real. I have no clue. But the idea of suddenly being a father floors me every time I think about it. I went from a party of one to five, practically overnight, and I know they're nervous about me, thinking that I might freak out at any moment because this is too much.

And while I can't promise I won't freak out, this isn't too much for me. It's just right. It's a chance to have a family the right way, to give them the life I never had. To give my kids the father I always wanted, and I know Hunter feels the same.

It might have started with a kinky arrangement, but it led us here, right where we're supposed to be.

Rule #42: There's no such thing as too much love.

Bonus Epilogue—Two years later
Isabel

"Da-da!" Austin nearly leaps out of my arms as Drake walks through the front door.

"Oh, thank God," I mutter as I set her down and she sprints her tiny little toddler legs across the living room to leap into his waiting arms. The smile on his face is infectious as he gathers her up in a tight hug.

"You're still awake, Ausie-bug?" He nuzzles his face in her mess of nearly white curls, and she squeals with giggles.

"Now, you can help with bedtime," I reply with a laugh. Approaching both of them, I plant a kiss on his lips, and brush back Austin's messy hair.

"Let me guess. Nix is already asleep, and this little bundle of energy is giving Mama hell?"

"Good guess."

Like magic, Austin rests her head on his chest, her two middle fingers going straight into her mouth, a telltale sign she's ready to pass out.

"The power of Dada," he whispers, clearly proud of the effect he has on her. I take his work bag and he heads upstairs with her. "Is Sophie still coming to babysit?"

"Yeah. Charlie's dropping her off at any minute."

"Perfect. Then we need to get this little devil to bed so Dada can take a shower before we go to the club."

"Dada," Austin mumbles with affection against the fingers in her mouth. Drake kisses her head when we reach the girls' room.

Slowly, we press open the door to find Hunter in the rocking chair and a copper-headed sweetheart snoring in his arms. He puts a finger up to his mouth to signal for us to stay quiet.

The sight of my gentle-natured Nix asleep on his chest makes my heart do flips. Tiptoeing closer, I lean down to kiss the top of her head. He smiles up at me, stealing a kiss of his own.

No one would ever claim favorites, but I do love the way the girls' personalities mirror the guys'. Nix is my quiet warrior, clearly more dominant than her sister without ever having to be half as loud or wild. Austin is a loose cannon, making more noise and messes than the rest of us combined. But never without a smile on her face.

Before they turned one, we got the official confirmation, and our suspicions were correct. The girls are biologically Drake's…as if Austin's blond mop wasn't proof enough. And I'm willing to bet anything it was that day in the bathroom when Drake shaved his head. That day really marked the end of one era and the beginning of another.

For months, I watched Hunter nervously as he swore the news changed nothing. I figured it must have been strange for him, to know after three years of marriage, I was pregnant with someone else's children. But that was never the way Hunter saw it. What's ours is ours—end of story. The girls are his just as much as they are Drake's, loving them equally.

And every day he proves it.

Drake is Da-da. Hunter is Daddy. And the way he beams at

them with love silences every fear in my head. As if he could possibly feel anything other than the unconditional love of a father.

Both of them turned into better dads than I could have imagined. Drake is the fun one—obviously. Rarely ever able to crack down on the girls when they need it, he never fails to be the nurturer, jester, and the boo-boo kisser.

Whereas Hunter is the protector, the one they run to if they are scared or in a new and strange place. I've watched him grow over the years into the rock of our relationship and now the rock of our family.

"Lay her down so we can get ready to go," I whisper. Very carefully, Hunter rises from the rocking chair and carries Phoenix to her crib, laying her down where she stirs for a moment, but with a few reaffirming pats from her daddy, she drifts back off. I brush back her straight red hair and lift the blanket up to cover her while she sleeps. My heart explodes for the hundredth time today as I watch her snore peacefully.

On the other side of the room, Austin mumbles for Drake again, so he sticks around to pat her back for a few minutes while Hunter and I sneak out.

"He'll stay in there and pat her back all night if we let him," I whisper in the hallway, and Hunter laughs.

"Well, we can't let that happen. We have a date."

"Do I have to get dressed up?" I ask, feeling too tired to imagine even doing my makeup at the moment.

"What would be the point of that? We're just going to get you naked the minute we get there."

"Thank God," I reply.

I change into a pair of black jeans and a loose-fitting top because they'd have to sneak me in the back if I tried to go to Salacious in dirty sweats and a yogurt-stained T-shirt. A mother's life isn't glamorous, but damn...I do love it.

I better if we're going to keep trying for number three.

Fifteen minutes later, Drake flies into the bathroom like a

storm, ripping off his clothes and jumping into the shower. Hunter laughs. "You're such a sucker."

"I know, I know," he replies, as he quickly washes his hair. It's finally grown out, but he keeps cutting it, keeping it styled on his head instead of letting it get to the length it was before.

"She's not going to be ovulating forever. Let's go," Hunter says in a command.

"Technically, you guys don't even need me."

"Don't say that," I snap. "Of course, we do."

"Yeah, well, the sooner Hunt gets you pregnant, the sooner my ban can be lifted and I can get my favorite pussy back."

"Jesus, Drake," I mutter with a blush. I'll never get used to that mouth of his.

"Hello…" a sweet voice calls from downstairs.

"Sophie's here," I say, jumping up and rushing to the door. Before I disappear down the hallway, I turn back to Drake in the shower and a half-dressed Hunter. Pointing a stern finger at both of them, I give them a strict warning. "No hanky panky, you two. We have company."

"Yes, ma'am," Drake replies.

Hunter smiles, but it's a wicked grin, and I don't trust him for a minute.

"Hunter Scott, I'm serious. Save it for me."

He finally nods with his hands up in surrender. "I'll keep my hands to myself. I promise."

Rushing down the stairs, I find Sophie and Charlie standing in the living room. "Sorry about the mess," I say, greeting them as I pick up a stuffed animal off the welcome mat.

Charlie is looking around at our toddler-toy-and-sippy-cup-strewn living room with an expression of amusement. Destined to be the fun aunt for all of her days, it's very clear to me that she's perfectly happy enjoying the twins for short periods of time. She loves to play with the girls, but she also loves giving them back and going home to her sexy rich man, alone.

Mia, on the other hand…is obviously dying for her own.

"Oh it's fine," Sophie says with a bright smile. In her oversized sweatshirt and pink-streaked hair, she slips off her Chucks and climbs onto the sofa with a sketchbook in her lap. "You know me. I'll just be here drawing all night. The girls almost never wake up anyway."

After saying goodbye to Charlie, I dash over to the bookshelf and find the latest shifter romance I wanted to show Sophie. Her eyes light up as I toss it to her. "Here you go. It just came out yesterday."

"Oh, never mind sketching. These are my plans right here."

I laugh. Who cares that the only person I can share my love for smutty romance with is a teenager? At least I have someone who gets me.

It's a while before Drake and Hunter finally come barreling down the stairs. Hunter is wearing a guilty expression and Drake a mischievous one. I just shake my head at them while grabbing my purse. I try to give Sophie the rundown, but she just waves me away.

"I got this," she says as Hunter starts to push me out the door, and I breathe in the fresh night air in relief before we get into the car. As much as I love being a mom, there's nothing quite like getting away to just be me again—with my two favorite people.

"God, I can't wait to fill you up," Hunter mutters, clenching his teeth.

Drake took his sweet time getting me tied to the bedposts, my wrists in cuff-wraps tethered to each side. His face is currently buried between my legs, my thighs wrapped around his ears as he brings me to an earth-shattering climax. All while Hunter watches, naturally.

I love the burn around my wrists, the way it feels to be restricted, the way I can't seem to get away no matter how hard I try. Not that I want to.

There's just something about the way I feel in Drake's bondage, free and relaxed, and so, *so* turned on. Add in his hands and tongue and I'm in heaven.

"I'm coming," I cry, my voice coming out in a raspy wheeze.

My back arches and I lift off the mattress as his relentless mouth takes me all the way through my orgasm, drawing it out impossibly long.

I'm left panting as Drake rises up from between my legs, replaced by Hunter languidly stroking himself. I squirm in anticipation, ready for Hunter, but Drake selfishly steals his attention away before I get what I want.

Lying on my back with my head on a pillow and my wrists bound to the headboard, I'm just out of reach of them as Drake drags Hunter in for a brutal kiss. A moan slips out of my mouth as I watch them devour each other, Hunter's hand moving from his own cock to his man's, stroking him in the same torturously slow way.

"How about you suck me off before you fuck our wife?" Drake asks, grabbing him by the back of the neck and steering him downward.

"That sounds cruel as fuck. You know how much that drives her crazy," Hunter replies, and I let out another groan as they both turn to look at me.

"Do it," I whisper, my mouth going dry at the sight of them touching each other.

"Such a dirty girl," Drake teases, his words cut off by the sudden onslaught of Hunter's mouth around his cock. "Oh God," he groans, thrusting his hips forward.

Hunter sucks dick now like he's making up for lost time. If I had a dime for every time I've walked in on him on his knees and his eager lips wrapped around Drake, I'd have enough to build another yoga studio. He still likes to be the one on the giving end during sex, but God does he love making Drake come down his throat. And God, do I love watching it.

The way our relationship is now didn't happen overnight. Hunter still has work to do, and transitions like calling Drake his *boyfriend* or *husband* are still a slow process, but there isn't a doubt he loves him. He always has. But for his entire life, Drake was his soul mate under the guise of his best friend. And at the end of the day, who cares what he calls him. These two were made for each other, and I'm the lucky bitch who gets to be the glue between them.

As for Drake and me, I was the one who asked him to call me his wife. I could tell how badly he wanted to, and it wasn't fair to hold him in boyfriend status after all this time. So now when people ask, I'm his wife too. Although when we're alone, I prefer that he call me his girl.

"Fuck, I'm gonna come, baby," Drake groans, his long fingers stroking back the black curls on Hunter's head as he bobs up and down. "I love your mouth so fucking much."

Hunter groans in response as he picks up speed, and I drink in the sight of Drake coming, slack jawed and eyes closed. My hands fight against the restraints because of how badly I want to touch myself while watching this.

Instead, Hunter swallows him down before kissing his way up Drake's body and planting a kiss on his mouth which makes Drake smile in his post-orgasm drunken state.

"Hunter, please. I'm dying here," I cry out.

"Sorry, Red," he says with a smile as he crawls between my legs, draping my thighs around his hips. Leaning over me, he presses his mouth to mine as he thrusts himself inside me. His movements are slow but brutal, and I know he's struggling to keep from coming too soon. After watching Drake go down on me and then giving him a blow job, he's already so hot that it won't take him long now.

Trying to get me pregnant must be another one of Hunter's kinks, because he's never been hornier in his life.

The bed shifts to my right and I feel Drake's hand under my

chin, pulling my kiss from Hunter. Drake's full, soft lips devour mine as Hunter picks up speed. Then, I feel someone's fingers drawing tight circles around my clit.

I love it like this when we are so consumed with each other we become one, and I don't know whose hands are whose. And I don't care because we are all equal to one another, three pieces of one soul.

Hunter's thrusts are rapid now, and my body is tight in anticipation of another climax. Drake's hands roam my body as I finally come undone. Hunter slams home one last time before his cock jolts inside me, filling me up the way he promised he would.

The three of us collapse together, and Hunter makes quick work of loosening the rope around my wrists so I can pull them free. Then the three of us just lie together, our legs tangled and hands intertwined.

We've only been trying for this baby for a couple months, and I feel good about this one. I already can't wait to have a little piece of Hunter inside me, and I hope it's a boy. A tiny little brown-eyed, curly-haired sweetheart who may have the two greatest dads on the planet but prefers his mama. And it may be stupid to dream of something that may never come, but I know that no matter what happens, I'm still the luckiest woman alive.

I wanted a family, a home overflowing with love, and the attention of the people I care about most. Now, I have all of that and more.

Author's Note on Bonus Content

Dear Reader,

In Chapter 31, Drake and Hunter experienced their first time together in bed. I had the tough choice to make as to whose POV this scene would be in, and it didn't feel right excluding Isabel from that moment, hence why it was told through her perspective, watching from the hallway. This scene was so pivotal, especially for Hunter, that I decided to rewrite it as a bonus, captured through his eyes. This (much requested) retelling of that scene is included here for you. Enjoy!

Rule #31: If your wife lets you have a moment with your best friend, don't waste the opportunity.

Hunter

MY KNEE BOUNCES THE ENTIRE DRIVE BACK TO THE HOUSE. DRAKE and I came in separate cars, so while he's behind me in his truck, I'm wondering if he's as nervous and freaked out about this as I am.

I'm about to fuck my best friend. A man. I don't know which part is more shocking at this point.

But fuck, I want this. I want *him* in a way I never did before.

As we reach the house, I notice a couple lights on upstairs. I hope to God Isabel is still awake. There's not a goddamn doubt in my mind that she's going to be down for this. Hell, she'll probably encourage it.

After we park, Drake and I jump out at nearly the same time. Our eyes meet for a split moment in a heated gaze before we both hurry to the door. I feel his breath on my back as I unlock it, and the moment we finally breach the threshold feels like unleashing something wild.

He slams me against the wall first, his lips on mine in a fury of desire. I love the way he hums into our kiss as our tongues tangle in warm friction.

"Are you sure about this?" he mumbles against my lips, moving his kiss downward to my neck. The moment his tongue swipes at the skin there, I lose it. Grabbing his shirt, I spin us until I'm on the outside and he's the one pinned to the wall. His giant body slams against it with more force than mine did.

"I'm so fucking sure," I reply, crashing my lips against his while my hands roam the hard muscular planes of his chest. Fuck, his body is so goddamn sexy. I've never been turned on by a male body before, but Drake has unlocked something feral inside of me. I just keep thinking about the way his chest muscles looked as I came all over them in the shower.

Now, I want to paint every inch of his body. I want to claim him as mine.

"We need Isabel," Drake whispers.

"I'll get her," I reply as I lift his shirt and run my hands over his stomach and chest.

Then I reach around, grabbing his backside as I grind myself against him. "Get your ass upstairs."

We don't so much climb the stairs as fumble our way up, both of us grabbing the other, kissing and grinding as we ascend to the second floor. If Isabel is sleeping through this, it would be a fucking miracle. For a moment, I have Drake bent over on the steps, my cock sliding between the cheeks of his tight ass in those jeans.

I'm going to lose my fucking mind.

"Go to the guest room...now," I mutter to him with my hand around his neck. "Get yourself ready for me."

Then I catch movement in the corner of my eyes—a wisp of red hair disappearing into the bedroom.

Nice try, Red. Can't get away that easily.

I shove Drake away, and he smiles back at me with a devious grin, and I feel my heart stutter in my chest. He looks as excited and happy as I feel right now. There's just one thing missing, and if she seriously thinks she's going to hide from me, she's crazy.

But when I turn the corner into our bedroom and find her giving a pretty impressive sleeping performance—eyes closed, breathing even, and hair tousled across the pillow, I realize that she really doesn't want to be involved.

But why?

I tiptoe closer, picking up the romance novel she must have been reading off the floor. Setting it on the nightstand, I stare down at my beautiful wife. If Isabel wanted to be present for this, she would. If she didn't want me to do this, she would stop me. My wife doesn't play games, and she doesn't beat around the bush.

With a smile, I lean down and press my lips to her forehead. "I love you," I whisper before turning out the light.

Then I quietly ease out of the room. When I reach the dark hallway, my feet freeze halfway to the guest room while the gravity of this moment hits me.

There is no stopping me now. But part of me wonders if we should slow down. If I'm making a mistake. What if he wants more from me? What if I go down this road with him and it ruins everything? What if this is the one line we shouldn't cross?

I shove all of those thoughts down. They're compelling, but not compelling enough to stop me from going into that room.

Besides, every thought in my head vanishes once I reach the guest room and see Drake lying naked on the bed, slowly stroking his thick erection and watching the door for the moment when I would arrive.

He doesn't look panic-stricken or nervous, so why am I?

When he glances behind me, noticing I'm alone, I quietly whisper, "She's sleeping."

Without waiting for his response, I tear my shirt off and unclasp the buckle around my hips. With our eyes glued to one another, I drop my pants and boxers and slip off my shoes until I'm standing in front of him naked. The room is lit only by a small nightlight on the wall, but my eyes have adjusted enough to see the rippled surface of his abs and pecs.

"Come here," he mutters.

I don't hesitate. Climbing onto the bed, I drape my body over his, our legs tangled and our hard cocks pressed together as I find his lips with my own, kissing the smile right off his face.

"I need you," I whisper through our frantic breaths. This is all moving too fast and if we keep grinding together like this, I'm going to come too soon. I'm not opposed to coming more than once tonight, but I want to savor this. I want for the next one to be while I'm...inside him.

His hands roam the skin of my chest and arms as he asks, "Then what, Hunt?"

My brow furrows before I lean down with a smile. "What do you mean, then what? Since when are you worried about what happens after sex?"

He pushes me back an inch. "Since I started fucking your wife. Since you kissed me in a dark club. Suddenly, it fucking matters a hell of a lot."

He's right. I know he is. But this is a question I'm not ready to answer. What he wants is something I don't know if I can give. Acceptance. Commitment. They're just too hard to articulate at the moment—as if they're both in a language I don't know. I don't speak *vulnerable*.

"What do you want me to say?" I whisper before pressing a kiss to his chest, then trailing my lips over to his nipple and giving it a teasing bite. I'm not playing fair—I know that. But it works, because on his next breath, he wraps his right leg around me and groans.

"Nothing. Just fuck me."

I swear I hear a little gasp or whimper just outside the door, but I ignore it as I move my lips downward, eager to know the taste and feel of him in my mouth. He sucks air in through his teeth when he realizes what I'm doing. My lips graze his shaft, and he immediately stiffens.

Then I do to him everything I felt him do to me. I ease my

mouth around him, letting him feel the warm, wet surface of my tongue along his shaft as I take him all the way to the back of my throat. I close my lips and suck, coming back up, tightening around the head.

He groans so loud it sounds like a wild animal. The muscles of his legs are tight and he fidgets and squirms as I suck his cock. When he digs his fingers in my hair and thrusts his dick down my throat, I almost come. Suddenly, and for reasons I don't understand, I want him to use me.

He does that two more times, and I gag loudly, saliva streaming down his length. If I even so much as stroke my own cock once, I'll be a goner. This insatiable need to be the one to make him feel good is overpowering. If I wasn't so intent on being the one to do the fucking tonight, I might lie down at this very moment and let him do ungodly fucking things to me.

Just like that, his pleasure becomes my pleasure.

But before that happens, his grasp at my scalp stings as he drags my mouth off his cock, bringing me up so our lips are fused again. When the ravenous kiss breaks, he mumbles, "Fuck me right now before I lose my goddamn mind."

My heart is pounding so hard in my chest I can feel it pulsing through my entire body. I'm practically dizzy with need. As Drake turns his head, I follow his gaze and spot the lube and condom he's placed on the nightstand. I snatch them both up and move to a kneeling position between his knees. His saliva-coated cock glistens in the soft light.

I put on the condom so fast, which is a fucking miracle because my hands are trembling like crazy.

"You have to…" he stutters as he lets his legs spread.

"I know," I whisper, coating my fingers with lube. I have to *prep* him. He thinks I don't know a damn thing about having sex with a man, but I know the basics. I do own a fucking sex club after all.

When I bring my coated fingers to the space between his balls and his tight hole, he sucks in a breath. I massage him gently before slowly easing past the ring of muscle. My other hand rubs his inner thigh, squeezing the firm muscles of his leg as I inch my middle finger in a little deeper.

He moans, letting his head hang back. I'm so fucking turned on right now. Something about knowing Drake loves this is making me crazier for him. The fact that I can make him feel good. Seeing how much he *likes* it.

"You like that?" I ask because I'm dying to hear it.

"More," he replies in a raspy grunt.

I can barely work in another finger, so I don't fucking know how the hell I'm going to get my cock in there. "Fuck, you're so tight."

"More, Hunter," he growls.

A drop of cum leaks from the tip as I fuck him slowly with my fingers, feeling his muscles relax and his body open up for me.

I don't think I can wait another minute. This is the hottest thing I've ever done, and I'm already worried that I'm going to blow my load the minute my cock touches him.

"I'm ready," he says breathlessly as he lifts his knees up a little higher.

Gazing into his eyes, I pull my fingers out and reach for the bottle of lube. I coat my dick and leak some more on him. Then I align myself at his entrance and thrust slowly until the head of my cock disappears inside him.

Neither of us are breathing as I slide in farther, leaning over his body to bring us closer. The moment I'm buried to the hilt, Drake clutches the bedding in tight fists, letting his head hang back as he groans a drawn-out, "Fuck."

His ass is strangling my cock and it's like nothing I've ever felt before. His hard body beneath me, his loud moans, his soft as fuck lips that I've suddenly gotten addicted to kissing. It's all so surreal.

I pull out just a little and slide back in torturously slow.

"Goddamn, that's good," I say as I kiss my way up his chest and neck. I pull out and slide in again, going a little harder this time. "Fuck, that's so good, Drake."

"It is, isn't it? Just keep moving."

My pleasure, I reply in my head as I sit back on my knees and start fucking him in earnest now. The headboard slams against the wall as I do, and I feel myself careening toward my orgasm. I'm wringing out every second of pleasure from this moment because it feels so fucking pivotal.

With each thrust, I try different angles, watching his face for a reaction, noticing when it takes on that pleasure-high expression that I love. When I find it, I don't stop, slamming into him at the exact spot that drives him wild.

"Stroke my cock while you fuck me," he murmurs, and I wrap my hand around him so fast, pleased to find him leaking some more with each thrust. He's going to blow any minute too.

"God, yes. Like that," he mumbles. And just hearing those words from his lips does me in.

"I'm gonna come." With one hand gripping tightly around his hip, I slam into him one more time before shuddering out a violent and blinding orgasm. I come so hard, I feel my pulse in my ears and behind my eyes.

Then I feel Drake's grip on my wrist just before the warm jets of his cum cover my fingers. We moan and shake together until all of our pleasure is spent and our bodies slump together in post-sex exhaustion.

My head rests against his chest, listening to the erratic beat of his heart. After a few minutes, I ease out of him and land on the mattress at his side. We have to get up and clean ourselves off, but at this moment, I can barely move.

"She was watching from the hallway," he whispers with his mouth next to my ear.

A grin stretches across my face. "I know. I think she enjoyed the show."

"How are you feeling?" He turns to face me, but I can't do the same so I keep my eyes on the dark ceiling as I think it through.

"I'm feeling good as fuck," I reply.

When he opens his mouth again, I'm terrified that he's going to ask me to talk about it some more. Drake wants me to define what this is, what *I am*. Instead of letting that happen, I sit up in a rush.

"Let's get cleaned up because as soon as you're ready, I want to do that again."

He lets out a huff and a laugh before shoving me off the bed. "Then, go get me a fucking towel, lover."

"Yes, baby," I joke because we're friends.

That's all—just two best friends.

Acknowledgments

This book was a fever dream. I honestly don't even remember writing it. It just fell into place so seamlessly I can hardly believe it really happened.

I guess that's what happens when you put three horny hotties on a road trip at a bunch of sex clubs. The story really tells itself at that point.

That's it…threesome-road-trip stories is all I'm writing from here on out!

While the actual writing portion was easy, there was really so much more that went into making this book happen. So I need to thank my amazing team.

My publicist and friend (and fellow workaholic) Amanda Anderson.

Danielle Sanchez and the team at Wildfire Marketing.

My beta readers, Amanda Kay Anderson and Adrian Babst, for the constant enthusiasm and dedication to my stories. You guys are phenomenal.

The Queen herself, Claudia, for being my kink and Shibari expert. Thank you for your wisdom!

My editor, Rebecca's Fairest Reviews. You'll be glad when this series is over, won't you? I'll start being on time again. Thanks for working so hard and making my work shine.

My proofreader, Rumi Khan. I appreciate your dedication and flexibility so much.

My agent, Savannah Greenwell! Thanks for holding my hand throughout this insane year.

Rachel Leigh. You know.

Lori, wherever I go, whatever happens, I'm taking you with me. Thank you for being so amazing.

My shameless sisters, for the laughs and the penis confetti.

The Sweetest reader's group in the world.

And my beautiful Sinners.

To all of the readers, booktokkers, bookstagrammers, too many to name, who welcomed me and my books with open arms. Y'all don't receive enough recognition for what you contribute to this community.

To every single person who reached out after I shared Garrett's story. I'm so glad you're here and that you're not alone.

Sometimes, I can't believe this is my job. To write books, tell stories—really dirty ones that encourage women to read and enjoy sex without shame. This job is what fuels me, lights a spark in my soul, and makes this life worth living.

Thanks for feeding that spark.

About the Author

Sara Cate is a *USA Today* bestselling author of contemporary, forbidden romance. Her stories are known for their heart-wrenching plots and toe-curling heat. Living in Arizona with her husband and kids, Sara spends most of her time working in her office with her goldendoodle by her side.

You can find more information about her at:

Website: saracatebooks.com
Facebook: SaraCateBooks
Instagram: @saracatebooks
Twitter: @SaraCate3
TikTok: @saracatebooks

Also by Sara Cate